An immortal u

Lucien Thrax, son of the earth and child of the ancients, is a healer of immense power. But years of work on a deadly vampire virus have not led to a cure, nor have they softened the wall he built around his heart. When he's forced to work with Dr. Makeda Abel, Lucien is convinced he's reached the limit of his patience with humanity.

Makeda Abel may be human, but she's far from impressed with the brooding vampire healer even if his mind draws her admiration. She's learned how to survive in the immortal world, and it's not by being timid. Working together may lead them to answers, but it also pushes Lucien and Makeda's reluctant attraction to the boiling point.

When nightmares become reality, Makeda will have to trust Lucien with her life. Finding answers has never been more vital. Finding love has never been more deadly. To heal the Elemental World, Lucien and Makeda must follow ancient paths and ask for help from the most inhuman of immortals. Because even with a cure in hand, the battle has only begun.

"Elizabeth Hunter's books are delicious and addicting, like the best kind of chocolate. She hooked me from the first page, and her stories just keep getting better and better. Paranormal romance fans won't want to miss this exciting author!" — *Thea Harrison, NYT bestselling author of the Elder Races series*

A Stone-Kissed Sea

Elemental World Book Four

ELIZABETH HUNTER

A STONE-KISSED SEA
Copyright © 2016
Elizabeth Hunter
ISBN: 9781539589907

Cover art: Damonza.com
Developmental Editor: Lora Gasway
Copy Editor: Anne Victory
Proofread: Linda at Victory Editing
Formatted: Elizabeth Hunter

For information, please visit:
ElizabethHunterWrites.com

To the people and country of Ethiopia

She sends out her children
Threaded through time
Mother.
Land.
And every blood, every line
Her diaspora.
Her sons, rooted in earth
Her daughters, reaching to heaven
Immense.
Larger than a single branch, unaware
we are the tree.
Errant children who wander
Crossing seas and mountains until
We return.
Rest.
Look out across her belly, see
the world born at dawn
and finally
Finally.
Understand home.

—E.H.

Prologue

"Makeda!"

His face swam in and out of Makeda's vision. *Not him.* He couldn't be the last thing she saw.

Not *him*.

Chipped-granite eyes in a coldly handsome face. Hard eyes. Hard face. Planed and ancient like the earth he controlled. Old eyes. Young face. His shaggy, rain-soaked hair dripped water onto her lips. She closed them as another stab of pain hit her chest.

"Dr. Abel," he said, "stay awake. Emergency services are on the way."

Images swam to the surface of Makeda's mind. Her mother laughing in the kitchen and her father behind his desk. The sun setting over the ocean near their home on the Puget Sound. She could hear the crashing water that reached the cliffs in this place she loved and hated.

Love and hate.

Like two beings struggling beneath her skin.

Always always always.

Torn in two. Something in her was so torn.

"Makeda!" He slapped her, and she took a sharp breath.

The quick inhalation hurt so badly she felt the tears come. They wet her cheeks like the mist rolling off the ocean. She could hear it. Hear the tide going out.

No. No, she was too far. Too far from the sea.

Wasn't she?

Her heart. It pulsed in her ears, surging, then falling off. Waves receding.

"Makeda, stay awake."

Tired. Hurts.

"I know it hurts." Another slap. Harder this time. "Stay awake, dammit!"

Not him. She didn't want to see *him*. She was dying, and it was his fault. Makeda felt him bend over, put his mouth at her ear, his breath cold because he couldn't be bothered to heat it. Couldn't be bothered with even a semblance of humanity to comfort her. She wanted her mother. Her sisters. She wanted *home*.

"*Yene konjo*," he whispered, "you may hate me, but I will not let you die."

Unbidden, old images came to her, aching scenes from her childhood. Mountains rising above the mist, sweeping ranges covered by a blanket of green. Raw beauty covered by dense clouds and a sky pregnant with rain.

Rain.

She felt it falling on her cheeks. Her forehead. Her lips.

Another slap to her cheek, but Makeda decided not to breathe. Not this time.

It hurt too much.

Everything hurt...

"Makeda!"

Baojia knelt next to Lucien, surprised to find the usually composed doctor in a silent panic. When he knelt down and examined the human, he understood why. The woman's body was a crumpled heap. She'd been dragged away from the wreckage of the Jeep, which had spun out on the wet roads, the vehicle tumbled on its side and wrapped around a tree, lying on the drenched ground, as broken as the human stretched out in the mud.

Lucien began to administer CPR.

"The ambulance will not get here in time," Baojia said quietly. "Lucien—"

"I've stabilized her as much as I can, but she's lost too much blood." Lucien didn't take his eyes off the woman. Didn't stop the chest compressions or the respiration. "She needs blood. I can't do anything more without it, and we don't have enough at the clinic. We don't..." A strangled laugh burst from his throat. "We don't have enough blood! How can we be *short of blood?*"

The blood they kept at the clinic was preserved blood for vampire sustenance or samples for laboratory testing. None of it could be transfused into a human. No one had planned for donor blood. They hadn't thought there was a need.

Lucien said, "The ambulance will get here in time."

Baojia put a hand on Lucien's shoulder. "My friend—"

"No!" Lucien shoved Baojia's hand away. The vampire's face turned feral and his fangs dropped. He looked toward the muddy road leading to the isolated compound on the Northern California coast, his eyes searching.

Nothing but sheets of rain blanketing the isolated cliffs that jutted over the sea. The storm had rolled in suddenly and brought high winds and a deluge.

"This is my fault," he said.

"It was an accident."

"This is my..." Lucien's eyes turned from wild to calculating in a second. "I call."

"What?" Baojia's eyes widened. "No."

"That's not the deal. No questions, remember? No obligations. I'm calling. Do it now."

"For *her*?"

"Yes."

Everything honorable in Baojia rebelled at the thought. "She doesn't want this. We both know that."

"It doesn't matter," Lucien said. "She was coming here tonight because she said she'd had a breakthrough."

"A breakthrough? This is about more than the Elixir. She did not want to be a vampire, Lucien."

Lucien grabbed him by the throat, and Baojia felt the earth rise up and grip his legs. He was reminded in a heartbeat that the immortal in front of him wasn't just a healer with stunning intellect but an ancient killer, one with thousands of years of survival behind him.

"You will change her," Lucien said calmly. "We have a deal. Do it now because she is dying. *Do it now, Baojia.*"

Baojia hesitated a fraction of a second before he saw something in his friend's eyes.

Something he recognized.

He shoved Lucien back and let his fangs fall. He felt the earth around his legs recede as he picked up the body of the tall woman who had become a respected colleague—a friend—and put his teeth to her neck.

From that night on, she'd be far more than a colleague or a friend.

She would be his immortal child.

Baojia struck quickly. Makeda's heartbeat was already faltering. He would have to be very, very fast. He could feel Lucien watching his every move, feel the ancient vampire's focused attention.

"I give you my word, Baojia," he said quietly. "I'll kill her myself if she hates this life. I promise you. But right now I need her mind."

Oh, my friend. Baojia said nothing as he drained the blood from Dr. Makeda Abel's body. *You need far more than that.*

Chapter One

The first thing Lucien remembered when he woke from death was the familiar sound of his mother's people. The staccato rhythm of Amharic dropped around him like rain hitting dusty earth. He opened his eyes to darkness, but the musky scent of burning bamboo and the mixed accents told him he was high in the mountains.

The last thing he remembered was intense heat and the sound of trickling water in the courtyard in Rome where he'd waited for dawn, hoping to end the confusion and suffering of his plague-ridden mind.

"I'm tired... I'm so tired."

Now he lay in a round *tukul*, the faint glow from the fire enough to illuminate the distinctive bamboo house recognizable for its twin smoke vents and bamboo screens. He was far from the heat of the Mediterranean. He was in Ethiopia, in the mountains of the Dorze people, high in one of his mother's remote compounds above the sister lakes of Abaya and Chamo.

And he was alive.

Damn.

His hair fell nearly to his shoulders, a shaggy brown and silver mix incongruous with a face humans usually assumed to be near thirty years. Saba must have given him a hell of a lot of blood for his hair to have grown that long. He reached up and touched his face, remembering the ache of the sun burning his skin.

"My son. My lovely child, what have you done?"

A wave of guilt at the memory of his mother's voice.

He was tired in spirit, but his body had not felt this strong in years. He could feel the hum of energy as the earth held him. He was stripped to his skin, the dark red soil rising from the Great Rift Valley cradling his body. The ancient energy soaked into him, making his blood and his mind race.

Home.

If there was any place on the earth that was home to him, it was this one. These mountains. Perhaps some might call it a strange thought for a pale, foreign creature who lived in the shadows, but this was the place Saba had brought him when he'd first been sired to immortal life. This was the place where the earth first fell under his aegis and the land spoke to him. Home wasn't the blood-soaked forests of Europe where his human life had come to an end. It was here.

Something in his soul realigned as he lay in the furrowed earth of his mother's land.

Life. The long, aching, glorious stretch of it appeared before his mind's eye.

Life.

Or some imitation of it.

Lucien closed his eyes and let himself fall back into sleep.

❖

2013

"You need to leave," Saba said.

Lucien swung the sharp-bladed hoe into the earth in time with the human next to him. Though he could turn the earth faster on his own—could upend the whole of the topsoil with his amnis—the rhythmic labor with the men around him satisfied something essential. Though he did not sweat, the mist on the mountainside had gathered on his bare chest and arms. A fire burned nearby, warming the men who worked beside him. They were readying the fields for planting maize, the steep mountainside too difficult for the horse-drawn plow to traverse.

"Stop," his mother said. "And listen to me."

Ever the faithful child, Lucien stepped away and handed the hoe to one of the men by the fire.

He wiped the mist from his face, feeling a smear of grit across his cheek. He glanced down at Saba, who stood in the gathering dusk watching the humans who continued working.

"I'm listening, *Emaye*," he said.

"*Yene Luka...*" She put her hand on his cheek. "When will you decide to live again?"

Lucien took a deep breath, tasting the night air and the turned earth. "What do you want from me?"

"You are my beloved son. I want you to be a man of honor and usefulness."

Lucien smiled. A mother in the modern world might have answered "happiness" or "contentment" when asked what she wanted for her child. Saba was not a modern mother. From her regal profile to the scars decorating her body in whirling spirals, his sire was a proud reflection of an ancient past. The oldest known vampire of their race didn't remember how she had come to be. She'd forgotten more than he'd ever learned. But some traits were eternal.

From ancient times to modern, mothers nagged their sons.

"Am I not a man of honor?" he asked.

"You are one of the finest men I know," Saba said, her chin lifting. "But you are not useful here."

He glanced at the half-plowed field and raised his eyebrows.

Saba lifted her hand as if she would strike him. She didn't, but the empty threat made Lucien smile.

"Do you think me stupid?" She nudged him away from the field and down the muddy path back to the village. "You're hiding."

A stabbing pain in his chest. "I'm mourning."

Her eyes, dark as the night sky, softened. "Mourn her, but do not despair. She was not your true mate."

"How do you know?" he asked, his voice frustratingly raw.

Rada's ghost haunted him. He'd returned to her at the end of her short mortal life, desperate to try anything to cure the cancer riddling her body. His own blood could not heal her. But he had tried everything to save her, including infecting her with Elixir. What he thought was a cure turned into a plague that eventually took her life.

And nearly took his.

"She didn't choose you." Saba turned to him. "Love her memory, but do not forget that truth. In the end, Luka, she chose a human life and a human death. Your true mate would have chosen *you*."

Bitterness stained his tongue as images of his lost love flipped through his mind. Rada as a young woman, a gifted scientist struggling for validation and respect. The passionate woman who'd become his lover. The woman who'd said good-bye, leaving him to pursue human desires. She'd had a husband. Children. She'd had a good life that ended too soon.

"I loved her."

"I know you did," Saba said. "Would she have wanted this apathy from you? Would a fellow healer have wanted you to stay on this mountain, hiding your gifts from the world?"

"What does it matter?" Lucien asked. "I've lived thousands of years. Seen humans progress and regress. Nothing changes, and humanity is exhausting. Can't the world wait for me to like it again?"

"In another age, I would say yes. But not this one." She handed him a folded piece of paper. "A message from Ziri."

The ancient wind vampire was one of his mother's dearest friends, though far more politically inclined than Saba. He'd been intimately involved in the creation and the exposure of the Elixir that had poisoned Lucien and killed Rada. Only a complete transfusion of Saba's blood had healed him.

And, for a time, he'd thought that would be the end of it. The poison had been exposed. Its creator had been destroyed.

But knowledge was the most pernicious virus.

Elixir hadn't disappeared. The infection only seemed to be spreading in the human world, putting more and more immortals at risk along with the humans they drank from. Not that it was his problem anymore.

"What does Ziri want?" Lucien asked quietly, a sense of inevitability falling on him as he took the letter.

"He bears a request from Rome." Saba pulled out another letter.

"And what does Emil Conti want?" Lucien asked, taking the second letter. "He controls Rome now. What more does he need?"

She pulled out another letter. "It's a request from Giovanni Vecchio."

Lucien closed his eyes and sighed. A request from Vecchio couldn't be ignored. Not when it was Vecchio and his mate, Beatrice De Novo, who had hosted Lucien in Rome. Not when Vecchio's ward, Benjamin Vecchio, had been the one to pull Lucien out of the sun and save his life. Whether he'd wanted the rescue or not, Lucien owed them—in particular the young human—an enormous favor, and Vecchio was far too calculating to forget it.

"Ziri. Conti. *And* Vecchio." He counted off the letters. They were being far too formal for a small request. "What do they want?"

"The vampire who controls the Pacific Northwest is an ally of theirs. They have had an influx of humans whose blood is tainted by the Elixir." Saba's face was grim. "This Katya Grigorieva is keeping the women. Building some sort of research facility to study them."

"*Study* them?" Anger was a faded emotion for Lucien, but he felt a flare at the word *study*.

"In a sense." Saba must have seen the disapproval on his face. "What should she do? Leave the humans alone? These women *will* die. We both know it. Should they infect more of our people because of their ignorance?"

"Human beings are not lab animals to be experimented on." He had taken an oath centuries before to do as little harm as he could. He was a healer and only a reluctant predator. "Why should I help this woman? Is she an ally of yours?"

"Her people will study the humans no matter what you decide," Saba said. "Ziri and Vecchio want you there to lead the research team. Security is already arranged, but they need a healer with some history with the Elixir."

He crossed his arms and looked over the cloud cover blanketing the valley below. The highlands rose above the valley, the stars a million points of light in the darkness as the clouds made islands of the mountain peaks.

"Why don't you and Ziri solve this?" Lucien asked. "Find Kato and Arosh. Make them help. You and your friends are the ones who came up with this scheme in the first place."

"I think you forget the inevitability of human curiosity," Saba said. "Geber was the alchemist, Luka, not us."

Lucien stared into the silent black night, but no solution came to him. In fact, his conscience began to nibble at the corners of his mind. "I owe Vecchio, so I don't have a choice, do I?"

"Do you want another healer—one who might not be as honorable as you—to be in charge of this research? A cure must be found, Lucien. My kind of healing has no place in that world, but you —"

"Fine." He closed his eyes. "You knew I was never going to be able to say no, Saba. I'll send the message to Vecchio. No need to go through all the political channels. Is the courier still here?"

"She is."

"Tell her to wait. I'll go and write the letter right now." He pulled on his shirt and took off his shoes, sinking his feet into the earth he'd soon have to leave behind for the modern human world of concrete, constant noise, and wireless buzzing.

A world that, like it or not, he was going to have to save.

Lucien observed the vampire for only a second before the man turned. He was eastern Asian—Han Chinese if Lucien had to guess—and of medium build. Far shorter than Lucien but powerfully built.

And quick.

The man's black eyes assessed Lucien with inhuman swiftness. "You are Lucien Thrax."

Not a trace of an accent. This American vampire must be his new chief of security.

Lucien nodded. "And you are Chen Baojia."

The man inclined his head only incrementally. "Baojia is sufficient, Doctor."

"Please call me Lucien."

Another quick nod. "I received information you would be arriving tomorrow night."

"That information greatly overestimated my desire to remain in the city." Lucien shifted the old rucksack where he carried his few belongings. His books would be coming in a truck the next night. "I don't like cities." Though he did appreciate the custom-built plane Giovanni Vecchio had provided for the journey. Saba had insisted on that concession as a matter of pride. No child of hers would be traveling in a ship's hold to do a favor for others. "I landed in San Francisco and told them to drive me here. There were plenty of night hours left."

"Very well," Baojia said. "If you'll allow me to show you to your quarters now, you should have plenty of time to settle in before dawn."

"Sounds good."

He let Baojia lead the way from the central guard building and into the new bunker-like structures lining the cliffside. Lucien could hear the waves crashing below and was grateful the compound seemed to be built with vampires in mind. Though there was a farmhouse near the road, the majority of the buildings were low and windowless. He suspected they were joined by tunnels underground, which suited his nature and provided good security for their human subjects.

"The laboratory is still in the process of being built," Baojia said, "but the first office is finished. That will be yours unless you want one of the others when they're complete. I'm sorry if the facilities aren't what you're used to, but living quarters for the women were the priority."

Baojia didn't sound apologetic. Lucien could almost hear the challenge in the vampire's voice, daring the newcomer to question his decision to prioritize the human patients he was guarding. Lucien had no objection. In fact, he had a feeling his priorities and those of his security chief would align nicely.

"No apology necessary," Lucien said. "This facility will probably be one of the nicest I've ever worked in."

An approving nod. "It's being built with vampire scientists in mind. Katya has multiple pharmaceutical companies with immortal staff, so this is far from her first lab, though it's definitely her most secure."

"Good to know," he muttered as they descended steps into a low concrete structure. "The humans' quarters?"

Baojia shot him a look. "They are secure. Doctors and researchers do not have access to the humans' living quarters, only to the medical facilities. It was one of the protocols I put in place. The women need to have a measure of privacy and autonomy, or they will not cooperate."

"Very good." Oh yes. His priorities and Baojia's should line up nicely. Far from the cold predator he first appeared, the vampire was clearly an advocate for those he protected. Lucien approved. He also wondered how old Baojia was, but he wasn't rude enough to ask.

"Baojia?" a voice called from outside. "Are you in there?"

Lucien's brain clicked on.

Human female. American. Accent indicates California, most likely southern.

Footsteps on the stairs, and Baojia went on guard, placing himself between Lucien and whoever was walking into the sunken office.

"George, are you— Oh! Sorry." A slight Caucasian woman appeared in the doorway.

Lucien tilted his head and watched her walk the last steps into the office. She was pretty enough, with pale skin, auburn red hair, and a face full of freckles. Her eyes were sleepy, but she was mortal, and it *was* the middle of the night.

"I had no idea you had company," the human said.

Thirty to thirty-five years of age. Recent trauma to both legs, but a more serious injury to the left.

One of his new patients? There was no scent of the Elixir from her. No aroma of the sickly-sweet pomegranate he'd tasted in Rada's blood.

Baojia was in front of her in a heartbeat, making no pretense of human speed. "Natalie, this is Lucien Thrax, the researcher here to help with the girls." Baojia turned to Lucien, clearly on edge. "Lucien, this is my mate, Natalie Ellis."

A human. And he called her mate?

How very... unexpected.

For the first time in years, Lucien felt interest tug at his mind. This pair piqued his curiosity. And curiosity was an itch he'd been numb to for a very long time.

Lucien felt the draw of water in the air and knew it came from the vampire standing at the doorway. Impressive control for such a young immortal. He felt the answering tug from his own instincts and reached out with his amnis.

He was underground. Whether the young immortal realized it or not, Lucien was old enough and strong enough to call the earth, even from within a concrete building. The wild energy of this rough land whispered to him, dancing along his skin. He could draw it close, collapsing the building from the outside, smothering anyone foolish enough to attack him with a deadly shroud of rock and soil.

The assassin and his little human mate would be gone in seconds.

But Lucien stepped away from the woman, relaxing his posture and reining his instincts. Aggression did not interest him. Instead, he plucked at the new curiosity, enjoying the vibration of it in his mind.

A human for a mate? No wonder the assassin's energy had spiked. This Natalie Ellis was ridiculously vulnerable.

"I'm sorry if I interrupted you," Natalie said quietly. "I just woke up and you weren't in the house, so I wondered if one of the girls—"

"Everything is fine." Baojia reached up and brushed a single finger over her cheek. "I was doing a quick sweep. Heading back to the house when Dr. Thrax arrived."

"Lucien," he interjected. "Please, call me Lucien. Doctor is a very recent title, from my perspective." Lucien relaxed his shoulders, making himself as nonthreatening as a vampire of his size could be. He heated his skin to human warmth and held out a hand slowly. "Miss Ellis, it's very nice to meet you. I assume you are not one of my patients."

The energy in the room dissipated, though the assassin remained alert. Natalie didn't just take his hand, she enclosed it, wrapping both her small hands around his large one. She was so warm. *So very alive.* Her warmth traveled up his arm and spread over his skin.

"You assume correctly," she said, releasing his hand after a pleasantly long moment. "Though I've gotten friendly with most of the girls, so if you need a familiar face to put them at ease, I'm available." She smiled. "I warn you though, Baojia's Spanish is way better than mine."

"Do all the patients speak Spanish?"

Baojia answered. "Yes."

Natalie's sleepy eyes warmed when she looked at her mate. "And they all trust Baojia. So it's very nice to meet you, Lucien, but we probably won't see each other much unless you want to come over to watch wrestling and have a beer."

Lucien frowned. *Was she joking?*

Baojia seemed to read his thoughts. "She's joking."

Natalie elbowed her mate, and he captured her in a playful hold that belied his solemn expression.

"Maybe I'm not joking," Natalie protested. "It's not like our social calendar is jam-packed, George. Besides, I've already made friends at work—it's time you have some too."

The vampire raised a single eyebrow at her, but Lucien could see the twitch of amusement at the corner of his mouth. This was a familiar lover's game. The emotional tie between the two was evident in their body language. Now if he could just figure out why the human was calling her mate "George." The look on the assassin's face told him that story would have to be offered in its own time.

"Natalie, if you are inviting me to your home, I am honored by the invitation," Lucien said, liking this couple the more he saw them interact. "Though we should probably allow your mate to become accustomed to me before I intrude on his territory."

Natalie let out a sigh. "Vampires."

"Horrible, formal creatures, aren't we?"

"Yes."

Baojia leaned into Natalie and whispered a barely audible endearment before another suggestion Lucien was *certain* the vampire had not meant to share. A slight flush rose to Natalie's cheeks.

Increased heart rate. Arousal. *Pleasure.* The mortal enjoyed her mate.

"I'll just head back to bed," Natalie said, nodding toward the door. "Bedtime for humans and all that. Lucien, it was very nice to meet you. After you two sniff each other's butts and make friends, come over for that beer."

Lucien watched her leave with a smile on his face and decided any vampire who had mated with a human like Natalie Ellis was a vampire worth knowing, and one he might even count as a friend one day.

Baojia cleared his throat as Natalie's footsteps were lost in the sound of the night surf. "Yes, she is always like that."

"Ah."

"And no, you cannot have her." Baojia let slip the first smile Lucien had seen from the man. "She's mine."

"Lucky you."

Chapter Two

Dr. Makeda Abel was reading a journal article by a Taiwanese researcher when she heard the childish giggle. She looked over her shoulder and saw Rochelle, one of the youngest patients in the sickle cell treatment wing, peeking around the corner. The girl was small for her age, as many of Makeda's patients were.

"What are you doing here?" Makeda asked. "You were taking a nap when I stopped by your room. Isn't it lunchtime for you? Does Nurse Mimi know where you are?"

Rochelle only giggled more.

Makeda bookmarked the article and turned her chair toward the little girl, who walked into the small office and toward Makeda's desk.

"So"—she held up her arms and Rochelle scrambled onto her lap—"what are you giggling about?"

The delicate girl had been coming to the hospital for blood transfusions since she was a year old. She was as comfortable with the doctors and nurses as she was with her family. And Makeda, though she had no children of her own, was a very practiced auntie. It was one of the reasons she continued to keep an office at the hospital. Her office at the lab was far more spacious, modern, and quiet, but she didn't have random little girls with bright smiles wandering in to say hello.

"Dr. Mak, you have curly hair like me." Rochelle's small hand reached out and patted Makeda's hair.

Makeda smiled. "I do." She'd left her tight curls to air-dry that morning since it was Saturday and she didn't want the bother of straightening it. "But I don't have any beads in mine."

Rochelle popped a thumb in her mouth and laid her little head against Makeda's shoulder, still patting her hair. "I like it. It's pretty like my mommy's."

"Thank you."

"But you should get beads."

"I'll think about it." Realizing she'd have company for a while, Makeda brought up the article again and found her place.

"You should wear your hair like that so Serena can see it."

Serena was another patient. A five-year-old with a thick shock of dark brown curls and loads of freckles that stood out on her pale skin. "Well, I usually straighten it for work, but maybe I'll leave it in for you and Serena one day."

"Why do you make it straight for work?"

"Some people think straight hair is more proper for doctors," she said carefully. "More professional."

Rochelle giggled again. "That's silly."

Makeda glanced down at the little girl with the brightly colored beads in her hair. Somewhere in the years of medical school and residency, the dark brown hair Makeda's mother, Misrak Abel, had crooned over when she'd been a girl, the mane she had braided and twisted with brightly colored thread, had become an unprofessional mop her daughter had learned how to brush and straighten into submission.

She leaned down and kissed the top of Rochelle's head. "You're right. It is silly. I'll wear my hair curly for you and Serena next week, okay?"

Rochelle said, "If you don't want beads, Serena has lots of pretty bows. Silver ones. And purple ones. And red ones..."

Makeda smiled and tried to imagine the makeover her tiny patients would give her if she let them.

Maybe she would let them.

She was a respected thirty-eight-year-old physician and researcher with years of experience on her resume. She was second in charge of one of the most prestigious hematology research facilities in the country and had coauthored numerous journal articles on the subject of sickle cell treatment. If she wanted to dye her hair purple and wear giant gold bows, no one should say a thing about it. After all, if her colleagues could put up with Andrew Kominski's ever-widening comb-over, nothing should be off-limits.

Quick footsteps coming down the hall had Rochelle's head lifting from Makeda's shoulder.

"Uh-oh," Makeda whispered. "She found you."

Mimi Ocampo put her fists on her hips in a mock gesture of disapproval. "Dr. Mak, are you stealing my patients again?"

Rochelle giggled.

"Is this a patient?" Makeda looked down at Rochelle. "I could have sworn this was a kitty cat. I'm so sorry."

"I'm not a kitty!" Rochelle slid off Makeda's lap. "I'm a... bunny!"

And with that, the little girl bounced out of the office and down the hall. Mimi turned to Makeda. "You weren't in the middle of anything, were you?"

"Just doing some filing before I head to my mom and dad's." Makeda nodded toward the door. "Her energy is good."

"Yep. The chelation therapy is going well. I think this will be her last inpatient treatment for a while."

"Good news."

Mimi smiled. "Your mom is so pleased you still keep an office here."

Mimi and Misrak had been fast friends and colleagues for nearly thirty years. Mimi, a new immigrant from the Philippines. Misrak, a new immigrant from Ethiopia. They'd bonded in their first hospital and had been friends ever since.

"My mom knows I need the reminder."

"Of what? Burned coffee and constant interruptions?"

"No." Makeda turned off her desktop and grabbed her bag from beside the desk, glancing at the wall of photographs and drawings her little patients had given her over the years. "I need to remember it was worth it to bury my life in a lab."

❖

Makeda never felt buried at her mother's house. The high-pitched squeals from her nieces pierced her ears as she chopped the mound of onions for the *doro wat* her mother was preparing for Sunday dinner. During the week, her mother cooked a medley of dishes she'd learned in over thirty years living in an international city like Seattle—dumplings and fish, pasta, and curry—but Sundays were for "home cooking," which meant Ethiopian food.

The spicy smell of garlic and *berbere* filled the kitchen of her parents' house as the chatter of little girls and low voices from the den filled Makeda's ears. Her mother was chopping the chicken while her older sister made the *injera*. Her younger sister, Adina, eyes watering, stood at her side, wiping away onion-fume tears.

"You're quiet today," Adina said. "Work?"

"Hmm?" Makeda grabbed another onion. "No, I'm not thinking about... anything, really. Just enjoying the background noise. It's kind of nice."

Adina laughed. "That's because you only *visit* the noise." A squeal came from the stairs. Adina shouted at her daughters in clipped Amharic, and the girls quieted down.

"Why do you and Fozia always yell at the kids in Amharic?" They'd always spoken a mix of Amharic and English at home, leaning more toward English the older they got.

"I don't know. Probably because Mom always yelled at us in Amharic."

Another scream rent the air, and Makeda's mother dropped her knife and walked toward the hall.

Fozia said, "They're in trouble now."

"How do they make a noise that high?" Makeda asked.

"Boys are loud too, but they don't break your eardrums."

Fozia said to Adina, "Can you imagine how quiet Makeda's house is?"

"I don't have to imagine. I live there." Makeda smiled. "And it's *very* quiet."

"Until *Emaye* comes over to complain about her poor daughter who has no babies!" Adina laughed.

"The horror," Fozia said. "What are you doing with your life, Makeda? Saving lives and curing cancer?" Her oldest sister looked up and winked. "Oh, wait."

Adina bumped Makeda's hip with her own. "She was always the smart one."

Fozia said, "And the best auntie."

Makeda grabbed another onion after finely chopping her third. "And I can't keep plants alive, so staying an auntie is probably a good move."

She adored her four nieces and two nephews. Auntie Mak's closet was well-known as an open dress-up playground when the nieces came to visit, and Makeda kept a battered microscope and plethora of old slides for those of a more scientifically curious nature. She lived within ten minutes of both her sisters and wouldn't have it any other way. And though Misrak and Yacob Abel despaired of their thirty-eight-year-old childless daughter ever giving them grandchildren, Makeda's sisters and their husbands were keeping the family stocked with plenty of little girls and boys to drive them all crazy.

It was enough for Makeda. She loved being an aunt but knew she'd make a distracted mother. Plus she didn't have time for men, and they were a fairly essential part of the equation.

Her last boyfriend had politely broken up with her over two years ago. Makeda didn't notice he was gone until three days after he'd removed the few things he'd kept at her house. He'd taken a microbiology teaching position on the East Coast, and they still e-mailed occasionally.

She wasn't good at relationships. She'd accepted that. And frankly, there were few men who interested her. She was a genius. It said so somewhere on a chart in a doctor's office she'd visited soon after moving to the United States. Her parents had been quietly ecstatic to have a genius for a daughter. For Makeda, it just meant one more thing setting her apart in an already strange new place.

She wasn't a snob about her intelligence—being arrogant about your intelligence was as logical as being arrogant about your eye color—but she'd learned to be discriminating. Makeda knew she'd lose interest in a man who couldn't engage her mind even if she did admire him.

"Makeda?" Her father's voice broke through her sisters' chatter and the smell of red onion. "Can I speak to you for a moment?"

Adina grabbed the onion she was reaching for. "Go. And bring me some wine when you come back."

Makeda followed her father into his office. She took after him in almost every way. She was nearly as tall and had the long, aquiline features from his mother's branch of their family. She also had his quiet personality and avid mind, though it was focused on an entirely different area of study.

Yacob Abel was an archivist and scholar of ancient Ethiopian and Syrian Orthodox manuscripts and the director of the Grigorieva Library. His office walls were decorated with posters of events and exhibits he'd helped curate along with childish drawings given to a proud grandfather.

Few outside their family knew the private library he curated belonged to the vampire leader of the Pacific Northwest. Few outside their family acknowledged vampires even existed.

But immortals had not been supernatural to Makeda since her mother and father had told her why they'd moved from Ethiopia when she was eight years old. They weren't a mystery. They weren't magic. They were simply an unexplained part of the world.

Humans were still mapping an ocean that covered seventy percent of the planet. They were still unlocking the mysteries of their own brains. How could they assume they knew the truth about every human myth and legend? Makeda was far too intelligent to assume she knew everything. The human body—a subject of study for centuries—still managed to surprise her regularly.

"Sit please," Yacob said. "I received a letter a from Katya Grigorieva yesterday that pertains to you."

Makeda frowned. "About me? Why didn't she or her secretary contact me directly?"

"The letter was from her, not her secretary." Her father shrugged.

ELIZABETH HUNTER

"This is how Katya operates. You know this. She considers it a sign of respect to contact me as the head of our family. It's a formality."

Makeda sat up and leaned forward. The only reason her father would be contacted by the big boss of the Pacific Northwest was if it had something to do with her research. The lab she worked at was owned and funded by Katya Grigorieva and specialized in studying blood disorders and cancers. The work they did was used to develop new treatments and drugs for everything from sickle cell to leukemia.

Katya's obsession with blood diseases might have seemed odd for someone who didn't have to worry about illness or aging. But Makeda knew humans and vampires were inextricably tied. Vampires had never discovered a way to live without human blood. Though there were some who existed on wholly animal diets, she had heard they were not as powerful. And power, in the immortal world, was how one survived.

Healthy humans were a vampire's guarantee of eternal life *and* eternal influence.

Thinking of herself as food made Makeda's skin crawl. "What was the letter about?"

"You've heard of the problems with this Elixir drug, yes?"

"I've heard of it, but it's only a problem in Europe, isn't it?"

If it wasn't, then Makeda's lab would soon be neck-deep in research, which meant the thalassemia project Makeda has spent the previous three years on might be shelved.

Please don't let it be spreading to the Americas...

"It has spread out of Europe," her father said. "There are cases here in the United States now. In California."

Damn.

Makeda took a deep breath as a wave of quiet anger washed over her. She would be taken off a project that could save hundreds of lives and possibly cure a blood disorder affecting thousands of children.

Because she needed to study a *vampire* drug.

"She wants you to see her tomorrow evening," Yacob said.

"I'm sure she's going to redirect our research targets if Elixir is becoming a problem," Makeda said, unable to cloak the bitterness in her voice. "Why not speak to Dr. Pak?"

Yacob shook his head. "I have no idea."

As ambitious as she was, Makeda had no argument with Jerry Pak as the head of the hematology lab. He was a brilliant researcher and surprisingly good at herding the distracted PhDs he was charged with directing.

So why did Katya want to meet with her?

"What time?" she asked her father.

"Eleven. The sun this time of year..."

"Of course." Northern climates were ideal for vampires in winter, but summer could be an issue, even in Seattle. "I'll make sure I'm there. Main office?"

Yacob nodded.

"Okay then." Makeda stood. "Better get back to the onions."

Her father called her as she reached the door. "Makeda."

"Hmm?" She turned, surprised to notice the grim expression on his normally cheerful face.

"Whatever she asks of you, be careful. Katya is a benevolent monarch in her world, but she is still a monarch."

Makeda arrived at the handsome redbrick-and-beam building just off King Street at five minutes to eleven the next evening. She hated being late, but arriving too early might make her appear nervous. The building was guarded heavily, as all Katya's buildings were, though most people passing by would have no clue anything was out of the ordinary. Rows of windows were carefully blocked from the inside, and human and vampire guards patrolled the block in the guise of office workers, news vendors, and dog walkers.

The dogs were not pets, and the walkers were not hipsters.

She passed a guard she'd met at several of Katya's employee events, but he didn't give Makeda a second look. She could almost feel the heat of electronic eyes on her as she walked into the lobby.

She rode the elevator to the third floor and was ushered to a comfortable chair by a friendly human secretary.

At precisely 11:02, another assistant came to the door. This one was not human.

"Dr. Abel?"

Makeda rose and walked out of the waiting area with the open windows revealing the glint of Seattle's many lights. She walked away from the human secretary, the buzz of normal conversation, and into the silent inhumanity of Katya Grigorieva's private office.

Makeda was the only human there.

Lifting her chin, she concentrated on keeping her heart steady and her breathing even.

She was escorted into an office far brighter than expected. The day-like lighting and colors made her think of an afternoon at the beach, not a vampire lair. Behind a beech-gold desk sat a very pretty teenager with pale skin and long dark hair. Katya held out a hand for Makeda to shake. Makeda took it, noting the warmth of her skin, an affectation Katya had made the effort to produce since vampire skin was normally much cooler than human.

"Dr. Abel," she said, releasing Makeda's hand. "I believe we've met before."

"We have," Makeda answered. "At the Christmas party for the lab two years ago. Dr. Pak introduced us. I'd seen you on the tours before that though."

"I enjoyed that Christmas party, but I think I made the majority of my employees nervous. I decided not to attend after that." Katya smiled and Makeda noted her slightly crooked teeth. "Better to let employees have their time to socialize without the boss hovering and listening in."

"It's not a logical reaction though." Makeda sat when Katya did. "Not from humans. You could conceal yourself in another room and easily listen to our conversations from a distance if you wanted to."

Katya's eyebrows rose.

Well, shit.

"Not that I'm implying you would," Makeda quickly added.

"Simply that you could if you wanted to."

Luckily, her employer looked amused and not offended. "You're correct, of course. But it's not conducive to good employee relations to remind humans of that too often."

"Of course."

Katya crossed her arms, and Makeda noticed the way the vampire was dressed. Again, it wasn't as she had expected. While Makeda wore a professional suit, Katya was in a pair of jeans and a fleece pullover more suited for backpacking or camping.

"You're brilliant," Katya said. "And I don't hand that label out lightly. In general, vampires are far more intelligent than humans. It's not prejudice; it's fact."

"Your nervous systems are heightened by the presence of the electrical current you control," Makeda said. "I'm not insulted. Amnis makes your processing faster. Other factors being equal, you *are* more intelligent."

"But you can keep up," Katya said. "How long did it take you to figure out Dr. McGrath was a vampire?"

"Three days." Makeda frowned. "In my defense, we did not interact much at the beginning, and he's not as pale as most vampires."

"He's also young and blends into groups of humans extremely well because of his mannerisms," Katya said. "That's part of his job for me. At the last lab he worked in, no one discovered he was immortal for over a year."

"That's surprising."

Katya shrugged. "Scientific observation can be less precise when it's not under a microscope."

"Are you implying my colleagues and I are myopic?"

"Of course you are. That's why I hired you."

Makeda couldn't argue with that.

"But," Katya continued, "it's not salient to the reason I called you here tonight. You're brilliant for a human, which means you can keep up with our kind who are also very bright. You also have keen insight to the subject matter because of your research into thalassemia, which I believe will be useful on this project."

"I assumed the thalassemia project would be shelved because of the Elixir problem."

Katya's eyes sharpened. "What do you know about Elixir?"

"Not much more than the basics," Makeda said carefully. "Information is... limited. And obviously there are no journal articles published about it."

"But you've heard about the strange wasting disease that has affected small populations in Europe?"

Makeda paused. "Rumors only. Word of mouth. But I'm a hematologist, not a gastro—"

"It's tied to Elixir," Katya said. "And it's related to the blood. *Everything* is related to the blood in humans."

Makeda didn't agree, but she wasn't going to argue. After all, the vampire controlled her funding.

Katya said, "I have a very small, very private lab in Northern California that has been working on finding a cure for Elixir for three years now. And I've decided, Dr. Abel, that the lab needs your brilliance."

Her heart pounded. "You want me to head a lab looking into an Elixir cure?"

Finally. *Finally*!

"Of course you're not going to head it," Katya said.

Makeda's heart dropped. "What?"

"There is already a project lead, and he's brilliant. In fact, he is considered by some to be one of the defining minds of our race. But he's at an impasse. He needs fresh eyes. Perspective."

Her boss wanted her to play second fiddle for a brilliant vampire doctor? That was so far from a promotion she felt an angry rush of blood to her neck before she could temper her reaction. "Ms. Grigorieva—"

"Katya."

"With respect, Katya..." Her father's words lurked in the back of Makeda's mind. *Be careful.* She took a breath. "I lead projects and have not been an assistant for many years. It's a different set of skills to support and work with someone who is in charge of the direction of the research. A move like this hardly seems like a good use of my abilities." Makeda paused to take a breath. "What I mean is—"

"You're not an assistant," Katya said. "You're a boss. Don't apologize for it; it's one of the reasons I chose you for this position."

I chose you.

Done. It was already done, and Makeda had to live with it. She tried not to let the wretched disappointment show on her face.

She knew the reality of going to work for a vampire. Her father had warned her, and she'd taken it under advisement. Huge funding opportunities, but there was no grievance committee. If your boss wanted you to do something, you did it or you quit. And quitting was only an option if you had the right kind of boss.

"You're not going to be Lucien's assistant," Katya continued. "You're going to be his partner. You'll have your own staff and your own assistants. But I want your take on his research so far. I think you can add to it."

"I don't know anything about this vampire, but I know scientists, and your head researcher is going to hate this. Has he asked for a collaborator?"

"No."

Makeda closed her eyes. "Then collaboration will not work."

"Yes, it will. He doesn't have a choice."

She opened her eyes. "Does he *have* to obey you?"

"No. But I fund him, and he's got three years and personal loss invested in this project."

Makeda shook her head. "It's not going to work. We will butt heads constantly. It might actually set the project back instead of advancing it."

Catching Katya's eye, Makeda could see the skepticism in her expression.

"I'm not trying to be contrary," she continued. "I understand what you're saying, and you could be right that another perspective on the research is all that's needed to find a cure. Brilliant advances can happen during collaboration, but unless he's looking for help, he's not going to welcome it. Scientists can be as territorial as vampires. I don't even want to think about a scientist who *is* a vampire."

Katya didn't say anything for a long time, and Makeda mentally updated her resume.

Finally the vampire spoke. "Dr. Abel, I appreciate your candor."

Well, that's a relief.

"But I still want you to take the project. Consider it a personal favor to me, because you're right, Lucien will not be happy. But something also tells me this might work better than either of us could predict. To sweeten the deal, if you can put up with him for... let's say two years—"

"Two years?"

"Work on this project for two years, and if you're not making progress—if he's impossible to work with—I'll give you your old job back with a significant raise in salary and funding."

Makeda knew how research facilities worked. "My position will have been taken over by then. I'll have lost time and momentum on my current project. I'll have to start an entirely new study group to—"

"Then I'll give you your own lab. Your own funding," Katya said. "But I want you to commit to two years. *Full* dedication, no side projects."

A light appeared at the end of the tunnel. "Two years and then I'd have my own lab?"

"I want full attention on this, Dr. Abel. I need—the world needs—your mind on this project. Completely and utterly focused on it. If you can do that, focus like that, and you still want to leave after two years, then yes. I'll give you your own lab and enough money to restart your thalassemia research with my full and complete backing. Also know that while you're on the Elixir project, funding will not be an issue. Lucien has an open checkbook; so would you."

Makeda took a few moments to think, but there was really no option. Katya was a benevolent monarch, but as her father had said, she *was* still a monarch. Unless Makeda wanted to leave her organization, she knew what she had to do.

She rose and held out her hand. "I'll do my best."

Saba

She watched the trucks move in and out of the warehouse, their drivers mostly headed toward the port in Istanbul. She stood in the shadows, her old friend hovering at her side.

"It hasn't stopped," he said. "Though things have slowed down. They are finding it harder and harder to offload without detection."

"Is Elixir the only thing made here?"

"There is a perfume as well. And, of course, this is only one of the facilities, though it is the primary one."

"And you're sure this is Laskaris?"

"I'm positive."

"If you say it's true, it is."

Ziri's network of spies was unparalleled, though she did understand he'd suffered a rather hard loss with the death of one of his primary information merchants the year before.

"And the Russian?"

"Has taken care of his daughter. There was no sentiment involved."

"Sentiment can be a distraction."

"As we're both aware."

She looked back at the warehouse where vial after vial of poison was being shipped out, spread to the farthest corners of the immortal world.

For now.

Ziri asked, "Does our son make any progress?"

"Of a kind."

Ziri had always claimed Lucien; he and Saba had been lovers

29

when Lucien had been sired. A good portion of the blood in her son's veins probably did belong to the old wind vampire, but the heart of him was Saba's.

"He's running out of time."

"Leave that to me." Saba's patience with her children was growing thin. Her patience with the world was growing thin.

The elemental world hung in the balance.

Saba wondered if her son knew how much.

Chapter Three

Lucien stared at the calendar hanging on his wall and listened to Katya on the speakerphone and tried to contain his anger. Anger with Katya. Anger at himself. Anger at his mother and her friends and medieval alchemists with god complexes and relentless curiosity. It didn't matter that Geber was centuries dead. Lucien wanted to raise him just to kill him in a more satisfying manner.

But anger solved nothing.

"I'm close," he said. "You know I need more time."

"You can have all the time you need," Katya said. "But I'm sending another scientist down there."

"I have assistants. The lab is excellently staffed."

"She's not an assistant. She's a hematology researcher with a focus on sickle cell diseases and thalassemia. She's smart. She's persistent. She's—"

"She's human." Lucien tapped a pencil on his desk. Three years working on this damn thing and he was at an impasse. He'd identified it as a virus, but not like anything previously known. He'd been able to isolate and identify the protein surrounding it—he'd even developed a test that could be used in humans—but curing it?

"Yes, she's human," Katya continued, "but she's not likely to be intimidated by you. She's worked with our kind in the past and can keep up."

Not with me. Lucien continued to stare at the calendar. Three years. Three years within centuries should not have been significant. But that was before everything he'd lost.

"You say this doctor can keep up with me," Lucien said. "But Katya, you don't know that. You don't even know what I'm working on."

A long silence on the line told him the pointed barb had met its mark.

"Don't forget who controls your funding, Lucien."

He leaned forward and glared at the phone as if Katya could see him. "And don't forget whom I answer to. Do you need a reminder? *It's not you.*"

Katya wasn't a bad sort, but to Lucien, the Russian vampire was an infant. He was here as a favor, and it might be a good idea to remind her of that.

"Would you like me to leave?" he asked. "Would you like to appoint this Dr. Abel to head the project? I've devoted three years to this study. I've developed a test that detects the virus in humans with near perfect accuracy."

"And you're already sharing in the profits from that test."

"Don't insult me," he snapped. "I don't need your money." He had caches of gold that were older than her mother tongue. "I have logged countless hours of research and treated patients with no hope of survival. I did this as a favor to Vecchio and because I believe in this project. Do you think your human doctor has that kind of dedication?"

Of course she didn't. No human did. He couldn't blame them. Their lives were too short for prolonged devotion. Lucien knew that from personal experience.

"You have one living test subject left," Katya said. "*One.* And her time is limited. I'm sending Dr. Abel down while the subject is still alive, and I expect you to treat her with respect."

Lucien grimaced. It was Katya's lab. She'd do as she wanted. If this human wanted to look over his shoulder, he couldn't stop her, but he wasn't going to hold her hand either. She probably didn't even read Latin.

"Do what you want," he said. A knock came at his door, and Lucien rose. He recognized Baojia's step on the concrete. He flung open the door and motioned the other vampire in, taking the small boy who raised his arms out for Lucien. "Katya, I need to meet with Baojia unless you have something you need to discuss with him."

"We have a call scheduled for later," Katya said. "You do not need to be present for our conversation."

It was hard to miss the frost in her tone. Baojia's eyebrows rose in question, but Lucien shook his head.

"Send Dr. Abel's file to me," he said. "I want to look over her previous work and get a sense of how her mind works."

"I'll forward it to your human. Respect, Lucien. She's not a lackey."

"Fine." He leaned over and hit the End Call button with a pencil, bouncing the wriggling little boy in his arms.

"Lucy!" Jake said. "Daddy said I can play with my blocks. Can I?"

"Of course you may." Lucien set the little boy down in front of the bookcases and let him pull out the set of intricately carved wooden blocks Lucien had made for him when Jake was a baby. They sat stacked neatly next to a pile of books the boy played with anytime his father and Lucien needed to meet.

The child was the son of Baojia and Natalie, but he looked remarkably like his father. Lucien had studied the possibility of vampire and human conception extensively at one point in his life and knew it was an impossibility, so he suspected a donor from Baojia's remaining human family in San Francisco, but he had never asked. It was none of his business. Natalie had given birth to their second child the previous year, and the little girl was the image of her brother.

"What did you do to piss off my boss?" Baojia asked, settling into a chair and angling it so he could keep an eye on the door and his child at the same time. "And who is Dr. Abel? Is that what our conference call is likely to be about?"

"Probably." Lucien wiped a hand over his face. "She's a hematologist from Seattle working at one of Katya's other labs. Successfully, it sounds like. Your boss is sending her down here next week."

Baojia frowned. "And you object to that?"

"I don't know her."

"She might be able to help."

"Or I might spend ages just getting her up to speed on the project, wasting time I could spend making actual progress, and she might not be able to understand my research direction at all. Or she'd have her own, which, frankly, would be a distraction."

Baojia thought for a moment. "Why now? The trials for the testing kits have been a success. Katya's making money hand over fist right now shipping them."

"Time," Lucien said. "Limited access to human test subjects. She's sending Dr. Abel down here while we still have Carmen."

Baojia's expression went blank. "How long?"

"I don't know." Lucien's voice softened. "A month. Maybe two or three. I doubt it will be longer than that."

Jake banged his blocks together with a satisfying crash as Baojia stared at the wall.

Lucien knew the loss of their last patient would be gutting to the former assassin even if the reserved immortal would never show it. He was, at his core, a protector. And he took the responsibility to guard the women he'd rescued from traffickers seriously. Losing them one by one over the past three years had been quietly devastating, though there was nothing Baojia could have done differently to prolong their lives.

Nothing either of them could have done.

The women had come to them with a death sentence already imposed. Carmen, the last and strongest of the women, had lasted six months longer than Lucien had predicted. Curing a virus like Elixir could take years of research, even with supernatural abilities.

Lucien doubted a human researcher would solve a mystery that had puzzled the finest vampire minds for centuries.

No, it wasn't doubtful. It was impossible.

❖

Lucien and Baojia stood at the gates of the compound waiting for Dr. Abel's car to arrive. Though there were living quarters at the lab available, the woman had insisted on taking a small rental house in the town twenty miles away. She'd also insisted on taking her own car.

Basically, she was already driving Baojia to distraction.

"Just because the worst *doesn't* happen doesn't mean it can't," he muttered, standing next to Lucien. "Does she think whoever is funding this wants you to find a cure? Do you think threats aren't constant? My people intercepted two spies from India last month asking questions in San Francisco. Three months before that it was a Macedonian assassin."

"Ah yes. He was delicious."

Baojia wasn't amused. "I can't believe Katya agreed to let her live in town."

"I'm rather surprised myself."

"Who is this woman?"

He'd done a little research on her. "Apparently she's the daughter of Katya's archivist. The man has worked for her for thirty years, so he's loyal."

"Dr. Abel should not be allowed to have this much independence."

Lucien raised an eyebrow. "Better not let your wife hear you say that."

"Natalie has learned that security is no longer an option."

"She only learned that when the children were born."

Baojia frowned. "Nevertheless."

Lucien hid his smile. He wasn't at all pleased about the new doctor coming and disrupting his lab, but he couldn't stop Katya. So he decided he would be... amused. He'd pawn Dr. Abel off on one of his underlings and give her all his original notes in Latin. That would keep her occupied for a while.

Under different circumstances, he would look forward to collaboration with a colleague—some of his best work had been done with partners—but he was not in a collaborating mood. He could scent the growing instability in his world, and he didn't like it. Some of the most ancient of their race were dying. Rumors of war drifted in the wind, and currents of power were shifting.

His mother, the most reclusive vampire he knew, had even gone roaming from her mountain home. He'd received a letter not too long ago from the Caucasus Mountains.

I go to see the fire king and your theios. *I would have their counsel on a matter of some concern.*

Night had fallen, and the ocean mist hung heavy over the low buildings that created a horseshoe facing the sea. Though Baojia and Natalie lived in the original farmhouse on the property, the rest of Katya's people, including doctors, lab assistants, support and maintenance staff—human and immortal—lived in the low bungalows and dormitories. The patients, the reason the lab had been built in the first place, had lived in the comfortable and luxurious quarters closest to the ocean.

All but one of them was gone.

"How was Carmen feeling today?" Baojia asked.

"As well as can be expected. She's not as dehydrated."

"Good."

The virus caused by the Elixir drug made vampires lose their grip on their amnis, which slowly starved them as their bodies stopped processing the living blood they needed to survive. They lost their bloodlust, control of their element, and eventually their minds. In humans, the virus was harder to pinpoint. It seemed to affect everyone differently, though a surge of health followed by an eventual slow wasting was universal in all the patients Lucien had treated in California and those he'd observed at Patrick Murphy's facility in Ireland.

Headlights shone on the road. Lucien and Baojia waited as Dr. Abel's car twisted over the low hills leading toward the house. As she approached, Baojia triggered the gate to roll back, and the small hybrid vehicle coasted to a stop in front of the farmhouse.

The woman who exited the vehicle provoked an unexpected surge of pure male admiration in Lucien. Surprised by the unexpected heat of his reaction, he tried to shove it back.

Makeda. Queen.

Her ancestors hailed from the Horn of Africa or very close to it.

Her figure and features were typical of the region. Her first name should have tipped him off, but Americans were so odd about naming their children, and Abel was not a typical Ethiopian or Eritrean surname.

Late thirties. Clear skin. Nonsmoker. Muscle tone indicates regular exercise.

She walked toward them. "Baojia? Is that correct?"

Second language speaker. First language Amharic? Ethiopian?

"Katya sent your picture for security reasons," she continued, taking Baojia's hand. "She said you preferred to use your first name."

"That's correct." Baojia said. "Welcome, Dr. Abel."

"Thank you."

Konjo.

The Amharic word for beauty popped into his mind. Makeda Abel's skin was pure mahogany with gold undertones. And though her hair was pulled back in a very professional twist, he could see the tendrils around her neck curling in the mist. Her eyes were large and cinnamon brown, her lashes sweeping her cheeks when she blinked.

She turned to Lucien and held out her hand. "Are you Dr. Thrax?"

"Lucien." He kept his body under strict control. Lucien realized after he'd taken Makeda's hand that he hadn't even heated his skin to be polite. Which was fine. She was his colleague, and she knew he was a vampire. Subterfuge was hardly necessary.

"Lucien, it's nice to meet you." She dropped his cold hand. "And please call me Makeda. Your reputation is unparalleled. I hadn't read any of your published articles before Katya assigned me to this lab, but I have taken a look at some Dr. Pak directed me toward. You are an excellent writer."

Flattering words, but her examination of him felt indifferent. No increase in heartbeat. Her expression, unlike her body, was impossible to read. Her eyes held no warmth, only speculation.

"You're very young," Lucien said. "I was expecting someone older."

A slight narrowing of her eyes was the only reaction she gave him. "If you expect me to apologize for my age, you'll be waiting awhile."

"That's not what I meant."

He detected skepticism in her eyes before she turned back to Baojia. "Thank you for the assistance at the house today," she said. "The people you sent were very helpful, and the security system seems *very* thorough."

"If you insist on living in town, increased security is something I must insist on."

"And I appreciate it. If you could show me to my offices, I'd like to get settled in. I won't be able to work a full night tonight, but I'd like to unpack a few things, take a tour of the facility, and meet some of the staff if you have time."

"Of course," Baojia said. "Why don't I ride with you? There's a road leading to the lab, and you'll be able to park right behind your office. I can help you unpack and then show you around and introduce you. Almost everyone is working tonight."

"Excellent, thank you." Makeda walked back to the car without even glancing at Lucien.

Baojia waited a beat after she'd closed the car doors. He cleared his throat and spoke softly. "'I expected someone older?' Really, Lucien?"

Lucien shrugged. "I did."

"This is where Natalie would say you have no game."

"She's a colleague. I don't need to have game."

"Right." Baojia walked to the car and opened the door. The heater was on, and a current of warm air drifted from the driver's seat and reached Lucien's nose before the cold night wind snatched it away.

Citrus and cinnamon.

❖

Seven nights later, he was reading another letter from his sire. This one was from Istanbul.

The vampire Zara has disappeared, but the boats loaded with this drug still move through the Black Sea and the Mediterranean unobstructed. There is no stopping it unless we want to draw the humans' attention, as it is hidden within legitimate goods. A cure is the only hope to save the humans. And ourselves. It is a creeping death, but a death that will be inevitable unless you are successful, my son.

Let it never be said that Saba didn't have high expectations for her progeny.

He folded the letter and put it in the locked drawer with the others just as someone knocked on his door and opened it only a second later.

"Not acceptable," he barked, rising to his feet. "If my door is closed, I—"

"Are you serious?" Makeda placed a folder on his desk, tension evident in the clutch of her hands. "I know vampires tend to be archaic, but are you serious with this?"

Lucien crossed his arms and hated that his first thought was that Makeda looked stunning when she was irritated. His second thought was that she was far angrier than she was allowing him to see.

"You asked for copies of my original observation notes," he said. "Is there a problem with them?"

"Reams of photocopies I can deal with because I know e-mail is an issue. But *Latin*?"

He shrugged. "You asked for originals. I take my notes in Latin, and I have for roughly two thousand years. If you expect me to apologize, you'll be waiting awhile."

Makeda said nothing, but Lucien couldn't help but notice the color rising to her cheeks. Apparently the unflappable Dr. Abel *could* be pushed beyond the clinical. So far he'd heard only praise from the team he'd so carefully put together.

She was so *friendly* for a research scientist.

Such a good listener.

So quick with feedback and surprisingly organized.

There were even rumors she had a sense of humor.

It grated more than it should have.

Lucien asked, "Will you need an assistant to translate them for you? I believe more than one are fluent."

Of course they were. He'd chosen them.

Makeda's eyes frosted over. "It's fine. It's been a few years, but I'm sure it'll come back to me. If I run into problems, I'll call my father. His Latin is probably better than yours."

"Since I spoke it as a child, I very much doubt that."

If Lucien had to guess, there were more than a few Latin phrases she was thinking of at that moment. She picked up the file and walked out of the room a few moments before Natalie walked in with the baby.

Natalie handed Sarah to Lucien and took a seat, fighting a smile. Lucien's instincts immediately calmed when Sarah was in his arms. He loved children, even if he'd never had the desire for his own. He found their presence soothing. Sarah smelled of milk and baby shampoo. She fussed at being away from her mother, so Lucien tucked her into his shoulder and rocked his chair a little so she'd fall asleep.

"Making friends already, I see," Natalie said. "That didn't take long."

"I can't imagine why she doesn't like me."

"I know. You're delightful. In a moody, arrogant way."

He sighed and closed his eyes, focusing on the delicate weight of the child on his shoulder. "I know."

"She's really very nice, you know. We had her over for pizza and a movie the other night. She's great with Jake."

"I heard. She's also funny and smart and organized."

Natalie glanced at Lucien's desk, which was piled with books and papers. "No comment."

"None needed."

"So you're jealous of the new doctor in the lab?" Natalie pursed her lips. "Do all the kids want to play with her now and not you? It's okay, you can tell me."

"You're ridiculous."

"No, I'm charming. And cute. And funny." Natalie cocked her head. "No wonder Makeda and I already like each other."

"And humble," he growled, shuffling papers with one hand. "Don't forget humble."

Natalie laughed. "I love you, Lucien, but if you were my vampire, you'd drive me up the wall."

He looked at her from the corner of his eye. "If you were mine, I *would* drive you up the wall. And you wouldn't be complaining about it."

Her mouth dropped open. "Was that a *smolder*? What has gotten into you? Give me back that baby. Men aren't allowed to smolder while they're holding babies. It's not playing fair."

He smiled, but he didn't give her back the baby.

"Seriously though, what *has* gotten into you?" Natalie asked. "I can tell you've been down lately. What's up?"

When he'd first met Natalie and Baojia, Lucien hadn't been certain he still wanted to live. Now that he had a purpose, he'd determined to stay alive so he could finish. After that? Who knew? But humans didn't want to hear about the darker moods of immortal life.

"I don't like research work," he said. "I'm a clinician at heart. Research is... not my favorite."

"And Makeda loves research."

"Yes."

"Can this be like a gang rivalry or something?" She leaned forward. "George and I could take sides. Would there be blood?"

"Natalie, there is always blood." He bared his fangs. "We're vampires."

"Not yet, I'm not. Probably soon." She paused. "It's important though. What you're doing is important. It's going to cure people someday. I know it will. That's huge, Lucien."

"But I can't help Carmen." He went back to sorting papers, trying to keep his free hand busy so he wouldn't break something. "I knew going in that I wasn't going to be able to save them, but I didn't realize how angry it would make me."

"You developed the testing kit."

"That helps vampires. Not humans."

Natalie narrowed her eyes. He hated that expression. She was too perceptive when she narrowed her eyes.

"I don't think you like vampires very much, do you?"

Lucien said, "That's ridiculous. I am one."

"Doesn't mean you like them."

Lucien stopped messing with his desk and put both hands on Sarah's back, enjoying the rise and fall of her little lungs. He could hold her, just like this, for hours, marveling at the intricate symphony of the human body. The divine machine that had fascinated him for thousands of years.

The beat of Sarah's heart and the draw of her breath. The ebb and flow of blood racing through veins and arteries. The quiet gurgle of milk in her belly and the soft coos she let out as she slept. And humming through every inch, conducting that symphony of life, were billions of nerve cells. A galaxy of energy contained in one tiny frame.

"Vampires are fine," he said, rocking Sarah. "We're boring. But you're right. The work is important. I'll try to be nicer to Dr. Abel. Maybe she'll be able offer something of value." He couldn't stop the smile. "Once she gets through my notes."

"They're in some obscure language, aren't they? I hate it when you guys do stuff like that."

"She won't complain." He rocked back in the chair. "After all, I could have written them in Greek."

Chapter Four

Makeda was unpacking boxes of dishes on the kitchen table while Natalie cleaned the counters and Jake ran yelling up and down the hallway of the small bungalow set back on a quiet street.

"Gotta love that echo," Natalie said under her breath. "Jake! Not so loud—the baby's sleeping."

"Ooooooooookaaaaay," the little boy shouted, his feet slapping on the hardwood floor as he made one last trip up and down the empty hallway.

Natalie smiled. "Thank you for being cool about me bringing them."

"Thank you for being cool about helping me unpack," Makeda said. "I am very happy I don't have to live out of a suitcase anymore. And please don't worry about the kids. I have nieces and nephews galore. There's something about an empty house that invites running."

The cheerful redhead peeked over at the port-a-crib set up near the fireplace. "Her brother is so loud. I have no idea how she sleeps through it all."

"Takes after her father?"

Natalie barked out a laugh, but the baby still didn't wake. "Well, that's the truth," Natalie said. "She's dead to the world."

"Is it difficult getting them on a normal sleeping schedule?"

"Difficult?" Natalie rolled her eyes. "Try impossible. Their father wakes up around eight at night and goes to sleep when they'd normally have breakfast. Regular sleep schedules are a foreign concept."

Makeda shrugged and opened another box. She could hear the little boy opening and closing all the empty cupboards and drawers in the back of the house. Most of her things were still in boxes, so he couldn't get into too much trouble.

"Until the children are in school, odd schedules won't be an issue," Makeda said. "As long as they're resting enough to be healthy, do what works for your family."

"That's our philosophy too." She glanced at Makeda from the corner of her eye. "Have you ever had a relationship with a vampire?"

"No, and to be honest, the sleep thing is one of the reasons. I'm a morning person," Makeda said. "There was one—he worked security at my lab, a lot like Baojia—and he was very attractive. We got along well. We went out a couple of times, but..."

"No chemistry?"

"Oh no. There was chemistry. But it was hard getting past the 'feeling like food' thing. I never felt like we were on equal footing."

"That's on him," Natalie said. "Not you. You're incredibly bright and accomplished. You're beautiful—"

"Oh, he was too," Makeda said with a smile.

"Plus you seem like a really cool person. So if he was making you feel inferior, that was about him, not you."

Makeda shrugged. "I'm sure it was partly me. I'm... a nerd. I'm the smart, quiet girl in class who sat in the back and tried not to attract attention. I have no interest in status or power dynamics, and I think you have to be willing to play that game—at least a little bit—to live in that world."

"Hmmm."

Makeda glanced at Natalie, who was now unpacking a box of glassware. She didn't mean to be offensive, but she often had a difficult time gauging how her words would be interpreted. What she considered honest, others sometimes thought was rude. That was not her intention. She truly liked Natalie and thought she could grow to be friends with her. She certainly appreciated her help unpacking.

"I don't mean to say you're power hungry or anything like that," Makeda said.

"I didn't take it that way! And I'm not. But I'm also okay with playing politics a little bit. Newsrooms are very, very political, and writers can be ambitious and manipulative. Fortunately, I find it interesting, not tiresome."

Jake ran back into the living room.

"Jakey, why don't you do a quiet puzzle? Momma brought some in your backpack."

"Okay!"

"Laboratories can also be political," Makeda said. "And researchers are very territorial about their information. But people mostly keep to themselves. Everyone has projects, and as long as they're not fighting over funding, most people just want to be left alone."

"Keep your eyes on your own microscope?"

"Pretty much," Makeda said. "I like it."

The quick stab of anger was no less painful after a month. She had to be here, working on the Elixir cure, but it had been infuriating to be pulled off her thalassemia research. She woke up at night thinking about it. She called to check with her assistant even though the young woman had already been reassigned.

"How are you liking the lab?" Natalie asked.

"It's not mine," Makeda said abruptly. "Sorry. It's... difficult. I didn't choose to be here—I was assigned. Pulled off a project I'd been working on for several years. I know the work here is important, but it's not *mine*. I don't know if that makes sense to other people."

Natalie grimaced. "It does. I've had stories—I still think about some of them—that I had to abandon because I got to a dead end in the investigation or my editor refused to keep backing me. Not many news organizations are willing to devote time to investigative journalism anymore. It's maddening."

Makeda had never thought about that. Both were researchers in their own way. "I imagine it's quite a similar feeling."

"Yep." Natalie reached for the glass casserole dish Makeda was unwrapping. "You move on—usually to something equally as important—but it's not *your* story. Not the one that's lived in your head for months or even years."

"Yes, it sounds very similar." Makeda bent and started putting dishes and pans away in the small kitchen. "I'll adjust. It would be easier if Lucien was more cooperative, but I also understand his point of view. He didn't ask for me to be here."

"Don't be too nice to him. I love him, but he's a grumpy old man. Don't let the pretty young face fool you. I *know* he could use some help. The problem is, he's entirely too brilliant for his own good."

If that wasn't a familiar feeling, Makeda didn't know what was. She had always been socially isolated by her intelligence. It was part of what made research so appealing to her. The thought that she had something in common with the irascible vampire she was forced to work with was somewhat annoying.

Makeda said, "Lucien is..." Irritating. Stubborn. Brilliant.

Highly attractive.

Makeda blinked as the thought popped into her mind.

How inconvenient.

"He has a hard time connecting with people," Natalie said. "Not many people understand how his mind works. I'm sure that's very isolating."

"His notes certainly indicate that he's quite brilliant. Now that I've managed to interpret them."

Natalie bit her lip to hold in a laugh. "He can also be a bit of a shit when he doesn't get his way."

"Early observations also point to that conclusion."

"I have faith." Natalie pursed her lips. "I think you two will find some common ground."

She wanted to move on to the next subject because her brain was supplying all sorts of inappropriate common ground she might find with the irritating Dr. Thrax. "How about you?" she asked Natalie. "Are you working at the newspaper right now?"

Natalie shook her head and looked over at Jack and Sarah. Jack had finished the puzzle with lightning speed and was wandering back down the hall. "I'm going to have many, many years to write. I get these little people for a blink. I'm going to enjoy every minute."

"So you'll turn?"

Natalie nodded silently.

"When they're young?"

"Probably." Natalie looked up from a box of cookbooks. "He worries. He never says anything, but it's constant. And I do too. We live in a dangerous world, and I'm vulnerable. Right now he has to protect all three of us. He says he wants me to wait, but I can't help thinking that if I were less vulnerable, I could be the one protecting too. And it wouldn't all be on him."

As hard as it was for Makeda to imagine wanting to be a vampire, Natalie's reasoning made sense. The heart of a mother was a fierce thing. Would she give up her life if it meant protecting one of her nieces or nephews from harm? Absolutely. Family was everything to her.

"You'd be separated from them at first, wouldn't you?"

Natalie nodded. "For a year at least. Which is why it won't happen right away. Sarah's too little. But once they're older... We have friends. Good friends. We've been talking to them about how to make things work. Baojia has a few favors he needs to call in, but he has favors he can offer too."

She smiled. "Politics. Again."

Natalie nodded. "It's inevitable. Believe it or not, Baojia is much more like you. He hates politics."

"But it's a reality."

"Yep. And he does what he needs to do to protect the people he loves." Natalie glanced over at baby Sarah. "I can't imagine a better or more attentive father."

Makeda and Natalie both realized at the same time that Jack was being suspiciously quiet. The women stopped and angled an ear to the back of the house.

Springs.

"He's jumping on your bed," Natalie whispered. "Do you care?"

"Nope. But we're not going to tell him he has permission because that would spoil the fun."

"You *are* an experienced auntie."

Makeda smiled. "I am the best."

A cheerful tap at the door made both women turn their heads.

"Expecting anyone?" Natalie asked.

Makeda poked her head around the corner and caught the edge of gold-tipped brown hair through the glass of her front door.

"It's Philip," she whispered. "My neighbor. He's very... friendly."

Natalie wiggled her eyebrows. "Oh, is he?"

"I better get the door or he won't leave."

Natalie's amused expression turned suspicious. "Wait, is this guy hassling you?" Leaving the boxes on the kitchen table, Natalie followed on Makeda's heels. "Because that's not okay. This is a friendly town, but that's not an excuse for harassment."

"No, I don't want to give you the wrong impression. He's not *harassing* me," Makeda said. "He's just a friendly, and I'm antisocial. He lives in Mrs. Gunnerson's guest house, and he helped me move some stuff into the garage last week. He's been stopping by ever since. He probably saw the garage door open and boxes out." Makeda opened the door and forced a smile. "Hi, Philip."

"Mak!"

You are not familiar enough to use a nickname with me.

Shiny white teeth in a tanned face reminded Makeda of a beer commercial. Philip, the quintessential California surfer dude kicking back on the beach with his friends. Probably a volleyball would be involved.

He pointed toward her garage with his thumb. "I saw the boxes out. Need any help? I'm trying to avoid work right now."

Natalie poked her head around and stuck her hand out. "Hey, I'm Natalie."

Philip shook her hand, his eyes squinting in the afternoon light. "Hey, Natalie, nice to meet... I've seen you at the market, haven't I?"

"Could be. So, you're trying to avoid work, huh?" Natalie stepped beside Makeda and crossed her arms. "What do you do?"

Philip looked pleased at the cross-examination. "Software development. I work for a company in Palo Alto, but since all my stuff is remote, I live up here."

Makeda said, "Philip likes his surfboard."

"I do." Another bleached-white smile. "And the north coast may be cold, but the waves are wicked."

"Nice." Natalie's expression hadn't softened, but her stance did. "So you don't mind if we put you to work?"

Oh no. Makeda was having a nice time talking with Natalie. She didn't want an intruder. She was fine socializing one-on-one, but the bigger the group, the more awkward she felt. There were too many variables with large parties.

Philip looked eager to help, but Makeda shut him down. "We're fine," she said. "Honestly, with the baby sleeping, probably the less people in the house the better."

Surfer boy's eyes went round. "Oh, shit—I mean shoot. I didn't realize there was a kid around. Sorry about the knock."

"It's fine," Makeda said, dropping her voice to a whisper. "But she's really fussy about her sleep so..."

"No worries. But promise me if there's anything too heavy for you guys to handle, you'll set it aside. I'm happy to help another time, you know?" He craned his neck to try to look inside. "When the baby isn't around and everything."

Just then, Jake let out a war whoop designed to wake the dead and came racing down the hall, his tiny bare feet sounding like a herd of small, rampaging elephants.

Philip frowned and opened his mouth, but Makeda broke in before he could say anything else.

"Okay, bye! Thanks for the offer, how about another time? Bye." She shut the door and spun to face Natalie, who wore an amused expression.

"Subtle," she said.

"I am not good with men. Especially men who are flirting with me. It makes me very uncomfortable."

"I thought he was cute."

"He is. He's very cute. And sweet. Philip strikes me as the human equivalent of a yellow lab."

Natalie snorted and herded Jake back to the kitchen. "He's smart too. A software designer?"

"I think that may be code for 'Grandma gave me a trust fund so I can play around developing apps,'" Makeda said. "He's never actually mentioned what company he works for, and he seems to spend far more time with a wet suit or walking Mrs. Gunnerson's terrier than in his home office."

"Interesting." The wheels were turning behind Natalie's distracted gaze. "I might have Baojia run a check on him."

"Oh, please don't. I'm sure he's fine. He just doesn't understand hermits like me."

"Still..." Natalie shrugged. "If he's your neighbor, Baojia probably already checked him out. He's thorough that way."

"Exactly."

"So sit back, relax"—Natalie peeked out the window at Philip's retreating figure—"and enjoy the scenery."

❖

Carmen, the last of the Elixir victims from Southern California, was slipping in and out of consciousness when Makeda finally met her. She'd heard the story, how Baojia and Natalie rescued a group of women trafficked in from Northern Mexico who had been deliberately infected with Elixir. The women were intended to be objects of a hunt designed to amuse powerful and rich immortals. Baojia, Natalie, and their friends had stopped the hunt and killed those immortals involved, but they hadn't been able to cure the human women. Like all infected by the drug, they wasted away.

The one survivor had only lasted as long as she had because they had caught the virus early. Carmen had been on immunosuppressant drugs, tried various vaccines and countless diet and alternative therapies designed to help her body fight off the illness. Nothing had worked. The virus was consuming her body, and no amount of intravenous feeding seemed to help.

Makeda sat in the chair next to Carmen, reading through the translation of Lucien's notes one of his assistants had given her in a moment of pity. Though the immortal physician might have come across to her as cold and territorial, in his notes she caught a glimpse of the man behind the stoic facade.

November 6, 2013—We lost Felicia today. Though an autopsy would show acute liver failure, the cause was Elixir, of course. Renal function had decreased in the week before her death. I considered dialysis and talked it over with her, but she did not want to suffer through the treatment when she had only months, if not weeks, left anyway.

We made her comfortable and allowed the other women to say good-bye. She will be missed.

March 4, 2014—Magdalena will be dead by the end of the week. Her heart is giving out.

April 25, 2014—Alma's liver is failing. I can't discern a connection among these causes of death.

October 16, 2014—I can't save them. I can't save any of them.

At times, Lucien's notes read like case studies. Other times, they descended into a familiarity akin to correspondence. But throughout her examination of the notes, she felt as if she knew him a little. Makeda saw that the man who wrote so passionately about treatments and diagnostics felt as deeply as any caregiver for the patients he treated. It softened her attitude toward him but made his current behavior more and more of a mystery. Far from warming to her, every night that passed, Lucien's hostility to her presence seemed to grow.

"Knock, knock." Baojia's voice came a moment before a faint tap on the door. "Am I interrupting anything?"

Makeda shook her head. "I'm just reading over her case notes."

Baojia pulled up a chair. "He's tried everything."

"It appears so."

"And nothing worked." The quiet immortal pulled out a paperback book. "She liked to read."

"Carmen?"

He nodded. "When her eyes started to go, I read to her. Me or Natalie, depending on when she was awake." Baojia reached over and smoothed Carmen's hair back from her forehead. "She looks older now, but she's only twenty-two."

It was hard to miss the sadness and affection in the vampire's voice.

"You're a good man, Baojia."

"I'm a failure."

"No, you're—"

"Don't." Baojia held up his hand before Makeda could refute his words. "I know logically that I am not a doctor. I know that I protected Carmen and the others from numerous plots and attempts on their life over the years. But at the end of the day, I'm more powerful than they could ever be. I'm stronger. I am their guardian. It was my job to protect them, and I couldn't protect them from this."

She kept quiet, not wanting to disregard his guilt. Baojia had a right to feel however he wanted. Makeda knew what it was like to watch a patient die.

"I'm not a doctor," Baojia said. "I'm a grunt. A soldier. A killer." He paused to let his words sink in. "Now imagine how Lucien feels. Imagine watching them waste away by degrees. And all the knowledge, all the experience, all the wisdom you've picked up over thousands of years... means nothing."

"I know what it feels like to lose a patient."

"He's not cold, Makeda."

"I didn't think he was."

"Didn't you?" Baojia cracked open the paperback with a fresh-faced girl on the cover. "I need to finish this for her. We're almost done."

Makeda felt her throat tighten, but she didn't rise. Instead, she put her notes aside and listened to the soothing voice of a self-admitted killer reading a romance novel in Spanish. She heard a noise at the door and turned to see Lucien standing with his back against the opposite wall, his cool grey eyes fixed on the dying human.

❖

Two nights later, Makeda heard a knock on the door just as she was pulling out the ingredients to make her favorite comfort food.

Oh Philip...

The man was nice enough. And he was very helpful. But Makeda had been looking forward to an evening alone. Every time Philip came over and asked to help with something, that meant she had to work too. She didn't want to work. She wanted cooking and wine.

Earlier that night, Carmen had taken a turn that caused everyone to rush to her room. Makeda ran in with the nurses only to have Lucien shove her out before he took over with his team.

It was jarring. And a stark reminder of where the lab's loyalties lay.

She walked to the door expecting to see Philip's blond-brown mane, but instead she saw a dark brown head, hair thick and sprinkled with silver. Lucien's hair reminded her of a fox's coat.

Makeda opened the door. "What's wrong? Did Carmen—?"

"She's stable." His hands were shoved in his pockets. His eyes were locked on hers as if he was making every effort not to look into her house. "That's why I came by. To let you know."

"I have a phone."

"I hate phones, and I needed a run."

"It's fifteen miles from here to the compound."

He couldn't help himself. He glanced around her entryway, his eyes lighting on the painting over her left shoulder. "Is that Lalibela?"

"Yes."

"Have you been there?"

"Only when I was a child. I haven't been back to Ethiopia since I was eight. I don't remember much."

Which was a lie. The imprint of her childhood home had never faded.

"I don't believe you," Lucien said, walking into her house, his eyes locked on the painting. "The light in this..."

"It's very good. The artist is a friend of my uncle's. He lives there. I'm surprised you recognized it. Most Americans don't."

"I'm not American."

Of course he wasn't. If his accent didn't remind her, his age should have. Lucien had implied he was over two thousand years old. He would hardly consider himself an American. And he was clearly making himself at home. His perusal of her art had shifted to the Salish moon mask she'd bought at a gallery in Vancouver several years before.

"This isn't African."

"American. Pacific Northwest."

"Extraordinary." His eyes moved to a photograph from the Omo Valley in southern Ethiopia. His fingers rose to the glass covering the photograph. "Look at her scarring. That pattern is very beautiful."

"It's ceremonial." She glanced at his arms and legs, now wholly covered by his clothing. "Are you interested in body modification?"

She'd never known a vampire to have tattoos like his. He must have gotten them during life. She didn't think vampire skin could take ink. She wasn't even sure it could take regular needles.

"You're thinking about my tattoos?" He glanced at her. "We all had them in my tribe, even our women. Legs. Arms. Backs."

"Face?"

"Sometimes, but not for me."

"A historian would probably have a field day examining them."

"Probably." He shoved his hands in his pockets and moved on to another painting. "But I'm not a subject for study."

Makeda couldn't stop the slight smile. "I hope you appreciate the irony."

"Oh, I do."

He didn't seem in a hurry to go, so Makeda left Lucien admiring the art she'd hung. It was a personal quirk. A house didn't feel like home to her unless there were things decorating the walls. In her mother's house it was family photographs and crosses. In her own house, it was the art collection she'd taken so many years to acquire.

She walked back to the kitchen only to have Lucien appear in the doorway before her.

"Please don't do that in my home," she asked. *Not prey. You are not prey.*

"How do you do that?" Lucien asked.

"Do what?"

"Regulate your heart rate so effectively. You have very few pulse spikes, even during emergency situations like we had with Carmen tonight."

"Increased heart rate does no one any favors," Makeda said. "It makes higher brain function less effective. During an emergency I have to think, not revert to primitive impulses like fight or flight. I learned how to control my heart rate during my emergency medicine rotation."

"And you still use the technique now?"

"I don't forget lessons."

"Ever?"

"No," she said. It wasn't a point of pride. There were some lessons she'd prefer to forget. "I don't forget anything."

Lucien stepped toward her. "What was I wearing the night we met?"

"A black or dark blue dress shirt. It was too dark to tell. And a pair of light brown slacks. They looked a bit like chinos, but with better tailoring. There were three buttons undone, though you normally only unbutton two buttons at work. Perhaps you were trying to subconsciously gauge my reaction to you. Black walking shoes. Black socks."

"The shirt was blue. So were the shoes and socks. If you were a vampire, you'd have been able to tell the difference."

"Perhaps. But as I don't ever want to be a vampire, I'll have to live with that slight disability." She paused and tried to remember her manners even if she wanted him gone from her space. His presence was unnerving. "Would you like a glass of wine? I was just about to pour one."

"Yes." His answer seemed to surprise him. "I would like some wine. What were you doing tonight? Did I interrupt you?"

"No. I was going to cook and drink. Not very exciting."

"Who are you cooking for?"

"Myself. And I freeze some for during the week when I don't want to cook." She poured two glasses of wine and tried to understand just how Lucien Thrax—a vampire she didn't particularly like who clearly didn't like her—had come to be sitting at her bar watching her cook. She pulled out the garlic and onion from the refrigerator, setting them beside the jar of berbere spice and shiro powder.

"You're making shiro?"

"Yes." She handed him wine. "You know shiro?"

A smile touched his lips. It was the first time she'd seen a smile from him. "Yes, I know shiro."

"Clearly, you've spent time in Ethiopia if you know Lalibela and shiro."

He sipped his wine, and Makeda could feel his eyes on her as she worked. "My mother is Ethiopian."

Makeda glanced up. "Not your human mother."

"No." His eyes almost laughed. Almost. "My sire. She lives in the highlands around Chencha."

"It's beautiful there."

"Have you been there?"

Makeda shook her head. "Only seen pictures. My mother and father have friends who live in Arba Minch."

He paused and took another sip of wine. "Why did they move? Your parents, I mean."

Makeda looked at him from the corner of her eye. "Academics were not always so welcome."

"True in too many places," he muttered. "So you came here?"

"My father had a friend under vampire aegis in Addis Ababa. This friend knew my family wanted to leave—*needed* to leave—so he wrote to people who might have need of a translator. My father is highly educated in ancient languages. One thing led to another..."

"And he came to work for Katya."

"Yes." She poured the chopped onion into a bowl with the garlic. "And he has worked for her ever since then. He's very loyal."

"Who was the immortal in Addis?"

"I don't know." She wiped her hands on a dish towel. "There are some things a child is not permitted to know. By the time it was appropriate to ask, it didn't seem important anymore. We're American, my sisters and me."

"You've never felt the urge to go back?"

A sharp stab of longing. "Of course I have," she said. "But how could the reality of a country live up to my childhood dreams of it?"

"Maybe it would be better."

"I doubt it," Makeda said, reaching for the knife without looking. "That's why"—she sucked in a breath when she turned and Lucien was standing inches from her, his hand clutching her own—"they're dreams. What are you doing?"

He held her hand inches from the knife. "You were about to cut yourself."

She glanced down to see that yes, she'd been careless. The blade was pointing toward her, and her hand was poised to grab the blade and not the handle. "Thank you. I was distracted."

He didn't let her hand go. Makeda had the distinct impression she was being analyzed in an entirely *un*clinical way. Her heartbeat picked up even as she willed her breathing to slow. She tipped her head up and watched Lucien's eyes.

They were extraordinary eyes. Warm brown around the edges with a cool grey surrounding the pupil. Stunning eyes. Inhuman eyes. She'd been told some vampires' eyes changed color when they turned, but she didn't want to ask. The question felt too intimate. He was looking, not at her face, but at her hair. His head cocked to the side as he ran his gaze all over the natural curls she'd let down that night.

"What do you want?" Makeda asked. "Why are you really here?"

"I want you..." He blinked and his eyes came back to hers. "I want you to leave me alone."

"I have a job to do. Just like you."

"I know." His eyes flicked down to her lips. She felt an inexplicable pull toward him. She'd forgotten about her pulse. Her heart threatened to beat out of her chest at his proximity.

Damn him.

"You should go back to Ethiopia," Lucien murmured. "Reality is always better than dreams."

"It's not."

"It is. Because it's real. How can you love something that isn't real?"

Makeda blinked, and Lucien was standing in the doorway again. "Someone is at the door."

A quick, cheerful knock told her Philip had finally come calling, but her eyes never left Lucien.

"I don't have any desire to share your company with another," he said. "I'll see you at work tomorrow night."

"I'll bring some shiro... if you want." Makeda heard Philip knock again, and she turned her head toward the door.

When she looked back, Lucien was already gone.

Saba

The Caucasus Mountains

Arosh stroked his finger over her short, cropped hair, smoothing a line down her spine and over the round curve of her buttocks. Saba sighed and moved closer to his touch.

"My queen, why do you come to me with such a heavy heart?" he whispered. "Do you need my fire for your vengeance?"

She blinked her eyes open, staring at the silks draped over his bed high in the mountains of Georgia. She could hear the soft, slippered feet of the women who served him shuffling in the corridors outside. A brazier burned low, not that she needed it when she was in Arosh's bed. It could be the middle of winter and the man would still walk shirtless through the snow.

"I don't know what I need," Saba said.

"Command me, my love. For I am ever your servant."

She smiled. "You're my servant when it suits you."

"True." He stretched his arms up and out. "But when I see your eyes turn inward, I know what you are thinking."

"I'm not there." She rolled over and laid her head on his flat abdomen. His amnis sparked under her cheek. The trail of hair low on his belly tickled her lip, and she reached out and bit it, making him laugh. "I'm not there *yet*, my fire king."

His fingers traced over the whirling spiral scars that decorated her shoulders. "You will tell me, Saba. For both of us have been quiet for too long. We are not retiring creatures. When you are ready, we will remake the world and begin again."

"Kato will not approve."

Arosh shrugged. "His heart is too soft toward the humans. It always has been."

"Neither will my son approve."

"Is Lucien your king?"

She bared her fangs and scraped fine lines over Arosh's hip. "Be careful. You assume much."

He yanked her up and latched his mouth over her breast, drawing long and hard at the sensitive rise until his teeth pierced her skin and Saba's back arched with pleasure.

Arosh lifted his bloody mouth to hers, and Saba tasted herself on his lips.

"You like it when I assume," he said.

"I will give my son a little more time," she said, "before I take any steps he would find unconscionable."

"Leave your son out of my bed," Arosh said. "He has no place here." He kissed a line between her breasts, over her belly, and south toward the garden where he'd always found his pleasure.

Saba smiled and grabbed a fistful of Arosh's silken hair. "And who is your queen, fire king?"

"Only my Saba." Arosh's teeth sank into the soft flesh of her inner thigh. "Only you."

Chapter Five

"Baojia said you were close. That was a year ago. What happened?" Brigid was a fire vampire and chief of security for Patrick Murphy, the immortal leader of Dublin. She was tiny, irritable, and flammable, especially when she didn't get the answers she was after. She was also mated to one of Lucien's friends. Carwyn ap Bryn was a former priest and current patriarch of one of the largest clans of earth vampires around the globe.

"Whatever update you can give us," Carwyn said, "would be most welcome. Murphy has been wanting an update, as has Terrance Ramsay in London. We appreciate the tests you've developed—they've helped enormously—but new infections are still happening despite the crackdown on Elixir shipments."

"There is no straight line in this kind of research," Lucien said, staring into the fire. "I've managed to isolate the cause. That's why we can test for it in human blood. But diagnosis doesn't mean treatment. I can tell you what's happening with the Elixir virus, but I can't tell you how to treat it."

Brigid said, "So it is a virus?"

"It's a virus in humans that can spread to vampires. Only it mutates from human to vampire, so the treatment for one will have to be different than the treatment for the other. The test you have can detect the protein tied to the virus. But killing this virus..." Lucien shook his head. "You can't kill it. You can only starve it."

"So how do we do that?"

"By starving the host."

Brigid's face was stricken. "So that's it? The humans die and the virus dies with them? That's not good enough."

"If you have some brilliant idea, I'd love to hear it," Lucien snapped. "I'm sure your twenty-some years of life and brief stint as a vampire have prepared you for advanced clinical research."

Brigid bared her fangs, but Carwyn leaned forward and put a steadying hand on Brigid's knee. "You know this is personal to us."

"It's personal to all of us." Had they forgotten Lucien had lost a human lover to this plague? Had suffered from Elixir poisoning himself? Rada's pained eyes haunted him. "Pressuring me isn't going to help."

Carwyn said, "Baojia said Katya has given you another one of her people to help. A doctor?"

Lucien groaned. "Enough. I just came from a long night at the hospital. I thought we were having a drink and relaxing. I don't want to talk about the new thorn in my side."

"A thorn in your side?" Brigid said. "Sounds like I'm predisposed to like her."

Lucien glared, but Carwyn only laughed. "Let the man have a few moments of peace, Brig. It's not as if he doesn't eat and breathe this project." He turned back to Lucien. "I'm also curious about the new thorn though."

"Dr. Makeda Abel. She's human."

"And?"

Lucien sighed. "Humans are fine for assistants. But not as collaborators. Her brain cannot work as quickly as mine."

"So?" Carwyn said. "It seems to me that we need new ideas, not faster ones. Who cares if ideas come a bit slower for her if she has good ones? What's her background?"

"Blood disorders." He pulled at his lip as a thought began to form. *New ideas, not faster ones.* "She was working on some kind of... sickle cell treatment or something like that before she got pulled off her own work and put on mine."

"So she's there unwillingly?" Brigid asked.

"She knows how the game is played," Lucien said. "She's no dummy, and she grew up under Katya's aegis. I'm sure she's getting something out of this project other than just a paycheck."

"Nevertheless," Carwyn said, "sounds like both of you are stuck. She was forced into this and you were forced to work with her."

"We stay out of each other's way. She's still coming up to speed on the research so far."

"Try to make the most of it, Lucien. She may have ideas you've never even considered."

❖

Those words followed Lucien on the plane back to San Francisco. He rested in the belly of the converted cargo plane belonging to Giovanni Vecchio and let his mind wander.

What could Makeda Abel know that Lucien didn't?

The Elixir infected human blood, unlocking a dormant virus in vampires. It took different forms in humans and vampires, but both forms led to a slow wasting disease. Starving humans of blood oxygen and vital nutrients, and starving vampires of amnis. But it all led back to blood.

Human blood.

Sickle cell was a blood disorder.

No, not sickle cell.

Thalassemia.

It was thalassemia she'd been working on, a human blood disorder affecting hemoglobin, the protein that carried oxygen to red blood cells. Patients suffering from it suffered from anemia because their red blood cells died, essentially of oxygen starvation.

Cell death. Starvation. Wasting.

"Thalassemia," he murmured. Maybe...?

It was possible Makeda's old research and Lucien's had some overlap. What if, instead of bringing her up to date on what he'd done, she looked at Carmen's blood as if it was a new case? No assumptions. No research parameters.

Not fast enough.

Nothing would be fast enough to save Carmen. Nothing would

bring any of the victims back. But nothing was stopping the spread of Elixir either.

"...a death that will be inevitable unless you are successful."

For the thousandth time, Lucien wondered just what his mother was doing traveling around the world. Saba wasn't a recluse, but she loved her mountains and usually had no desire to go wandering. The fact that she'd left her home piqued his interest. She was poking around in the Eastern Mediterranean, probably accompanied by one or more members of her old cadre. The very cadre that had spawned the idea of Elixir in the middle ages.

It was not a comforting thought.

Ziri, cunning wind vampire and elder ruler of the northern deserts, was unpredictable at best. He was manipulative, vicious, and very smart. Ironically, it was Ziri who had been Saba's lover when Lucien was sired. The blending of their blood was probably what had led to Lucien's wandering ways, which were odd for an earth vampire.

Kato, ancient king of the Mediterranean, had once been a favorite uncle to Lucien. His *theios*. Kato was jovial and fierce at the same time. It was Kato whose lover had first taken the Elixir. Kato who had fallen into the mindless haze that had almost claimed Lucien's life.

And Arosh. Fire king. Ruler of Central Asia. Saba's favorite lover. They could never be in the same place for more than a few decades, but each held the other in greatest esteem. Arosh was fiercely loyal to Saba and all his friends. He'd been the one to shelter Kato during his illness. Now that Kato had regained his senses, Arosh could be out for revenge.

Lucien had a sinking feeling he'd be meeting all of them before this was over. Someone with a very old grudge was spreading the poison Saba and her friends had helped create. They'd tried to destroy it, but nothing in their world remained hidden forever. The poison was spreading like a drop of wine in a water glass.

❖

"I want you to throw away whatever you're working on right now," Lucien said, striding into the lab where he'd seen Makeda's assistant coming and going. "I want you to take all my research and set it aside."

Makeda looked up and spun her chair toward him, but she didn't stand. "Oh? Welcome back and all that."

"Toss it. Look at this case as if you were seeing everything for the first time. Carmen is your only patient. You have no idea what she has or what I've tried in the past regarding treatment. Throw it all away and start fresh. It doesn't have to be fast. I want slow. Deliberate. Consider anything and everything. You have no direction right now; you're starting over."

Lucien stood with his hands on his hips, but Makeda didn't react. There was just that maddening slow pulse and a face devoid of emotion.

She said, "What makes you think I was following your research to begin with?"

"What?"

"I've already started fresh," she continued. "It was no use going over old lines of inquiry. I'm looking at this as if it were a human blood disorder that has nothing to do with vampires."

She'd anticipated him. Lucien was taken aback and... slightly aroused. Unexpected and inconvenient.

"Fine," he said. "Good. If you have any questions—"

"I won't ask you," Makeda said. "That would be counterproductive." She turned back to her computer.

Her disregard only made her more appealing. "You're very quick for a human."

"I'll try not to be insulted by that. You're not the first arrogant vampire I've worked with."

"And you're not the first human I've worked with."

"I know." She flipped through a notebook of handwritten notes. "You've got a bit of a reputation, Dr. Thrax."

He stiffened. "What does that mean?"

"Only that a few of the younger techs would be happy to catch your eye." She raised an eyebrow. "It's quite well known you enjoy human women. According to gossip in the lab, *only* human women. But if you're looking for company—"

"I'm not." Lucien didn't react. It was normal for humans to tell tales about the unfamiliar. "Do you make a habit of listening to gossip?"

"It's practically impossible to avoid it in a lab this small. We amuse ourselves any way we can." She finally looked at him. "And since you're not the kind of administrator who takes kindly to practical joking—or so I've been told—gossip and innuendo will have to do."

"Lives are at stake, Dr. Abel. I expect my employees to focus on the task at hand."

Her mouth turned up at the corner, and Lucien caught a hint of a dimple in her cheek. "So do I, but I also recognize that they're only human. Or most of them are. We all need a break now and then, or we burn out. My kind doesn't have eight hours of sleep forced on us every night."

"Not all my kind do either." Lucien was old enough that sometimes sleep eluded him. Or he only grabbed a few hours of it in a night. "Fine. Enjoy your jokes and your gossip, but don't expect me to feed into it."

"I wouldn't dream of it," Makeda said, turning back to her notebook. "I need to record some notes now. Please close the door on your way out."

Lucien had been dismissed. The nerve of the woman...

Dammit, he was definitely aroused.

❖

One month later...

"No more," Carmen whispered to him. "Lucien, no more."

He leaned over the bed and spoke softly. "I'm just trying to keep you comfortable. I know you don't want me to—"

"The feeding tube... out." Carmen spoke through cracked lips. "I want it out."

Lucien dabbed some petroleum jelly over her lips to ease the cracking. He ignored the sickly-sweet smell surrounding her. Once, that sweetness had lived in her blood. Now he smelled it on her breath. Her hair. The cold sweat that coated her skin.

"You'll die without the feeding tube," he said quietly.

"I'm dying anyway. I'm tired. I just want to go."

She was nearly skeletal. Her heart was failing. She slipped in and out of consciousness.

"Please, Lucien." Carmen closed her eyes. "You have never treated me, or any of the others, like experiments. Not once. Please don't keep me alive now just because—"

"You were never experiments," Lucien said, his throat closing up. "You are my patient. I want to help you."

"You can't." Her emaciated hand reached out to grasp his. "It's finished. You'll cure others. Take anything you need from me for your work. It's only a body. But let me go. Please. Stop the feeding tube. Stop the water. We both know how to end this."

Guilt was a lead weight in the pit of his stomach. "What are you asking of me?"

"You know what I'm asking." She squeezed his hand with surprising strength. "Please call Baojia and Natalie. I want to say good-bye. Then, if you are truly my doctor, you'll end this. *Please.*"

"Carmen, you don't want me to—"

"I was never meant to live this long," she said, her voice stronger than it had been in months. "I was supposed to die months ago. This is not life. This is only suffering. God would not want this for me. He is not that cruel."

He sat back in his chair, his eyes locked with hers.

Please, she mouthed. *Please.*

An hour later, Natalie and Baojia sat on either side of her, Natalie singing a lullaby he'd heard Carmen sing to baby Sarah. Baojia held her hand with both of his, a pillar of quiet calm compared to the riot of Lucien's emotions. Carmen's breathing was labored, her pulse erratic. The feeding tube she hated was out. The intravenous fluid had been taken away. Lucien stood with the syringe of morphine in his hand, watching his friends say good-bye.

He reached over Natalie and inserted the syringe in the port on Carmen's arm.

A few minutes. Less. The monitor had been switched off, but Lucien heard when Carmen's heart stopped beating. One last breath rattled out.

She was gone.

And he had failed.

Lucien turned to see Makeda standing on the far side of the room, tears running down her cheeks.

"What are you doing here?" He didn't recognize his own voice. It was hard. Cold.

Makeda's watery eyes met his without flinching. "She was my patient too."

"You barely knew her."

"Lucien," Natalie said from Carmen's bedside. "This is not the time."

Makeda said, "I know you're feeling—"

"You know nothing about how I am feeling right now," Lucien snapped. "You know nothing. Get out."

Baojia stepped between them. "*Both* of you get out. Right now. You disrespect Carmen with your petty bickering."

Lucien didn't argue. He walked out the door, down the hallway where a clutch of other researchers had gathered, and through the double doors leading outside. He walked to the edge of the cliffs and stood, staring at the sea.

Mist soaked his coat and shirt. He stripped them both off until the water coated his body and drenched his hair. He could feel it dripping down his back as his amnis coursed through his body, reaching for something—anything—to release it. He broke into a jog.

Then he ran. He ran along the cliffside, kicking off his shoes and socks. He sank his feet into this raw, untamed land and went to his knees.

His fists slammed into the earth, and he heard the edge of the cliff break away, sliding into the ocean below. He gripped the earth and pulled it apart. His amnis punched down into the soil and spread through tiny fissures in the ground. More of the cliff broke away and fell into the sea. He gripped a boulder between his hands, roaring as he sent his energy into the rock, fracture after fracture cracking the boulder until his amnis had turned it to gravel.

He ached with failure. Thousands of years of power and learning had done nothing to heal them. All his efforts. Years of research.

It's finished.

Lucien curled into the ground and let the soil embrace him.

Please.

The raw earth closed over his body as he sank down to the bedrock.

Let me go.

He woke knowing it was dusk. He'd passed the previous night and day in the comfort of the earth, but that was all the self-indulgence he could allow. There was work to be done. He rose to the surface and surveyed the damage to the landscape.

Deep cracks lined the edge of the cliffs, and several boulders had been beaten into gravel. He shored up the cliffside and spread the gravel so it wasn't noticeable. He walked back to the lab, soil coating his skin. Clamping down the grief that threatened to make him rage, he pushed open the doors and walked to Makeda's office. He knocked but didn't wait for permission to enter.

"Dr. Abel," he said as he walked in, "make sure you take the necessary samples of the patient's body before it's sent to the incinerator."

Makeda turned slowly, her eyes raking up and down his body.

Lucien knew he looked savage. Pants torn and dirty, no shirt, caked mud covering an upper body marked with the ceremonial tattoos he'd inked in mortal life. His tattoos were why he rarely went without long sleeves.

He made his voice as clinical as possible. "Samples need to be taken as quickly as possible. Even with the body chilled—"

"I took them last night after you left," she said quietly. "Lucien—"

"You were there to collect samples," he said. "I apologize if I misunderstood your reason for being in the patient's room. You were following protocol."

"That's not why I was there, and you know it."

He heard the angry bite in her voice, and the dark part of his mind reveled in it.

"Nevertheless, if samples have been taken, then the body should be disposed of as quickly as possible. It's still unknown how the virus —"

"Baojia and Natalie are arranging the cremation. Her ashes will be sent to her family priest in Ensenada. Why are you acting like this?"

"Like what?"

"Like you don't care. There was a minor earthquake just north of here last night. I suppose that was a coincidence."

He paused. "My caring didn't save her life. The only thing that's important now is the research. I don't expect you'll need time off since you barely knew the patient. Please have your assistant send me a progress report as soon as possible. I've been lax on oversight with you, but don't expect that to continue."

"Are you really this much of a bastard?"

"Does it matter?" he asked. "We're colleagues, Dr. Abel. Our focus should be on developing a cure for this virus, not making friends."

She was upset. Of course she was. No matter how many patients he lost, he still felt them. And she'd had only a fraction of his life. Her cheeks were flushed, and her eyes shone. Part of him wanted to walk over, put his arms around her, and take comfort in her warmth. She tempted him on every level. Her mind. Her body. Her softness and her arrogance. The scent of her blood called to him.

But she was human. She was mortal. She would die like all the rest, and his heart...

That ancient organ could only take so much.

Rada's emaciated form filled his memory. The memory of her words haunted him. *Please, Lucien. Please, end this for me. I hurt so much. Please, my love...*

"I expect a progress report on my desk tomorrow night," Lucien said. "Please attach any relevant data to the report."

"So you are this much of a bastard," she muttered. "Fine. I'll get the report to you when I have the time. I'll remind you that I do not work for you. I'm cataloguing the samples, and then I'm going to Baojia and Natalie's for a drink. I should probably invite you, but I really don't want you there."

"I have things to do and no time for socializing."

"Good for you, Dr. Thrax."

He turned and walked out the door, heading to his office and the monkish personal quarters behind it. He showered. He dressed.

Then he got back to work.

Chapter Six

Two months after Carmen's death, Makeda took her first night off since she'd started her own line of inquiry into the Elixir virus. She was listening to a new musician from Mali while she drank wine and grated carrots.

Her months in California had become a blur. She'd come to some of the same conclusions as Lucien in that time. The Elixir didn't introduce a virus, but something about the ancient alchemical formula unlocked one in human blood. That virus could then be transmitted to vampires. She'd checked and double-checked her conclusions based on new blood samples coming in from Ireland, but she continued to be stumped by how it affected immortals when they were immune to every other virus she could think of.

She was smart enough to realize she didn't know enough about vampire biology, but the one colleague she wanted to ask had become a ghost in his own lab. Lucien had isolated himself in his wing and rarely came out, sending Ruben or one of his other associates out with reports that seemed to indicate he was fixated on origin instead of treatment.

Makeda was losing patience. His staff was losing patience. Even Baojia and Natalie were starting to get short with him. Makeda heard Baojia mutter about sending Lucien back to his mother for a time-out.

She'd laughed. Then she'd grimaced.

Makeda needed his help. There were aspects of immortal biology she simply wasn't familiar with. Things she knew Lucien would be able to illuminate. If they actually succeeded in collaborating, she knew the results could be groundbreaking, but the stubborn man had become a hermit, and he was fanatically territorial over his research.

An early winter storm had rolled in suddenly that night. She stared out the window at the pouring rain as she let her mind wander. Inevitably it wandered back to her ongoing research on thalassemia.

In retrospect, that genetic disorder looked so simple. It wasn't as if her human patients on that trial were dealing with an unknown virus that caused their blood cells to mutate. In thalassemia, the cause of the disease was all about the genes. Genes could be mapped. Viruses however, while utterly simple particles at first glance, shouldn't be able to alter vampire and human blood to the point that...

Wait.

Makeda's hands stopped. Her eyes glazed over as she tracked the droplets of water running down the window. Tiny droplets flowing into other droplets, forming tributaries that dropped water to the earth. Moisture filtering through the ground. Flowing along paths leading back to the massive expanse of the sea that was the source of all water.

The source of all life.

The source.

It all filtered back to the source.

She stopped breathing as the intricate pattern of thoughts wove into a tapestry. She froze and became utterly conscious of her own body, of the coursing blood in her system pumped from her heart, through the lungs, carrying vital nutrients through the arteries, the delicate arterioles, the tiny capillaries that fed each cell. Then the steady flow of oxygen-starved blood making its return journey through the veins. An endless system of red cells fed and renewed...

By the source.

Makeda gripped the edge of the counter. It was only a theory. A theory whose foundations were still being debated by human researchers. But Makeda knew she was right.

"I know how the virus lives," she whispered.

And if she knew how it lived, then maybe—just maybe—she and Lucien could figure out how to make it die.

Dropping everything and turning off the stove, she reached for her phone. It was nearly ten at night; she knew he'd be awake. She tapped Lucien's name and waited for his office phone to ring. If he wasn't at his desk, then at least one of his assistants—

"Lucien Thrax."

She let out a relieved breath when he answered. "Lucien, I think I've had a breakthrough."

A long pause on the other end. "Fine. I'll pass you to Tara and she can—"

"Did you understand what I said?" Her anger spiked. "I am telling you, I've made a breakthrough. I know how the virus is replicating. How it's able to affect immortal blood. I mean, I think I do. I need your help to understand..." She sighed, frustrated. "I need your help, okay?"

Another long pause. "If that's the case, then Ruben will be able to —"

"I don't want to talk to your damn assistant, Lucien! Not even the vampire one. I need to speak to you. I know we barely tolerate each other, but if you can't hear me out on this, then stop pretending you're a scientist interested in the truth."

His voice when it came back was acid. "If you have something to share, drive out here and speak to me in person. I am busy."

The line went silent, and Makeda threw her phone on the couch, where it buried itself between the colorful cushions her sister had made to remind her of home.

"Lucien, you are an utter and complete jackass!" A knock at the door. Makeda strode over and threw it open. "*What*?"

Philip stood with his hand raised, eyes wide, and mouth gaping. "S-sorry?"

She tried to get ahold of her temper. "Philip. No. I'm... sorry. I'm pissed off at a work colleague and he just hung up on me. Is there..." She took a breath. "Hi. Why are you here?"

He held up a bottle of wine. "I finished a project. Kind of in the mood to celebrate and I saw your light, so I figured you might want to share this with me." He held up a hand. "But that's okay. I mean, I don't want to intrude if it's not a good time."

She had tugged at her hair until it stood up under her hands. She probably looked like a mad scientist in the horror stories. "I'm sorry, but I think I need to drive out to the lab."

Philip turned his head with a frown, looking at the deluge. "In this? You can't be serious. It's pouring. And those roads going north are—"

"I know. I know. But I think I finally have a handle on the root of the problem I've been working on, and I just need... I need to get it down. Talk it out, you know? Hash it out with this guy because he's got the other half of the puzzle, if that makes sense." She let out a frustrated breath and looked down at the pajama pants she was wearing. "And I probably don't need to go out to the lab looking like this."

"Here." Philip took a step inside the door and set the wine down on the entry table before he put his hands on her shoulders. "We'll save the wine for later. If you have to go, go. But why don't you borrow my car? It's four-wheel drive. It'll be a lot easier to navigate that mud if you're determined to go. No way is your hybrid going to make it out to the cliffs."

She looked over his shoulder. Philip was probably right. Her little car would get stuck on the muddy gravel road, but the Wrangler he took off-roading would be fine. "Are you sure?"

"Totally sure. I'm not going anywhere tomorrow anyway. You go get ready and I'll put the top on the Jeep, make you a cup of coffee. Just head across the street when you're ready."

Helpful smile. Sweet man. Why couldn't she be tempted by her generous neighbor instead of the irascible vampire?

Wait. Not that she was tempted by... No. That was ridiculous. Lucien just made her blood boil because he was an incredible and brilliant *jackass*.

"Thanks, Philip." She patted his arm. "I... Thanks. I'll take the offer and owe *you* a bottle of wine. Let me get dressed and I'll be right over."

He glanced over her shoulder. "Stove off? I can smell you were

75

cooking something."

"Yes." She nodded. "Thanks. I'm so distracted right now."

"I can tell!" He grinned. "Must be some breakthrough."

"It is. I think—I'm pretty sure—it's *the* breakthrough, you know?"

The corner of his mouth lifted. "That's fantastic!"

❖

Taking the old Jeep was a good choice, Makeda thought as she bumped along the gravel road leading toward the lab. Even though it was a manual transmission, which she wasn't overly comfortable with, just the weight of the vehicle was helping keep her on the road. It was a few miles out of town before she turned off on the cliff road and immediately felt the buffet of wind hit her sideways. She climbed the hill leading from the highway and carefully took the turns, downshifting as she crawled along the muddy road.

Jackass.

She didn't need to be out in this weather. Lucien could have talked it over with her on the phone. Sure, they avoided using the phones for sensitive information, but the reality was, even if someone was listening in, approximately 0.001 percent of the population—human or immortal—would have understood the conversation to begin with.

"Whoa." She downshifted and jerked the car to avoid a deep pothole. "Stop thinking about the stubborn vampire, Makeda."

Honestly, would it have killed him to just bend a little? And yes, she found his focus somewhat attractive. She couldn't deny that. She'd always been drawn to genius of any kind, and Lucien's was a burning fire kind of genius. His passion for the human body and its intricacies was akin to that of an artist. She'd once overheard him dictate analysis on a blood sample to an assistant with the same tone as a poet describing a lover's body. The young assistant had been flushed when she left his office, and Makeda couldn't blame her.

Passion was sexy. Focus was attractive. And in her most exhausted hours, she'd allowed her mind to wander to what that focus would feel like if it ever turned her direction. Lucien was an attractive man, and she was only human.

But her feelings were contrary to reality. Most of what Lucien projected toward Makeda was irritation, disinterest, and at best, a grudging tolerance.

Lightning cracked the sky as she crested the hill separating the lab from the main road. She downshifted and applied the brakes, careful not to let the Jeep gain momentum on the slick road. It twisted between the oaks and cedars, the gravel worn away in some spots by the downpour.

A deer jumped from the bushes, but she overrode her instinct and kept the Jeep straight, knowing that swerving could mean her death in these kinds of conditions. Luckily, the animal darted away from the car and into the bushes on the other side before she reached it.

"Stupid Bambi," she muttered.

She moved her hand to the stick shift and pressed down on the clutch, ready to downshift as the slope increased. She nudged the wheel to the left as the road twisted into a curve—

The steering wheel didn't budge.

She lifted both hands, attempted to wrench the car back on the road.

Nothing.

Her pulse increased as the oak trees in front of her grew larger. The car was slipping and sliding down the hill. She braked too hard, and the rear of the vehicle fishtailed to the left. Then Makeda was sliding sideways down the hill, mud and rock flying up and slapping the side of the car. There was no time to think. No time to react.

The Jeep rolled.

Something crashed.

Everything went dark.

❖

"Makeda!"

His face swam in and out of Makeda's vision. *Not him.* He couldn't be the last thing she saw.

Not *him.*

Chipped-granite eyes in a coldly handsome face. Hard eyes. Hard face. Planed and ancient like the earth he controlled. Old eyes. Young face. His shaggy, rain-soaked hair dripped water onto her lips. She closed them as another stab of pain hit her chest.

"Dr. Abel," he said, "stay awake. Emergency services are on the way."

Images swam to the surface of Makeda's mind. Her mother laughing in the kitchen and her father behind his desk. The sun setting over the ocean near their home on the Puget Sound. She could hear the crashing water that reached the cliffs in this place she loved and hated.

Love and hate.

Like two beings struggling beneath her skin.

Always always always.

Torn in two. Something in her was so torn.

"Makeda!" He slapped her, and she took a sharp breath.

The quick inhalation hurt so badly she felt the tears come. They wet her cheeks like the mist rolling off the ocean. She could hear it. Hear the tide going out.

No. No, she was too far. Too far from the sea.

Wasn't she?

Her heart. It pulsed in her ears, surging, then falling off. Waves receding.

"Makeda, stay awake."

Tired. Hurts.

"I know it hurts." Another slap. Harder this time. "Stay awake, dammit!"

Not him. She didn't want to see *him.* She was dying, and it was his fault. Makeda felt him bend over, put his mouth at her ear, his breath cold because he couldn't be bothered to heat it. Couldn't be bothered with even a semblance of humanity to comfort her. She wanted her mother. Her sisters. She wanted *home.*

"*Yene konjo*," he whispered, "you may hate me, but I will not let you die."

Unbidden, old images came to her, aching scenes from her childhood. Mountains rising above the mist, sweeping ranges covered by a blanket of green. Raw beauty covered by dense clouds and a sky pregnant with rain.

Rain.

She felt it falling on her cheeks. Her forehead. Her lips.

Another slap to her cheek, but Makeda decided not to breathe. Not this time.

It hurt too much.

Everything hurt...

"Makeda!"

She dreamt of drowning. But when she opened her mouth, it was to drink the sea that surrounded her. She drank and drank and she was not full. She swallowed the ocean, but it did not quench her thirst.

She dreamt of floating, but when she opened her eyes, it was to see the moon through a veil of water. Blood and salt. A warm thread slipped past her lips, down her throat.

She was filled with it.

Her skin was freezing, but a fire burned in her veins. Her heart slowed. Stilled. But the fire still raged. It raced through her blood.

Tiny droplets flowing into other droplets, forming tributaries that dropped water to the earth... Flowing along paths leading back to the massive expanse of the sea that was the source of all water.

The source of all life.

The source.

It all filtered back to the source.

The fire pumped from her heart, through her lungs, stealing her breath before it crept through her arteries, the delicate arterioles, the tiny capillaries that fed each cell. The fire churned through her veins, an endless system of cells fed and renewed...

Blood.

The source of all things.

The elemental energy filled her mouth as she drank. The space and matter of it. Liquid fire. It filled her mouth. Transformed her mind. Newly woken synapses latched onto the thought, dissected it, and came to their conclusion even as her body lay unmoving.

Vampire.

They had made her vampire.

❖

She could feel him in the room when she woke.

"Yene konjo, you may hate me, but I will not let you die."

Makeda was assaulted by her senses, bruised by the rush of input to her system. The sheet over her naked body was too heavy. The low light from the lamp was too bright. When she inhaled, she tasted everything.

Including the warm blood near her face.

She turned her head and sliced her teeth into the bag of warm blood. She ignored the oily taste of the plastic and focused on the salty-sweet liquid sliding down her throat. Within a minute, the worst of her thirst was quenched. She flipped over and pressed up, her muscles coiled and ready as she rested on her hands and knees, wholly aware of the creature who'd been watching her as she woke.

"You." Her voice sounded strange to her ears. "You did this."

"I didn't sire you," Lucien said, pushing away from the wall.

"You. Did. This."

Makeda took in his appearance in a second. Exhausted eyes. Firm lips. Body tensed and ready.

He nodded. "I did this."

Despite her fury, a raw wave of sensual hunger swept her body as she looked at him. Her mind was in chaos, even as her body readied itself and pheromones scented the air. Lucien's mouth fell open as he drew in a breath. Makeda could see fangs dropping past his lips. See his erection harden beneath the civilized trousers.

"Makeda—"

"Why?"

He paused. To her newly woken senses, his response felt like hours.

"Because I need you."

She sprang at him, jumping off the exam table where they had placed her. She rose before him, her thigh brushing the steel of his erection while her hand closed around his throat.

Lucien did not blink. Not when she tightened her hand. Not when her fangs cut her lip.

His eyes locked on the bead of blood at her mouth, and Makeda heard his heart beat once.

"Makeda," he whispered.

Her other hand shot up to grip his hair at the nape. She pulled. Hard. His head didn't even move. He stood, body like stone, as she stared until he was forced to meet her eyes.

Cold eyes. Cold skin.

Just like hers was now.

Rage and desire flipped like a coin in the air. She grew damp between her legs. Her nails dug into his skin at the neck and she bent her head, her fangs aching as she licked out to taste him. Sweat. Skin. Blood.

Male.

He grabbed her hair and yanked her face up. She crawled up his body, locking her legs around his waist as his other hand gripped her thigh. If she were human, he would have broken her.

A low growl came from Lucien's throat when he bared his fangs. He took a deep breath and delicately traced the tip of a fang along her lower lip where it bled. His tongue flicked out. Eyes locked with hers, he licked at the blood dripping down her chin.

A sound between a snarl and a moan came from her throat. The hunger filled her mind. It made her ache. She wanted him to bite her. Fill her. Drink her blood as she drank his. Her hand tightened on his throat.

"We can't," Lucien said, even as his tongue reached her lip. He didn't stop. He bit her lower lip with his dull front teeth, then slid his tongue along her fangs. "Makeda, we can't."

She yanked his hair harder. "I hate you."

"I know."

"But I don't care." She released her hand from his neck and sank her teeth into the skin above his carotid.

Lucien roared and pressed her head to his neck for three heartbeats before he wrenched her away, his flesh tearing beneath her teeth. He flipped them around and pushed Makeda against the wall, his hips cradled between her thighs as he thrust against her. She felt the rasp of cloth against her labia. The press of his erection. He froze, her hair gripped in his hand. He pressed his forehead to hers and growled.

"*Stop.*"

Instinct made her submit. His body was rock hard against hers, and she could feel his dominance battle against her own. She felt his amnis as she never had in life, a warm press of influence against her skin. It made her want to scream. It made her want to purr.

"Stop," Lucien said again, tugging on her hair. "Take a breath."

"I don't need to breathe."

"Breathe anyway."

Very deliberately, Makeda slid one leg down until she could touch the floor. She breathed. The rise and fall of her chest let her pause. Think.

She was naked, but she felt no embarrassment or shame. She felt... free. Her body was inhumanly strong. It was responsive. She felt the pull and stretch of her muscles with a new level of awareness.

She said, "Release me."

Lucien released her thigh but not her hair. She slid the other leg down, her toes teasing the back of his thigh, his knee, before she righted herself. She took another deep breath, but all she smelled was Lucien's rampant need. One instinct battled the other. His need to control. His need to give in.

She'd done this to him.

Her lip curled up, and she felt the pressure behind her fangs ease. "Let go of my hair."

"Are you in control?"

"Are you?"

He let go of her and took a step back. She saw him carefully wipe any emotion from his face as he moved away from her. Within seconds, his careful mask was back in place.

"Who did it?" she asked.

"Baojia."

"Why?"

"I told you: I need you. You called me tonight. Said you made a breakthrough. It may be the only chance we have at curing this disease. Did you think I was going to let you just die?"

So calculating. So cold. Her desires had never mattered. Apparently they weren't even considered.

She asked, "Why not change me yourself?"

He paused.

"Well?"

"I don't have any children," he said. "I don't want the obligation or the responsibility."

Makeda's lip curled. "So now I'm Baojia's *child*?"

"As of right now, you're no one's child. He turned you to fulfill a deal we've had in place for years. We would each turn one human of the other's choosing. No argument. No obligation. You are not under Baojia's aegis unless you want to be. You are not under Katya's because I won't allow it."

I won't allow it. A rising sense of panic shot through her. "So where do I belong?"

Lucien looked at her long and hard. "Though Baojia cannot demand your loyalty as per our arrangement, he has offered his own. You may choose my aegis or Baojia's. Those are your options."

Bitterness soured her mouth. "What if I don't want to belong to either of you?"

"Those are your options, Makeda. Baojia or me. You know enough about the way our world works to know you must belong to someone." He took another step back. "So choose."

Before she could respond, Lucien walked out the door, closed it, and Makeda heard him turn the key in the lock.

Saba

Saba waited across from the young fire vampire, Kato at her side. The man was one of her blood, his sire of her direct line, but his element had manifested in fire. She didn't know him. Didn't know what to think of him except that when he'd been required to kill his own daughter to protect their race, he had done so.

"Do you distrust me?" Oleg asked. "To bring a water vampire to our meeting?"

Saba cocked her head. "That would imply I had some fear of you, child. I do not."

"No?"

Without another word, Saba held her hand out, palm up, on the table between them. Oleg looked at her hand for a long time. He frowned, deep lines forming between his eyebrows, then he reached out and put his hand in hers.

Saba closed her fingers over Oleg's warm palm and gripped it. Hard. "No," she said. "I do not."

"I had no desire to hold your hand," he said. "I do not like to touch others."

She could hear his heart. "And yet you did."

A flicker of fear in his eyes. He was a wise one to be scared of her. For though some thought of Saba as a grandmother and others as a benevolent and wise spirit, Saba was of the earth.

And the earth could be a cruel mother.

Oleg asked, "Who are you?"

"Who have you heard that I am?"

"The oldest of us. The oldest of all of us."

"You may be correct." Saba didn't release Oleg's hand. "I do know your blood comes from the earth. From one of my line. So, Oleg Sokolov, you are mine, whether you want to be or not."

The vampire's eyes flared. He didn't like that news.

"What do you know of the Elixir?"

"I know that I wish I'd never listened to my mate. She's dead now, with good reason."

Interesting. Had he killed his own mate for involving him in Elixir? That was... very interesting.

"Do you have any dealings in it?"

"Do I look like a madman?" He shook his head. "You know I am not lying. Anyone in my organization who was involved in that filth is dead. Dead by my hand. Those who had my blood and those who did not. And I have paid the price for my foolishness many times over. Ask anyone." He waved a hand around the tavern. "Oleg's ships cannot pass without paying half their profit in tariff to the Greek."

"Because you killed his lover?"

Oleg's eyes flared, and his heat permeated the booth. "Because I will not be played the fool. Especially not by those seeking to spy on me within my own house. Anyone taken in by that madman has been put to death."

"Where did the madness lie?" Saba asked. "Was it Laskaris? Or your daughter?"

"I do not deny the madness sprang from my blood, but those who dismiss the Greek as lazy or only opportunistic do so at their peril. Zara was no criminal mastermind, though she was evil. Now she is dead, and the Elixir still flows through the Bosphorus. That is all I know."

"I am glad," Saba said, "you did not put your own sentiment over the greater good of our race."

"You're speaking of Zara?" Oleg shrugged. "She was nothing to me."

"She was your blood."

"She was *nothing*."

Saba smiled. If the fire vampire wanted to deny his connection to the malicious troublemaker, it was no business of hers. The job had been done, and Oleg had been the one to do it. She approved.

"There may come a time when you must put the good of our race over sentiment again."

Oleg said, "I am a self-interested man. I do not believe in a greater good, a higher power, or a master plan for our world."

"Then you do not know me."

A smile touched the corner of Oleg's mouth. Just a hint of one. "And I thought I was the most arrogant thing at the table."

Kato spoke for the first time. "It's not arrogance."

Oleg opened his mouth, then closed it. He nodded at Saba and pulled his hand away from her grip.

"Is there anything else you need of me, *Baba*?"

She smiled at the title. Perhaps Oleg might win her affection after all. "Not now. But perhaps soon."

He bowed, lifted his head, and said, "You are the oldest and wisest of our people. I am at your service should you have need of me."

Oleg walked from the room, and the scent of burned spruce left with him. It wasn't an unpleasant scent, nor was he an unpleasant man no matter what he chose to think of himself.

Kato picked up her hand. "He's an interesting one."

"He is."

"Did you notice the human?"

"He paid her no notice," Saba said. "None at all."

"His lack of notice was noticeable," Kato said.

Saba smiled and leaned against his shoulder. "You're such a gossip, Kato."

"It's hard not to be when you've been hearing everything secondhand for centuries."

"Come." She rose and pulled him up with her. "I have an appointment with an old friend."

"Should I be jealous?"

"For this? Definitely not."

Chapter Seven

Lucien leaned against the cold concrete of the hallway, listening to Baojia and Makeda's conversation in her room. Everything was quiet. Muted. The blood they'd quickly acquired was the only sustenance she'd taken other than a little rice. Baojia had put her in one of the secure rooms belonging to the Elixir patients after he'd made sure to shield it from daylight. It was comfortable and guarded.

Ruben eyed him with disapproval but said nothing.

If Baojia or Makeda knew he was listening in, they didn't give any indication of it. He cared nothing for their privacy; his interest was in Makeda.

A week after her transformation and she had still not decided. Or if she had, she'd given no indication of it. She'd spent the first four days swinging between rage and weeping. On the fifth day, she'd allowed Baojia into her room during the night, and his presence had settled her. Her emotions were predictably unpredictable according to her sire, who had overseen the newly transformed under Ernesto Alvarez in Los Angeles. Lucien could understand why his friend would have that duty. Baojia's quiet, steady strength would put a violently unstable new vampire at ease.

Now she was finally speaking, and Lucien didn't care if he was being rude.

He had to know.

"You're going to have to decide soon," Baojia said. "I don't want to pressure you, but indecision leads to instability. Katya accepted Lucien's and my reasoning for changing you without her approval—accidents cannot be predicted, and your life needed to be preserved—but she needs to know what your intentions are."

A long pause. "I'd like to speak with my parents."

"Katya has already informed your parents of the situation."

Another pause. "I see."

Lucien regretted that. Makeda should have been the one to decide how and when to tell her parents about her new life, but the Abel family was not under his aegis. He had no authority in the matter.

Unless she chose him.

The possessive need for her surprised him. Yet if she chose Baojia, he could not stop her.

Choose me.

"Makeda," Baojia began, "while I do not want to influence your decision unduly, I do feel an obligation to you. You are a child of my blood. I have no claim over your loyalty per my agreement with Lucien, but whether you choose my aegis or his, I want you to know I will *always* consider you my child. You are part of my family. Natalie and I are in complete agreement. No matter what you decide, I want you to know that."

Lucien could smell her tears.

"However much we care for you," he continued, "I do want to explain some things."

"What?"

"Lucien..." Baojia took a deep breath. "Lucien is very well-connected."

"I was guessing that by how he speaks to Katya."

"He is not under her aegis. He's a child of the elders, which means he is very, very powerful."

"You're saying his aegis would be the better choice," Makeda said. "But my family—"

"Your parents are under Katya's aegis. As long as your father works for her, he will remain so, along with your immediate family."

"And if I choose your aegis, I'll remain with Katya too."

"In a sense. But that's not the only thing to consider."

Lucien often forgot about Baojia's political savvy. Those at the top of the food chain didn't have to think as strategically as those in the middle. Baojia, being a young vampire who had broken from his sire's aegis, was much more adept at power plays and strategy for the simple reason that he had to be. He was still a relatively small fish in a very big pond.

Baojia said, "I serve Katya's organization as a choice. She has no blood tie to me. Should you choose my aegis and I leave hers for whatever reason, your loyalty would follow me."

Makeda let out a frustrated breath. "This is so complicated."

"Politics is an unavoidable part of your life now. I'm trying to explain what could simplify that."

"What are you talking about?"

"Lucien."

A long pause. "Lucien hates me."

Lucien shook his head and rolled his eyes at her declaration. His feelings for Makeda were so far from hate, he had trouble sorting them in his own mind.

Baojia said, "Lucien does not hate you."

"Then he really, really doesn't like me."

"Whether that's true or not doesn't really matter," Baojia said. "Stop thinking in decades and start thinking in centuries. Lucien has offered you his aegis. As far as I know, only two or three people in the world are under it. Do you understand what that means?"

"Not really."

"It means he's both very powerful and very independent. Vampire loyalty goes both ways. Favors go both ways. If someone owes you loyalty, you also owe them protection. If someone answers to you, they also depend on you. I come from a long and complicated line of water vampires whose blood eventually traces back to a single water vampire in the Mediterranean. One of the ancients so old he no longer remembers human life. Your blood is of that line. Any children you sire in the future will be another branch of a complicated and layered tree."

Loyalties in the immortal world intertwined over centuries. Lucien thought about the many humans who owed his mother allegiance. Some human clans had been serving her and her children for centuries. When you added in her immortal children and their offspring, it became even more overwhelming. He'd never be able to prove it, but Lucien suspected every vampire in the world could eventually trace their blood line back to Saba.

She was the immortal Eve. The source of vampire life, not that she could remember how it all came to be.

Baojia was still explaining things. "There are some advantages to a large family tree like mine. It provides many connections in our world."

"I don't want politics, Baojia. I'm a scientist. All I've ever wanted was to do my research." He heard her choke. "Care for my family. I can't even see them anymore, can I?"

"You'll be able to eventually," Baojia said, soothing her. "And the time will pass faster than you can imagine." He paused. "I want you to think about your family when you choose your aegis, Makeda."

"You think I should go with yours because of Katya."

"No," Baojia said. "I think you should go with Lucien. Because of Katya."

Lucien froze. Oh, the young assassin was smart.

"What?" Makeda sounded horrified. "You think I should choose Lucien?"

Was his protection really so distasteful to her? He remembered the smell of her blood—the agony and ecstasy of her bite—and his own blood rushed south.

"Lucien is a child of the ancients. His mother is the oldest vampire known to our kind. She is the source of our blood. Our power. Saba owes allegiance to none. In many places around the world, she's worshipped as a goddess. She is not *a* power, Makeda. She is *the* power. If any came before her, they are not remembered. And if they are not remembered, they do not exist."

The silence in the small room was oppressive, and Lucien wished he could see Makeda's face.

"And Lucien is this woman's son?" Makeda finally asked.

"He is."

"So if I chose his aegis—"

"It would put you *and your family* under the protection of

arguably the most powerful vampire in the world. If Saba ever called her blood..."

"We would all feel it."

"I believe so."

Not that she would, Lucien thought. His mother wasn't interested in empire anymore. Once, she'd ruled a continent. She said the responsibility gave her a headache.

"You think my family and I would be safer under Lucien's aegis."

"Katya already has your father's loyalty and obligation. If she had yours as well—"

"All our eggs would be in the same basket," Makeda said, grasping the implications immediately. "But if I choose Lucien, my family would have both Katya's protection and Lucien's."

"It would."

"Dual protection like that would give Katya pause should my father ever fall out of favor with her."

Lucien closed his eyes and focused on her voice.

Makeda's mind ensnared him. A curl of anticipation tightened in Lucien's gut when he thought of her already brilliant mind enhanced by amnis. She would be dazzling. Luminous. Captivating.

A queen.

Desire for her burned in his blood.

Lucien waited in Baojia's office until the vampire returned. Baojia glanced at Lucien sitting in the office chair on the other side of his desk, and his mouth tightened.

"In the future, I will not hide your presence from her," he said. "Don't put me in the middle of your arguments."

"Will she choose my aegis?"

"She hasn't decided," Baojia said. "For now, leave her alone. Your presence is too disruptive."

"I haven't done anything to—"

"Stop," Baojia hissed, glaring at Lucien. "You know exactly what you do to her. Sometimes I think you delight in it. Makeda is my child whether she chooses my aegis or not. If I was worried only for her emotional well-being, I would keep her as far from you as I possibly could."

Lucien steepled his fingers. "You know I'm the better choice."

"I do. It doesn't mean I have to like it."

"I thought we were friends."

"I don't like it when my friends manipulate my other friends." He didn't sit as Lucien did. It didn't matter. Both of them knew Baojia's power was a fraction of Lucien's. "You've made it clear you need her mind, and that's the only reason you saved her life. How do you think that makes her feel?"

"Makeda is a rational woman. She understands why her life had to be preserved."

"Stop pretending there is only science between you. You didn't do this for *rational* reasons, Lucien. Don't lie to me."

Lucien said nothing.

"If she chooses you," Baojia said, "this antagonism must stop. She will depend on you, especially within the first year. Whether you are honest about your feelings for her is your choice. But your feelings are not *her* fault, so find a way to handle your resentment." Baojia paused. "I expected better of you, Lucien."

The quiet admonition pricked Lucien's conscience. He closed his eyes. "She tempts me. I don't like it."

"Everyone in the lab saw your bickering for what it was," Baojia said. "And we all know why you didn't sire her yourself."

Because siring Makeda would have killed off the possibility of anything more than a paternal relationship.

"I won't insult either of you by cautioning against an intimate relationship," Baojia continued. "The roots of... whatever you two have were evident months ago. But you are more powerful than she is. You are older and have more control. Show your honor and let her lead in this."

He kept returning to the addictive pleasure of her bite. "And if I can't?"

"Don't use weakness as an excuse." Baojia picked up a note near the phone on his desk. "We both know your self-control is unparalleled. It's the only reason you can work with patients as you do."

Because a vampire performing surgery in the throes of bloodlust wasn't something Lucien could allow to happen. His mind touched on the cool self-control Makeda had mastered in her own body, and he wondered if her transition to immortal life would be easier because of it. She was, in her own way, as controlled as he was.

Except when she'd bitten him.

"I need to go into town," Baojia said. "I managed to convince the human police that Makeda sustained only minor injuries, but I had to use amnis when they wanted to question her. If I don't resolve things, there will be too many questions. The human who owned the car filed a report."

"Whose car was it?"

"Her neighbor. Philip Marin."

Something about the neighbor scratched at his mind. It was the same neighbor who had interrupted Lucien at her house weeks before. They weren't lovers; Lucien would have smelled the human on her skin. There had been only the faint whiff indicating casual contact.

So why did Makeda have access to his car in the middle of the night? And why had that car slid down the hill when Makeda was a competent driver? It could have been a random accident caused by the storm, but not knowing irritated Lucien. Makeda had only scattered memories of the minutes before the accident, which wasn't unusual in humans who'd experienced head injuries, so she could offer no insight to the cause of the crash.

"Have you spoken to Philip Marin?" Lucien asked.

"No." Baojia looked up. "The police said he left a few days ago for a meeting in Palo Alto." His eyes narrowed. "Right after his car was crashed and a friend was seriously injured?"

"The meeting could have been unavoidable and he was informed she had no major injuries. Has he called her phone?"

"No. Natalie has it. No calls except from her family and a few colleagues from her former lab. Natalie's been dealing with them."

A phone call would be the bare minimum a friend might expect in this situation. Philip Marin's actions were leading Lucien to speculate he'd left town for other reasons. Protective anger simmered in his belly. "Was the car examined?"

"The car is barely recognizable." Baojia nodded toward the door. "But I know someone in San Francisco who can sort through it. I'll need to call him up and get him into the impound lot. Shouldn't be a problem. In the meantime, I'm going into town to talk to the police. You coming?"

Staying at the lab would only make his thoughts circle around Makeda. "Who's monitoring her?"

"She wanted to be locked in alone. She has a store of blood and her notes. Ruben is watching her, and I have two extra guards on call. One human and one vampire."

Ruben was Lucien's second-in-command of the lab, but he was also trained by Baojia. The guards were simply a precaution.

"I'll go with you," he said. "Let's see if Makeda's accident was really an accident."

Lucien stared impassively at the human who was trying not to panic. Philip Marin was buried up to his neck, his pale face had lost the sun-kissed tan, and pallor had stolen the calculation from his expression.

"I don't know any more than that," the operative said. "I was supposed to watch her. The night of the accident, I panicked. She said she'd had a breakthrough. *The* breakthrough. I knew my bosses didn't want that to happen."

"And your bosses are...?" Lucien had his suspicions, but he'd rather know for certain.

Philip was silent.

"Your birth name isn't Philip Marin," Baojia said, standing next to Lucien in the cavern cut by the Pacific Ocean. They'd found Marin two nights earlier in San Francisco, trying to find passage to Europe on a freighter. "Interpol identified your prints as belonging to Stavros Marinos, a low-level criminal with drug connections and a history of identity theft."

"You're a nobody, Philip." Lucien dug his feet into the wet sand around the human. The earth pressed in, turning Marin's face red as he struggled for breath. Lucien eased back. "Tell us who hired you."

"They'll kill me," Philip choked out. "They'll kill me no matter what—"

"Don't you understand?" Lucien crouched down, his bare feet flexing in the gravelly sand of the sea cave. "You're going to die. You are not leaving this cave alive. You stole her life, Philip. You must answer for that."

Terror filled Philip's eyes. "I can give you names."

"I know you can."

"I was hired in Istanbul. Zara Olegovna hired—"

"Zara is dead," Lucien said. "Who else can you give us?"

Panic as waves lapped at the rocks near the entrance. Tiny sea creatures were beginning to skitter along the pebbles.

"I don't know! Aris was my boss, but it was Zara who—"

"I told you Zara is dead, Philip. Give us something new, and we'll kill you before the crabs begin to nibble your face." Lucien took a stick and flicked it along Philip's ear. "They have very small claws. It might not hurt much at first. It will probably be the tide that kills you."

"Laskaris!" he cried. "Rumors were everywhere in the city. He wants to take over the Greek court. Kill his rivals. Regain the glory of Athens and that kind of bullshit." Philip descended into panicked blathering in his mother tongue.

Laskaris. It was exactly who Lucien had suspected based on his mother's reports and the information he'd received from allies, but he needed more than rumors. The old Greek was the de facto leader of the oldest vampire court in Europe. Athens had once ruled the Western world, and many vampires still looked to it as the epitome of wisdom even though the four immortals that made up the court had become lazy and self-indulgent.

"Laskaris is funding production of Elixir?"

"I didn't work for him. Not directly. I worked for Zara. She's the one who brought it to him. She came up with the idea... Laskaris ran with it. He wants an empire. Wants to fucking take the world back to the Stone Age and shit. That's all I know."

"Why kill off humans?"

"He says there's too many. They'll be too hard to manage. The Elixir is population control. He takes out enough humans and vampires, the rest will be easier to conquer. He'll take out his rivals, starting in the Mediterranean, then move on from there. He thinks he's fucking Alexander the Great or some shit." Philip blinked rapidly, his eyes never leaving the waves. "You're going to kill me."

"Yes."

"I don't want to drown," he whimpered. "Please God, don't let me drown."

Lucien looked at the waves creeping into the cave. "Yes, I imagine it's quite terrifying." He looked back at Philip. "Do you think Makeda was terrified when she couldn't steer your Jeep and she started sliding toward the trees?"

Philip began to sob.

"I've never liked cars," Lucien said. "They can trap immortals just as they can trap humans. The difference is, vampires are much harder to kill. Not like Makeda." He ran a cold finger under Philip's jaw, tapped on the pounding pulse. "She was like you, Philip. Soft. Breakable. She didn't survive the crash."

The human would be useless for any further interrogation. It didn't matter. He'd confirmed what Lucien had suspected. He stood and turned to Baojia. "Keep the waves back until I can speak to her."

Baojia raised an eyebrow. "Offering up her murderer?"

"It's her decision to make," he said, looking over his shoulder at the quivering human buried in sand. "Besides, she needs the blood."

Lucien walked out of the cave and up the rocky path leading to the bungalows where his patients had once lived. No patients anymore, just the burgeoning power of a woman who tested every one of his instincts. When he reached her door, Ruben stopped him with a single raised hand.

The stocky vampire had been his assistant for almost three years, leaving his home in San Diego and following Baojia to Northern California when he'd learned of the scientific research Katya was funding. He'd been a biologist as a human. Now he was Lucien's assistant and Baojia's pupil.

"Sorry, boss," Ruben said. "She doesn't want company. She specifically mentioned yours."

"I have her murderer buried in a cave down by the beach. I need to know what she wants to do with him."

Makeda pounded on the door, and Ruben turned and unlocked it. As soon as the dead bolt slid free, an irate Makeda wrenched the door open.

"Who?"

"Your neighbor, Philip Marin."

Shock. Then awareness. "The steering. I remembered something about a deer. Thought I must have swerved... But no, it was the steering. I couldn't move the wheel. I started down the hill, and the road started to twist."

"Marin tampered with the power steering. He was desperate to stop you from reaching the lab, and he took a chance you'd reach the cliffs before it gave out. If it had gone out on the highway, you'd have had no issues. But once you reached the hills—"

"He wanted me dead." Her eyes narrowed. "Why?"

"He works for the vampire funding production of the Elixir. He was ordered to watch you. He panicked when he thought you were close to a cure."

"Where is he?" Makeda bared her teeth, her fangs long and already red with her own blood. "Where is that bastard?"

Lucien caught her arm before she could take off into the night. On her own, Makeda could go on a killing spree. There were still humans at the compound, including Natalie and her children. If bloodlust overwhelmed her senses, she wouldn't know a loved one from an enemy.

"With me," he said, "or you don't take a step out of the building."

She tried to tug her arm away, but Lucien held firm. Ruben didn't raise a hand, not even when Makeda looked to him for help.

"Sorry, Mak. I made bad decisions my first year that I've had to live with for seventy. I'm with Lucien on this one."

Makeda said nothing more but left her arm in Lucien's hold and began walking. As soon as she hit the outside air, her face turned toward the ocean.

"It wants me," she said on a breath.

He'd wondered whether she'd have an affinity for fresh or saltwater. Apparently Baojia's blood ran true. Makeda needed the sea.

"Come with me," he said. "Slowly. Be deliberate in your movements, or you'll appear too fast to the human eye."

"But there's nobody around."

"Practice now. Build the discipline now. Your mind will be particularly malleable for the next six weeks."

"Six weeks? Exactly?"

"Very near to exact."

Makeda paused and thought as she slowly walked down the cliff.

"Piaget's theory of cognitive development?"

He wasn't surprised she'd made the connection. "Related, in my opinion. Amnis enhances processing and that involves the physical as well as the mental. It seemed natural there would be a link between human and vampire cognitive development. The next two years will be crucial for you."

She continued to pepper him with questions about the science as they walked at what felt like a snail's pace down the cliffs. "Does a twenty-four-month time line hold in vampires?"

"Anecdotal evidence seems to indicate that, but there's no way to test it."

"Has human cognitive theory affected how newborns are trained in the modern era?" Makeda asked.

"For some of the more scientifically inclined."

Lucien relaxed as they walked and talked at deliberately human speed. Her arm remained in his grip and—whether she realized it or not—her face remained angled toward the ocean. No wonder, as it was the element aligned with her amnis. The tension in her skin eased as the sea air touched it.

"I have my own theories," he continued. "My mother scoffs at them."

"Oh?" She glanced at him from the corner of her eye. "I imagine so. How were you trained as a newborn vampire?"

"She made me hunt lions." Lucien shrugged when Makeda's eyes went wide. "They weren't endangered then. Lions are very good at hiding, and they are very patient."

"But vampires are faster than lions."

"So are gazelles, but lions still kill them."

Chapter Eight

Makeda couldn't stop breathing in the misty air. It was manna. She felt as if she could survive on the sea air alone.

Until she scented a hint of human blood.

Lucien's hand tightened on her arm, and she heard growling.

"Calm, Makeda," he said. "Calm."

The feral sound was coming from her own throat.

"Stop." She forced her feet to a halt and tore her eyes from the mouth of the cave where the delectable scent originated. "I want to walk in the ocean."

"Why?"

"Because I need to think."

Lucien looked surprised, but he said, "Fine."

He walked with her down to the water, and Makeda slipped off the loose slippers she was wearing. She'd worn nothing more than scrubs for the past week. Nothing else felt comfortable against her skin.

Makeda walked into the water up to her knees and sank down, taking Lucien with her. She didn't care if he got wet; she didn't care about anything but getting the water on her skin.

"Give yourself a minute," Lucien said. "You should have been brought to the sea before this. I am sorry, Makeda."

"I've been sitting in the tub a lot," she said. "It helps me think. But this..."

It was heaven. The cold saltwater soothed her skin and filled her senses. Instead of sorting through a myriad of jumbled sensory information, Makeda could finally think.

Lucien said, "Most water vampires show an affinity toward either saltwater or fresh. You obviously take after Baojia."

Makeda didn't want to think about Philip or the other choice still sitting in front of her. Not now, not when the water gave her the first real peace she'd felt since she'd woken in this nightmare. She didn't know how much time passed, but the tide had risen considerably when she felt ready to speak again.

"I don't want to kill Philip," she said. "Or I do... but I don't want to give in to the urge, if that makes sense. I don't want to lose control."

Lucien was looking at her, and she couldn't interpret his expression.

"Is that abnormal?" she asked. "Should I want to kill him? Will this affect my predatory instincts adversely?"

"Your predatory instincts will never be a problem," he said. "We are predators to the core. I'm simply amazed you're thinking this clearly."

"When I become agitated, I list the bones in the human body. If I'm still agitated when I finish, I start on the muscular system." She ducked her head under a wave, spitting out the overwhelming taste of salt and seaweed. "It helps."

"I'll remember that."

"What will you do with Philip if I don't kill him?"

"He has to die. Not only is he spying in Katya's territory, he tried to kill a human under her aegis. I will kill him. Or Baojia will." His eyes turned calculating. "Depending on which of our aegis you decide to claim."

She stared at him. "You're lying."

"Maybe."

"You are." She glanced over her shoulder at the mouth of the cave. "He's buried in there?"

"Up to his neck in sand."

"Thank you. I think."

"I was happy to do it."

"I know. You don't like that I'm a vampire." She didn't think about the words until they'd already left her mouth, but she felt his hand tighten on her arm. "If Philip is buried, then I don't have to choose either of you." Makeda stood and Lucien followed. "Philip can stay where he is and the ocean will take care of him for me."

"Drowning is a cruel death."

Makeda thought about the friendly man who'd helped her move boxes and washed Mrs. Gunnerson's car. The man who'd pretended to be her friend, all the while spying on her. The man who had tampered with his own car in an attempt to kill her.

"I know it's cruel." She walked back toward the cliffs, Lucien still holding her arm.

Makeda went back to her room, and Lucien left to speak to Baojia. She wondered how long it would take for Philip to die and briefly considered asking Ruben to take her to the edge of the cliffs so she could see the tide enter the cave.

She didn't. Allowing cruelty was one thing. Enjoying it would make her a monster.

❖

Three days passed in darkness. She was underground during the day, hidden in a room with no windows and only one door. She slept more deeply than she ever had in her life. At night there was only a moonless sky when Baojia took her to the sea. They walked down every night and she calmed in his presence, surrounded by the water that spoke to her soul.

Baojia didn't waste time chatting. She knew he was waiting for her to decide between his aegis and Lucien's. Every night, she felt more comfortable in this new skin that felt everything. Every night, she thought about choosing Baojia and bidding Lucien good-bye.

She didn't do it.

Makeda had always been a creature of her mind, keeping her body in good condition because she knew her brain operated at peak capacity when she was healthy. But her physical self was a supporting mechanism for her mind.

In this new skin, she felt trapped by it.

The sensory information she absorbed was nearly overwhelming.

The only saving grace was the new speed and agility of her mind. Utilizing familiar methods for analysis, the strict discipline taught by her family, and her new cognitive agility, Makeda was able to quickly rein in her most base hungers, which were concentrated in two areas.

Blood and sex.

The blood she had to have, but Makeda refused to do anything about her suddenly raging sexual drive. She drank four quarts of human blood each night. Two upon waking and two before the day caused her to black out. And it *was* blacking out. Nothing about vampire sleep reminded her of human sleep. She was awake. Then she was asleep. She did not dream and wondered if the lack of sleep cycles would adversely affect brain function at some point. She posed the question to Baojia.

"Meditation," he said, cutting through the water with a neat stroke she emulated. "Or some form of it. Every vampire I know practices it in some way whether they call it that or not. Some actively meditate. Others daydream. When you live as long as we do, nights become monotonous. We become artists, craftsmen, avid readers. I know one earth vampire who climbs the same mountain every night before dawn comes. He's been climbing the same stretch for forty years now. It's not a challenge; it's become his meditation.

"What do you do?"

"I practice tai chi and I recommend it for all new vampires. It focuses the mind and body."

"Can you teach me?"

"Yes."

He didn't ask the question she knew he wanted to ask: Had she decided under whose aegis she would live?

"I haven't decided yet."

Part of her longed to stay with Baojia. The friendship they'd shared had been superseded by more familiar feelings. She felt a kinship with the vampire like that she felt near her father. It was an immediate trust and comfort she could not explain but chose to cherish nonetheless. Though she hadn't ever wanted to be a vampire, she'd come to realize Baojia had the type of honor her own father did.

Authority shown in service to those he was responsible for. She knew that kind of power. She respected it.

But Lucien...

The sensual hunger hit her as soon as her mind turned to Lucien. Though physically impossible, she woke some nights feeling as if his skin was still under her mouth. The taste of his blood lived on her tongue. Though she knew it only to be a very strong sensory memory, something in her felt as if he'd entered her bloodstream and lived under her skin.

"Focus," Baojia said, sensing her erratic emotions begin to scatter. "I'm not going to rush you."

"Lucien and Katya both want me to decide."

"Let me worry about them," he said. He reached for an outcropping of rock that jutted from the sea. The rock below the waterline was encrusted with mussels, but the top was smooth. He held out a hand and Makeda took it. "I can hold them off for a while longer."

"Thank you," she said, sitting next to him and letting the spray fill her lungs. "But I need to decide for myself too."

"Do you want to talk about it?"

She didn't want to talk to Baojia about her reservations toward Lucien because most of them involved sex, her confusing feelings about their relationship before her change, and her illogical hunger for him. But who else was she going to consult with? Her contact with her sisters was limited—she didn't know what she'd say to them anyway—and Natalie was human too.

Why weren't there any female vampires at the compound? The thought brought an irrational spike of anger.

"Why aren't there any vampire women here?" she asked. "Do you and Lucien have a problem working with women?"

Baojia raised an eyebrow but only said, "No. My top lieutenant in San Francisco is a woman, and in case you didn't realize it, so is my boss."

Makeda forced herself to relax. She was being unreasonable, reacting before she thought. A majority of the human staff at the lab were female. It was likely the lack of immortal women was purely chance.

"But..." Baojia looked thoughtful. "Lucien may. I don't know. He's a lot older than me."

"You think the son of the most powerful vampire in the world—who is a woman—has a problem working with women?"

"Not working with them," Baojia said. "But if I'm reading you correctly when he's around, you're attracted to him, and I don't believe he takes vampire lovers as a rule. Is that what's bothering you about accepting his offer of protection? Because we both know that rationally he's the better choice."

Well, it looked like she'd be confiding in Baojia after all. "I'm very... aware of him. I don't like it."

"It could be purely chance," Baojia said. "He is a male of no blood relation who is in close physical proximity, and your body is still coming into balance. Immediately after my turning, my sex drive was very high. I took a number of lovers, all of them immortal." His voice softened a little. "It was not emotional in the sense of attachment, but they understood the heightened senses. One of them is still a very good friend. It could be the same with Lucien."

It was likely Baojia was right and this vicious pull she felt toward Lucien was simply the product of her physical transformation and her mind's ongoing attempts to reorganize itself.

"However," he continued, "I do think you have to acknowledge that before your turning, you and Lucien were drawn to each other. You were antagonists, but that is still an emotional relationship. I don't think you should discount that."

He was right. Hate was not the opposite of love. That was indifference. And she and Lucien had never been indifferent toward each other.

"And you don't seem to have this problem with any of the other staff. Ruben guards you most nights when I'm not with you, and as far as I know—"

"Oh my gosh, Baojia, Ruben is like... my brother or something."

"Well, that's another thing you shouldn't discount."

"I won't discount anything." Makeda watched as the waves crept up the rock, fascinated by the small eddies and currents created by the grooves and dips worn by time and erosion. A small pebble spun around a pocket worn into the rock, smoothing it on a microscopic level as she watched. Given enough time and water, that small pebble could wear a hole in the massive boulder where she sat. That tiny pebble would be joined by others. A crab could take up residence. Anemones could find shelter.

"Amazing, isn't it?" Baojia said. "The places where earth and water meet can often be the most violent." He lifted a tiny starfish from a crevice in the rock. "But the most delicate things can thrive within that violence. Some can only thrive there."

Water meeting rock. Could she and Lucien's relationship be a simple reflection of that dichotomy? Him, the immovable object, and her, the force of change? Or was he the volcano and she the cooling sea? There were no easy answers to what their relationship was or what it might become should she choose his aegis. But she knew choosing his protection was the far wiser choice. For herself and her family.

"I know what I need to do," she said quietly. The weight of reason had never felt so heavy before. "Will you speak to him?"

Baojia reached over and closed his hand over hers. "I will always be here. No matter what."

"You're a good friend," Makeda said. "And a good sire."

"He'll take you away."

"I know. It's probably for the best right now." Not being able to see her family and friends was agonizing.

"I wish I could come with you, but I can't."

She patted his hand and finally felt a hint of mischief as the burden of decision lifted from her.

"I know. Thanks anyway... Dad."

"Okay, now you're just being weird."

❖

Makeda woke to a low light and the quiet drone of the cargo plane. Lucien hadn't told her where they were going, but hopefully it was someplace with far fewer humans and far less temptation.

Lucien was sitting in a corner of the plane, reading a stack of papers and taking notes.

"What are you reading?" she asked.

She had no need to clear her throat. Biological processes appeared to stop during vampire sleep, which meant mucous production and its resulting hoarseness did as well. She wondered why Lucien and Baojia were so insistent she drink half her ration of blood before she went to sleep. Perhaps it had something to do with cell repair.

"I had my assistant search your laptop and print any pages from your browsing history that were within our research parameters," he said, not looking up from his work. He didn't stop writing either. "I know your memory is not entirely recovered, but I'm hoping—"

"You snooped through my computer?"

"No, Tara did." He glanced up, then back to his notes. "I doubt she had any particular curiosity about your browsing habits. I simply needed to know where your thoughts were taking you the day before your accident."

She bit down her retort. It was a gross invasion of privacy, but she trusted Lucien's assistant not to snoop. Tara was a bright young thing, but she was particularly focused. If you set her on a task, she rarely deviated.

"Does she still have my computer?" Makeda didn't know if she'd taken any notes on her laptop, but if she had, the files would be password protected.

"No."

"Have her send it to... wherever we're going."

"You won't be able to use it in Bahir Dar."

Everything in her stopped. "We're going to Ethiopia?"

He looked up, frowning. "Is that really surprising? You're under my aegis now. You need to meet Saba."

Yes, but...

"Ethiopia is landlocked." And she was a water vampire. She tried not to panic.

Immediate understanding colored his features. "That is true. However, it does have numerous lakes. Lake Tana has a number of islands, many of which are inhabited. Two of which are inhabited only by my mother's people."

"And that's where we're going?"

"Yes. One of the islands is mine, and I keep a lab there. It's not luxurious, but it's completely self-sustained. Solar power and an independent water system. We'll be able to work without humans."

Makeda had nothing to say. She'd never worked alone, even when she worked solo on projects. "How will we—"

"Why don't you save your questions until we get there?" he asked. "You may find you don't have as many as you think."

Message received. Shut up and only ask questions if you absolutely have to.

Lovely.

She lay back down and concentrated on using her amnis to dampen her senses. She muffled her hearing and taste. She observed the feeling of the scrubs she was still wearing, concentrating on what the seams felt like pressing against her skin. It didn't hurt; she was simply more cognizant of the details. Taking that knowledge, she focused her mind on softening her awareness of the fibers pressing into her skin.

"What are you thinking about right now?"

She blinked her eyes and noticed that Lucien was watching her.

"The seams on my clothing. I think they may have used a synthetic thread to sew in the labels."

He frowned. "There will be other clothing on the island for you. It will be traditional."

Traditional clothing was likely to be the loose dresses her mother still wore around the house or for formal family events. Loose dresses would probably be as comfortable or more comfortable than scrubs.

"Traditional clothing will be fine," Makeda said. "As long as the fibers are natural. My skin seems to sense synthetics more acutely than natural fibers."

"I'll make a note to tell them."

"No humans?" she asked.

"No, I've never wanted humans too close to the lab. There is a sister island nearby where my brother lives. It has more communication and a satellite dish. My mother's humans have always lived there and gone back and forth between the two, but I've messaged ahead. They know not to come to the island until I tell them otherwise."

"Is there refrigeration?"

"If you're thinking about blood, don't worry about having enough. My brother's people will feed us. Once the first six weeks have passed, we'll begin to supplement human blood with cattle. It's mostly what I drink when I'm there."

"The Mursi people in the Omo Valley traditionally drink cattle blood and milk," Makeda mused. "They bleed a cow once a month, but they rarely kill one."

"They probably descended from my mother's people at some point."

"Do you think it's where vampirism came from?" she asked. "Human blood drinking?"

"I don't know, though I've often wondered the same thing. I'm fairly sure Saba's human tribe originated in the lower Omo Valley or near it because of her scarification. It's similar to some the tribes still practice. Of course, she's thousands of years older than they are. I could be wrong, but I don't think so."

Makeda fell silent and thought about the years stretching before her.

Endless years. She would never grow old. She would never lose her mental or physical strength. She would never develop disease. She'd never even catch a cold.

And she'd never see the sun.

She'd never have a child of her own.

She would watch everyone she'd loved in life die. Her parents she expected one day, but her sisters?

Her adored nieces and nephews?

Her friends.

Her colleagues.

Every patient she'd ever treated would likely die before her unless her life was ended by violence. Makeda would exist in a shadow world the sun never touched where human lives were barely seasons. If she thought about it too closely, she might just go mad.

She focused on immediate goals. She still needed to finish the cure for the Elixir virus. She needed to control her hunger.

After that?

"Baojia said I'd need to be isolated for at least a year."

"That's the typical period of time," he said, still scribbling in his notebook. "Individuals vary based on training, personality, violence of the change, and many other factors. I've seen immortals blooded for five years and still out of control. I've seen others at six months who were nearly Zen masters. It varies greatly."

"I've never heard the term blooded before."

He glanced up. "It's archaic and comes from the Latin word for the process of turning someone, which is *sanguinem*. If you use the term, you date yourself."

"How old are you?"

He stopped writing, looked up, and held her eyes. "Why do you want to know?"

"I'm spending eternity with you," she said. "Small talk has to start somewhere."

"Two things." He started writing again. "You're not spending eternity with me. Do you see me hanging on my mother's hem? You'll be independent soon enough. And two, don't ask vampires their age."

"Impolite?"

"Imprudent," he said. "Age is a good indicator of power—though not the only one, as you've seen with Baojia—so asking someone directly how old they are is the vampire equivalent to the crude human phrase 'dick measuring.'"

"Hmm," Makeda said. "I've never had any need to participate in that particular activity."

"Neither have I. You still shouldn't ask my age." He closed his notebook and put it to the side. He walked across the converted hold and sat in the seat across from her. "I know we don't get along very well, but it's my responsibility to teach you what you need to know in this life, so please listen to me."

"Baojia has already taught me—"

"Baojia is an infant." He didn't let her finish her thought. "He's my friend, and I have a great amount of respect for him. He's highly intelligent, and I trust him, which is a rare thing, even among those I count as friends. But you have to understand, Makeda: I sat at the foot of kings in my infancy. My teachers were emperors, and my mother is a god. What Baojia counts as wisdom is *nothing* to me."

Makeda's heartbeat picked up and she felt her fangs drop. She didn't understand her reaction.

Was she fearful? Excited? Hungry?

Aroused. She frowned at the realization. The promise of so much knowledge aroused her.

Drawing in a deep breath, Lucien sat back and stared at her. "You like that," he said. "The power attracts you. It's a predictable—"

"Not the power." Her voice was heavy and slow. "The... knowledge."

"Interesting."

He stared at her as if she were a bug under a microscope. It should have felt clinical and cold, but it didn't. His examination heated her skin. She couldn't look away from his eyes, which perused her body with such focus she lost track of time. He traced her legs, lingering on her ankles and her thighs. The silent attention to her breasts should have enraged her, but it didn't. His gaze slid over her body like a caress.

Had it been hours or minutes?

The plane began its descent, and Makeda snapped out of her spell at the quiet murmur of the captain's voice. She strapped herself in and made ready to land, ignoring Lucien's unwavering attention. She pretended the roaring in her ears was the sound of the engines and not the pulse of her blood.

It didn't matter. He knew.

The tires bumped on the runway, and his eyes finally returned to hers. There was the hint of a smile on his lips. "Welcome home, Makeda."

"I guess I'll see."

"See what?"

"If reality is better than dreams."

Saba

Alitea, Aegean Sea

She flew in his arms, wrapped around Ziri as he transported her across the water and into the heart of Laskaris's domain. They landed in the highest balconies of the sea fortress, the walls rising up against the crashing waves below.

Alitea was no natural island.

It had been formed millennia before by the careful partnership of Sofia, an earth vampire of ancient lineage, and Eris, her sister and a fire vampire of singular skill. They had formed the island off the coast of the mainland as a haven for immortals, shaping it from the volcano Eris had called. After Kato had retired from his empire, Laskaris came and shaped the currents in his own way, adding his mark to the island haven. Jason and his people had been the most singular of craftsmen, flying above the trees and bays of the island, carving the rock that formed the outer perimeter walls into terraced luxury before he took his place on the council throne. Mortals from all over the ancient world had been brought in to build the lavish temples and palaces before they offered their lives as blood sacrifices to the living gods of Alitea.

Ever since, the council had hidden Alitea from human eyes. In ancient times, they had draped it in legends that kept the mortals away. Tales of shipwrecks and cursed waters still kept modern humans at bay. Mortals were not welcome on Alitea. Its residents hunted elsewhere, bringing back offerings for their gods.

Saba watched a group of water vampires climb from the moonlit water of the harbor and walk toward the temple at the base of Eris's volcano. All carried skins she would guess contained blood. All looked flushed and healthy.

They were reverent and joyful in their bearing. No shadow of Elixir lived here. No fear stained Laskaris's happy island kingdom.

Saba curled her lip in disgust.

"What did you want to see?" Ziri asked.

"I don't know."

"They all reside in the temple, you know. Even Sofia does now."

Sofia. How Saba had once loved the woman and envied her joy in Laskaris as a mate. Was this Saba's fault? Had she been too lenient? Given all of them too much freedom?

The vision of her daughter's ashes flashed across her mind.

This is what comes of freedom.

Death.

Ruin.

Extinction.

"Have you decided?" Ziri asked.

"Not yet."

He lounged against a pillar, his black robes fluttering in the ocean breeze. "You'll have to decide soon."

"He has time."

"Not much."

Chapter Nine

Lucien watched Makeda as she leaned over the edge of the small boat carrying them to the island. For as long as any human on Lake Tana could remember, Tana Genet, the island where his home was located, was simply one of the many monasteries dotting the water. It wasn't a monastery—though it was isolated—but the humans who lived on the sister island spread the monastery rumor until it was the only truth anyone remembered. The fishermen gave the island a wide berth, and no boats landed except his own and those of his brother, Gedeyon, who lived on the neighboring island.

"Are there hippos near your island?" Makeda asked over the buzz of the off-board engine.

She was still wearing scrubs. There had been no clothes waiting at the airport, only an old van driven by one of Gedeyon's vampire children. It was the same young vampire who escorted them through Bahir Dar and piloted the boat that took them to the island. Lucien had sent a message to Gedeyon before they left the United States, informing him that no humans could be around the newborn, though she wasn't as uncontrolled as some. His brother, as always, listened to him and had arranged everything.

Now with the moon high in the sky and the quiet of the lake broken only by the small motor, Lucien felt his soul relax on the deepest level. He was home. Makeda was home. He watched her with new eyes, seeing everything through her childlike fascination. He didn't think she'd blinked since the plane landed.

"Hippos?" he asked. "Not many. If there are, they'll flee when you set foot in the water. They're remarkably perceptive, and they recognize our kind as predators."

"Crocodiles?"

"Not here. You'll be able to swim as much as you like, though I'll have to accompany you."

"Why?"

"The islands are far out in the lake, but we're still among humans. They know to keep their distance, but there are fishermen. Tourists. Pilgrims who are ignorant of our true identity. It's my responsibility to keep you—and the humans around you—safe from your bloodlust."

He saw Gedeyon's arm lift as they approached.

"Who is he?"

Lucien couldn't stop the smile. "My brother."

Makeda frowned.

"I suppose he's a cousin, in the vampire sense. His sire was one of Saba's older children. Lake Tana is his home."

Gedeyon was dressed in the white robe typical to monks on the islands, but his head was uncovered and his bright smile shone under the half-moon. He wasn't a monk, but those on his island thought of him as such. He had no mate, and most of his children were independent except for one daughter who also lived on Tana Beza, the sister island to Lucien's own.

"My brother!" Gedeyon called as they approached. "Welcome home."

"*Salam.*" Lucien hopped out of the boat and onto the dock, bowing his head before he grasped Gedeyon's hand and embraced him. "How are you? How is your family? Is your daughter well?"

"They are all in very good health. Hirut has prepared a meal for us." He looked to Makeda. "Sister, welcome to Tana Genet."

"Gedeyon," Lucien said. "This is Makeda. Sired to water by my good friend in America, but under my aegis by choice."

The young vampire who'd been piloting the boat was helping Makeda onto the dock, careful with the American vampire in the strange clothes.

"Thank you." Makeda spoke in Amharic, delighting Gedeyon from the expression on his face. "I am sorry. I did not travel with fresh clothes."

"My daughter will find something to suit you," Gedeyon said, bowing to Makeda and holding her hand in his. "I am Gedeyon, and I am honored to be your host during your stay here. If you have need of anything, you must tell me, and my people will see to it. We both know Lucien would rather be in a book than making conversation."

He took the ribbing from Gedeyon because... his brother was right. And also because for nearly six hundred years, Gedeyon had been one of his closest friends. Lucien didn't like all of his immortal family. In a clan as vast as Saba's, it would have been impossible. But he liked Gedeyon and he'd liked Gedeyon's sire, who had come from the land across the Red Sea.

Gedeyon asked, "Have you fed this evening?"

"We had preserved blood on the plane." He put his hand on the small of Makeda's back, ushering her up the dock and knowing Gedeyon would notice the gesture. "But if you have fresh, it would be appreciated. Makeda will need to feed before dawn."

"Of course." Gedeyon spoke quietly to the young vampire on the boat before he led them up a path twisting through a sacred grove of coffee plants. The night birds went silent as they passed, wary of the new predators on the island. Gedeyon glanced at Lucien's hand, which remained on the small of Makeda's back, and lifted an eyebrow before he said, "Tarik will bring some blood before dawn. Hirut and the women cleaned the house for you, but I told them to leave the laboratory alone."

"Thank you. I shut everything down before I left last time, so it should be fine." Lucien took a deep breath. The air on the island was rich with green plants and rain, and the fecund scent of forest humus lay under the sharp bite of cooking fires. "No storms?"

"Ah." Gedeyon lifted his shoulders in a shrug. "Nothing significant. My people checked the generators and cleaned the solar panels. I started the water system. You and Makeda should be comfortable."

"Thank you."

"My brother, I am so happy to have you here." Gedeyon grinned. "But you must tell me about this plane of yours. Who ever heard of our kind traveling on planes? What is the world coming to?"

❖

Makeda was bathing and changing into clean clothes when Gedeyon passed Lucien a beaker of *tej,* the honey wine he brewed on his island, while they sat near the dock. "So you finally bring a woman home and Mother isn't here."

"Makeda's not 'a woman.'"

Gedeyon grinned. "My brother, what is wrong with your eyes? Is there any cure for it, do you think?"

Lucien smiled. "She's not *my* woman. She is—was—a human colleague. She was almost killed by someone trying to stop us from finding a cure for the Elixir virus. That's why Baojia turned her. I need her for the research."

All amusement fled Gedeyon's face. "This vampire stole her human life?" A quiet curse. Rarely did Gedeyon curse. "Did you kill this person?"

"I killed the one who did it, but he was a small fish."

"Is she still in danger?"

"I told no one we were coming here. They will suspect Ethiopia because it's my home, but the only human aware of our location is Giovanni Vecchio's pilot."

"So Vecchio knows you're in Bahir Dar."

"Mother says he's trustworthy."

"Saba says many things," Gedeyon said. "But she's not here right now, is she?"

"Do you know where she is?"

"Tobruk, last time I heard. Inaya sent a request for a visit months ago."

"Is Inaya still stable?"

"As far as I know. The visit could be for any number of reasons. It might just be diplomatic."

A distant kinswoman by mating, Inaya had taken control over her territory in North Africa only five years before, ousting a corrupt immortal with tenuous ties to Athens. The territory she controlled consisted of both Libya and Egypt, so she was carefully watched by everyone in the Mediterranean and North Africa. Since her first move was establishing a new overseer for the Suez Canal and lowering the tariffs paid by vampires traveling through the canal, she'd become almost instantly popular. She was seen as moderate, pragmatic, and cautious in her associations. A diplomatic visit from the mother of the African continent was a smart, but not particularly daring, political move.

"Is Ziri still involved with Inaya?" Lucien asked.

Gedeyon shrugged. "Probably not, but who knows?"

Lucien stared across the lake. "Saba wrote to me from the Caucasus."

"Is that so?"

He sipped his *tej*. "Arosh and Kato are in the Caucasus. She was near the Black Sea before that."

"Are you saying our sire is playing politics?" Gedeyon asked. "Lucien, you know she hates politics."

"Yes, she does." He leaned forward, putting his elbows on his knees and watching a kingfisher dive from a branch. "She's stayed out of politics for a thousand years, and now the Elixir threatens us all."

"Sounds like you better get to work." Gedeyon rose from his seat. "I suppose it's a good thing you have such a pretty assistant this time. Though this one has fangs, so I'm not sure if you'll know what to do with her."

"Your opinion was not asked for, Gedeyon."

"I'm just saying that vampire women have more bite, brother." Gedeyon's eyes lit in amusement. "Why do you think I prefer them?"

Only with his brother would Lucien joke of such things. "And when was the last time you were warm in bed?"

Humans were warm and soft. That's why Lucien preferred them. They didn't care about his age or political connections. His lineage wasn't nearly as enticing as his skills in pleasuring them. Human lovers were simple.

And yes, short-lived. But that made their lives all the more precious.

"You *are* blind if you don't see what is in front of you," Gedeyon said. "Besides, I'm sure you and your lovely queen could create your own heat between you."

He waved Gedeyon away and rose from his seat on the dock. Dawn was nearly on them. Lucien needed to check on Makeda and make sure she'd eaten. Then he'd be able to—

Oh damn.

He'd forgotten how spartan he kept the living quarters on the island. Other than the lab, which was very well-appointed, there were only a few outbuildings for storage, an outdoor washhouse and kitchen, and one tukul, the windowless round house he preferred for sleeping.

One tukul and one bed.

❖

When Lucien returned to the tukul, Makeda was already asleep on the bed. Piles of blankets and embroidered pillows surrounded her. The bed lay low to the ground, raised on a wooden platform he'd carved one year from a cedar tree that had fallen on the island. It was long and wide. Lucien was not a small man, and he liked to lounge when he had the time.

Makeda's hair was damp and curling around her face, and she wore a long linen dress Gedeyon's daughter, Hirut, must have found. Makeda was so tall the dress only came past her knees.

Modern men were so foolish, Lucien thought, gazing at the delicate bones of Makeda's feet and ankles. Artificially molded bodies had nothing on the delicacy of a woman's bared ankle. He resisted the urge to stroke her skin from her arch to the curving heel and drew a sheet up to her waist.

Then he secured the tukul, setting the alarms that would wake him should anyone try to disturb him or Makeda as they slept. She would not wake. She was sleeping the unmoving, heavy sleep of the newly turned. He doubted she would even twitch.

He glanced around the tukul as he stripped off his traveling clothes and put on a loose pair of pants that wouldn't scandalize an American woman. He'd have to share the bed with her. There was no place else to sleep, and he wasn't taking the floor. There were low stools, but not even a couch or chair because he never had visitors here.

Makeda must have been near collapse to not consult with him about sleeping arrangements. Or perhaps she assumed the house was hers and he had another on the island. Either way, he had no desire to sleep on the floor. Shifting Makeda's body to one side of the bed, he climbed in. There was plenty of room, and she was safe with him. He would wake before her anyway.

But when her eyes fluttered open at nightfall, Lucien still hadn't left the bed.

"What are you doing?" she said.

Trying to understand why I still find you fascinating. Lucien raised a hand and moved an errant curl that had fallen over her face. "Observing you."

Her eyes were wide. "I meant why are you in my bed?"

"It's my bed, actually."

"You mean—"

"There's only one tukul on the island and only one bed. I don't mind sharing with you. You're a very quiet sleeper, and it's a very wide bed."

She said nothing, but he could tell she wasn't pleased.

"It's practical," he said. "This way I can guard you. I will wake during the day if we're disturbed. You will not. You're completely vulnerable when you sleep."

She glanced down at his bare chest. "Apparently."

"Don't insult me by implying I would violate you. One, you should know me better than that. Two, I would be a pariah among my associates for taking advantage of a newly turned vampire under my aegis, and three, my own sire would cut my throat if I ever violated a woman."

He saw her shoulders relax. "Your mother would really do that?"

"Yes."

"She sounds…"

"Harsh?"

"No. I wasn't going to say harsh."

But she didn't expound on her original statement. They lay, openly staring at each other as rain fell on the roof of the tukul. The thatch rustled in the wind and the rain, but the reeds swelled to keep them dry.

"I prefer tukuls," he said. "They're very sensible. Ecologically sensitive. Efficient."

"And the rain sounds lovely on the roof," she said. "I've never slept in one before. I grew up in the city."

"I don't like cities." He picked up another curl and rubbed it between his fingers, examining the weight and texture of her hair, which was extraordinarily fine. "Tukuls are light-safe too."

"I know. I checked before I went to sleep."

"Smart girl."

"I'm a genius."

"I know. I read Katya's file on you."

She paused and watched him play with her hair. "Don't be impressed," she said. "Genius is not an accomplishment." Makeda frowned but didn't move away from him. "Do you have a file too?"

The corner of Lucien's mouth turned up. "I'm sure I have files in archives all over the globe."

"Why are you doing this?"

He propped himself up on one elbow and continued playing with the curl he held. "I like your hair. Do you mind?"

"No, the Elixir virus," she asked. "Why are you working on it? Curiosity?"

He considered how to answer her.

It killed my lover.

But that wasn't true. Not really. The cancer would have taken Rada if the Elixir hadn't come along.

I'm trying to save the world.

Arrogant. And fundamentally untrue. He was ambivalent about the world as a whole.

I'm obeying my mother.

It was accurate. It also made him sound like a child.

"I was visiting a friend—a former assistant—when I first heard of it," he began. "She was dying. She had pancreatic cancer, and there was nothing more the doctors could do. Her family didn't know who I was, but I visited her at night."

"You cared for her," Makeda said.

"Very much. And I couldn't save her."

Makeda shifted closer on the bed, and Lucien resisted the urge to take her in his arms. She wouldn't be warm, but she would be soft. He coveted the weight of her body and imagined her head resting on his chest.

"We can't save everyone," she said. "We've all had to learn that."

"True. But I wanted to save Rada. And then a man—a vampire—showed up and offered me a miracle. I didn't think it would work, but it did. For a while. She had this unaccountable burst of health. The cancer disappeared. We..."

Makeda's eyes grew wide. "You bit her, didn't you?"

He nodded. "I thought I had lost her. But then she was back, and... I didn't take more than a few drops. The bite wasn't for feeding."

Makeda allowed his confession to go unquestioned. "How are you alive?"

"Saba," he said simply. "She drained my blood and gave me her own. I was not in good health when she brought me home four years ago. Saba healed me. Then she sent me out to find a cure for this poison."

"You survived." Her eyes turned inward. "Have you tested your blood?"

He followed her train of thought immediately. "Yes, that was my first thought. Unfortunately, because I received nearly a complete transfusion of my mother's blood, my own immunity did not kill the virus. I simply had new blood."

"What about human patients? A few have shown resistance."

"Inconclusive." He relaxed his head back on the pillow. "There are some humans who are naturally immune to certain viruses, and we do not understand why. Their immunity doesn't seem to transfer to others." It felt natural to talk with her this way. Head sharing a pillow and minds sharing ideas.

If you were sharing bodies, it would be even better.

He shifted away from her when he grew erect. He didn't want to break the strange spell wrought by the rain and the dark night. He wanted to lay in bed and watch Makeda think. Watch the darting motions of her eyes and the slight movement of her lips when she formed an unspoken thought. She was fascinating.

And if he didn't leave the bed soon, his predatory instincts weren't going to be focused on anything as mundane as blood.

He leaned over and brushed a kiss over her lips before he could think too much about it. Then he rose and swung his legs over the side of the bed. "We should get to the lab. I want to show you around, and your notes should have been delivered during the day."

He pulled on a shirt and stood, walking into the night before Makeda could get out a word.

"I thought you said there were solar generators," Makeda said.

"Yes, but I don't waste the electricity," he said. Florescent lights glowed over each workstation, far better than the smelly kerosene or oil lamps he'd once been forced to use in the lab. "Stations are lit. Lighting the whole building wastes energy. There are lamps for the rainy season."

She walked into the laboratory and slowly turned, taking everything in.

Perhaps it wasn't what she was used to, but the basics were still there. Besides, what they were working on involved unlocking her mind. For the moment, they were dealing in the theoretical, and Lucien didn't need a modern lab to think.

"And computers?" she asked.

"No computers." He shrugged at her wide eyes. "We can't use them anyway."

She made a disgusted sound. "Haven't you heard of Nocht?"

Lucien scowled. "Is that the voice-recognition system Patrick Murphy's labs are working on?"

"Yes. Every lab in Katya's territory is using a beta version of the program. Even our lab in California. Did you see Ruben using it?"

His chin lifted. "I don't need a machine to record my thoughts for me."

"It goes far beyond voice recognition and data collection. It's a complete operating system designed for voice. There are proprietary devices designed for vampires that run Nocht software, and it's significantly faster. Even some humans are starting to use it exclusively."

Interesting. "Is it cloud based?"

"Are you kidding? Can you imagine any immortal trusting their information to a cloud?"

She had a point, but it didn't make any difference.

"It doesn't matter what is available in other places, Dr. Abel. You'll have to make do with what we actually have. Anything more modern is going to be too close to human populations. Right now you are not to be trusted around humans, remember?"

She spun in circles, taking in the hanging wires and metal shelving. "I was expecting something basic, Lucien, not something from the nineteenth century."

He crossed his arms. "That is an electron microscope in the corner, and I can assure you those didn't exist in the nineteenth century. I know because I was alive then. You'd be amazed what real scientists could accomplish when they just used their minds."

She put her hands on her hips and stepped closer. "Are you implying the hack-science boys' club you were a part of a hundred and fifty years ago is somehow better or more thorough than a modern research lab? Weren't you still using leeches?"

"At least we didn't have to rely on machines to think for us."

Makeda's fangs dropped and a low snarl came from her throat.

His arousal was instant, and it made him angry. Lucien could admit he'd found Makeda attractive as a human, but he'd expected her appeal to lessen when she became vampire. The fact that it hadn't irritated him, which made him perversely angry with her.

His voice was acid. "*Supposedly* you had some kind of brilliant breakthrough in your own home, so if you can't think here—if you can't sort through your ideas and theories in this lab from the twentieth century—then you're a piss-poor scientist and your so-called breakthrough would have amounted to nothing."

Her fangs shone in the light. "Screw you! I didn't ask for this."

"You'd rather you were dead?"

"If I have to spend my eternity dealing with your patronizing ass, then a sunburn sounds great!"

No.

Not acceptable.

Never.

Lucien grabbed her by the nape of her neck, brought her mouth to his, and kissed her.

Chapter Ten

When Lucien's lips crashed into hers, every cell in Makeda's body screamed at her to take more. She'd woken aroused and hungry. One hunger had been fed, but the other pulsed under her skin, begging to be released. With Lucien's lips on hers, she was a creature of raw nerves.

He bent, never releasing her lips, and lifted her, pushing up her dress to wrap her legs around his waist. Then he gripped the curve of her bottom with one large hand. He was a big man. Taller than Makeda and muscular over his lean frame. Perfectly proportioned with wide shoulders and narrow hips she squeezed with her thighs. She pressed her body to his and felt his rigid arousal at the juncture of her thighs.

"Yes," he groaned. "More."

She lifted one hand from his shoulder and slid her fingers into the silky weight of his hair as he angled her mouth to take her deeper. His tongue invaded and was met with her own. He tasted the length of her fangs, and Makeda felt the hunger grow heavy in her belly.

She wanted him so much, and she hated her own weakness.

"I'm still angry with you," she muttered through biting kisses.

"I know." He bit her lip and sucked the blood into his mouth, groaning at the taste.

"But I want you," she hissed.

"I want you more." His hand tightened on her buttock, and he ground his pelvis against hers. "I don't... do this."

She licked out, tasting his neck. "You don't seduce colleagues?"

"I don't take vampire lovers." He growled when she bit his neck, even though she didn't break the skin. "I don't... It's not—"

"Shut up," Makeda said, pulling his mouth back to hers.

He held her as if she weighed nothing. His muscles bunched and flexed under her fingers. His hands dug into her bottom and her lower back. If she'd been human, the bruising would have been extensive. The primitive creature that had taken residence under her skin approved, but her rational mind...

It was screaming at her.

The hand Makeda had buried in his hair moved to collar his throat. She forced him away with a hard shove, though he didn't release his hold on her buttock or lower back. She was no longer the feral creature who had woken and attacked the first vampire she saw. She could be better—be stronger—than this.

Lucien asked, "What is it?"

Makeda stared at the dip of his suprasternal notch, aching to taste the delectable hollow between his collarbones. She didn't. She wanted to, but she didn't. She forced her fangs to retreat but wasn't sure how successful she was. They still felt heavy in her jaw.

Her life in the past two weeks had become a marathon of self-control. The air around her tasted like temptation because she could always scent the faint smell of humanity. She felt controlled by her hungers. A captive to a body she was still learning. She was aware of every temptation at every point she was conscious. The hours she spent asleep terrified her.

Waking next to Lucien that night had terrified her. It had also thrilled her.

"I can't do this," she said.

"Why not?" His voice was a low rasp. He tried to kiss her neck, but she pushed him back, her hand a vise around his throat. "We both want this," he said. "We've wanted it for months. All the fighting was just—"

"No." She took a breath, began naming bones in her mind. "I cannot do this. Let me down."

"If you're afraid—"

"*I'm not afraid.*" Her temper spiked. "Let me down, or I will hurt you."

He dropped his voice and whispered, "You could try." Then, very deliberately, he relaxed the hand on her buttock, moved the hand from the small of her back to her hip, and lowered her to the ground, dragging his erection over her abdomen. She shuddered, need gnawing at her belly, but she took a careful step back.

"What game are you playing, Makeda?" Lucien's voice was hostile again. "You fight with me. Kiss me—"

"You kissed me."

"You kissed me back." He looked down at her with the dispassionate expression that made her want to scream and tear at his chest until he bled. Then she'd lick at his skin until the wounds closed. Then she'd bite him again.

"I'm completely out of control," she muttered, closing her eyes. "I'm mad."

"You're not insane."

Without another word, Makeda spun and left the laboratory, running through the forest of coffee trees and ficus until she reached the stone dock. She ran to the end and dove into the water without taking a breath, sinking until she could no longer feel anything but the pull and tug of tiny currents in her hair and around her dress. The water caressed her, and she plunged into the darkness, searching for peace in a place that felt both foreign and familiar.

Lucien swam behind her.

Makeda floated in the lake, watching the sea of stars above her. Black had no place here. To her newly keen vision, the stars didn't look like ice but tiny jewels. Faceted gemstones floating in the sky.

New eyes.

For the first time, something about immortal life made her smile.

"What do you think so far?" Lucien was floating a little way from her. He'd been silent for hours, ever since their fight in the lab, but he moved toward her as he spoke.

"About what?"

"Being back in Ethiopia."

"I don't know." She kicked her legs out and listened to the splash of water in the still night. "I don't remember much about this area besides visiting the monasteries when I was a child. Most of my memories of Ethiopia revolve around our house in Addis or my grandmother's village."

"Where is that?"

"Near Yirgalem."

"Sidamo region," he mused. "Very beautiful."

"And the cave where the princess hid," Makeda said.

She heard Lucien swim closer. "What was that?"

Makeda smiled. "It was a story my grandmother told us. I don't know if it's true or not. There was a cave on the mountain where the village was. My grandmother said that a princess once hid there when armies came to attack her father's palace. She hid in the cave and hyenas guarded her."

"They didn't eat her?"

"Of course not. She was a princess."

"Ah." He drifted closer. "I had no idea scavengers held royalty in such high regard."

She couldn't stop her smile. "It's just a story. We were so curious about that cave. I'm sure my grandmother wanted us to stay away from it. There was a family of hyenas that lived there, and we might have been bitten."

They swam until Makeda could hardly feel her legs, but it seemed to make no difference to her body. She never once ached or grew tired. And though the water didn't feel as heady as the ocean, it still embraced her, soothing her nerves and feeding her soul until she felt as comfortable as a child nestled in her mother's arms. Lucien stayed behind her, letting her lead.

When Makeda spotted a rocky outcropping jutting out of the water to her right, she headed toward it. It sloped sharply, with weeds and algae making the base of the rocks too slick to climb. Makeda treaded water next to it, considering how she might be able to get on top.

"Use your amnis," Lucien said behind her.

"What?"

"Your amnis," he repeated. "You're a water vampire, remember?"

"I'm aware of that, but..." She frowned, considering the rock. She lifted her hands from the water and let it dance in her palm. It came instinctually, but she didn't know how to lift herself onto the rock with it. "How?"

Lucien was at her side, treading water. "This could be an issue."

"You don't know how?" An unexpected laugh burst from her throat. "Of course you don't. You're an earth vampire."

"Correct." He swam closer to the rock. "So until we find a better teacher than me..."

She felt his amnis fill the air. The punch of energy was as potent as when he kissed her. Makeda watched Lucien place his hand on the rock, and it reformed under his power. Like a giant stretching its shoulders, the rocky outcropping shrugged up and out. Before her eyes, natural steps formed in the rock, leading to a smooth platform flat as an open palm.

He walked up the steps and held out a hand. "*Yene Nigist Makeda*, I have made you a throne."

Fighting back a smile at his playful words, Makeda took his hand and he lifted her out of the water.

"That was very impressive," she said as she settled on the rock. The linen shift that had felt so light and flowing around her in the lake flopped on the ground and clung to her skin.

"That was nothing," Lucien said. "I'm not being modest. I've raised—and demolished—city walls with nothing more than my hands."

"How?" It wasn't wonder—though there was that—she honestly wanted to know. Her education with Baojia had been rudimentary at best, because their time had been cut short. Getting a handle on her amnis was a top priority.

"I don't think I could explain it to you in any way that makes sense." He paused. "The land here is familiar to me. I recognize it, and it recognizes me. It's a huge advantage earth vampires have that other elements do not."

"Because all the other elements are mobile."

"Yes." He leaned back, propping his lean, muscled arms behind him. "Even freshwater like this is constantly moving. Streams feed lakes which feed other rivers. Water evaporates, condenses. It's constantly in motion and everything leads back to the sea."

She couldn't escape her awareness of his body. She grew hungry for him but forced herself to concentrate on what he was saying.

"There are ocean currents that are constant, but the sea *itself*, the element, is continuously shifting and changing. The earth shifts and changes, but on a massively slower scale."

He cocked his head looking over the water, and Makeda's eyes went to the hardened trapezius muscle at the back of his shoulder. Just in front of it was a curving dip she wanted to sink her teeth into.

"...need to find you a teacher who can— *Makeda*."

She blinked and pulled away from his neck. She'd been leaning in, drawn to the sound of his voice and his scent, inches from his skin. She sat straight and repeated the periodic table in her head. If she started in on the bones and muscles, she would only picture Lucien.

"I apologize," she said.

"Why?" His voice was slightly rough. "Do you think I don't feel it too? It's obvious from our earlier interaction that I do."

"We kissed. We don't have to make it about anything more than that."

He bent down, forcing her to look into his eyes. "I wanted to devour you. And I don't usually like vampires as lovers. I wanted to lay you down on the floor and tear off your clothes like an animal. Wanted to sink my teeth into your inner thigh and hear you scream. I wanted to kiss your—"

"Stop." She put a finger on his lips, but Lucien only opened his mouth and took her finger between his teeth, letting his fangs grow long before her eyes. His unrelenting gaze challenged her control. She was hanging on by a very thin thread. "Lucien, stop."

He released her finger. "Why?"

"Because I don't know if I want you or not."

His hands shot out and gripped her thighs. "Shall I prove you wrong?"

"I know I want *someone*," she said. "But are you sure it's you? Or would anyone in the vicinity cause this reaction at this stage of my development?"

Lucien froze, and Makeda knew she'd made her point.

"I *want*. My hunger is voracious right now. But I don't know if it's because I want *you*, Lucien Thrax, or whether this is a reaction to the change and my lack of control over my hunger. That is why I ran tonight."

"Not playing games?"

"I don't play games. I never have. You told me I could kill indiscriminately right now. Does that apply to other things?"

His jaw clenched and he spoke between gritted teeth. "I don't know."

"I want to wait until I do know," she said. "I'm not a nun, nor am I looking for a husband, but I am discriminating in my partners. I would not choose to have one unless I knew it was me, Makeda, choosing him and not my out-of-control urges."

He nodded, but his eyes were calculating. "I can respect that."

"Thank you."

"But I don't believe that's what's going on."

She paused and considered his words. "Why not?"

"Because we wanted each other before you became a vampire."

It was true. They had been antagonistic, but Makeda had been drawn to him from the beginning of their acquaintance, even when he infuriated her.

"You don't like vampire women," she said.

"I like you." His smile bordered on smug. "Don't change your argument now just because your other one didn't hold water."

"You've never taken one as a lover," she said. "I've heard the rumors, and you just said so yourself. Were you lying?"

"You heard absolutes when I didn't say them. I've never been attracted to power games. With you, however, that doesn't seem to apply. You don't play games. Were *you* lying?"

"No."

He reached out and played with a lock of hair curling by her ear as it dried in the cool evening air. "Next argument, *yene konjo*?"

"We need to focus on the Elixir virus."

"If we're so distracted by our attraction to each other, then we've no hope of conquering the problem. You can't think of any problem nonstop or you'll go mad. Trust me on that one. I've hit the edge more than once."

She was at a loss. One by one, he had demolished every wall she'd built to contain her reaction to him.

"I still think my first argument is valid." When he opened his mouth to object, she raised her hand. "You don't believe me. That's your right. But right now *I* believe me. I don't know if this attraction is real or a product of the amnis surging through my system. Until I do know, I'm not comfortable pursuing anything more than a friendly, professional relationship with you."

She expected him to object when he opened his mouth, but he paused and his eyes turned calculating. "How long?"

"Pardon me?"

"How long until you'll trust yourself?"

She hadn't thought of giving herself any kind of deadline. "I don't know. Didn't you say the worst of the hunger and mood swings would be over in six weeks?"

"So six weeks?" His eyes gleamed. "That's only four more."

"I haven't agreed to anything, Lucien."

"I can live with four more weeks."

He stood, and Makeda could see the outline of his arousal behind the loose pants he wore. He'd stripped off his shirt, and her gaze traveled up his body to the rivulets of water falling down his chest. She could see his tattoos clearly now. Scattered drops on his shoulders mimicked black spots on his chest and shoulders. The water ran over dark chevrons inked on his torso until they formed tiny tributaries that cut and traced over the valleys of his musculature.

She blinked at the memory of rain. Rain hitting glass. Drops tracing down the window...

"Makeda?"

Coursing blood in her system pumped from her heart, through the lungs, carrying vital nutrients through the arteries, the delicate arterioles, the tiny capillaries that fed each cell. Then the steady flow of oxygen-starved blood making its return journey through the veins. An endless system of red cells fed and renewed...

By the source.

"It all goes back to the source," she murmured, her eyes unfocused.

"Makeda?" He knelt in front of her. "What is it?"

"I remember the night of the accident."

The printouts from her computer history lay spread on the table before her. She stood, unable to remain sitting, and sifted through them with inhuman speed.

"This one," she said. "Read it."

"Bone marrow and viral infections?" He skimmed the article. "You think the virus is replicating in the bone marrow."

"I think it has to be. Everything goes back to the blood, right? It's what vampires feed on. It's what keeps them alive. Bone marrow is the single biggest site of blood cell production in humans and—I'm assuming—vampires."

"It is." He stared at the paper in his hands, frowning as she spoke. "I suppose I could write Brenden in Dublin. Have him check —"

"Bone marrow is also vital to the immune system. If the virus is attacking and living in the marrow—"

"That explains how it's surviving in vampire blood," Lucien said. "And if the bone marrow is the source of the disease, it would also inhibit any immune reaction."

"No antibodies. No immune reaction. The body is helpless against the invading disease because the disease is replicating in the marrow itself."

Lucien set the paper down. "How do we treat diseases that attack bone marrow? Think out loud."

"Marrow transplant. Peripheral stem cell treatments. There are other ideas proposed, but those are the current options."

"Bone marrow transplant." He sat down and let out a long breath. "On vampires."

"It's theoretically possible."

"There are so many problems with this." His eyes were fierce. "Makeda, you have no idea—"

"Yes, the healing factor would be a problem," she said. "And we're dealing with big unknowns because transplant surgeries often take—"

"The healing issue is only the start of it." Lucien stood again, as on edge as Makeda was. "If we're talking about marrow transplant, we're talking about fundamentally changing the structure of a vampire's blood. Possibly killing off the very thing they need to survive in order to cure them. This could change everything about their biology. Amnis is fed by the blood, yes, but it's tied to the nervous system. Changing marrow could change blood type. Could change elemental identity. Amnis. It could change a vampire's connection to his sire or mate."

None of those things had occurred to Makeda, but she immediately saw their importance. Vampire identity, family, and political power were closely tied to their element and family structure. Changing either of those things could fundamentally alter an immortal's place in the world.

But even then...

"They're dying, Lucien." She put her hand on his shoulder. "We offer. We ask for volunteers like we would in any experimental treatment, and we let them decide. But they're *dying*. If we can work out the mechanics of the transplant, this may be an option. The *only* valid option that's presented itself in four years."

He looked around the lab. "Even if we work out the existing problems, where are we going to run these trials? You can't be around human patients, and I can't leave you. At the same time, I don't think the immortal world can wait for this."

The thought of running trials she couldn't monitor enraged her, but she knew there was no other option. "We'll have to run them in Ireland. You're familiar with the doctors in the facility there, aren't you?"

"Brenden McTierney," Lucien said. "He's human, surprisingly. He was a great friend and colleague of Ioan ap Carwyn, one of the first immortal scientists who discovered Elixir."

"Why can't we have this Ioan—"

"Ioan's dead." Lucien's expression said the subject wasn't up for discussion. "But Brenden worked with him and Ioan trusted him. Patrick Murphy hired McTierney when he started the Elixir facility outside Dublin. He's my chief point of contact there."

"Would he be able to run trials? How familiar is he with vampire biology?"

"He's not innovative, but he's thorough and he's meticulous. More, he has the trust of the vampires he's treated. If anyone can make the case for an experimental procedure, Brenden would be it." He paused. "Katya won't like it."

Makeda scoffed. "Neither of us is under Katya's aegis at this point. As far as she's concerned, I thought up this theory after I became vampire. She has no proprietary claim on my ideas, and she can't prove otherwise."

Lucien stared at her for so long she became self-conscious.

"Do you think I'm morally wrong in this?" Makeda asked. "Yes, she funded my thalassemia research, but this idea—"

"I don't think you're morally wrong. I was just trying to control myself. I find it incredibly arousing when you're arrogant."

"Really?"

"Yes."

Makeda found that pleasing, and she didn't know why. Arrogance was an unavoidable part of her personality, but she didn't consider it a positive one. Her very traditional parents tried hard to instill humility in all their children. It just hadn't taken well with Makeda. She wasn't a boaster, but she remembered going through much of her childhood quietly tolerating those she felt were inferior on an intellectual level. It wasn't an attractive trait.

Except, apparently, to Lucien.

Saba

Inaya lounged in Ziri's lap, laughing as he offered her grapes. She snatched them from his fingers, at ease in the scowling presence of the old wind vampire. Two of her harem lounged nearby, blowing kisses when Inaya or Ziri glanced their way.

Saba and Kato exchanged looks, but they'd long ago accustomed themselves to Ziri's particular appetites and frequent whims.

"Take Ziri and leave us," Saba said to Kato. "I want to speak to Inaya alone."

"Why?"

"Because I want to," Saba said. "And it's none of your business."

Kato leaned over and breathed the words into her ear. "Don't think I don't see you, my queen."

"See what?"

"The look in your eye."

"I don't know what you're talking about."

Kato drew back and kissed her temple. "Liar."

The two old vampires departed, leaving Inaya with Saba and the delicately trickling fountain in the center of the courtyard.

"What did you want to talk about?" Inaya dropped her flirtatious demeanor once the males had left.

"I'm considering."

"Considering what?"

Saba stared at the woman. In many ways, Inaya was the culmination of centuries of immortal progress and civilization. She'd been turned at the peak of her human health, chosen deliberately by a thoughtful and cultured immortal leader to be his protégée. She'd been trained in the Ottoman court of Rosetta. Progressed through the ranks of her sire's business and political organization until she'd struck out on her own, slowly building alliances until she could conquer the corrupt leader of Libya and Egypt. She took his territory for her own and established her own modern immortal empire.

She was cultured. Educated. Civilized. Progressive.

And still her court was stricken by Elixir.

"How is your friend?" Saba asked.

Inaya's eyes sharpened. "How is your son?"

"Progressing."

Not fast enough.

The sentiment remained unspoken between them, for Inaya knew she was nothing to Lucien. Speaking against the last of Saba's true offspring was a quick way to find death.

"We trust your guidance, Mother." Inaya murmured the expected platitudes, but Saba could see rebellion in the curve of her mouth.

Saba had once ruled all the African continent, and she'd found the responsibility tiring. She recognized now that she'd been shirking her responsibilities. These were her children. All of them.

And sometimes children needed a mother's discipline.

She cupped Inaya's chin in her palm. "A twisted bone must break in order to mend correctly," Saba whispered, pinching Inaya's chin. "Do you understand, daughter?"

"I understand."

Chapter Eleven

Lucien listened to music when he worked. Unless he was working in a lab with myriad assistants and staff bustling around, he listened to music. Bach sometimes. Other times African artists or Latin American. Western folk music. He found anything with a droning element soothing. When he needed to focus, he often turned to bagpipes.

None of those options seemed to suit Makeda.

He held up a few cassettes. "Pick *something*."

She looked up from her notebooks. "Why? I don't like to listen to music when I work. I prefer silence. Don't you have headphones?"

"No."

"Why not?"

"Because it's my lab. Which means we listen to music." He was only being polite giving her the option of which music to listen to. He found a cassette of Tibetan throat singers and snapped it into the player with half a smile on his face.

A few seconds later, she slammed down her notebook. "You have got to be kidding me." Makeda marched over to the cassette player and reached for it, but Lucien grabbed her and swung her around.

He was perched on a work stool, and he pulled her between his legs, braceleting her wrist in one hand with his other hand on her hip. "Leave my music alone."

"This is awful."

"I find it quite soothing. There's something about the nasal droning—"

"Let me look." She huffed out a breath. "If you have to have music, I'll pick something inoffensive."

"You can't do that." He brushed his thumb back and forth over the inside of her wrist. "Good music should always be a little offensive. Otherwise, it's boring."

He wanted to lick her wrist and bite her shoulder. The night before had been highly interesting. In typical newborn fashion, Makeda had swung from excitement to confusion to anger to passion in the space of minutes. She fascinated him. He was too curious not to explore it.

"Classical music isn't offensive," Makeda said, still frozen between his legs. Her eyes were on the hand holding her wrist.

"It was when it was written." He stroked her again. "Beethoven was a bastard. Stravinsky caused riots. I'm fairly sure Mozart was thrown out of a church or two."

She tried to turn, but he wouldn't let her. "Will you let me go please?"

"I don't want to."

Anger and pleasure flickered across her face so quickly he nearly didn't catch them. Oh yes, he'd have to watch Makeda Abel very closely to understand the secrets she tried to conceal.

She wanted him. That wasn't a secret. And he had four weeks to convince her it wasn't a byproduct of her bloodlust. He didn't have any illusions that her newborn cravings hadn't contributed to her loss of inhibition. They did. But bloodlust didn't create feelings. She hadn't latched on to Ruben or Gedeyon or Hirut. She only reacted to Lucien, which—in his mind—proved she'd wanted him before.

Makeda pulled her wrist away. "You don't like vampires."

"I like you."

Her eyes met his in challenge. "And when I don't die after a few decades?"

"What is that supposed to mean?" The thought of her dying made him snarl. Made him remember those terrifying—he could admit it in retrospect—moments on the night of her accident.

"There were plenty of rumors around the lab about your kink. You only like human women. Maybe it was a blood thing. Maybe it was the body heat. I don't judge. But personally, I don't think it was either of those."

Lucien crossed his arms. "Enlighten me."

"You're an arrogant jackass."

And she had the guts to tell him to his face. That was probably part of the attraction. "I'm arrogant. And?"

"You see humans as inferior, and you don't want an equal for a partner. You want a pretty creature you can drink from and fuck for a few decades until they want more than you can give them and they leave you."

He felt a muscle in his jaw jump. "You know nothing."

"Afraid of commitment, Lucien? Is that why you don't take an immortal mate?"

His arm shot out and wrapped around her waist, pulling her tight into his torso. He pressed his chest to hers. Locked his thighs around her hips.

"So perceptive, Makeda. You think you can put my relationship history in a neat box? You think that will help you avoid the clawing need for me in your gut? It won't."

She didn't look away. "It's the bloodlust."

"Liar." He leaned forward, enjoying the cool brush of her breath against his lips. "And for the record, I *do* like human women. They're soft and warm and delicious all over. I like to take my time with them. Like to wring pleasure out of them until they're wrecked from it."

There was that anger again. But hidden behind it was pure desire.

"But right now, I find you more interesting." He leaned back and pushed her away. "Pick some music. Anything you want. Just make it loud."

A moment later, the driving sounds of Creedence Clearwater Revival's "Green River" filled the lab.

"You're archaic," Makeda muttered. "I'm getting you an iPod."

"If you want to waste your money, go ahead."

He forced her out of the lab a few hours before dawn, dragging her away from her work before she collapsed or broke something. She'd begun to go in circles on possible trial protocols for the Irish hospital where the Elixir patients were being kept. It was driving her to distraction. He couldn't seem to reason with her, so Lucien turned off the generator, tossed her over his shoulder, and threw her in the lake.

She came up sputtering, but then she let out a long breath, sank into the water, and he knew he'd been right.

They swam out to the rock where they'd sat the night before, and Lucien instructed Makeda to shadow him in a deliberate tai chi routine Baojia had taught him before they left California. They stood in the center of the lake, feet planted on the smooth grey rock, as the moon circuited the sky and the stars grew faint. He felt the threads of energy weaving around them like a tapestry. Earth and water. Sky and stars.

Peace.

He felt Makeda behind him, her young amnis bright and wild. It shimmered like the cool reflection of the moon. Burst around him like the curls that dried in a riot around her face.

He turned to face her and she halted in her forms.

"Did I do something wrong?"

"No." He started another form. "I just want to look at you."

She kept her eyes locked with his as they moved. "Why?"

"You're beautiful. And I don't understand you."

"No, you don't understand why I'm interesting to you," she said.

Clever, clever.

"I suppose you're right."

"Were you this interested in me when I was human?"

"Yes." He paused and thought back. "No."

"Make up your mind, Lucien."

He stopped moving and stepped closer. "I think I have." He ran a finger across her collarbones. She was wearing a sleeveless tunic and a pair of loose pants that night. The tunic dipped low enough he could see the faint pulse of her erratic heartbeat. He could hear it.

She closed her hand over his and pulled it away from her skin. "You might have decided, but I haven't."

Lucien cocked his head. "Why do you hesitate to take what you crave?"

"I don't do out of control well."

"I beg to differ. I remember your bite on the night you woke. You do out of control very well."

She shook her head and crossed her arms. "Do you indulge every craving you have?"

"It depends on what it is," he said. "If it's something that would be good for me, then yes. And Makeda"—he bent down and whispered in her ear—"I would be very good for you."

"Don't."

"Don't what? Seduce you?" He didn't touch her. Instead, he let the amnis flow from his feet, into the rock, and spread over her legs. He knew when she felt it, the warm trickle of heat that crawled across those delicate, tempting ankles, up to her knees, caressing her thighs until it reached her—

He sputtered back when the slap of water hit his cheek.

"Stop it," she ordered.

Lucien was too shocked to do anything but laugh. The sound carried over the water, drifting on the wind that whipped over the lake.

"I *like* you," he said.

"Then don't try to manipulate me."

"*Yene konjo*," he said, "that wasn't manipulation. That was teasing."

"So you say."

"That was also very impressive," he said. "Just a few days ago, you could barely splash me."

"I don't know how I did it." She lifted her regal chin. "Instinct, I suppose. Don't ask me to do it again."

Lucien had to distract himself, or he'd lose any semblance of self-control. "Talk to me about your problem," he said, starting to move through the tai chi forms again. "Think aloud. Sometimes it's better that way."

She hesitated but followed his motions. "I'm not accustomed to collaboration."

"You weren't accustomed to drinking blood either, but you're taking to it like a native."

"I am a native," she said, looking around the broad sweep of black water. "Kind of."

"But not native to immortal life. You're doing very well though. Gedeyon mentioned it."

She murmured something and fixed her eyes over his shoulder to stare at the horizon. "It's the chemotherapy sequence. I'm trying to predict immortal reactions to mortal medications. I can't predict it with any surety."

"No surety here. Experiments. Tell me what you're worried about."

As Makeda processed the problem aloud, Lucien offered ideas that she picked through like a finicky cat. None of them was quite the right solution, but as she took in more and more information, he noticed her gaze grow less present. She was focusing inward, skipping around a mind that now worked twice as fast as her old one. With time, she grew still, frozen in the White Crane posture, but Lucien could see her mind racing.

He paced around her on the damp rock, watching as she worked through the thoughts dancing in her mind. Every now and then, she'd blurt out a question and he'd answer it, sometimes asking one of his own. Sometimes she would answer. Sometimes she ignored him.

"Makeda." Lucien could see the beginning of dawn creep behind the mountains. "We need to take shelter."

"No."

"We have to."

Her eyes flew open. "I haven't fed."

Damn. She hadn't. He'd been fascinated by the workings of her mind and completely forgotten she needed to feed her physical body. She'd wake in the evening with her instincts roiling if he couldn't get her back to shore fast enough.

"Don't argue. I'm still faster." He grabbed her around the waist and dove into the lake, cutting through the water and holding on to her by the hand. He could feel her lagging. Could feel the tug of daylight beginning to pull at her.

"Makeda?" He picked her up and carried her when they reached the dock. "Wake up."

"Can't." She sounded drugged. "Not... optimum development... potential loss of..."

Her head fell against his shoulder and she was out. She'd fallen asleep worried about the potential detriment to her cognitive development, if he had to guess. Not worried she'd attack someone or wake starving. Lucien tried not to smile.

She would be hungry and pissed off in the evening, but hopefully she wouldn't forget what she'd been working on. That would probably anger her more than anything.

She was soaking wet when he laid her on the bed. It was too damp and cold for her to be comfortable resting with wet clothes against her skin. Trying not to look at her as anything more than an unconscious patient, Lucien disrobed Makeda and pulled one of her traditional cotton dresses over her head. Then he tucked her into bed and secured the tukul before he rested beside her.

Lucien was ready when she woke.

He'd woken an hour before her and called for a quart of fresh blood to be delivered. Where Gedeyon was getting the blood, Lucien didn't ask. He knew Gedeyon and Hirut provided for enough humans on the island to meet their own needs, but they might have to go to the mainland for fresh blood. His brother was well aware of the Elixir threat, so whatever source he had, Lucien knew it would be safe.

Her fingers twitched and brushed against his skin. Lucien rolled closer and Makeda turned to him instinctively. He saw her take a deep breath, and her fangs grew in her mouth. "Makeda."

Another deep breath. Her eyes still closed, she rolled into him and buried her face in his neck.

Lucien's body reacted immediately. She sighed and licked out against his skin.

He wanted her bite. By *God*, he wanted it badly.

Lucien took a deep breath. "Makeda, wake up."

He didn't want her to wake up scared or shocked. She'd be more dangerous. He put a hand on her cheek and brushed his thumb over her skin, his fingers teasing her curls.

"*Yene konjo*, you need to drink."

Her teeth scraped over his pulse, and every instinct in Lucien screamed at him to bend his neck and press her mouth to his skin so she could bite.

He hungered for her bite with every breath. He'd never wanted to be bitten, but the memory of her fangs the night she first woke haunted him.

A low groan came from his throat, and he tried to gently move her back. "Makeda, wake up."

A low, hungry snarl.

Lucien clenched his eyes shut and fisted her hair, dragging her away from his neck just as her fangs pricked his skin.

"No." He rolled her to her back and braced himself over her, controlling her legs as they kicked and she tried to twist out from under him. "Makeda, wake up."

Her eyes flew open, but they were in no way rational. She bared her teeth and snapped at him.

Lucien banded his arms around her and pulled her up, turning her around and clamping his legs around her to hold her down as he reached for the pitcher of blood. Holding it in front of her face, he said, "Drink."

Makeda grabbed it and shoved her face in the blood, drinking it in rapid gulps.

Halfway through the pitcher, she raised her head and let out a strangled sigh. "I hate this."

Lucien frowned. "Is there something wrong with the blood?

Gedeyon assured me—"

"No. It's not the blood." Her voice was tired. "I hate feeling like an animal. Controlled by my hunger."

He brushed her hair away from her face, making sure none of it touched the blood. "We were all this way once. In fact, most of us were far worse. I was nearly uncontrollable for three months. I attacked anything that came near me, including my mother."

"Why?"

He nudged the pitcher back to her mouth as he told the story. "When I was turned, I hadn't eaten properly in weeks. It's why my musculature is so defined. We were fighting the Romans, and they were very good at weakening their enemy. I was a soldier, so I was very strong, but in those weeks before my death, my body was beginning to eat itself."

She took a break from drinking. "How did you die?"

"Not in battle." He smiled. "Which surprised and disappointed me. I was hunting, actually. Stalking a bear that had ransacked our stores. I knew if I managed to kill it, we would also have a good amount of meat for the men. The local crops had been burned by the Romans, but there was still game in the forests."

"Man against bear," Makeda said. "Bear wins?"

His shoulders shook with laughter. "I got in a few strikes, but yes, I didn't fare well in the end. The only reason the monster didn't drag me off and eat me was that Saba was watching. I'd... amused her."

"By fighting a bear?"

"She told me later it was the cursing." He smiled. "My mother told me I cursed better than a Roman, and it made her laugh. She wasn't laughing later when I woke like a bear and began mauling another of her children. She had to bury me."

"Bury you?" Makeda asked. "How did she—"

"She actually buried me. The ground opened up and swallowed me every time I threatened to lose control. I wasn't in command of my elemental strength at that point, and I was nowhere near as powerful. She kept me underground a good part of the first year."

"Is that Saba's version of a time-out?"

Lucien threw his head back and laughed. "Yes, I think so."

"Did it make you angry?"

"Not really. In my lucid moments, I understood. I was grateful, in fact. I knew I was far from civilized. And of course, I had no idea what a vampire really was. They were folk tales in the mountains. Monsters that scared children. I wasn't a fool to believe in them. So I had to overcome my incredulity *and* my bloodlust. It took far longer than a year because it took me a long time to accept what I was."

Makeda had relaxed in the circle of his arms and legs. The pitcher of blood was gone, and her energy was even and easy. Lucien rested his chin on her shoulder and brushed his cheek against her curls. "So you see, we were all uncontrolled at the beginning. We were all monsters."

"We still are."

It was the first time she'd referred to herself as part of the "we." The first time he felt her softening toward life as a vampire.

"We're only monsters if we allow it," Lucien said. "We can become so much more."

She turned and pressed her cheek to his. "Will you show me?"

"Yes."

❖

Except he was a horrible instructor. Lucien and Makeda stood on the edge of the lake, staring at each other, each with their hands on their hips. Gedeyon and Hirut sat on the stone dock, watching them both with poorly concealed amusement.

"You're an awful teacher," Makeda said. "This is not going to work."

He tugged a hand through his hair. "I have to think that some of the concepts are universal. Our elements may be different, but can't you sense the... matter of it? The substance, if you will. When your amnis reaches out—"

"There is no matter. No substance." She threw up her hands, and he could tell she was getting frustrated. They'd been at this for over two hours. "I'm imagining my amnis wrapping around the water like you say, but it feels a little like trying to fill a bucket with a colander."

He crossed his arms. "Can't you just... follow your instincts?"

"My instincts are telling me to go for your throat right now. Mind if I follow those?"

That sent Gedeyon and Hirut into peals of laughter. Both of them had immediately taken to Makeda, and she was cautiously opening up to them. Her Amharic had gone from rusty to fluent. She and Hirut joked as they worked around the island washing clothes or gathering firewood—normally both jobs the humans would be hired to do, but with no humans allowed near Makeda, Gedeyon's daughter had offered to help.

"Lucien," Hirut called, "do you build your house with water? No more can she build with earth. Makeda cannot learn this from any of us. Let me call my friend, *agoti*."

Hirut had a trusted friend in who lived in Djibouti, but Lucien was reluctant to expose Makeda to anyone not under his or Saba's aegis. If only Baojia had been able to accompany them...

"Please," Makeda said. "I have to learn more than the basics. Besides, it will give me something more to focus on. If I can discipline myself learning my element, I know it will help the bloodlust."

He pursed his lips and saw—with some satisfaction—Makeda's attention was drawn to his mouth. "I don't know this vampire."

"You said yourself that Hirut is one of the most cautious vampires you've met. If she trusts him—"

"But do I trust him with you, *yene konjo*?" He stepped closer and brushed a hand over Makeda's hair, which had grown damp and wild as she experimented with the lake water.

She let out a shaky breath. "Lucien..."

"Four weeks," he said under his breath. "You think that will be enough to convince you?"

"I told you I hadn't agreed to any..." She blinked and looked down at her feet sunk in the mud at the edge of the lake.

"Makeda?"

"Something is coming," she whispered. "I can feel it in the water."

Lucien whipped around, snapping at Gedeyon and Hirut, who had stood as soon as he felt Makeda's alarm. His friends flanked Makeda as Lucien stood on the edge of the water. His shoes were off and his feet drew energy from the earth he stood on. He sank his energy down into the soil, past the rock and into the lake bed. He felt the foreign energy vibrate in the murky water, felt the massive surge of power.

Who would dare?

This was Saba's land. No one was foolish enough to come at her people. Not unless they wanted to be wiped from the earth.

"Lucien?"

"I feel it."

It was in the air. A sucking vortex of water appeared in the distance. It looked like a waterspout, but Lucien knew this was no air vampire. The column moved across the water at ferocious speed, heading straight for them. Makeda vibrated behind him, and he could sense her control about to snap.

"Gedeyon."

"I have her."

This was no time for Makeda to lose it. Newborn vampires could be fierce in combat, but only against an unskilled opponent. Any water vampire able to construct and travel in that column was more than skilled.

He was a master.

Lucien caught a scent on the breeze. It was familiar... and it wasn't. Something about it didn't make sense. Gedeyon and Hirut must have noticed it at the same time. They both frowned in confusion.

"Mother?" Hirut said. "But how could she create—?"

"She can't." Lucien stepped farther into the lake, wading up to his knees as the stunning column of muddy water came closer. As it did, the water column shrank, grew shorter and wider until its maker was visible through the swirling water.

His beard was trimmed and his bronze hair tamed into a barely savage mane, but the olive skin was the same. The piercing blue eyes and fearsome visage. Lucien stepped toward Kato, and the ancient vampire's face broke into a wide smile even as the vortex calmed and fell around him to settle back into the lake. And still Kato walked upon the surface, a creature of such enormous strength that ancient peoples had seen him and named him a god.

"*Theio*." Lucien bowed from the waist, his heart surging with fond memories. Behind Kato, Saba emerged, holding Kato's hand as the two walked toward him. "Mother."

"Lucien." Kato's voice boomed. "Son of my heart." Kato stopped in front of Lucien, his feet sinking into the water as he brought his arms around Lucien in a tight embrace. "It is so *good* to finally see your face."

Lucien felt tears come to his eyes when Kato kissed his forehead. He wrapped his arms around his uncle and offered a silent prayer of thanks.

Lucien had not seen Kato in centuries. Not since Ziri and Arosh had concocted the fiction of their battle with the old king—a battle widely believed to have caused the death of both Kato and the legendary fire king. Lucien had mourned bitterly at the loss of them both, but especially of Kato. He'd discovered Kato and Arosh were alive only when they revealed themselves in Rome, but he had not seen his favorite uncle since then. They had both been recovering from Elixir poisoning. Both had been in seclusion. Kato was still believed dead by many in the immortal world.

"I have missed you, *Theio*," Lucien said.

"I was so pleased when your mother told me you had recovered."

"And you... how?"

Kato's amnis had been broken by the Elixir virus for centuries. His sire was dead. From everything they knew about Elixir infection, his uncle should not have recovered.

"We will tell our stories," Kato said, patting the back of Lucien's head, "after we greet new friends, yes?"

"Of course." Just then, Lucien realized Kato's arrival could not have come at a better time. "I am *so* glad you're here."

Saba grinned at Kato's side, then she grabbed Lucien's face and kissed his cheeks. "You look so much healthier, *yene Luka*. Who have you brought to me now? Is it the doctor you spoke of in your letters? Did we surprise you?"

"You frightened us," Lucien said. "The waterspout was a nice touch."

Saba laughed from her belly. "So much fun to travel with Kato! I forget. Ziri has speed, but Kato—"

"Has style." The ancient winked at Saba and pinched her chin. "We came up the river. It seemed the fastest way."

"The river" must have referred to the Nile, which flowed from the Mediterranean all the way up to Lake Tana in the mountains. Because who else would walk the Nile river as if it was his own personal pathway?

Only Kato.

"Who... are you?" Makeda whispered behind him.

Lucien turned with a wide smile, Kato's arm still around his shoulders. "This, *yene konjo*, is your new teacher."

Chapter Twelve

Makeda stared at the two vampires across the fire. If she'd had no knowledge of the vampire world—knew nothing of immortals or amnis or elemental power—they would still not seem human. The air around them crackled with energy. They moved through the world with inhuman grace. Saba's wrist turned up, and six rocks appeared around the fire pit, perfectly smooth and suited for each person's height. Hirut brought a pan of coffee to the fire and handed it to Saba, who roasted the beans as she and Gedeyon chatted about the island and her people who had been left in his care.

Kato sat beside them, legs stretched out on the ground as he leaned his massive shoulders against a rock. When Saba handed him a clay *jebena* filled with water, he held it in his hands and Makeda saw steam pour out of the neck. He handed it back to her and she set it over a warming fire until the coffee had roasted.

"Incredible, aren't they?" Lucien whispered in her ear.

"Completely." She glanced at him but looked away before the intimacy of eye contact tempted her too much. "Are they... together?"

Lucien stared at his mother as she performed the coffee ceremony for Gedeyon and Hirut, waving the smoke from the roasting coffee toward them so they could enjoy the offering of fragrance.

Makeda wondered if she'd be able to stand the richness of traditional coffee with her new taste buds. Most of her food Hirut had made bland so Makeda could become accustomed to flavors again. White bread and shiro were about as daring as she got these days. Well, white bread, shiro, and blood.

"Hmm?"

"Kato and Saba. Are they...?"

ELIZABETH HUNTER

"Lovers?" Lucien frowned a little. "I don't think so. They were a long time ago, but Kato generally prefers men." Lucien shrugged. "But who knows? If either of them needed affection, the other would offer it with no hesitation. They are very close."

Makeda watched Lucien observe the others. She had never seen him more profoundly at ease. "You love them."

He looked down and smiled before he put an arm around her. "Very much. And you will too. Ziri and Arosh... I'll let you form your own opinion." Lucien tensed. "*Don't* have sex with Arosh."

Makeda's eyebrows rose. "Excuse me?"

"Not just because I want you for myself, but because... Well, he's Arosh. You'll probably want to. Just know it's a bad idea."

Saba called out, "Sex with Arosh is never a bad idea, son. Don't be so possessive."

Makeda's eyes went wide. Had Saba heard their whole conversation? If her cheeks could flame with embarrassment, they would have.

"Saba and Arosh are devoted lovers," Lucien said. "They just aren't constant ones."

Saba waved her hand. "What is constant when you are as old as we are?"

Kato leaned back and looked up. "The stars. They are constant."

"Even stars burn out occasionally." Saba leaned over and gently kissed his mouth. "And then sometimes they shine again."

"Why would I want to have sex with someone I don't know?" Makeda asked. "I'm genuinely curious why you think I'd be tempted by that."

Saba laughed out loud. Even demure Hirut smiled a little.

"Arosh is the fire king," Kato said, also grinning. "His women love him, and he loves women. His harem is well-satisfied, but he always enjoys a challenge." Kato nodded firmly. "You would be a challenge."

"Why?" She frowned. "Not that I'm going to have sex with a complete stranger, so I suppose it doesn't matter."

"Your loss," Saba said.

Kato looked at Lucien, and his smile grew impossibly bigger. Makeda looked over her shoulder.

Oh.

Lucien was staring into the fire, his jaw clenched. His fingers dug into her hip.

"Lucien." She nudged his knee with her own. "I'm not going to have sex with the fire king. Just the name makes him sound like a pretty bad bet."

His fingers relaxed, and his frown eased into a smile. "Good."

"Not that I'm agreeing to anything else, so get that smug smile off your face."

Kato laughed. "I like her."

Saba poured the coffee, but her eyes met Makeda's and she winked.

The excitement of the previous night couldn't be matched by the routine of the second night, but Makeda enjoyed it more. She passed another quiet day in Lucien's bed. This time, because she'd fed before she went to sleep, there was no raging hunger to overwhelm her. She woke to a soft kiss on the cheek and quiet words urging her to drink.

It was affectionate and so soothing she had to fight the urge to curl into him and sate her hunger for Lucien's body. Every night she felt more and more in control of her emotions and instincts, except where Lucien was concerned. Her hunger for him only grew. Even when they fought, she wanted him.

In fact, she might have wanted him more.

That night, while Makeda and Kato walked out into the water, Lucien was running an analysis on a sample of Kato's blood he'd asked for.

"Like you," the giant vampire said, "my preference is for saltwater. But the basic practices are the same. You'll only be stronger, more in control, in the sea."

"The Elixir virus broke your connection to your element,"

Makeda said. "But you've recovered fully?"

He didn't seem offended by her question. "I wouldn't say fully, but I am nearly whole. My children are all dead, but they had their own children, and their blood strengthens me."

Makeda flipped through what she knew of current Elixir treatment. "Partial transfusion?"

"Total exsanguination followed by partial transfusion."

Something wasn't adding up. Even total exsanguination wouldn't have killed off the virus in his marrow. At least, not that alone. "It's startling that you have survived."

"I'm vampire." Kato smiled. "And I'm still the strongest of my kind."

"Do you mean the strongest of water vampires?"

"Yes."

Makeda paused. "The strongest in the world?"

Kato shrugged. "I believe so."

"Because you're the oldest?"

"I don't know that I am," he said. "Though it's possible. There are rumors of some ancients in the South Pacific who may be older than me. But in my world, I am the greatest."

Makeda supposed that for an ancient Mediterranean king, the world still revolved around his sea. "You're the common ancestor Baojia talked about. The one all the water vampires are descended from."

"Am I?" He cocked his head. "Possibly. It's been so long that none of us really remember our origins. The elders in the East claim to have accounts of the earliest vampires—they call them *Sida*—but they could be lying. Ziri believes them, but that could be because the Sida were supposed to have been wind walkers like him. He said his sire was one of the horse people." Kato put his hands on his hips and looked at Makeda. "History isn't interesting to me. We should play with water."

Makeda couldn't stop her smile. Lucien was correct. She was quickly growing to love Kato. He was jovial and humorous. And though his power was frightening, Makeda's fear was tempered by his charm. There was an innocence to Kato. To him, the world was still a simple place. He spoke warmly of his friends and children's children. He spoke of obliterating his enemies with a deft levity that confused and charmed Makeda at the same time.

As for Saba, Makeda found the other woman too intimidating to be lovable.

Kato and Makeda waded into the water and dove deep. Kato had demanded Makeda wear as little clothing as possible for her lessons, so she'd stripped down to only panties and an undershirt. The freedom in the water felt incredible.

"I feel *everything*," she said, surfacing after long minutes and floating on her back to watch the stars. "I can feel the fishes and the hippos. The birds as they float or dive. How is that possible?"

"Because you're connected to the water, you feel the void where the animals exist," Kato said. "That is why Lucien couldn't understand. Earth vampires reach for the substance, while we look for the void. Much as your mind assumes information to paint a cohesive picture of a mosaic, your amnis fills in the information you're sensing from the water." He pointed to his right. "A group of six hippos is over there sleeping."

Makeda laughed. "Hippos are easy to sense."

"Because they displace so much water. Do you understand?"

"Yes."

"What you need to learn is how to coax the water." He swam to her and grasped her hand. "Hold on to me. Feel what my amnis does first, then try it yourself."

They floated for hours, most of which consisted of Kato demonstrating how to coax the water and Makeda fumbling through some poor imitation of it. Nevertheless, her teacher was endlessly patient.

"Remember, Makeda, your own body is over half water." He stood behind her, her hands cradled in his giant palms as she felt his amnis move. "Water is in the air. In the soil. It's everywhere. Water is what came first of all things."

"But how do I manipulate it?"

"You have to find its energy first," he said. "Don't think. Feel. Allow yourself to listen to your instincts."

"I thought I was supposed to fight my instincts."

She felt his chest rumble in a quiet laugh. "Why would you do that?"

"So I don't kill anybody?" she said. "That seems like a good reason."

Makeda felt him shrug massive shoulders.

"People die all the time. It's the way of things. You shouldn't kill innocent people because there is no honor in killing that which offers no harm. You shouldn't let your hunger consume you. But self-control is a weapon like anything else. Be careful you don't let your armor weigh you down."

"So learn self-control. And also learn when to let it go?"

"If you can't ever let it go, it becomes a prison." He leaned over and kissed her cheek. "Not a tool."

Makeda wondered if Kato could read minds. Waking that night, she hadn't been hungry for food; she'd been hungry for Lucien. She'd slaked one thirst, but the other still burned.

"If you don't listen to your instincts and learn to read them, you'll never master your element. Find the water within you. Let it connect to the water without. Once you feel the tie between yourself and your environment..." He broke away from her, stepping to the side and lifting his arms as if in prayer. The lake rose in a sheer curtain of rippling, living water. Fish danced in it. Curious birds swooped by and shook their feathers. "...you will know your power, Makeda Abel."

He let the water come crashing down and turned to Makeda, the spray billowing around him, drawn to his bare skin. "This world belongs to us. Water is the true cradle of life. The whole of this world is nothing but a stone-kissed sea, a playground for our kind." A wide smile broke through the darkness. "No matter what the others might think, in *our* world, she who controls water can rule the earth."

❖

Makeda was still trying to figure out the trial protocols for Dr. McTierney two nights later. She wondered if she shared Kato's assertion with the Irish physician whether he'd be more amenable to her requests.

Just so you know, Dr. McTierney, I've been told by a former emperor that I could possibly rule the earth, so you should probably just send me daily reports and not bitch about it.

That might not work as well as she hoped.

Makeda had spoken to Brenden McTierney on the satellite phone the previous night and was reasonably content with his competency. She also warned him she'd expect nightly updates once the trials were underway, even though the doctor balked at that amount of oversight. She was micromanaging, but he'd just have to live with it. She'd never run trials from a distance before. It was infuriating on several levels.

Lucien strode into the lab carrying a handful of papers. "I think I've figured something out."

She glanced at him and quickly glanced away. The normally aloof vampire had kept up his steady and affectionate behavior, leaving Makeda wondering what had come over her former antagonist and when whatever switch he'd flipped would flip back. She wasn't accustomed to Lucien's affection, and in the absence of her normal support system, she didn't want to become dependent on it. That couldn't lead to anything good.

"What did you figure out?" Makeda asked, keeping her eyes trained on her calculations.

"I've figured out where the virus originates."

"In the marrow," she said. "We knew that."

"I mean before that."

She looked up. "What do you mean?"

"It's a virus. It doesn't spontaneously generate, it's transmitted. Replicated. But it's the only virus in history that seems to affect vampires," he said. "Why?"

"I... don't know. You're the vampire-biology expert. I assumed you had—"

"Immunity." Lucien pulled up a stool and sat on it, so close she could feel his amnis crackling with excitement. "And we do. We have centuries of it. Every antibody our sires and their sires ever had. But we have nothing to fight off this virus because it looks like nothing we've ever seen before."

"Because it's a mutation."

"Of what?"

She opened her mouth, but she couldn't think of anything. She'd looked at the virus's structure but not that closely. She'd been more focused on how it was replicating, not its origins. "The Elixir causes it."

"It causes the mutation," Lucien said. "Unlocks it. But where did the virus *originate*?"

"There are no new viruses," Makeda said. "There are variations of older viruses or those that have lain dormant or those we haven't discovered yet."

"But we did stumble across it, Makeda. My mother and her friends unlocked it hundreds of years ago."

"And they eradicated it when Kato went mad," she said. "You've told me this story before. It was rediscovered in the early part of this century by a vampire bent on world domination. Or destruction, depending on who you ask. And it's been spreading since."

"To every vampire it touches. Every human. No matter their genetics or geography."

"So?" Makeda frowned. "Lucien, you have to know that we're all genetically similar. Markers of race or ethnicity aren't biological. They're a construct. Even vampires and humans are basically the same."

"Except for my mother."

Makeda blinked. "Excuse me?"

"The virus has affected everyone it touches except my mother. I took a sample of her blood when I took Kato's. Come look." Lucien's fangs had dropped in his excitement, and one clipped his lower lip.

The scent of blood distracted Makeda, but she managed to rein in her instincts. She walked over to Lucien's workstation and looked at the printout he handed her. "What am I looking at?"

"A reading of Kato's viral load."

"It's a lot lower than I expected," she said. "If this were a cancer, I'd say he was in remission. I was talking to him the other night, and it sounds like—"

"Not important." Lucien shoved another paper under her nose. "This is Saba's."

Makeda tried to make sense of what she was seeing. "She... Her blood—"

"Is nearly the same as Kato's, which makes sense." He scowled. "Because they've been exchanging blood."

"*What?*"

"Oh yes. She told me last night when I confronted her."

"But does she have the virus now? Lucien, how could she—"

"No." He tapped the paper. "Look again."

She sorted through the numbers, wondering where he'd had the blood analyzed. Their lab was too small for the equipment needed, and Makeda didn't even know if she'd be able to use most of it with the way she reacted to electricity these days.

She was getting sidetracked.

"Look at her antibody count," Lucien said.

"This doesn't make sense." Saba's blood didn't show any of the markers they'd come to expect from Elixir patients. In fact...

"She's *immune*?"

"She's immune."

"How? Are you...?" Makeda looked at the numbers again, but Lucien was right. Saba was producing antibodies that were fighting off the Elixir virus. And if Saba had immunity to something that could infect even Kato...

"It's a retrovirus," Makeda said.

"It's probably been around for millennia, and she must have been exposed when she was human," Lucien said. "Or very near when she became a vampire. She's the oldest of us. If she had exposure to this virus when she was human, her system fought it off and she's carried the immunity with her. She might be the only one alive who has it."

"She's the key." She frowned. "So why didn't her blood cure Kato when he was first infected? You told me they'd tried—"

"How could it? They never touched his marrow. They treated the symptom, but not the source." Lucien smiled. "You were right. It all goes back to the source. And with vampires, Saba *is* the source."

"So if we're going to truly cure this virus—cure it and not just treat the symptoms—we need Saba's help."

"For patients whose sires are alive," Lucien said, "exsanguination followed by new blood works. We don't know exactly how, but it works."

"But for those without a living sire, a transplant from Saba—"

"Going all the way to the marrow," Lucien said. "Essentially remaking them as immortals. They would be her children. They would be connected to her amnis. Her element."

"Not all of them will be happy about that."

"No." He took a deep breath. "We have to accept that some will prefer death to losing their elemental identity."

Makeda said, "We have to give them the option, Lucien."

"You're forgetting one very big thing." He grimaced. "For this to work, we also have to convince my mother."

Chapter Thirteen

Lucien tapped a pencil on the desk in Gedeyon's home as he wrapped up the video conference with Brenden McTierney. The desk was intricately carved with crosses and other ecumenical symbols typical of the area around Lalibela, where his brother had spent his human years.

He wanted to take Makeda to Lalibela. And Gondar. Axum. Did Hirut still keep in touch with her family near Awassa?

McTierney was going on and on. The man was gentle as a lamb with patients, but with his peers... "Your Dr. Abel has got to understand that taking time to write up the kind of reports she wants is going to require hours that our team could be spending on—"

"If it's just a matter of manpower, why don't I send one of our colleagues from California to you, Brenden?" Lucien asked. "In fact, Ruben worked with Dr. Abel for months and will understand what level of detail she'll want in order to monitor the trials from a distance. Why don't I arrange for him to assist you during the next few months?"

"I'm insulted you think I need one of your people looking over my shoulder," the Irishman clipped out. "I thought we had more respect between us, Lucien."

"This isn't a matter of respect." Lucien soothed the irritated physician. "Or a matter of questioning your competency."

"Trust me, with Makeda Abel, it was *definitely* a matter of questioning my competency. The woman asked me to mail her a copy of my CV and my most recently published study! Does she think working with Elixir patients lends itself to publishing in damn medical journals? Who does she think she is?"

"She's young, Brenden." Lucien managed to hold in the smile

that wanted to erupt. Makeda was arrogant, but damn it, she had reason to be. "She was turned five weeks ago, and she's stuck in isolation right now. She's doing remarkably well during her transition, so please cut her a little slack. If time weren't such an issue with this, she'd never have allowed anyone—including me—to run this trial without her."

"Jaysus, Lucien." McTierney looked suitably shocked. "She didn't lose her composure the entire time we were arguing. I didn't even realize she was vampire." The Irishman's cheeks went a bit red. "I'll admit, I thought she was one of your..."

Lucien paused long enough to make the human squirm. "One of my assistants?"

"That's generally what you call them." McTierney shrugged. "Come on, you do have a reputation. I've never heard of your collaborating with a peer before."

And that was just a bit pathetic, wasn't it? Lucien was getting slapped in the face with his own past more and more these days. First it was his mother thanking him for finally bringing someone home who could carry on a conversation. Then it was Kato blithely mentioning that Lucien was finally growing up. Gedeyon's gentle ribbing and Hirut's quiet surprise every time Makeda cracked a joke with her sharp, dry humor.

"Makeda is... special. She is under my aegis, McTierney, so tread carefully. She has powerful friends. Added to the obvious fact that she's extremely bright. Makeda is the one who initially came up with the idea to treat the Elixir by treating bone marrow, so you understand why she's feeling protective of the trial."

"I already have four human volunteers and two vampires," McTierney said. "They're ready and waiting as soon as you and Dr. Abel finalize the protocol. Any word yet?"

The biggest holdup was on his end, and Lucien grimaced when he thought about what he had yet to do. He'd been cagey with McTierney so far, and that didn't engender confidence from the other man, who would be effectively turning over his own patients to Lucien and Makeda's experimental treatment.

"As soon as I have a donor identified for the immortal patients, I'll let you know. The humans—"

"Are already starting on a course of chemotherapy. Radiation will follow that. Stem cell donors have been identified for all four. Are you sure you want to proceed with the HSCT?"

"You've explained the risks?"

"Yes."

"Then I say that's our best option. Time is against us on this." Hematopoietic stem cell transplantation was risky, but it was also the best option for rebuilding the humans' immune systems from the inside out. "Especially if we're catching patients in the early stages of Elixir infection when they're still in their first bloom of health. Dr. Abel pointed out that the initial upswing could carry them through the worst of the chemo and radiation, allowing their systems to bounce back stronger with the new stem cells."

"I agree." McTierney paused. "Ioan would have loved this. Seeing you collaborating with a partner."

The corner of Lucien's mouth turned up. "He would have loved taking the piss out of me." Ioan had often teased Lucien about finding a nice immortal instead of his serial monogamy with humans.

"It's not that," McTierney said. "Working with Julia has been one of the singular privileges of my personal and professional life, Lucien." Julia was McTierney's wife and partner in their medical practice. "There's something special about sharing a professional passion with the person you love."

"Calm down, Brenden," Lucien said. "We're colleagues."

"Of course you are." The doctor smiled. "Let me know when we're ready to go. We need that immortal donor, Lucien. None of these patients has a living sire. If they did, they wouldn't be with me."

"I'll do my best."

He used a pencil to push the End button on the laptop. Makeda had been regaling Gedeyon with tales of the Nocht system she'd beta tested, and his brother was almost falling over in excitement. Gedeyon loved gadgets and new technology, but he was stuck with the human variety until he could order equipment from Ireland.

Hirut tapped on the door. "Lucien, are you finished?"

"I am." He pushed away from the desk. "Did your assistant need to get in here?"

Hirut's human was a young woman who looked to be university age. She was the one who maintained the satellite link and computer equipment in Gedeyon's small office.

"She's fine, but I was wondering if you wanted to take Makeda's blood to her."

"I will." He glanced at the clock. He'd not realized how close it was to dawn.

Most of Makeda's nights were taken up with training now that there was little they could add to the trials until they were truly under way.

Just the donor. He still had to approach his mother. And yes, he was putting it off for as long as possible. Though they would need to test her blood for compatibility, Makeda theorized that Saba was the vampire equivalent to mitochondrial Eve for humans. It was likely most, if not all, vampires could accept her blood and stem cells.

But would she be willing?

Saba had stopped siring children soon after Lucien had turned. She had hundreds, if not thousands, of vampires in her extended clan, but for direct descendants, there were few still living. How would she feel about possibly siring more?

Because though they wouldn't take her bite, any immortal treated with Saba's stem cells would effectively become her child. On that, Lucien and Makeda both agreed. Whatever line they came from would be broken. Whatever element they controlled would be dead to them. They would be born anew into Saba's blood, and he wasn't sure if his mother would be willing, not to mention the victims.

If she wasn't, then any hope for vampire Elixir patients without living sires was dead.

❖

He wandered around the island, searching for Makeda. Tana

Genet was tiny, and he knew she must be going stir-crazy, but he was trying to keep her safe for as long as possible. He wasn't sure what Saba was plotting, but Lucien guessed she'd pull him into it some way or another.

"Makeda?" He turned when he scented her. She was on the water, perched on the smooth stone where she and Kato often practiced, looking at the horizon, which had begun to lighten. He stripped off his shirt before he dove into the water and pushed through the murky shallows until he reached her. Lucien surfaced and climbed onto the rock. "Makeda, you need to get inside."

She said nothing, and her face was wrecked with sorrow. Bone-twisting grief was painted on her face.

"Makeda?" A needle of fear worked itself into his heart. "What are you doing?"

"The trial protocol is in place," she murmured.

"So?"

"You know who the donor is," Makeda said. "You just have to talk to her, Lucien."

Her voice was cold. Dead.

"Makeda, you need to get inside now."

Her hair curled around her in wild abandon. She'd been sitting on the rock long enough that it was nearly dry. She didn't look at him. Didn't look at the glassy stillness of the lake or the birds flying over the water or the fishermen in the distance, rowing their reed boats out to the middle of the lake.

She was staring at the horizon, watching the sky grow lighter.

"Makeda, get inside," he whispered.

"Just a little longer."

Lucien was afraid to touch her. "Makeda, please."

She finally looked at him, and her eyes made his heart scream. Her anger sliced through the last of his armor. Her eyes convicted him.

"You don't need me anymore," she said carefully. "There is nothing I can offer this study that you cannot do yourself."

Understanding threatened like the dawn. "Please don't do this."

"There is nothing more you need from me, Lucien."

"Makeda—"

"I have served the purpose for which you turned me."

He tried to keep his heart steady, but he couldn't. "You know that's not why I did it."

"Then why?" she screamed, leaping to her feet. "*Tell me why!* Why will I never see the sun again? Why will I never have a child? Why will my sisters die before me? My nieces. My nephews. Why will I watch everyone I love leave me behind? I had a life, Lucien! I had a family. I may have been an amusement to you, but *I had a life*. And you took it away. Took my life. My choice to die. You took everything when I was nothing more than a mind you needed!"

"That's not true!" He rose to his feet. "Makeda, please come inside. Let's talk about this."

"You don't need me anymore."

"You know that's not true." He clenched his hands into fists to keep from grabbing her.

She was right. He'd taken the choice from her at the beginning of this. He could not take it from her again.

"Makeda..." He lost the fight against his instincts and reached for her, wrapping her in his arms. "I'm sorry."

The cry wrenched from her throat undid him.

"I'm sorry," he said it again. "I'm sorry, Makeda. I'm so sorry." He clenched her tighter when her shoulders slumped. "I couldn't see you die. I couldn't." *Don't make me watch you die.* He could feel the dawn coming, but she wasn't falling asleep. Damn stubborn woman. "Makeda, please come inside."

She didn't say anything. Her sobs were grieving, angry cries that tore at him, shredding his control. He gripped her tighter and stepped toward the edge of the rock.

"Please," he whispered again. "Don't do this to me, *yene konjo*. I don't want to face the night without you."

She didn't say yes, but she didn't say no. Her body collapsed into his, and Lucien took it as permission, gripping her tightly as he dove into the water and headed toward the shore. When he reached it, he picked her up and walked straight to the shelter of the tukul, slamming the door just as the sun rose over the mountains in the distance.

He set Makeda on the edge of the bed and reached for the pitcher of blood. She was limp in his arms, like a child fighting to stay awake. A child who had cried too much and worn herself out.

"Open," he said. "Drink it all."

For a moment, he thought she wouldn't comply. Then she opened her mouth and Lucien practically poured the blood down her throat. A thread of it dripped from the corner of her mouth, and he leaned over, licking it up before he placed a gentle kiss at the corner of her mouth.

When the blood was gone, her expression hadn't changed. If anything, her eyes were even more remote. They glassed over, unable to focus as exhaustion took her. Before she fell asleep, he helped her out of her clothes and pulled one of his own shirts over her head, wrapping her in his scent. Then he covered her with a sheet and crouched back on his heels, staring at her as she closed her eyes.

Her body relaxed completely.

Her breath stopped.

And soon there was nothing but the quiet hum of her amnis and the scent of the woman who had somehow come to mean more to him than his own life. The realization hit him like a hammer between his eyes. He sat on the ground and put his head between his knees.

It had been coming for weeks. Months even. Perhaps it had been as inevitable as their first argument.

Lucien stared at Makeda, whose body had gone limp with the sleep of the newly blooded.

He would have stayed with her.

He would have held her as the dawn broke and they both burned.

Damn the world. He would have stayed.

She didn't wake with a snarl or a start the next evening. Lucien was ready for her anger. Ready to face her claws. But Makeda didn't bare them when she woke. She opened her eyes to the thatch ceiling above them, not even looking at Lucien where he lay beside her. He heard her inhale and knew she smelled the blood in the pitcher next to the bed. But she didn't move.

Lucien didn't move either. His realization the night before had changed everything, and he held his feelings carefully. He felt almost as fragile as she looked.

She said, "I was in a bad place last night."

Her hand lay limp at her side and Lucien took it, tracing the fine veins that rose like rivers beneath her skin. He didn't know what she wanted or needed from him, so he just listened.

"I got off the phone with Dr. McTierney and looked around the lab." She swallowed. "I realized there was nothing more for me to do, so I walked around the island. Then I walked again. And again. And again. And... I started to realize that this is what my life is now. Every night. Waking in darkness. Going in circles. Years passing. Decades. And eventually, I would be completely alone."

"Never," Lucien whispered. "You'll never be—"

"My family will die. My mother and father I expected, of course. Every child faces that. But my sisters. Their husbands." She paused. "Then their children. Even their grandchildren. They will *all* die. And I will be left alone."

Lucien didn't remember his human family. He was the second son of his father and not the heir to any land. Lucien hadn't been expected to have a wife or children. He'd been expected to be a warrior. When he'd died and been reborn, he'd left nothing behind.

"Did you truly want children?" he asked softly.

"Yes." She paused. "I don't know. Maybe not. But the possibility was still there."

"You can still be a mother, Makeda. Look at Saba."

"It's not the same."

"No, I suppose not." He laid his head down next to hers, rubbing his cheeks on her curls. "I love your hair. Have I told you that? Do I pull it at night?"

"No. You're easy to sleep with. You never bother me."

Then clearly I'm doing something wrong.

Lucien didn't say that.

"This is my fault," he said. "You're too isolated here. Your geography is limited. Your circle of companions is limited. I should have recognized that and—"

"It's not your fault."

"Don't try to absolve me," he said. "It is my fault. I've been so focused on work I haven't been taking care of you."

"Kato is—"

"You are not Kato's responsibility."

She finally turned to look at him. "I don't want to be your responsibility either, Lucien. I don't want to be an obligation."

"Makeda..." He breathed in her scent, the subtle play of pheromones mixed with her skin and hair. The orange oil in her soap and the cinnamon in her toothpaste. Aromas he'd now associate with her for eternity. "Don't you know you are far more than an obligation to me?"

"Am I?" Her eyes and voice dared him. "Or am I a challenge? A vampire to seduce for variety? To prove you can? Because you have a type, Lucien, and I am not it. I stopped being anything close to it when my heart stopped beating. So why me? What makes me so special?"

He smiled. "Everything."

"Nothing. You didn't order Baojia to change me because of some great passion. You aren't madly in love with me, and you never were. So what about me is special? Nothing. And once we leave this place, I won't be in your face every night, you'll grow tired of the challenge, and you'll move on to something else."

He propped up his head and looked at her. "You're not going to believe anything I say, are you?"

"Why should I?"

"Because I'm not a liar, and I never have been. I told you I needed you."

"Because I'd made a breakthrough."

ELIZABETH HUNTER

He cocked his head to the side. "Is that what I meant?"

Makeda frowned. "You said I might be the only chance of curing this disease."

"And I was right. You were the one who found the solution."

She said nothing, clearly trying to reconcile his words and his coldness the night she'd been changed.

He leaned over and brushed his lips against hers. "Let me remind you what I said next. 'Did you think I was going to let you just die?' Did you, Makeda?"

The memory of his terror the night she'd lain twisted on the cliffs collided with his fear from the previous dawn. "When I tell you I ordered Baojia to change you because you matter—because you're unique—you should believe me."

Her eyes were a riot of confusion. "Self-delusion doesn't count as honesty."

So stubborn. He smiled. "Skeptic."

"Yes."

"I do think I'll enjoy proving you wrong, Dr. Abel."

"I'm sure you'll enjoy trying, Dr. Thrax."

He leaned down and captured her mouth with a grin still on his face, delighted by her skepticism. He didn't try to make his kiss fleeting or easy as he had before. Lucien took her mouth boldly, biting her lips until she let him in. His tongue delved into the heat of her mouth and he fantasized about tasting other lips, imagined her shaking and weak beneath him when he brought her to orgasm. He wanted to make her crazy with lust, then watch as she abandoned the control she wrapped like armor around her.

He would seduce her body as she'd seduced his mind. He'd teach her the pleasures of an immortal lover. Teach her how he filled long nights when he had leisure. He'd tease her body for hours, prolonging her release until she was begging for his bite.

And Makeda would bite him.

His body grew impossibly aroused at the memory of her teeth in his neck. It had been far more intoxicating than he'd imagined. The pull of her lips against his skin and her tongue licking his blood. He'd felt her bite with a thousand nerves brought suddenly and violently to life.

"Not tonight," she whispered. "Lucien, I can't..."

Her emotions were too volatile. Her control was still on the edge.

"Not tonight," he said. "Just kiss me, Makeda. Don't think of anything else. Just kiss me."

"Yes."

Lucien rolled over Makeda and braced his body over hers, letting her feel the weight and the strength of his arousal. She shoved slender fingers in his hair and gripped hard, forcing a groan from his throat. Her knees lifted and pressed against his hips as her pelvis arched up. Her heat seared him, but he still felt her, slightly removed, an observer to her own passion.

He would make her mindless if it was the last thing he did.

Lucien gloried in the challenge, but it wasn't just the challenge. He reached up and cupped her cheek, brushing his thumb across the dark gold ochre of her skin. His heart swelled that she was there, lying under his body, vibrant with amnis and humming with life.

She was alive.

Forever alive.

And she would be his.

Chapter Fourteen

They swam the next night, across the lake and down a river thick with silt, the red-brown water opaque even to vampire eyes. But Makeda no longer needed her eyes. She felt everything as she swam. The herds of hippopotamuses and lazy slither of crocodiles. The quick darting fish and swooping birds that skimmed the lake.

And as she swam, Lucien's presence was behind her. He clasped her ankle with a gentle hand, letting her lead them toward the falls he'd described but taking the lead when they needed to exit the river to avoid human construction or traffic. They moved so quickly the scents of humans didn't even register over the living smells of the Nile. They passed the lights of the city and moved deeper into the countryside. The moon rose and the stars grew brilliant in the sky.

Makeda stopped and floated in the river, turning her back to it as she gazed into the blackness.

"I always thought they were white," she said.

"They are." Lucien linked his fingers with hers as they floated downstream. "And they're not. They're every color."

She glanced at him. "Do you remember what things looked like as a human?"

"Not really. I used to hold on to memories of daylight so tightly. I had one of my mother walking across the courtyard. I don't remember if she was beautiful, but she was very tall and had dark red hair. When color photographs and motion pictures came, I think I lost those memories. I remember having them, but I can't really *see* them anymore."

"Because you had something more immediate to take their place."

"Yes." He rolled over and floated on his belly. "There are no humans around here. Not for miles. You can relax."

"And at the falls?"

"I doubt it."

A tension she didn't realize she'd been holding on to eased. "I'm terrified I'll kill someone."

"It's almost certain you will at some point," Lucien said. "Killing is unavoidable in our world."

Makeda sat up in the water, floating with no effort. "Then why do we exist? How does your conscience allow you to—"

"I save more than I kill," he said. "Is a cost-and-benefit analysis allowed?"

"I don't know. Is it?"

"We're predators, Makeda. You'll discover that the more you grow into your new life. The more you understand your abilities and limitations. We're predators," he said. "Like all the powerful."

She turned in circles and scanned the darkness that was no longer so dark. What would have appeared black to her human eyes was now a layered landscape of grey. "You're saying humans are predators too."

"The most powerful are rather blatant about it." He shrugged. "At least we're predators for a reason other than our own power."

"Fine. But the question remains, why do we exist?"

"Why does the lion?"

"To maintain balance in an ecosystem, apex predators must always exist," Makeda answered. "But lions don't eat other lions."

"But they do maintain balance," he said. "We don't have to kill to eat, and most of us don't. The truth about our existence would have been discovered long ago if we did. Now we're myths and legends. Predators who can walk side by side with our prey."

"But we are monsters."

"If something has the ability to think and to reason, it has the ability to be monstrous," Lucien said. "Why aren't all human beings benevolent? Why do even the best of them sometimes do things they abhor?"

Makeda frowned. "No one is perfect. That's human nature."

"Of course it is," Lucien said. "And humans—like us—can be monstrous. That some of our kind choose *not* to be—even with our greater strength—is the reason we exist. I believe we do what the lion does. We maintain balance."

"We keep the human monsters in check?" Makeda asked. "And who keeps us in check?"

Lucien grinned. "The sun, of course. And that, *yene konjo*, is a lesson in humility. We may have the ability to prey upon humans, but we need them to survive. And the very thing that gives them life will kill us faster than anything else."

"Even Saba?"

"Even Saba. She can cloak herself and survive longer than most, but even she can burn."

Makeda heard it then, a growing roar in the distance. "The falls."

He grinned like a boy. "Do you want to ride them?"

Her heart began to thump. "Can we?"

He turned and patted his shoulders. "Get on my back. I'll make sure you're not hurt. You may just be getting friendly with the Nile, but these falls have known me a long, long time."

She wrapped her arms around his neck, and he turned his face. With a quick kiss, he swam into the growing rapids. Dodging rocks, logs and the remains of fishing boats, Lucien swam them closer to the edge. She could hear the falls. Sense the excitement of the water and the dropping away of the—

"*Oh my God!*" she cried as the edge appeared suddenly before them. "Lucien?"

"Hold on!" He laughed. "Don't you trust me?"

She squeezed his neck so tightly she would have crushed his larynx if he'd been human. Then the water enveloped them, the current sucked them down, and the river threw them over the edge and into nothing.

❖

Makeda lounged on the bank, her body resting in the shallow

water as the mist billowed around her. It kissed her skin and clung to her hair. She had never felt more powerful. Lucien walked naked into the water. The current had ripped both their clothes off when they went over.

He'd been right though. She didn't have a scratch on her. When they'd landed, they plunged into a massive pool that appeared below them, the falls sucking them down, then shooting them up and toward the edge of the gorge. Whether that current had been subtly directed by the earth vampire standing before her, she didn't know.

"It used to be bigger," he shouted.

"Really?" Makeda eyed his naked form, which was very *very* nice. "It seems pretty big already."

He put his hands on his hips and turned to her. "Before they built the dam—"

"Oh, you were talking about the waterfall?" She nodded. "That makes more sense."

Lucien paused for a moment, his mouth agape, before he threw his head back and laughed. "Who are you?" he asked between breaths. "And what have you done with serious Dr. Abel?"

She lay back in the river, the air around her filled with living water. "I feel amazing here. More alive than I have since I woke that night."

Lucien moved slowly, prowling toward her. Makeda had never seen him look more predatory.

She'd never felt more like prey.

Lucien crawled over her, caging her body with arms and legs coated in copper-red water. His hair was dripping, and his eyes were narrowed on her lips. "I've always thought," he said, his voice rough, "that the most beautiful places in the world are where earth and water mate."

"You mean meet?"

"I mean mate." He lowered himself and kissed her. Makeda felt the pulse of his amnis over her whole body. She was lying on the edge of the water, lush grass at her back, covered in mist and Lucien. He explored her mouth with leisure, his body a broad wall of muscle over hers. She felt surrounded, the earth at her back, the water filling the air.

And Lucien.

He tasted of salt and earth. Makeda could scent his blood and her own arousal. She could feel his heart beat against her breast. His hands tangled in her hair, and his body was warm and solid. Enticing. And she was so hungry.

Her body was alive with need. He explored her face with his lips. They were both drenched, and when she opened her eyes, rivulets ran from the corners. She didn't know if they were her tears or the river's. It didn't matter. The river was her. She was the water. The sky. The mist. She felt it then, the universality of her element, infusing the air, the earth, and the space between her body and Lucien's.

Desire engulfed her. She arched her back and let out a low moan. Her skin felt too tight. It couldn't contain what she felt when his mouth was fused to hers. Her body was at once familiar and foreign. She'd become a creature of need.

"Say yes," he said when he released her mouth. "Say yes, Makeda. This thing between us isn't a challenge for me or a weakness for you. Don't you feel it?" He linked their hands together and pressed Makeda into the earth. She gasped and arched under him. "Don't you *feel* it, Makeda?"

She'd been overwhelmed by her own senses. She couldn't think. She felt too much. Too much!

Makeda opened her eyes and saw the wheel of the Milky Way through clear eyes, the ordered constellations distracting her as the crashing water urged her to lose control.

Let go.

The earth was beneath her. It hummed under her skin. She felt it. *How did she feel it?* Living. Breathing.

This is eternal life.

"Yes." She wanted Lucien. Wanted everything. She hungered not for blood but for the endless night and satisfaction of an entirely different appetite.

Lucien took her mouth, an edge of desperation coloring his movements. He parted her thighs and rocked between them. He bent and tasted the wet skin of her breast, running his tongue over the slick flesh before he traced a path back to her neck, sucking so hard she arched up again.

"Come in me." Her trembling hand found his shoulder.

"Not yet."

He was relentless. His teeth scraped over her breast again, and she cried out. His fangs teased her, the edge of pain bringing her hunger to aching focus. His fangs disappeared and his lips were warm. His body was hot, his skin a fever making the mist rise from his bare shoulders. Her thighs gripped his hips, her pelvis arching up as he twisted his body and tormented her.

"Lucien, please."

His mouth left her breast and his smile was evil. "Not yet."

Infuriating man!

The relentless lips drove her to madness. He teased her neck again, licking out over her pulse and pressing his chest against her breasts. He sucked hard at the tender skin of her neck, and Makeda let out a small scream of fury and hunger. Her fangs, already long and throbbing, sank into Lucien's shoulder and he roared, driving into her with one hard thrust.

Yes!

Makeda's head fell back and she released a harsh breath. She felt him, hot and full within her, the relief and the madness sweeping any rational thought away. She couldn't think. She only knew his driving possession fed the relentless hunger that had stalked her since the night they met.

"Again." He released one hand and pressed her face to his neck. "Here, Makeda. Bite."

She bit and sucked his blood, the hot surge of his life filling her mouth as he filled her body. He groaned and kept his hand on the back of her head as she fed from him. He tasted of salt and red earth spiced with the scent of cedar and coffee. Lucien filled her senses until she was mindless and surrounded. As she drank, his amnis enveloped her, entering her blood until she was intoxicated.

Makeda licked her lips, her head swimming. "Too much."

"No," he grunted. "Take more."

"Lucien." Her back ground into the earth as he thrust. "Too much."

He lowered the hand holding her mouth to his neck and pressed his forehead to hers. His eyes were closed and his face was incandescent.

"I can feel you," he said. "I can feel *myself* in you. My cock. My blood." He cursed in some ancient language. "*Yene hiwot.*"

He sounded desperate. She threw her arms around his shoulders, replete with his power, and wrapped her legs around his hips. The new angle drove her closer to the release that had been building since she'd driven her fangs into his skin.

Lucien flung her over the falls again, and she cried out when she came, dragging him with her into the rush of madness and release.

❖

They lay in the grass sloping up from the falls, the stars wheeling overhead as the moon sank under the horizon and night birds sang. Lucien played with her curls, spreading them out on the lush grass as they dried. His eyes were intent on his task, fascinated by her. Makeda glanced at the rough bite on his neck, which was almost healed. It was still an angry red but closing before her eyes.

"You didn't bite me," she said.

He paused, his hand hovering over her hair. "Did you want me to?"

"I suppose... I just assumed—"

"A bite is never assumed, Makeda. It's a very intimate act. More intimate than sex. I would never bite you without asking."

Her mouth dropped when she remembered her first violent night as an immortal. "You mean the night I woke when I bit you—"

Lucien stopped her mouth with his, crushing the apology from her lips.

"I wanted it," he said when he came up for breath. "Even if I couldn't admit it then. The tie between us... I wanted your bite, Makeda. If I hadn't, I would have stopped you. I wouldn't have even let you close to my neck."

She couldn't ignore it. "I violated a boundary even if I didn't know it, and I am so sorry."

"You didn't know. And I'm the one who is sorry. I didn't know what to say to you that night. You were so angry—with good reason—and I was thrilled and guilty at the same time. Ecstatic that you were alive and guilty that you'd been changed without your consent."

"You were so cold."

"No, I wasn't." He played with her curls again. "Trust me. If you'd had a civilized turning, Baojia and I would have talked to you before it. You would have had time, like Natalie, to come to terms with the transition. Understood what exchanging blood can mean."

"What can it mean?" She propped herself on her elbows. "I bit you tonight, Lucien. You told me to—"

"I told you to"—he looked away—"because I've never experienced that pleasure before. And I wanted it with you."

"Never?"

"No."

Makeda blinked. Lucien was over two thousand years old. She had a hard time imagining there was any type of sexual pleasure he hadn't explored with that many nights lived. He'd demonstrated more than a few mastered skills in the previous few hours.

"Didn't you *ever* have vampire lovers?"

"Not many. And never the kind who..." He ran his hands through his damp hair. "Do we have to talk about this?"

"We just did things that are probably illegal in this country, and you're reluctant to talk about your past biting history?"

He fell back on the grass with a rueful laugh. She crossed her arms and laid her head on his chest.

"Makeda..." He twisted a lock of hair around his finger. "Biting can be extremely pleasurable. During sex it's *otherworldly*. But exchanging blood, taking my blood while I take yours, is also a tie. A very long-lasting one."

"And you don't want that tie with me?" It stung. Even though it was too soon. Even though they'd never talked of commitment. It stung.

He scowled. "Did I say that? Exchanging blood like that is equivalent of marriage for our kind. *Mating*."

"Wait. *That's* what vampires mean by mating? It's an actual blood tie?"

"Yes."

Oh. Well, she couldn't argue with caution then, even if her own emotions were riotous. She was grateful he hadn't taken advantage of her ignorance.

"But Baojia calls Natalie his mate."

"Because for him she is, even if they haven't exchanged blood. Once she becomes vampire, she'll take his blood and he'll take hers. It will tie them on an elemental level. Their amnis will join and..."

"I felt your amnis in me," she said. "When I took your blood."

"I offered it to you. I wanted you to take it. There's no obligation, Makeda."

She paused, her chest feeling tight and full. "Do you want my blood?"

His eyes told her without words. They flared with heat, and she saw his fangs lengthen behind his lips.

She let out a slow breath. "How do you know? We've only known each other—"

"We've known each other for months. Worked together for months. And been through a very soul-stripping experience. I have been alive more than two thousand years," he said. "You are my match, Makeda. I am certain of it."

So am I. Makeda couldn't say the words even as her heart screamed them. She wasn't a sentimental creature and she never had been. She had to examine this urge to cling to Lucien. Was it healthy? Codependence? Grasping the familiar in an unfamiliar world? Until she had more time, more confidence, and more familiarity with this life, she could never admit how much she wanted Lucien to belong to her.

He tugged her down to his mouth by the curl twisted around his finger. "You'll know when you know," he said. "We have plenty of time. Until then, feel free to take as much of my blood as you like."

"Are you sure?"

"Yes." He nipped at her full lips. "I love how it feels. Plus it will make you stronger. My amnis is very old."

She crawled over him, throwing a leg over his thighs. He was roused and ready; so was Makeda.

"Only if you're sure," she said, closing her eyes when he palmed her breasts and stroked.

His hands slid down her sides, gripped her hips, and lifted her onto his erection. "Very, *very* sure."

Chapter Fifteen

Lucien slept that day in the bosom of the earth, Makeda curled against his chest, his blood humming in her body. He could hear the crash of the falls overhead and the everyday sounds of humans as they went about their business. Goats and sheep trod over them, birds hopped, and children laughed and ran. And they rested, cradled by the red earth and the roots and rocks that sheltered them.

Makeda wasn't a fastidious lover, for which Lucien was extremely grateful. He enjoyed getting dirty with a partner. Enjoyed cleaning up just as much. And with Makeda...

It was unlike anything else. She existed with him now, a part of his soul residing outside his body. He was heady with possession and knew Kato and Gedeyon would have to be careful for a few days. Until Lucien felt more balanced, any immortal his instincts told him could be competition would be in danger.

If Makeda were ready to offer her blood, it would be a moot point. But currently he resided in her blood. She didn't reside in his. Her trust humbled him. She'd fallen asleep in his arms knowing that he hungered for her. He would never take her blood without her consent.

Not like you took her life.

Lucien's conscience ate at him, but he pushed the quiet voice back. Makeda was happy. She'd laughed the night before. Smiled when they made love. She would be content when she was his. He would make sure of it. She'd never stare at the horizon again, searching for oblivion in the sunrise.

She would be his.

The other piece of his soul stirred and turned toward him, burying her face in his neck as she nuzzled closer.

Yene konjo. Yene hiwot.

My beauty. My life.

She was beauty to him. She had a bump on her nose, a scar on her chin, and slightly knobby knees. Her ears were uneven on her head, and nothing could be more beautiful. He'd noticed it the night before, and the imperfection had delighted him. As did the distant look she got when she was thinking over a problem. She'd stare into the distance and focus inward. Her internal musings would hold the entirety of her attention, and Lucien would be forgotten. But when Makeda came back to herself, her eyes lit with the joy of a traveler returning home. It was as if she'd found the greatest adventure in her mind.

"Kiss me with the kisses of your mouth," he whispered as she stirred in his arms. "For your love is more delightful than wine."

Her eyes remained closed. "My beloved is like a gazelle or a young stag," she whispered. "But really he's more like a lion."

Lucien smiled. "You know Song of Solomon."

"My father is a theological scholar. I read the Bible backward and forward whether I wanted to or not." Her eyes opened with a glint. "But as a young girl, I may have found Song of Solomon the most tempting."

"Makeda," he breathed her name across her cheek. "My queen."

"Is the sun down?"

He nodded.

"So we need to go back."

"Only if you want to. We could stay here another night if you wish."

"We shouldn't." She scraped a hand over her eyes and smiled. "We're filthy."

He glanced around the hollow he'd created in the earth. It was cozy to him, but he suspected it wasn't to everyone's taste. "It's good clean dirt."

Makeda laughed and poked at the earthen ceiling. "We'd better go. I should train with Kato tonight, and you need to talk with Saba about donating stem cells."

He groaned and hid his face in her hair.

"Just get it over with," Makeda said. "Your dreading it is probably worse than the actual conversation."

"I don't think she's going to like this."

"How do you know?" She looked up. "She's scheming something right now. I'm certain of it."

"What makes you say that?"

"It's the look on her face. My mother gets the same look. Like... frustration and resolution all at once. When I was a child, my mother got that look right before she turned the car around and took us all home for being brats."

"Well, she is a mother. She considers herself a mother to all vampires, in fact. No doubt she's plenty annoyed with us right..." The realization hit him so hard he stopped breathing. Stopped talking.

Oh. Saba was planning something all right.

"Shit," he muttered. "We need to go."

"Oh?" Makeda rolled to the side and Lucien lifted his arms, spreading the ground above them as if opening a curtain. "What's so —"

"She's ready to turn the car around," Lucien said. "You're right. She's fed up with the lot of us, and she's deciding what she's going to do."

Makeda climbed out of the hole and shook out her hair. "So what's the emergency?"

"Have you ever heard of the Axumite Dynasty?"

"It ruled Northern Ethiopia from the first to the ninth century," Makeda said. "Of course I know it."

"An Axumite emperor took one of Saba's daughters for a lover. Then that emperor abused her trust and locked her in a sunny room as she rested."

Makeda gasped. "What did Saba do?"

"She killed him, laid waste to the countryside, and ended a nine-hundred-year dynasty," Lucien said, remembering the blackened churches and bloody stones as he climbed out of the earth and grabbed Makeda's hand. "She didn't hold back, Makeda. No one with any relation to the power structure survived. Women. Children. She wiped them from the face of the earth. Thousands of innocents were caught in the backlash of her rage." He headed back up the hill and toward the river that would lead them to Lake Tana.

"But why would Saba—"

Lucien stopped and spun around, putting his hands on her shoulders. "I love my mother, Makeda. But she's not... good. Or bad. Not in any way that modern people understand. When I say Saba is debating what to do about the future of the vampire world, it is very much an emergency."

They were only a few kilometers from the island when Makeda stopped, forcing Lucien to halt alongside her. He surfaced and wiped the water from his eyes. "What's wrong?"

"You need to calm down," she said. "If I can feel your nerves, she'll be able to as well."

"Saba is probably planning wide-scale destruction as a way of wiping out the Elixir problem and rebuilding immortal society. That's what all the travel was about. That's why Kato is here. She doesn't see history in centuries, but millennia. Do you realize how many people that would affect? Some people think she's a benevolent earth mother, but those people also forget the earth can be an uncontrollable bitch when it's roused."

"I know that, but you approaching her when you're angry won't help her to calm down. If you want her to calm down, you need to be calm too. Think. Don't just react. Plan. Are you certain she wants to rebuild immortal society? You told me she didn't like politics."

"That's why she goes the 'razing empires and laying waste' route."

"So give her another option," Makeda said. "Lucien, *we have the cure*. Don't you think she'd rather donate a few stem cells rather than destroy entire societies and geographical areas?"

He paused and really thought about it... and he honestly didn't know what Saba would prefer.

But he did know what Kato would prefer. And Ziri. They were moderates.

Arosh would vote for wholesale destruction.

"We're asking her to donate stem cells that would change her family structure in massive ways," Lucien said. "We're asking her to basically adopt any infected vampire whose sire is no longer living. She'd be responsible for them. Stuck with them even if she didn't like them. She stopped siring vampires long ago, Makeda, and she had her reasons."

"So give her new reasons," Makeda said. "Figure out how all these new children can help her or benefit her or... something."

"Like how?"

She threw her head back in frustration. "I don't know! You know this world far better than me. You'll think of something. Just figure out a way that everyone becomes a winner—the infected, Saba, the world as a whole—and present that option to her. At least it may make her think twice about the wholesale destruction."

He felt a smile threatening. "Just reason with my sire, stop world destruction, and make everyone a winner? Is that all you want?"

"Yep." She smiled and pressed a quick kiss to his mouth. "That should do it."

"Great." He started swimming toward the island again. "I'll get started on vampire sunscreen right after that."

"I knew you were brilliant."

It scraped against every instinct in him, but Lucien left Makeda to train with Kato while he went to look for his mother. An hour of thinking aloud with Makeda was all he'd needed to formulate a plan that would cure their patients, prevent wholesale destruction—probably—and it might just straighten out the mess the immortal world was facing. In fact, it was Saba's own bloody past that had been the key.

Saba was leaning on a rock near the coffee brazier, chatting with Hirut and chewing on a *mefaka* as the coffee roasted. She eyed Lucien as he sat down and stretched out his legs.

"Good. You got that out of your system," she said. "Hopefully the girl will have more control now."

"*Salem*, Hirut. Hello, Saba. And how are both of you this evening?"

Hirut laughed as Saba patted his cheek. "So shy, my son. Is your woman well?"

"She's training with Kato right now." He grabbed one of the chewing sticks from the small sack Saba carried at her waist and bit down. The *mefaka* was as effective as a toothbrush, and Lucien preferred them when he could get them. "You visited Arosh when you were traveling, did you not?"

"I did."

"And Ziri?"

She glanced at him, then at Hirut. "Why do you ask?"

"What are you planning, *Emaye*?"

Saba leaned back against the rock and looked up at the stars. "Do you have a cure for Geber's poison yet?"

"Yes."

Saba and Hirut both stared at him.

"Truly?" Hirut asked. "Lucien, that is wonderful!"

"How long?" Saba demanded.

"It hasn't been tested. Makeda and I have to finalize the trial protocol with the doctors in Ireland. That's where we're going to run the tests. But we think it will work. She's nearly certain of it, and so am I." He met his mother's eyes. "It's not a cure, Saba, it's a treatment. And the immortal patients will need stem cell donors."

"Offspring? Siblings? Mates?"

"No. So far, there's only one sample we've tested that has the immunity needed to battle the virus."

Lucien knew the second it registered. "Me?" Saba's lip curled slightly. "What do you want *me* to do?"

"We want to try both peripheral stem cell donation and bone

marrow and see if one is more effective than another. The peripheral stem cells can be collected from your blood, the others can be collected with a needle into your pelvis. It'll be more painful, but you'll hardly feel it. I can do the procedure right here on the island."

"And that's all?" She narrowed her eyes. "That's not all. You're changing their blood, aren't you? Making their blood mimic mine."

Hirut sucked in a breath.

"Yes," Lucien said. "After the transplant, their amnis will align with yours. They'll be earth vampires, and they'll have a sire bond with you."

Saba started muttering under her breath. "I don't want more children."

"It's the only way to treat this. Once this cure is known—"

"You know why I want no more," she scoffed. "Why do you bother asking this of me?"

Lucien paused. He needed to speak carefully. "*Emaye*, I know after Desta's death—"

"You know nothing!" Saba screamed. "*Nothing*. You have no child. You want none." Fat tears rolled down Saba's cheeks. She didn't wipe them away because she had no shame in her grief. The world had bled for it, and Lucien knew it hung on the brink of bleeding again.

Even after a thousand years, the pain of his sister's loss was a raw wound. Many of Lucien's siblings had found peace and walked into the dawn. Many had been lost in battle. Some had given in to despair. Each loss was a wound on his mother's soul.

But nothing had been like Desta.

"I will have no more children," Saba said. "This world will be *cleansed*, my son. We will start again."

"No." He grabbed her hand. "*Emaye*, listen to me. We can't do this."

"You need not have a part in it," she said. "Arosh, Ziri, and I—"

"So Kato has already objected?" He jumped on the omission as he saw Hirut sneak away. "Kato wants no part in this?"

"He is still recovering," she said, her eyes burning. "And I don't need his support. I have made my allies. Those who have seen this sickness that spreads across oceans. It touched my own blood." Saba put a hand on Lucien's cheek. "What they did to you... I cannot forgive this."

"Then don't forgive it," he said. "But don't destroy it either. I am asking this of you. As your child. Too many will die. Too many will lose faith in our world. And the cost of human lives... Saba, you know there is a better way."

She narrowed her eyes. "What do you want of me? You're not only asking for my blood."

Lucien took a steadying breath.

"I want you and Kato to overthrow the council of Athens."

Lucien couldn't read Kato's expression, and he really wanted to. It was, after all, Kato's own council Lucien wanted overthrown. Kato had started the council to transition his territory into a more "democratic" government when he decided to step down. It was the oldest council in the Mediterranean and Europe. The most venerated and, at one time, the most powerful.

But those days were long gone. Or so they had thought.

Lucien, Makeda, Saba, and Kato had gathered around a cooking fire. Makeda sat at Lucien's side, adding wood to the fire when it was necessary.

"Livia may have been the original producer of the Elixir," Lucien began, "but soon after she was killed, Laskaris—and possibly the other members of the Athenian council—stepped up. I don't know if the Elixir was his ambition or the council's, but Laskaris sees it as a way of dominating the immortal world and regaining Greek power."

"Zara gave him the idea," Saba said.

"But Laskaris ran with it," Kato added. "And from what we have discovered, he shows no signs of stopping."

Lucien eyed his mother and Kato, knowing he didn't have the whole story but not wanting to press too quickly when his mother was only reluctantly listening.

"Zara is no longer an obstacle," Saba told them. "I am assured of this."

Lucien had questions about how Zara had been taken out of the equation, but it wasn't relevant to the present discussion. If Saba said Zara was no longer a problem, she was gone.

"The Elixir triggers this retrovirus," Makeda said. "It's something we all have in our systems, but it's dormant until it encounters Elixir-tainted blood. Saba is probably the only being on the planet who is immune to it."

"It must have been a common virus at one time," Saba said, "but there have been so many. How could I remember?"

Lucien said, "Unless there is someone older than you, you're likely the only one who has the correct antibodies."

"I probably am, but there is no way of knowing," Saba said.

"And it doesn't really matter," Makeda said. "As long as the vampire world *believes* you are the oldest, you are the sole vampire capable of healing them."

Lucien leaned forward. "Saba, if these trials work, you will hold the fate of any infected vampire in the palm of your hand. You will be the only cure for them, and any vampire who comes to you for a cure will owe you their allegiance. Not only by vow—because we both know vows can be broken—but by blood."

Kato spoke, his voice quiet. "Where does the council of Athens come in?"

"It has to fall." He let the silence hang over the campfire, but no one spoke. "Athens is your seat, *Theio*. You have every right to take it back if Laskaris is corrupt."

"I gave up my empire," Kato said. "So did your mother."

Lucien knew he needed to tread carefully. "When my sister was taken from you, Saba, you took the crown from her murderer, though you had not ruled in a thousand years. You wiped out his line, and his corruption ceased to be. Then you ruled for years before you allowed another king to rise to power. You put him in place and stepped back into the shadows."

Saba didn't grow angry. She was silent. Considering.

Kato said, "So what do you propose? Your mother and I oust the existing council and take over?"

"That's exactly what I'm proposing. Not only you but Ziri and Arosh as well. The four most ancient vampires in the West. When you take Athens, you could wipe out production of Elixir. No one will question your right to rule."

"Who is to say another will not start producing it again?" Saba asked.

Makeda said, "Spread the word that any vampire infected must come to you to be healed."

Lucien said, "Your cure would have a twofold result. *If* the trials are successful—"

"And that's still an if," Makeda said.

"—the treatment spares those who come to you and makes them blood-loyal to your aegis," Lucien said. "It also eliminates the effectiveness of Elixir as a poison *and* a political tool."

Kato nodded. "Who would knowingly spread Elixir when it would mean Saba, most ancient of our kind, would become even more powerful? Every infection of Elixir would only push more immortals to you."

Lucien gripped Makeda's hand and prayed his words had swayed his mother. He knew Kato was already on his side, though the giant man was obviously reluctant to step into power again. Lucien knew Kato would do it because it was right. He'd do it to save the world from the destruction Saba was capable of wreaking.

Kato spoke softly. "Just think of it, my queen. You would have an army Zhang could only dream of. His golden horde would be a pale shadow of the army you could amass."

Saba stood and looked at all of them. Lucien felt her gaze resting on Makeda the longest.

"I will take my friend's council and think on this," she said. Then she left them and disappeared into the night.

Chapter Sixteen

"I want you with me," he said.

"I can't. You know I can't, Lucien." She didn't look up from her notebook. She was double-checking notes for Dr. McTierney. If Lucien's plan went into action, the necessity of a successful trial became even more pressing. All they were waiting on at this point was a decision from Saba. "It's too soon for me to leave the island."

"You can." The vampire was persistent. "Your control is far more impressive than other immortals of your age. Far more impressive than my own was. You've had very few slips. We'll be traveling with Kato and Saba—"

"And negotiating alliances that could change the balance of power in the Western world." She finally looked up. "Working with both vampires and humans I'd have no way of avoiding. You don't need to be babysitting me while you're worrying about that."

He propped his chin on his hand and didn't look away. "If I leave you here, what will you do all night?"

Makeda's mouth opened, but nothing came out for a long time. "I'll monitor the trials with Dr. McTierney. You know how controlling I am about this."

"We're going to know in a matter of weeks if they're successful, Makeda. With the way our cells regenerate, we'll know yes or no very quickly."

"You don't know that. And if good news comes through that quickly, I'll... I'll read a book," she said. "Drink some wine. Cook with Hirut. Maybe she can teach me some new recipes. I'll live my life, Lucien. Whatever that's become now."

His eyes bored into her. "I don't like leaving you."

She put down her pencil. "Is it because you'll miss me? Or

because you're afraid I'll hurt myself?"

The look on his face told her it was the second option, even though she was hoping for the first.

"There is nothing I can say that will be enough reassurance to you if you don't trust me." She picked up her pencil.

"If you ended your life, I would feel it," he said quietly. "It would hurt."

She clenched her fingers around the pencil. Makeda was matter-of-fact about her feelings. She had been deeply depressed and isolated on the island. She'd chosen to make the difficult decision to stay alive and try to make sense of this new life even though her work was finished. She tried to think night to night. If she thought even five years down the line, she began to panic.

"You've had my blood now," he continued. "If you did anything to harm yourself, it would rip me in two. And I'm not talking about the physical pain, though that would be substantial."

"Lucien—"

"I need you to be aware of the power you have over me right now, Makeda. I'm being completely honest because you seem to constantly expect me to lie."

"I don't constantly expect you to lie."

"Yes, you do. You question everything I tell you."

"That's not distrust," she bit out. "It's arrogance. I don't trust anyone's reasoning as much as my own."

A slow smile grew on his face. He reached over and twisted a curl around his finger. He was completely obsessed with her hair. It might have bothered her once, but as her hair was in a constant state of tangle because of her water practice, there was nothing much he could do to make it worse. She was considering a very short clip like Saba wore, but the look she imagined on her mother's face was enough to stay her hand.

"If I recall correctly," she said, "you find my arrogance attractive. So chew on that, Dr. Thrax."

"I'd rather chew on you. Come with me."

"You're going to be too busy. Don't you have a world to save?"

"Hang the world!" He tugged her closer and kissed her hard. "You think I care about saving the world more than you?"

"You should. Statistically speaking—"

He took her lips again. This time he didn't let her go. He twisted his stool and curled his legs around her, dragging her between his thighs as he delved into her mouth. He tasted like Lucien. Coffee and black licorice from the candies he liked to nibble on at his desk. She sank into his mouth, let his arms circle her. She filed every touch and taste and smell away for their inevitable separation.

The thought of Lucien leaving the island—possibly for months—hit her hard, but she wasn't his mate. She didn't know what she was, other than the woman he had sex with who bit him. He cared for her —Makeda had no doubt—but she still distrusted her own feelings. Everything in her life had changed. The joy and contentment in his embrace felt like a gift that could be snatched away in a heartbeat. Makeda wanted to depend on it, but she also wanted to be cautious.

Angry kisses turned soft and coaxing. "Hang the world. Come with me," he whispered. "To bed. Right now. Let me convince you, *yene konjo.*"

She shook her head to clear it. "Lucien, I need to finish this."

"You've reviewed it a dozen times." Soft kisses rained over the arch of her cheekbone. "Come with me. I want to show you something new."

One week with Lucien had been the sexual education of a lifetime. Makeda's head swam at his touch. He knew exactly how to tempt her. Her relentless curiosity had proven the perfect match to his insatiable hunger. Just the promise of some new pleasure had her weakening.

That was until Saba strode into the laboratory.

Lucien groaned and buried his face in Makeda's shoulder. "Mother—"

"This procedure you're suggesting. Will it weaken me?"

Lucien didn't let Makeda go, but his head popped up and he turned toward his sire. "What?"

"You know of what I speak. These sick vampires, will siring them weaken me?"

Normally, any offspring a vampire sired would siphon off some of their power. At least temporarily. Not that Saba didn't have a reservoir of power to spare. For her, it would hardly be noticeable. But that wasn't the only consideration.

A sire's power was transferred to their new offspring. Old vampires equaled very powerful newborns. In Saba's case, even siphoning off a tiny part would equal an abnormally powerful new immortal. But marrow treatment wasn't anything like a true sire bond.

"I do not know for certain," Lucien said, "but I don't believe it will weaken you or create powerful new children. You are not truly giving them your blood. You're giving them your bone marrow or stem cells. My gut instinct is that it won't be the same, but we'll have to test it to find out."

Lucien didn't breathe as he waited for her to deliberate. Neither did Makeda.

"I'll do it," Saba said.

"Are you sure?"

"I'm sure." Saba nodded toward Makeda. "She can take the blood from me, or whatever it is you need. Right now you go to Kato. And leave the healer in the laboratory, because we need the soldier if we're going to do this."

"Saba, you could do this in your sleep," Lucien said. "You once ruled a continent."

"I ruled a continent thousands of years ago," she said. "I have no love for this modern world and not enough familiarity with it. You may not like politics, son, but you're well-acquainted with that aspect. You will join Kato and me. You will help us plan and execute this campaign." She looked at Makeda. "And you will come with us. His attention will be divided if you remain here."

Damn bossy vampires. Makeda shook her head. "I'm not ready."

"Child, you do not say no to me," Saba said. "You will travel in my entourage. Recognize it for the honor that it is and be quiet."

Lucien squeezed her hip, and Makeda bit her lip so she didn't talk back. She was thirty-nine and unaccustomed to being spoken to like a child.

Of course, she also recognized that the woman who spoke to her was royalty in the most fundamental sense. She was also a more powerful predator who had offered Makeda protection and position.

She took a deep breath and prepared to send Brenden McTierney a very welcome e-mail. At least it would be welcome on his side.

Makeda Abel wouldn't be monitoring her colleague's every tiny move during the transplant trial.

Instead, she was going to war.

❖

"I told you," Saba said, lying down on the crude examination table. "No anesthetic will work on me."

Makeda shook her head. "There must be something—"

"There's not." She unwrapped the skirt around her waist. "I can handle the pain."

"I don't think you understand just how much pain a posterior iliac crest bone marrow retrieval is going to produce."

Saba said nothing. She stared at Makeda, her dark eyes revealing nothing.

Makeda shrugged. "If you don't want anything to dull the pain, then I guess we'll do it your way." *And I'll try not to pass out in sympathy.*

"I'm more concerned that you won't be capable of following through on this. Do not worry about me. I have endured pain you cannot imagine."

Makeda said nothing more. She went to the corner and started to wash, mentally cataloguing every step she'd need to take in order to make this marrow retrieval work in less than ideal conditions. Lucien had laid out the tray and prepped the storage chest where Makeda would put the retrieved marrow. Transport was already arranged. Saba's marrow and her blood would be in Ireland within two days.

"You don't like me." Saba lay on her side, her hip exposed. "That is fine. In fact, I like that you don't like me. Too many immortals are awed by my power, and that is not good for Lucien."

Makeda paused for a moment, then continued to wash and put on gloves. Was it nearly impossible for Saba to get any kind of infection from a biopsy needle? Yes. That didn't erase years of training.

"Your power is unlike anything I've ever known," Makeda said. "But no. I'm not awed by you or anyone else. I study the human body. We're all the same inside. The most powerful human in the world can be brought to their knees by the tiniest virus."

"An infection conquered Alexander when no king could," Saba said. "You're wise for a human."

"And even vampires, who are stronger, faster, and smarter than humans, can't survive in the sun. Or without blood. Or away from their element. You have weaknesses too."

"You'd survive in the Sahara," Saba said. "You just wouldn't be as powerful. But you'd survive, Makeda." She looked over her shoulder. "We survive. Do you understand?"

Makeda paused, the biopsy needle in her hand. "Are you insisting I come participate in this war because you're worried I'll kill myself?"

"Yes. You're the kind who could reason her way into believing your purpose on earth is finished. A year ago, that would have been none of my business, but now my son loves you."

Saba's calm assertion hit her like a punch to the stomach, but Makeda didn't flinch. "We're still learning each other."

"You will be learning each other for eternity, if you are lucky, for none of us are relics to be studied. We are constantly changing. You are his true mate. Do you think I can't scent his blood in you?"

"We're not mates."

"You will be." Saba turned back to stare at the wall of the examination room. "When you understand what loves means, you will offer him your blood as he has offered his."

"I know what love is."

"Not as he does," Saba said. "Not as I do."

Makeda said nothing, because Saba was likely correct. She didn't often think about Lucien's age. His presence was too immediate to be ancient. If she thought about his age at all, it was to wonder about the things he'd seen, not the emotions he had experienced. She filed it away to think about later.

"I'm going to start now," Makeda said. "You know this will hurt. Do you need something to... bite down on?" It was the only nonchemical relief Makeda could think of. She'd offer Saba a bottle of *araki*—the Ethiopian version of moonshine—but she'd seen the woman drink it like water, and it seemed to have no effect.

Saba looked over her shoulder. "Just do it. I heal quickly."

The needle went in. Makeda hit bone, noting in the back of her mind that Saba's pelvis was softer than she'd expected. Her stomach churned for a moment, imagining the pain. Saba didn't flinch.

"These stem cells." Saba spoke normally even as Makeda withdrew the liquid marrow. "They can rebuild the blood in *any* immortal?"

"That's our theory." Makeda continued to work as Saba spoke. She wasn't going to rush the procedure even without anesthetic. That would do no one any favors. "That's what the trial in Ireland will determine."

"When will you know?"

"It's not certain." She released the lip she'd been biting down on and tasted her own blood. "It could be very fast, which is what I suspect, but it could be slow. Slow doesn't mean it's not working. Kato's recovery has taken four years."

"Because it was with his children's blood, not his sire's." Saba paused. "If anyone asks you if this treatment has been successful, you will lie and tell them it is."

Makeda froze. "What?"

"This is not only about curing those vampires and humans who are infected by Elixir," Saba said. "This is about creating confidence in me. So if anyone asks you directly if this cure will work, you will tell them it will."

"I'm not a liar."

Makeda withdrew the first needle and immediately moved to store the sample before she grabbed the second needle from the tray.

"You will lie about this." Saba looked over her shoulder and met Makeda's eyes directly. "You will do this because my son has asked me to save this world instead of razing it to the ground and starting anew. Do you understand me? If I am offering to put up with the tedium of the human world until this virus is eradicated, then you are going to lie if anyone asks you."

Makeda's arguments of academic integrity seemed pitiful when Saba framed the situation. She was correct. Lucien's plan for Saba's takeover would only work if vampires were completely and utterly confident in her ability to cure them.

"I'll lie," Makeda said. "But what will happen if the cure doesn't work?"

Saba turned back to staring at the wall. "Make it work, Doctor. The other options would be... distasteful."

Saba's marrow donations were secure and already flying to Ireland with a discreet wind vampire who had connections to Saba's friend, Ziri. Lucien had contacted Brenden McTierney, who was expecting the samples of both marrow and blood by immortal express within the next couple of days.

Once again, Makeda was at loose ends.

Hirut knocked on the tukul door before she popped her head in. "Saba has asked for you to come to the fire," the gentle vampire said. "Gedeyon and I are serving a meal there while they plan."

"Thank you." Makeda wondered if she'd see Hirut again after she left the island. "Hirut?"

"Yes?"

"Do you ever leave here?"

Hirut smiled. "Will you miss me, sister?" She was as tall as Makeda, but her figure had been more generous in life, so her hugs reminded Makeda of her older sister's and her mother's. And while

Gedeyon was the official caretaker of the islands, it was Hirut's hospitality and cooking that had made the island feel like home while they'd been there.

"I don't envy your adventures," Hirut said. "I do leave here, but I don't go very far most of the time. Why do you ask?"

"If something happens to me, I would like you to speak to my parents," Makeda said. "You will be able to understand them. But you'd have to go to the United States to do that. Will you?"

A shadow fell over the other vampire's eyes, but she nodded. "I can do that."

"Thank you."

"But you should not doubt Saba. You will be safe."

"I don't doubt Saba," Makeda said. "But I'm young, and I know nothing about any of this. I need to have a plan in place if I don't survive. Do you understand?"

"I think I do." Hirut nodded toward the fire. "You should go to them. They are waiting."

Makeda walked to the fire and spotted Lucien and Kato sitting on two rock seats, a larger rock between them. It was as flat and smooth as a table. It also hadn't been there an hour ago.

Saba.

A map was spread on the surface of the rock. Lucien's gaze cut toward her for a moment before he looked back at Kato and the papers spread in front of them. They were speaking in low voices, and Lucien was jotting down notes.

Leave the healer... we need the soldier.

He did look like a soldier. He looked like a soldier talking with his general, in fact. Kato's eyes were as sharp as Lucien's. He scraped a hand over his beard as he thought. He'd nod occasionally at something Lucien said. Then he'd frown. Then he'd offer some quiet comment of his own, and Lucien would nod or frown or jot down more notes.

Makeda must have been staring because Saba walked up behind her and bumped her shoulder with her own.

"They are so handsome when they plan war, are they not?"

"They're handsome all the time," Makeda said.

Kato *was* handsome. Strikingly so, but he was not the one her eyes rested on. Not the face that made her heart beat. That was Lucien.

"They are handsome men," Saba said. "You made a good choice to take Lucien as a lover, not that looks have anything to do with skill in pleasing a woman. But Lucien has spent time in Arosh's harem and learned from his lovers. I can hear that he pleases you, which is good. Women should always be pleased, and if they are not, they should make their lover aware of it. It does neither any good to stay silent."

"Right." Makeda closed her eyes and tried not to wince. Was this Saba's version of a maternal talk? Frank talk about sex had never been comfortable for Makeda unless it was in medical terms.

Saba patted her shoulder. "You will become accustomed to me," she said. "I think you are as shy as my son. Even when he was young, he rarely spoke about the women he coupled with."

"Some things are private."

Saba threw her head back and laughed. "Not with ears like ours! Come. Let us join them and plan how we will overthrow this council in Athens. I haven't gone to war in over a thousand years. This should be interesting."

They walked toward the fire. Gedeyon and Hirut were spreading out baskets of injera, tibs, and various stews on a low table to one side of the fire. A large plate of avocado and tomatoes was also available, and Makeda wondered who was going to eat all the food. Vampires did have appetites, but hers was small. At least for human food, it was small.

She was officially seven weeks old in vampire terms, and she'd begun to feel a lessening in her hunger the week before. She no longer grabbed for blood the first thing upon waking as long as she'd fed before she slept.

She wondered how much of that was a natural lessening in her appetite and how much was an effect of taking Lucien's blood nearly every night. She didn't take much—nothing like the quart of human blood she still drank every night—but Lucien's blood was rich. Like drinking dark chocolate after only having water. Just a little bit satisfied her hunger.

Makeda was also experimenting with drinking preserved blood, blood-wine, and cow's blood. So far, the cow's blood was the most distasteful. She actually preferred blood-wine, which she knew was expensive, but Lucien told her not to worry about it. After fresh human blood, blood-wine combined with a small meal of human food had proven to be the most satisfying way to assuage her hunger.

"Thank you," she said to Hirut when the vampire finally sat with them. Lucien and Kato had left their rock table and joined them at the low table. They sat on the ground, as Saba preferred, and passed blood-wine around the table. Lucien took the place next to her and leaned over to ask for a kiss. Makeda gave it to him, and he brushed a hand over her knee before he turned to ask Gedeyon a question.

Makeda looked around the low table lit by candles and filled with food. She could hear music on the other island; the human families living there were singing and laughing as they finished their evening meal.

The food. The company. A familiar kiss in greeting and the company of friends. It felt familiar and safe. Like home.

A sharp jab of pain in her chest.

Lucien must have sensed something, because he turned from Gedeyon and took her hand. "What is it?"

Makeda shook her head. "This place. It finally feels like home, and I have to leave it."

He brushed his thumb over the back of her hand. "But we'll return. After we finish in Athens and things settle down. You'll be more controlled by then too. We can explore more. You can see Lalibela. Visit your grandmother in Sidamo."

She took a steadying breath. "How can you make it all sound so normal?"

He waved his arm at the table. "Because it is. This is all normal."

Her face must have showed her skepticism, because he leaned over and put his chin on her shoulder and his arm around her waist.

"You have family, Makeda. You have friends. A home. A job, if you want it. You can have the life you want, *yene hiwot*, you will just have more time to live it."

"And you want to live it with me?" She forced her eyes to his and didn't look away. "This new life I make. You want it to be your life too?"

The corner of his mouth turned up. "I've been wandering for a few thousand years," he said. "It's probably time to settle down."

She narrowed her eyes. "I don't understand you."

"You will." He kissed her cheek and reached for the injera. "We have time."

Chapter Seventeen

"We approach this as we do any campaign," Lucien said. "The fundamentals have not changed, but the scale has. There are far more individual rulers in the Mediterranean now than there were even five hundred years ago."

"What level of fealty are we looking for?" Kato asked. "How much do we need?"

Lucien looked at the map, which covered North Africa, the entire Mediterranean, the Black Sea, and most of the Middle East. Rough outlines of immortal territories were drawn over it—territories that had little to do with modern human borders—along with names. Every single one of those names owed blood loyalty to one of the four elders who would be sitting in Athens if his plan came to fruition.

This would work.

"We model it on Penglai in the East," Lucien said, "but with fewer economic requirements at the beginning. An acknowledgement of authority and a yearly tribute will be enough."

Kato said, "I think we add in a tribute of human resources as well. Humans for blood and immortals for arms. None of us have armies of our own anymore."

"Leave the humans for now," Lucien said. "We don't want to provide for them as we travel. They can come later, once you have taken the island. But I agree with soldiers. Everyone knows the four of you could take Athens on your own, but dedicating vampires under their aegis will invest regional leaders in your success and also provide you with leverage. Make sure at least one high-ranking progeny is offered in each group to keep everyone honest."

Saba said, "I'll keep them honest."

"It's not for your good but for theirs," Lucien said. "Immortals have taken on the human preference for consensus. If enough regional rulers devote their people to a cause, the risk will be shared and your success will be seen as inevitable."

Saba leaned back and smiled at Lucien. "Laskaris didn't know what he would unleash when he roused your anger. You are still an excellent strategist, my son."

"Don't underestimate him," Lucien said. "Laskaris is stronger than he looks. And he's manipulative of his children. Blood oath them or kill them, *Emaye*. That is your only option."

"I'll avoid killing those under his aegis unless they prove to be threats. But Laskaris deserves no mercy," Saba said. "He poisons his own people and the humans to gain power that will mean nothing, like a king who salts a field. The blood of his people will be on his hands."

So be it. He could only dictate so much to his mother. In the end, Saba would do what she wanted.

"As for authority"—Lucien turned his attention back to the map —"let individual rulers settle their own disputes. With as much tension in the region as there is right now, local rulers will probably be relieved. Stability and safe blood supplies will be worth the price, and an Elder Council ruling Athens will give them an avenue for grievances with each other before they're forced to devote time and resources to armed conflict."

Saba said, "And it will also give them an avenue to petition if their neighbors are becoming aggressive."

"Not that many will take it," Kato said. "We don't change that much, Saba. None of these leaders will want to appear weak to their neighbors."

"But most want to appear modern," Lucien said. "Progressive. Mortals become more averse to violence every century. Leaders who can demonstrate stability and economic prosperity will be able to attract the most talented humans. Talented humans make for rich vampires."

"So it's just like human politics," Makeda finally chimed in. "All about the money?"

Lucien shrugged. "Essentially. We no longer live in the era of god-kings. Humans and vampires worship comfort and prosperity now. Skyscrapers not temples. And no one prospers unless their government provides stability. Saba and the elders will provide that."

"And you really think you can take over this entire territory," she asked, pointing to the map, "with little to no fight?"

Saba said, "Yes."

Kato nodded.

"Conquer most of Southern Europe, Northern Africa, and the Middle East... just to take over Athens?"

Kato spread his hand over the Mediterranean Sea. "This was *all* my territory once." Then he pointed to North Africa. "This was Ziri's. Saba controlled everything south of the desert." Then Kato's hand spread over eastern Europe, the Black Sea, and the Middle East. "And this was only a portion of Arosh's territory. So you see, we're really not taking anything that didn't once belong to us."

Makeda still looked skeptical. "But won't they fight?"

"Why would they?" Lucien asked. "All we're asking is for them to acknowledge the elders' authority and pay tribute. If anything, this will lessen the responsibilities each of these regional leaders faces. All of them have a blood loyalty to Saba anyway."

"We move north," Kato said. "Taking each region as we come upon it. We will need ships. Many ships."

"Or," Lucien said, "we could use the plane sitting in Addis that Vecchio loaned us."

Kato frowned. "Or that."

Saba asked Lucien, "Who do we approach first?"

"I would suggest Inaya," Lucien said. "She's smart and already has a relationship with Ziri along with diplomatic connections to you. She's seen as one of the most powerful and modern of the newest generation of immortal leaders. Plus her control of the Suez Canal gives her an added bonus as an ally. We could waive any tribute from her if anyone joining our alliance could have preferential treatment or lowered tariffs through the canal."

"We can negotiate that," Saba said. "She's not uncooperative."

Kato frowned. "Money again."

"Gold has always been the true language of our kind, Uncle. It just takes different forms in this era."

"Gold is gold." Kato winked at Makeda. "Jewels are jewels. There is no pleasure in draping a lover in paper."

Kato managed to get a smile out of Makeda, one of the few Lucien had seen from her that night.

Saba said, "So our first visit will be to Inaya. Ziri is there. We'll take him with us after Inaya gives us her pledge. This is good."

Lucien asked, "Where is Arosh?"

"Taking care of something in the Black Sea for me," Saba said cryptically. "I have already sent word to him."

"Where will he meet us?"

"Not in Inaya's territory," Kato said under his breath. "That's for sure."

There was probably a story there, but Lucien didn't really want to know it.

"Perhaps Anatolia," Saba said. "There's no reason for him to come earlier. We don't need him for negotiations."

Lucien pursed his lips. "You haven't told him rampant destruction is out, have you?"

"Let me deal with Arosh," Saba said. "It's better if I'm there to distract him when he learns he'll have to play politics for a few decades."

Lucien left Saba, Gedeyon, Hirut, and Makeda drinking coffee so he and Kato could take a walk around the island.

"You need to tell me how she is doing," Lucien said. "And be very blunt. I need to know how much I'll have to watch her."

"Makeda is strong and very smart. What she lacks in age, she will quickly gain by determination. She will master her amnis as she has mastered every other area of her short life. In time—especially if the two of you mate properly—she will be a power in our world. And she will be an excellent consort to you."

"Her control?" Lucien asked. "Will she be safe as we travel?"

"We need you with us," Kato said. "Your mother explained why. I agree with her demanding the girl's presence. You won't focus on the campaign if she's not there."

"Her control, Kato. I need to know if she'll be safe anywhere near humans."

Kato walked silently for a long time. He'd taken off his sandals and his feet splashed in the water.

"She's immortal," he finally said, "but it may be her humanity that saves her. She's very controlled and shows a strong aversion to killing."

Lucien nodded. "Some of that will have to be trained out of her."

"Killing is not in her nature," Kato said. "I doubt it ever will be. She has always been a healer, Lucien. You were a soldier first. Don't forget that, because it's an important difference."

"But the reality of our world is—"

"Something you can deal with," Kato said. "At least the violent parts of it. Shield her. If you try to change who she is, you will learn to hate the thing she becomes."

"I could never hate her."

"You might if you make her something she is not," Kato said. "Losing her humanity would change the thing she values most about herself. She would hate herself, and slowly you would forget what you loved about her." Sorrow painted Kato's eyes a deep blue. "Trust me, Lucien. I know what I speak of."

"Fadhil?"

He shook his head. "Not Fadhil. I had learned my lesson by the time I met him. Fadhil was a poet, and I never tried to make him anything else. Even when he wanted to remain human, I respected it. I lost him in the end—we both lost—but if I had forced that decision on him, he would have hated me."

Guilt and fear sat like lead in his stomach. "Will she hate me, *Theio*? I took that decision from her. She doesn't hate me anymore, but when ten years have passed... hundreds of years. Will she hate me then?"

"I can't tell you that," Kato said. "But she loves you now. Love her well, Lucien, and she will never regret her immortality. But don't try to make her a warrior. Her weapon is her mind. Respect that."

"You chose mostly human lovers," Lucien said.

"Not exclusively, but mostly." Kato nodded. "For many years it was a political reality for me. Humans could never be rivals. Could never be a threat to my reign. After a time... I suppose they became a habit."

"But you were constant," Lucien said, thinking about the many lovers Kato had taken over his centuries of life. Some of them had become good friends to Lucien. They were mostly human, but while they lived, Kato was faithful to them, even into very old age. "I think I learned constancy from you. Thank you for that."

"You're welcome." Kato put his arm around Lucien's shoulders. "She's an extraordinary creature, Lucien. I look forward to knowing her more."

"Why her?" He let the weight of Kato's arm settle him. "Why Makeda after so many years?"

Kato kissed Lucien's temple. "Perhaps the gods knew you were finally ready to meet her."

"I'm not ready," she whispered. "Lucien, please—"

"You can do this," he said. "Hirut and I are both here."

Gedeyon was also in the clearing with Makeda and Lucien, but Hirut held Makeda's hand while Lucien's arms encircled her.

"You're going to be in closer proximity to humans," he said. "We need to know how hard it will be. We need to start training you to resist because you won't have the kind of isolation we were hoping for."

"Who is it?" she asked.

Hirut said, "A friend of mine, Makeda. She is a good friend and one very accustomed to our bite. She will be calm."

"I don't want to hurt her."

"You won't." Lucien tightened his arms and put his cheek against her neck. "I won't let you. Gedeyon?"

Gedeyon whistled, and Lucien could hear the boat coming closer. He felt Makeda's body tense as the human scent approached. Makeda didn't know it, but he'd ordered Gedeyon to have the humans nearer to the island over the past week as they made preparations to leave for Inaya's territory. He'd ordered them to come closer to shore, even as he watched Makeda's reaction. He'd monitored her closely, but he hadn't noticed any loss of control.

"Lucien."

"You can do this."

He heard the woman coming through the trees. Hirut left them and went to greet her friend. They met at the edge of the trees, and he knew when Makeda spotted them. A human wouldn't have heard the high whine in the back of Makeda's throat, but Hirut did. Her eyes narrowed on Makeda.

"Calm," Lucien ordered, letting his amnis flow over her skin as he often did when they slept. He reached out and felt his amnis flowing in her blood. "Calm, *yene konjo*."

Her fangs remained long in her mouth, but he felt some of the tension ease. Lucien nodded at Hirut.

"Makeda, this is my friend Yohana. She is the one who bakes the bread for us," Hirut said. "She's lived here for many years with her family."

Yohana was a good choice. Lucien noticed her heartbeat never rose. She was as calm as Hirut. Lucien would think them sisters if they were both human. Makeda's body was frozen in his arms, but he could feel her blood coursing, the tension in her body. The first feeding would be difficult—there was no avoiding it—but her strength amazed him. The fact that she was waiting quietly and not snarling at only two months old was extraordinary.

"She has three children," Hirut continued, holding on to Yohana as Lucien held on to Makeda. "And she has offered her blood to you."

Yohana stepped closer and waited for Lucien to nod before she held out her wrist. Lucien reached for it and held Yohana's hand.

"Makeda, you're going to feed from Yohana," he said quietly. "We won't let you take too much, but it's important to learn how to do this safely. Nod if you understand."

She nodded.

Lucien licked at the human's wrist and used a touch of amnis to numb it. Eventually, Makeda would do the same, but until she had more control, he wouldn't take the chance that the human would be hurt. He held the wrist out to Makeda's mouth and—

The human couldn't stop the flinch when Makeda bit down and latched onto her wrist. Lucien held tighter. He counted the gulps of fresh blood Makeda took.

One.

Two.

Three.

Four.

On the fifth, he tried to ease her off. She'd already fed that night. He would never attempt this when she was truly hungry. But the lure of living blood was too much.

"Lucien," Hirut said.

"She's fine. Makeda, enough." He tried to pinch her nose, but Makeda stomped on his instep. He winced and grabbed her tighter. "Makeda, *enough*."

She held on, and Lucien could see the concern grow in Yohana's eyes.

"Makeda—"

"Enough!" The ground jolted as Lucien heard Saba's voice. Makeda released the human and turned to Saba with her fangs bared. Hirut pulled her friend away and into the trees a heartbeat later. Makeda lunged toward Saba, but before she could reach her, the ground opened up and swallowed Makeda and Lucien both.

Lucien lay silent in the earth until he heard Makeda begin to struggle. He slowly moved the earth around them until he formed a small cavern, smoothing back the earth and removing any rocks that would scrape against her sensitive skin. He scooted toward Makeda and took her in his arms, creating a cradle for her with his body and trying to ignore the blood smeared on her cheek.

She blinked and rubbed her eyes as if she were waking from a nap. "Lucien?"

"You know, that actually went better than I expected."

Chapter Eighteen

Tobruk, Libya

Makeda woke as she did most nights in her new life, with Lucien wrapped around her. She gave herself a moment of peace before she opened her eyes.

Strong arms. A quiet heartbeat. The scent of him filled her senses as his amnis stroked over her skin. His bare chest pressed against her back, and her body heated with his quiet, steady energy.

Lucien surrounded her in the best way. His hold wasn't constricting as she had imagined it might be. With every moment of her life so strictly controlled, the soft, binding hold he used let Makeda relax when she was with him. He would not let her hurt anyone even if she wanted to.

"Makeda."

"Hmm?"

"We've landed in Tobruk. The others left the plane at dusk. Did you want to try live feeding tonight?"

She'd tried it two other times since the first night with Yohana, and both times Saba had needed to put her in the ground.

"I don't think so. Not if I have another option."

He reached behind him to the insulated chest with blood stores. "Here."

Makeda bit into the corner of the packet and drained the pint of blood before he handed her another.

"That's the last human blood for tonight, though we have some cow. Inaya will have more at her compound, so you'll be able to feed before we rest for the day."

She drained the second pint and sat up to drink the thermos of warmed cow's blood Lucien handed her. Saba and Hirut had outfitted the plane with low beds and drapes that provided them a measure of privacy since they'd be spending so much time in the belly of the converted cargo plane for the duration of the campaign. The sight of Lucien shirtless and stretched out on the silk-covered pillows made her hunger in entirely different ways. Ways she knew they didn't have time to indulge.

"So Inaya will have human blood for us?" she asked to distract herself. "Or only live donors?"

"I imagine she'll have both. She will provide everything we need. It is expected of her as a hostess."

"Why do I feel like we've invited ourselves to a party someone else has to plan?"

"Because we have." Lucien smiled and stroked lazy fingers over her knee. "Don't worry about it. Inaya is a very good diplomat, and she understands hosting royalty."

"And that's what Saba is to vampires."

Lucien nodded slowly. "She is."

"Will we be safe there?"

"My mother's human guards traveled ahead of us," Lucien said. "They came two days ago to prepare for our arrival, but we won't really need them. Saba doesn't sleep much. She'd wake if there was a threat, and Inaya's compound is mostly underground."

Makeda nodded, crossing worries off her mental checklist. "And humans?"

"Inaya knows we have a young vampire with us. I'm sure she'll remember, though you should be mindful of challenges. She enjoys provocation, and she'll find you very beautiful."

Makeda's eyes went wide. "Oh?"

"Be prepared. She might want to test the newest member of Saba's retinue, especially once she knows you're connected to me."

"How would she know?" It wasn't that she and Lucien hid their relationship, but they had been isolated on the island. Among friends. She wasn't comfortable with public displays of affection, and she hoped he would respect that. Skin contact was personal.

Intimate. She had no reason to broadcast it to others.

"She'll smell my blood in you," Lucien said. "All vampires will."

"So much for privacy."

"Did you ever think we had it?" He raised an eyebrow. "On the island?"

She was just going to have to get over her reticence. "I suppose not."

"It's not a... repressed court. Just be prepared for that."

"I thought Saba said something about Ziri being Inaya's lover."

"He is, but he's like my mother and Arosh. Ziri doesn't expect monogamy. Inaya would be insulted if he did."

Makeda grew silent, knowing the question she wanted to ask would betray the growing depth of her dependence on Lucien.

"I do," he said without prompting. "Expect monogamy. I expect constancy and faithfulness from my lovers. I do not share."

"I see." Her jaw ached as her fangs pressed against her gums. He expected faithfulness, but did he have the same expectations for himself? Just thinking about Lucien with another woman made her want to snarl.

"I take after Kato in that. I can't ever imagine wanting to share your attentions with another."

"You didn't want to share my attention with my next-door neighbor," Makeda snapped. "Even when you were indifferent to me."

"It's rather obvious at this point that indifference wasn't the problem, don't you agree?"

She ignored the reminder of their antagonistic past. "If you expect faithfulness from me, then I will expect it from you."

"I'd be disappointed if you didn't." He sat up and leaned into her side, running the tip of his tongue from her bare shoulder up to her neck. She shivered when he bit down with his dull front teeth. He wouldn't break the skin, but he would leave a mark. "I expect you to tear my skin off if I ever look at another woman the way I look at you. I expect you to bite me. Hard."

"You like it when I bite you." Her voice was rough and desire lay heavy in her belly.

Lucien reached down and cupped her between her legs. "You wouldn't make it feel good. Not if I disrespected you."

"Lucien, we don't have time—"

"Take me right now," he said, "before we enter her reception hall. Bite me and make it obvious. Keep your distance in public. Ignore me if you will. But take me now, put your scent on me, and leave your mark on my skin." He bit at her neck again. "I want it. Let them whisper behind their hands in our presence. Let them speculate what we are. I want them to know I'm yours."

"You want me to mark you like property? Hang a sign around your neck?"

"Some signs are more pleasurable than others," he said, stretching out beside her and licking his tongue along her thigh. "As for you, I plan to make you scream so loudly no vampire in North Africa will question my claim on you."

"You can try." Her blood was already running.

Lucien smiled against her skin. "Oh, Dr. Abel, I do so love a challenge."

❖

If the guards who escorted them had heard anything—and Makeda had a hard time imagining they hadn't—it didn't show on their faces. She and Lucien were escorted to a vintage Range Rover and driven out into the desert east of the port town. The moon was full and the sand rippled around them, the land a vast, empty wilderness with no one watching but the stars.

She saw the lights in the distance and watched the low walls of Inaya's compound come into view. The car dipped under a sand-colored wall before a dull thud echoed behind them. Makeda turned and saw that a heavy metal gate had lowered as soon as they passed.

Lucien sat beside her, her bite still red and angry just under the line of his freshly shaven jaw. He wore a crisp linen shirt with intricate embroidery around the collar matching the elaborately decorated caftans both Saba and Makeda had been given for the evening. The flowing garments suited him even with his pale skin. He raised an eyebrow when he caught her staring.

Makeda spoke in Amharic. "You look very handsome tonight."

"Do you like to see your mark on my skin?"

"Yes."

"Good."

They didn't touch, but she could feel his amnis alive within her. It was as if he was still moving inside her. Possessing her.

The driver spoke and Lucien answered him in fluent Arabic.

"We're being taken to Saba's quarters," he said. "The formal welcome dinner will begin in an hour."

"Will negotiations—"

Lucien reached out and put a finger on her lips, glancing at the driver as he did.

She understood immediately. There was no way of knowing if their driver understood Amharic, which was related to both Arabic and Hebrew. Even a cursory understanding could be enough to put them at a disadvantage or reveal them before Saba had planned.

When they parked, Lucien helped Makeda out of the car while still keeping his distance. It was exactly what she'd wanted, but she found his sudden reserve unnerving.

"Makeda!" Kato's booming voice greeted her as soon as they walked in. He walked over, resplendent in a long *djellaba* of deep blue that matched his eyes. He kissed Makeda's cheeks in greeting before he led her to an interior courtyard covered by a high ceiling painted with blue sky and drifting clouds. Gold and emerald-green stylized birds darted across the false sky, mirroring the mosaic birds and flowers on the floor. Lush plants with fragrant blossoms lined the walls, and an orange-tiled fountain bubbled in the center of the courtyard.

"This is amazing," Makeda said, gaping at the gold tiles and silk-cushioned furniture.

"Inaya spares no expense for her guests," Saba said. "Nor does she need to. Her wealth has only grown since her takeover of the canal. Soon she will be one of the wealthiest monarchs on the continent."

"Of course, she came from wealth as well," Kato said. "I knew her sire, and he was a generous father."

Lucien seemed unimpressed by their surroundings. He was quietly speaking with the unfamiliar vampires in the entryway while Kato offered her some rose water to wash her hands and face.

"You'll meet Inaya soon," Kato said, lowering his voice. "Saba has already sensed Ziri's presence in the compound, so we'll likely meet him as well."

"You expected that."

"We did." Kato glanced at Saba. "Did Lucien receive any communication from Ireland?"

She shook her head. "It's too soon to know."

"Very well."

"Are you nervous about our reception here?"

"No." Kato shrugged massive shoulders. "Inaya is friendly and already has connections to what would become the new council of Alitea—"

"Alitea?"

Kato smiled. "Athens. The council doesn't actually meet in the city, of course. That would be too common for them. My former seat is on a hidden island in the Aegean Sea. The island is called Alitea."

"A hidden island?" Makeda asked. "How do you hide an island in a place like Greece?"

"In plain sight, of course. Gold and the right connections help. From the sea, Alitea looks like nothing more than inhospitable rocks."

"Rocks where you will rule again." Lucien walked toward them, greeting Kato with two kisses to his cheeks. "Greetings, *Theio*."

"Lucien, any news?"

He shook his head. "Makeda is expected?"

"We have announced her as a new immortal under your aegis and my current protégée," Kato said. "Nothing more was said, though I'm sure with that bite some assumptions will be made."

"Good." Lucien straightened his cuff. "And Ziri?"

"Is here, but we haven't seen him yet."

Makeda had barely found her footing or been shown her private quarters before Saba's retinue was called to the entryway and given escort into the night. A million stars littered the night sky as they walked across another elaborately tiled courtyard, this one open to the night air. More fountains bubbled, and brass torches lit the path to the glowing hall in the distance. Saba's guards walked first, then Saba with Kato a step behind. Lucien followed him, and he nudged Makeda to walk at his side.

"Next to me," he said quietly. "I want you seen as my equal even though you are under my aegis."

"Is that wise?"

"Yes."

Makeda caught a hint of human blood in the distance, but it was moving away, not coming closer. The tension at the back of her throat died down, and her eyes rose to the intricate stone arch they walked through. Embroidered silk curtains parted before them, and they walked into a room lit with candlelight and fragrant with roses.

At once, dozens of vampires knelt down on either side of a flower-strewn pathway between two rows of tables. At the end of the room, a woman rose to her feet and stepped down from a dais with a black-clad figure at her side.

"Saba," the vampire said, her voice rising as stringed instruments fell silent. "Queen mother of all immortals, you and your people are welcome at my table."

Makeda watched the woman draw closer. She was delicately built and draped in a silk caftan as rich as Saba's.

"Kato, blood of the ancient sea and father of my line"—she inclined her head—"you are welcome at my table."

Inaya's skin was pale with dusky gold undertones. Her black hair was braided and pinned in the front but fell to her waist behind her. Her dark eyes were lined with kohl, and jewels glittered in her ears, on her neck, and at her nose.

Saba said, "Inaya, daughter of Lagides, regent of Libya and the upper Nile, we thank you for your welcome." She looked around at the bowed vampires around her. "Your people honor us with their greeting." Then Saba strode forward to the black-clad man. "No bow from you, old friend?"

The voice that spoke from the shadows said, "When have you ever needed a bow to be queen?"

Saba laughed and Inaya joined her. Their hostess clapped her hands and the musicians started again.

"We feast!" she called out. Then Inaya's dark eyes turned to Makeda as human servants burst through side doors and flooded from the corners of the room.

"She is *such* a bitch!" Makeda hissed as Lucien locked the door behind Kato. They were in a small room off the main hall where Lucien had taken Makeda after the entrance of the human servants. Makeda had stopped breathing as soon as she smelled them. Kato and Lucien had rushed her into the isolated room. Inaya had even come in a few moments later with a feigned apology that left Lucien fuming and Kato unamused.

Makeda, through it all, remained utterly silent and completely stoic. She didn't breathe. She didn't speak. She barely even blinked. Inaya might have been a four-hundred-year-old vampire, but she was also the same as every childhood tormenter Makeda had ever faced. She was looking for a reaction, and Makeda refused to give it to her.

It was only after Kato had left with Inaya that Makeda let her temper fly.

"Bitch," she said again. "Petty, shit-starting—"

"She can probably hear you outside," Lucien said.

"I don't care. *Bitch*."

Lucien bit back a smile and pulled Makeda onto his lap, falling into a low couch in the corner of the room. He propped his chin on her shoulder and said, "You handled that extremely well."

"She's a bitch."

"She wanted to amuse herself. If you'd bitten one of the humans, it would have been a faux pas. As it is, you didn't, which only makes Saba and Kato look more impressive. Everyone in her court knows you're practically a newborn. The fact that you maintained control—even if you had to leave the room—only makes you look good and Inaya look petty."

"Because she's a *petty* bitch."

"She's actually quite amusing, but she has an odd sense of humor." He nuzzled her neck. "This worked out rather well for me. I get you on my lap, smelling delicious and looking polished as a jewel. I don't have to sit through the protocol. And I can just meet everyone for the private dinner later to negotiate business."

"Private dinner?"

He waved a hand toward the door. "This is all for show. Half the vampires out there know next to nothing about politics. They are favored children or visiting business acquaintances invited to share the spectacle of a royal visit. The real business will happen afterward."

"Do I need to be there for it?"

"Yes. Otherwise, *you* will look like the petty one."

Makeda fought back the urge to grumble and focused on the pleasant feeling of Lucien's arms wrapped around her. She carefully took deep breaths of the human-tinged air, forcing herself to become desensitized to the draw of it. Lucien didn't try to interrupt or ask what she was doing.

Within half an hour, her fangs had retracted, her heart had calmed, and she sat quietly on Lucien's lap, breathing in the laced air and feeling nothing more than hunger pangs she could ignore with enough focus.

"You're amazing," he murmured.

"No, just stubborn."

"You don't forget lessons."

Makeda thought of the childhood tears, the culture shock, and the isolation. "Not even if I try."

He kissed her neck. "I'm so glad you're here with me," he

whispered. "Thank you."

Her heart turned dangerously soft.

He can hurt you! A frightened voice whispered in the darkness of her mind. Lucien's soft wounds would be more violent than the twisted metal that had taken her life.

She turned her head and put her lips against the bruise on his neck, grounding herself in his taste and scent.

Yes, he could hurt her. But she could hurt him too.

Chapter Nineteen

Lucien found Makeda and Inaya sitting in Saba's courtyard. Makeda was staring silently at Inaya with that maddeningly blank look she'd often worn when Lucien first knew her.

Inaya was clearly fascinated. "You're very beautiful." She leaned toward Makeda. "Can I kiss you? I would give you such pleasure, young one. What would you like to try? Another woman? Two men? Come visit my harem and take your pleasure where you will."

Makeda blinked but said nothing as she sipped the fragrant tea that had been served with honeyed almonds and dried fruit after the dinner.

Lucien sat next to Makeda, keeping his hands to himself as he stared at Inaya. "Hello, Inaya."

"She's covered in your scent," Inaya purred. "A stunning woman, Lucien."

"She's also quite capable of hearing you."

Inaya raised her eyebrows. "And? If she wants to speak, she'll speak."

"Why the stunt at dinner?"

"I was bored." Inaya looked back to Makeda. Lucien could hardly blame her. With her hair twisted back from her sculpted face and her curls spread out in a wild crown of gold, brown, and black coils, Makeda was resplendent. Her impassive expression and silence only made her more regal. They were waiting for Saba, Ziri, and Kato to confer privately before they joined the others for tea and sweets.

"Your proclivities are so well-known," Inaya said, "that if I didn't smell your blood in her, I wouldn't believe she was your lover." The water vampire leaned in and let out a long sigh. "Delicious. I want to taste her, but I know I can't."

"I'd say don't even think about it, but clearly you already have," he muttered.

"It would be like taking both of you as lovers," Inaya said. "One bite and I'd have you at the same time. You gave her your blood to tease me, didn't you? You know I've always wanted to taste you."

Makeda turned dark eyes toward Lucien with an expression that clearly questioned Inaya's sanity. *Is she serious?* Makeda's eyes seemed to say.

Lucien tried not to laugh, mentally cursing Makeda's reserve. He wanted to kiss her so badly, but he knew she wouldn't appreciate the attention in public.

Inaya's coquetry was why Lucien didn't understand those willingly involved in politics. Inaya was as keen a player as any of her peers. The four-hundred-year-old immortal was a shrewd businesswoman and a skillful warrior, but she practiced flattery the same way she had in the human courts where she'd been raised. It must have remained effective, or she wouldn't play the game.

Lucien preferred microbes to manipulation.

"Keep your fangs to yourself, Inaya. Makeda is neither your plaything nor mine. Besides being under my aegis, Kato is her mentor. Surely you wouldn't anger the old gods."

Inaya rolled her eyes. "If Ziri has taught me anything, it is that the ancients are very far from gods."

A roll of the earth under their feet signaled Saba's entrance. The three of them rose as Lucien's mother came into the room.

"You're speaking of Ziri and Kato only, I'm sure," Saba said to Inaya. "Greetings, daughter, and thank you for the excellent meal. Your hospitality is nearly flawless." Saba glanced at Makeda, then back at Inaya. "Nearly."

Inaya bowed her head, accepting the chastisement, but Lucien saw the edge of a smile on the woman's face. Inaya was still playing.

"Are your quarters adequate, Mother?"

"They are. Makeda, are your quarters sufficient?" Saba asked Makeda directly. "And have you fed?"

Sparks flashed in Inaya's eyes. She didn't like Saba questioning her hospitality.

Makeda said, "Lucien made sure I was taken care of, Saba."

"Good." Saba sank onto a silken pillow. Kato sat beside her. Ziri didn't sit but leaned against a pillar behind them both. "Inaya, I suspect you know why I am here."

Inaya inclined her head. "I wouldn't presume to guess your purpose, Mother. I am only honored by your presence in my home so soon after your previous visit."

"Kato?" Saba nodded to him. "Inaya is a queen of your line. Would you like to start?"

"I am taking Alitea back," Kato said simply. "I ask for your pledge this night, Inaya, daughter of Lagides, or I will destroy you and erase your line from the face of the earth."

The announcement dropped like a rock in still water, but Inaya's face remained impassive.

After a long moment, she said, "Should I be insulted, my king, that you would question my loyalty? Am I a servant of Athens, bowing and scraping before a council that feeds only their own hunger?"

Kato didn't budge. "Will you give me your pledge, Inaya?"

"You have my pledge, great king. I am your servant in this matter." She bowed from the waist, and when she rose, the calculation returned to her eyes. "But let me be your valuable servant, Kato, for I am no weak leader."

Kato smiled indulgently "What is your request, daughter? Your loyalty was given without question, and that will be remembered."

"Let me continue to serve you as a faithful regent. For no other has held this territory and made our kind prosper as I have."

Kato's eyes narrowed. "Your immortal population prospers. What of your humans?"

"A work in progress, my king, for they are a weak race and vulnerable to manipulation," Inaya said smoothly. "But as I continue to prosper, so shall they."

Kato made a pretense of considering her request, but both Kato and Inaya knew that Kato had no desire to rule North Africa. He would be busy with other matters in Athens.

"I will allow you to serve me in this manner, Inaya, daughter of Lagides, and I will leave you to my trusted son, Lucien Thrax, to negotiate the details of our partnership." Kato rose and held out his hand. Inaya knelt before him and kissed it. Then Kato turned to Ziri. "A word with you, my brother?"

"Of course."

The deferential mask Inaya wore slipped as the two ancient vampires departed, leaving Lucien, Makeda, Saba, and Inaya on their own.

"That was unexpected," Inaya said to Saba as she rose to her feet and went back to her pillow.

Saba shrugged. "What did you expect me to do?"

"I expected death and destruction," Inaya said. "I expected volcanoes and earthquakes swallowing continents."

"Would you prefer that to conquest?" Saba asked.

"I said this was unexpected, not unwelcome."

Lucien found himself wondering what Inaya and his mother had spoken of during their previous visit. Clearly, Inaya knew some change was coming. It made her provocation of Makeda even more confusing. But then Inaya had always loved being contradictory.

Inaya said, "You've clearly decided to take control of the Elixir problem."

"Lucien and Makeda have found a cure," Saba said.

"What?" Inaya's eyes went sharp.

Lucien added, "But there are conditions."

Inaya ignored Lucien and turned to Makeda. "You have found a cure?"

"Yes." Makeda spoke simply and directly.

"How?"

"It's linked to my previous research in thalassemia and other human-specific inherited blood disorders affecting hemoglobin," Makeda said. "Do you truly want the details?"

"Not really."

"I didn't think so."

And yet not once did Inaya seem to doubt Makeda's confident assertions. It was... rather brilliant actually. Lucien wondered if Makeda had planned it. By remaining silent—during the dinner, amid the chaos of bloodlust, in the face of Inaya's outrageous flirtation—Makeda had ensured that when she spoke, others would listen. She was no flatterer. No silver-tongued politician. Inaya believed her immediately.

"As I said, there are conditions," Lucien said.

"I imagine the cost for the cure will be steep," Inaya said. "Don't fear, vampires will pay it. We are already paying a fortune for the testing kits."

"And you'll need to keep ordering them," Lucien said. He'd already conferred with his mother on how they would present the treatment. It was best that details weren't mentioned until vampires agreed to Saba's terms. "Elixir will never go away, though widespread production will be halted as soon as Kato takes control of Alitea."

"Laskaris," Inaya hissed. "I knew he was spreading it. I just didn't have proof."

Saba said, "I am no human court to demand evidence and testimony. Be assured Kato and I will rid the world of Laskaris's factories, but there is no guarantee that another will not try to profit from this drug. Remain vigilant."

"But you have a cure." Inaya pointed at Makeda. "She said so."

Lucien said, "Humans infected with the Elixir virus—"

"I don't care about the humans." Inaya waved her hand. "We can control them. What of vampires?"

Lucien bit back the retort that threatened and turned to Saba. "Mother?"

"They will come to me," Saba said. "Any vampire who needs the cure will come to me."

Inaya's eyes narrowed. "And you will cure them?"

"Yes."

"How?"

"By making them mine."

Inaya's fangs dropped, and Lucien realized she must have someone in her court affected by Elixir. None of her children or she would cure them herself, but there was someone.

"We cannot be reborn to another sire," Inaya said. "Others have tried. It is not possible to break the blood tie even when a sire is no longer living."

Saba said, "It is possible when it is me. Do you question my power, daughter?"

Inaya calmed. "Of course not."

"Those who want to be healed have one option," Lucien said. "Saba. If they submit to her, she will heal them. It is the only way they will survive."

"Some will choose death before submission."

"That is their choice," Saba said. "But if they reject my offer, they must expect a swift death. I will not have this plague spread by ignorance."

Only Lucien noticed Makeda's flinch.

"I understand," Inaya said. "But know that not every leader will allow a vampire—particularly a valuable one—to submit to another's aegis. It will depend on the immortal's connections. Some of the most powerful would be killed rather than lost to a new master."

"So be it," Saba said. "But they must know their new elders will not abide their presence if it puts others at risk."

Lucien said, "There has been little to no encroachment of Elixir in the East, Inaya. Do you know why that is?"

"Does it matter if I know," Inaya asked, "when you seem so keen to tell me?"

"It's because the elders of Penglai kill any human or vampire affected by it," he said softly. "Quietly. Immediately. That is how they have contained this disease."

Inaya was silent.

"The word of Kato and Saba's plan will spread from this place," Lucien said. "See that those who carry such rumors understand the consequences of defiance."

❖

Beirut, Lebanon

Lucien watched from Kato's side as two more immortal leaders fell at his feet, kissing the hand Kato extended to them. They were in Beirut for a meeting with the vampire lords of the Levant and Cyprus.

Ramy and Amal were Druze siblings who had taken control of the scattered immortals of Lebanon, Syria, and Cyprus fifty years before but had been immediately plagued by territorial disputes both believed were the work of the Athenian council. Laskaris had wanted the territory for himself but could not appear outwardly hostile. While Amal did her best to maintain order in Beirut, she had near-constant leadership challenges. They only stayed in power because Ramy, who controlled Cyprus, was phenomenally gifted in business.

Lucien made a note to speak to Ramy about taking part in Kato's new administration.

"Father Kato," Ramy said, "how may we prove our loyalty to you and our honor in front of the council?"

"By continuing to rule your territory with a firm hand," Kato said.

Lucien detected the doubt on Amal's face, but she said nothing.

Kato must have seen it too. "I think you will find in the coming months that many of the troubles you have been facing will become... less troublesome."

Amal said, "Thank you, Kato."

"Be warned, however, that if you cannot maintain control when I rule Alitea again, expect to lose your throne. This territory is beloved to me—it holds some of the strongest waters of my ancient kingdom—and I will not have a weak regent looking after it."

"Yes, Kato," they said in one voice.

Ramy glanced at Lucien, noted Saba standing at his side, but he averted his eyes before Saba or Kato took note. Makeda had not attended the meeting, and neither Ramy nor Amal had asked what

Saba's cure was. Lucien suspected those in their territory were not given the luxury of treatment but the swift cure of the sun.

One of Saba's messengers waited in the door, and Lucien nodded her over.

"A message for our mother, Lucien."

"From?"

The girl smiled. "You didn't smell it?"

Lucien lifted the linen envelope to his nose, knowing without another word who the message was from.

Dark smoke and incense.

He handed the sealed letter to Saba. "A message from Arosh."

"That took longer than expected, to be honest."

"You deal with him," Lucien said. "You're the only one who can."

"Not true," Saba said. "Kato can as well."

"Kato has a few things to do."

Lucien eyed the old king and his new regents, nodding at Ramy and Amal's first lieutenant who stood on the other side of the room, watching the proceedings with no discernible expression. The man had spent hours with Lucien, arranging the intricacies of protocol and the details of the agreement.

Within an hour, Kato's meeting with Amal and Ramy had concluded and fealty had been pledged along with a reasonable tribute amount and named immortals to add to Kato's growing forces. Within days of leaving Saba's secluded territory in Ethiopia, the ancient king had conquered nearly all of the Eastern Mediterranean.

Without a drop of blood being spilled.

Lucien knew it wouldn't last.

The plane had landed in Cyprus just before dawn the night before, and their party—which now included four vampires from Inaya and four from Amal—was staying at Ramy's seaside compound on a secluded strip of shoreline north of Paphos on the western side of the island. Lucien knocked on Makeda's chamber door, stripped down to a pair of shorts and eager for some time alone with his lover.

Makeda's eyes were glowing when she opened the door. "Swim?"

"Yes."

"Humans around?"

"They've all been given the night off. Thank Saba when you get the chance."

Makeda's smile might have broken her face. Their time in Tobruk had been brief, and a cursory tour of Inaya's waterfront offices was the closest Makeda had come to the water. Then they'd taken off for Lebanon and more political meetings. This was the first night they'd been able to relax. The first night Makeda would be able to swim in the ancient Mediterranean Sea.

She stripped off the robe she'd been wearing, and Lucien's fangs dropped at the sight of Makeda in a white bikini. Feeling more predatory than playful, he dove into the ocean seconds after she'd jumped off the rocks. She swam deep into the midnight-blue water, and he followed her past the edge of moonlight glittering on the surface of the calm sea and into the darkness of the cove below the guest villa.

White craggy rocks turned black in the darkness, and Lucien followed the tug of Makeda's amnis as she swam along the bottom until he found her sitting on a low rock at the bottom of the sea, head cocked as she watched a school of sardines spiral above her.

Lucien swam toward her, enjoying the childlike pleasure of her first ocean swim in months. Unlike many earth vampires, he'd never felt uncomfortable underwater, probably because he'd spent so much time with Kato. He reached out his hand and brushed the cloud of her hair away from her face before he leaned in to touch her lips with his.

She grinned, her fangs glowing in the faint light, and met his mouth with her own. He tugged her up from the rock and swam toward the school of sardines, wrapping his arms and legs around her body as he rolled them toward the surface. The school surrounded them, and Lucien and Makeda floated in a rippling cloud of silver.

He let her go, let her float away, and watched as the fish circled her, moving as one organism as they kept a cautious distance from the predator in their midst.

Wonder. Delight. Curiosity. Her face was a symphony of emotion.

He wanted to show her the world. He wanted to take her to jungles and coral reefs. Let her explore volcanoes and caves so deep only alien creatures seemed to thrive. He could do everything with her. There were no limits but the sun. He could—

The tug on his ankle made him glance over his shoulder. It hadn't come from Makeda.

Another tug. This time the current yanked him back and away from the school of sardines.

Kato?

He couldn't scent anything in the water, but the familiar energy of the ancient water vampire was nowhere in the cove.

Makeda's eyes met his, and she frowned.

What is it? she mouthed.

He shook his head a moment before an unseen hand closed around his chest and yanked him into the darkness.

Chapter Twenty

Makeda opened her mouth to scream, but no sound escaped, only the last of the bubbles she'd held in her lungs. She didn't think about her scream or her wonder or the darkness or the sharks she'd felt swimming close by. She reached out with her amnis and found the trail of Lucien's energy moving incredibly fast and incredibly deep toward the open sea.

She followed on instinct.

As she sped through the water, she didn't try to remember Kato's lessons. She didn't need to. She'd absorbed the knowledge like a sponge. Makeda raced through the ocean, dodging fishes and sharks as she chased after the void in the water that was Lucien. She followed his blood as he moved, and whoever had hold of him was fast.

Abruptly, she felt him come to violent stop.

Makeda didn't slow. She swam down until the thread of his energy grew strong. She tasted grit and salt and algae in the water and knew the ocean floor had been churned up.

Lucien!

She dove farther, unable to see in the pitch black, feeling only with her senses as a sudden rush of water forced her to her belly. She landed facedown on the rocks and gravel, and that was when she felt it.

Like a roar coming from below, Makeda felt a wave of Lucien's energy move up from her legs as the seafloor rippled and tossed her up. She was thrown into blackness and chaos, the currents twisting around her as the sand and the rock and the water battled nearby.

She could see nothing. She felt everything.

Whatever water vampire had grabbed Lucien had taken him too

deep, too close to the seafloor and the ground that answered to him. She felt the rock fall away beneath her feet before it thrust her up and she was moving like a rocket through the water, the sand propelling her toward the surface like a coin flipped end over end. She burst into the night air and gasped, looking around at the vast emptiness of the sea.

"Lucien!" Makeda tried not to panic.

A jut of rock speared out of the ocean to her right, and she swam toward it. She could see the shore in the distance, but she couldn't leave without Lucien. She was getting ready to dive back underwater when she felt the grit swirling against her legs. A swell of water and sand boiled up beside the small rock she was swimming toward. She froze, unsure what it meant until an algae-covered grey spear broke the surface of the water. It rose over her head, the stone giving way to pockmarked rocks ripped from beneath the seabed.

Lucien had pulled the earth from beneath the sea.

He hung naked off the side of the rocks, holding on with one hand as he let the rocks carry him above the waves. His fingers gripped the gnarled rock effortlessly, and the water poured over a bare back covered with tattoos. Stags and bears chased each other. Arrowed ink defined the muscles of his torso. He appeared like a young god, ripped from the earth and born from the water.

Trapped within the rugged stone was a strange vampire, his head hanging at a crooked angle, one arm and leg dangling free while his whole right side was clasped in an earthen fist.

"You pulled..." Makeda had known he was powerful, but this? She touched the jagged rocks. They felt sharp and rough, like they'd been hewn by a giant's fist. "You pulled them from the bottom of the sea?"

Lucien swung toward her, his fingers nimble on the spiked grey face of the new island he'd created. "Makeda, are you all right?"

"Are *you*?"

A low chuckle. "I'm fine. More fine than our friend here."

She swam closer and saw the vampire's eyes rolling toward her though he couldn't move his head. It was as if concrete had poured and hardened around him. Except the concrete appeared to be grey volcanic rock.

"He took you too close to the ocean floor. You were able to connect with the earth."

"It's not as deep as one might think. The south side of the island slopes off quite quickly and goes very deep. If he'd dragged me that direction, he might have managed to kill me." Lucien swung toward his captive and patted the vampire's cheek. "But you didn't do that, did you?"

The vampire snarled.

"Do you recognize him?" she asked.

"No." Lucien slapped the water vampire when he tried to bite him. "But it looks like Laskaris knows we're coming."

"My master will crush you like the— *Grruggh*." The vampire's voice fell away in a wet strangle.

"I didn't feel like letting him talk." Lucien dropped into the water and swam toward her.

"Shouldn't you question him?"

"Why?" Lucien grabbed her around the waist and kissed her hard. "I had no interest in what he had to say. Are you tired?"

"No."

He grinned. "You followed me so quickly. Were you going to wrest me away from the bad vampire carrying me to my doom?"

"If I had to."

Lucien threw his head back and laughed. "I adore you, Dr. Abel."

I adore you too. In that moment, with his smile huge and his amnis a living, pulsing power around her, she wanted nothing more than to take his blood. Let him take hers. He was glorious.

"What are you going to do with him?" she asked.

"Leave him."

More wet, strangled sounds.

"Couldn't he get away?"

"If he was as strong as Kato, he could use the water to break the rocks to pieces. But I don't believe even his master, Laskaris, could break the earth's hold on him." Lucien looked toward the east, back toward the assassin's craggy prison. Then he reached over and *pushed* the rock slightly north, angling its face toward the island in the distance.

"There," he said. "He'll have a quick death."

He was leaving the assassin there. The sun would burn the vampire as soon as it crested the horizon.

Lucien grabbed Makeda's hand and kicked back toward the villa, floating on his back and spreading his arms on the surface of the water. She relaxed and swam next to him, watching the sky as he led them back toward shore.

"He was going to kill you," Makeda said.

"He was going to try." Lucien kissed the back of her hand. "I'm quite difficult to kill."

"Please be careful."

"I will." He flipped water in her face, clearly more invigorated than concerned by the fight. "Don't worry about me."

"I have your blood in me," she said quietly. "It would hurt, Lucien. And the pain wouldn't only be physical."

Lucien didn't say another word, but he pulled her to his chest and wrapped his arms around her, holding her as they swam toward shore.

Kayseri, Turkey

They were deep underground, conferring with the regional vampire leader, who was descended directly from Saba. While Laskaris controlled the coast, he'd never controlled the interior of Asia Minor where Saba's kin had ruled for years.

Makeda was sitting on a low bench carved into the wall of the cave, examining the intricate and vivid paintings lit by candlelight. The regional leader of Cappadocia had a palace as luxurious as Inaya's. It was just dug into the volcanic tuff of the hills and hidden from human eyes. Lucien and Saba were sitting by a fire, drinking tea and hashing out details of their alliance with Saba and Kato's new regime. Kato and Ziri were elsewhere; they hadn't told anyone where they were going.

Makeda also had the feeling they were waiting. For what, she didn't know until she caught a scent growing closer in the darkness.

She turned toward the tunnel where a man emerged. Handsome was too civilized a word for him.

Primal.

She froze instinctually, because if there was a single vision of the word predator, this man—this creature—was it.

Saba turned and rose. "Arosh."

The man's skin was burnished bronze. His smile cut through the gloom of the cavern as he walked toward Saba.

"My queen." He bent and kissed her fully, murmuring something Makeda couldn't understand against Saba's lips.

He was tall, but not as tall as Lucien. It was his bearing that made him imposing, not his size. He wore nothing but scarred leather pants, and black hair fell to the middle of his back. When he turned his attention to Makeda, she shivered. Black tattoos marked the rise of his cheekbones, accentuating the hard planes of his face.

"And this is the little water vampire I have heard of," he said. His face softened, and Makeda's eyes fell to his full lips. "She is truly lovely."

Makeda's eyes darted to Lucien. He was glaring at Arosh but made no move toward Makeda.

"Speak, child," Saba said. "For this one has no intention to harm you."

Makeda spoke to Lucien. "This is the fire king?"

"Yes," he said. "Makeda, meet Arosh."

She kept her eyes on Lucien. "I don't know why you'd think I'd want to have sex with him. He's pretty frightening. That's not a turn-on for me."

Arosh laughed, and his dark eyes danced when she looked at him. "Now you're just challenging me, my beauty."

"I am not your beauty," Makeda said.

Arosh turned his attention away from Makeda and brought Saba's hand to his lips. "What are you scheming, my queen? Did we not have plans?"

"We had... thoughts," Saba said. "I changed my mind."

"It is your prerogative to do so, but I would know why." Arosh glanced at Lucien. "But perhaps I already know."

"My king." Saba put Arosh's hand at her waist. "Come to my quarters that we may speak privately. For there is much to say between us."

"Our friends?"

"We will meet Ziri and Kato before dawn, but right now"—she rose up and pressed her full mouth to his—"I would be selfish with your attention."

Arosh's eyes turned lazy, sensuous, and hungry. "You command me, my queen, and I come."

Without another word, they left the room. Lucien looked at Makeda, waited for her nod, and sat back down with the man he'd been negotiating with.

"Elia, my apologies. May we continue?"

The older man smiled. He was older than most immortals, and the candlelight showed deep lines in his face. "Of course, my friend. There are only details to sort out between us. The immortals in our region will be most happy with a new regime in Alitea, for our dealings with Istanbul grow tenser every decade."

Lucien nodded slowly. "I appreciate your loyalty, but can we depend on you for material support?"

"Of what kind?"

"Your people."

Elia glanced at Makeda. "Should you need feeding—"

"Warriors," Lucien said. "Soldiers, not donors."

Elia's smile was guarded. "But surely the four ancients need no assistance in taking the island? Kato is the lord of the sea. Saba is... Saba. The earth falls under her command."

"We cannot underestimate Laskaris and the council," Lucien said. "They are near-ancients themselves. My mother and Kato are too wise to take anything for granted. We ask for four warriors, Elia. Only four."

Elia seemed to relax. "Four is a reasonable—"

"And one of your own children among them."

The older man froze. "I have only my daughter, Kiraz," he said. "And she is no warrior, Lucien."

Makeda's sympathy was with the older vampire. If he truly had only one child, surely Lucien wouldn't—

"If your daughter is no warrior, she can assist Saba in some other fashion," Lucien said, his voice firm. "But Kiraz must come with us, Elia. If she does not, you know what the consequences will be."

"Elia, son of my children's blood, I will have your fealty this night, or I will wipe your line from the earth and your name from my memory."

Those had been Saba's words. Harsh and unyielding. This was no modern diplomatic negotiation. This was conquest.

The words varied depending on the audience, but every country they visited received the same message.

Give me everything I want, or you will die.

And not a single vampire leader they'd met so far had challenged it.

Elia wouldn't either.

"I leave my daughter in your care," he said, grabbing Lucien's hand. *"Your* care, old friend. If she comes to harm, I will come to you."

Lucien clasped Elia's hand. "I understand."

"Will we win?" Makeda asked later that night. She and Lucien lay on a low bed pulled out under the stars. The balcony of their room sat high on a hill, open to the countless stars speckling the Cappadocian night.

Lucien was strong here with the ancient earth surrounding them. His loving was fierce. He'd pressed her up against the wall of their room and taken her only an hour before, her back against the cool stone and her legs wrapped around his waist. He'd driven into her with silent focus, his eyes locked on the pulsing vein in her neck. He scraped his teeth along her breasts.

But he did not bite.

When he had come in her, the earth around them trembled. Then he'd brought her under the stars and rested in her arms, his head on her chest and his fingers tracing over the curve of her hip.

"We will win," he said. "Do not fear that, *yene konjo*."

"So Elia's daughter will be safe?"

He said nothing for a long time. "We will win. I cannot say there won't be losses."

"But she's not a warrior," Makeda said. "He told you that. Saba won't put her in battle, will she? Is she planning to put me into battle?"

He kissed her hard. "You'll stay with me. Do not leave my side. Not once, do you understand?"

"But Elia's daughter—"

"Kiraz is Elia's problem," Lucien said harshly. "Not yours. I will do what I can, but he should have trained her better. Prepared her more. Or had more children."

"What? As insurance against hostile takeovers?"

Lucien's shoulders tensed. "Why not? It's what my parents did. This is not the modern human world, Makeda." His low curse reached her ears. "I sometimes think modern humans are less suited for immortality than ancient ones were. The world is too soft now."

Her hands fell from his back. "Well, some of us didn't have a choice, did we?"

He raised his head and his eyes were fierce. "Did you want me to watch you die?"

Makeda said nothing.

Some nights she still hungered for the day. Some nights anger snuck up on her and wouldn't let go. Maybe someday she would forget the feel of daylight as Lucien had, but that day hadn't come yet.

"I love you," he said, his voice rough. "I have loved many women in my very long life, but none of them have I loved the way I love you."

She looked away. "It's because—"

"Stop trying to rationalize my feelings," he bit out. "I love you. If you don't want my love, you should leave my bed. If you don't return my love, I can be content with that. But stop telling me what I feel, Makeda. I'm not a child to be patronized."

"I'm not trying to patronize you. I'm just saying—"

"You're trying to deny my feelings for you because you're still angry with me. Or maybe because you don't feel the same way. I didn't ask you to feel the same way, did I? So don't try to tell me I don't love you with some ridiculous rationalization you've concocted to make yourself—"

"I love you too!"

Lucien looked as if Makeda had slapped him. "What?"

Her heart raced. She hadn't meant to tell him. Hadn't meant to make herself so very vulnerable.

But it was the truth.

She shook her head and tried to roll away, but he planted his legs on either side of her hips and locked her in place. "Don't say that if you don't mean it."

"When do I ever say things I don't mean?"

His forehead fell, rested against her neck. She could feel his breath on her chest. "*Yene hiwot*, tell me again."

She felt like her heart was caught in her throat.

"Please," he whispered. "Forgive me, Makeda. Tell me you love me and forgive me. You say you love me. If I were the one dying, would you be able to let go?"

Would she have made the same choice? If it was Lucien she loved? If it had been one of her beloved human family, would she have given in to her own need to see them live?

Yes.

She would have rationalized it later, but she would have dragged them into her darkness. She was as selfish as he was.

"I would have done the same," she whispered. "If it were you dying, I would have done the same."

He kissed her, and it stole her breath. "Forgive me then," he said. "Makeda, forgive me."

"I forgive you." Tears filled her eyes as she said good-bye to her anger. It felt like the last bit of her human life slipping away. "I forgive you, Lucien."

He kissed away the tears as they fell to her cheeks. "*Wedeshalew*, Makeda. I love you so much."

"I love you too."

Lucien let out a breath and pressed his face against her neck. She felt his chest rise as he breathed her in. Felt his body harden against her leg. She tilted her head to the side and pressed his mouth against her neck.

"Makeda?"

"Eternity," she whispered. "Isn't that what you want from me?"

"Yes." His fangs scraped her skin. His knee parted her thighs, and he settled against the cradle of her body.

She was damp from his scent. From the rush of amnis spreading from his body to hers. It burst like tiny kisses over her skin. But even as her body came alive, Lucien waited. He lay poised over her, his mouth against her neck, his arms holding him utterly still as his amnis aroused her and drove her toward madness.

"Take it," Makeda said. "Now, Lucien."

"I want everything," he whispered. "For I am faint with love, most beautiful of women."

"Then bite." She closed her eyes and gave in to her instincts. "Take everything."

He nudged her knee up, opening her as he entered her. Then his fangs slowly pierced the skin of her neck, and everything she was became his. He fisted her hair in his hands, angling her head to the side as he ravished her.

"Lucien!" She cried out as he drank her blood. She could feel her amnis enter him, shooting through his body as he rocked inside her. It was... otherworldly. He released her neck and thrust up, blood staining her lips when he took her mouth. He hooked an arm around her thigh and drove harder.

"Now," he said.

Knowing what he wanted, Makeda yanked his head to the side and struck. He cried out and arched his back as he came. She could feel his pleasure as her own, and she groaned against his neck. Lucien grabbed her hand and bit her again, sucking on the sensitive skin of her wrist as he drove her higher and higher.

He didn't stop. He kept going.

Makeda felt as if she were on the edge of leaving her body. Her head swam as their blood and amnis mingled. She sucked harder, feeling the pull of his lips as he took her blood. As she took his.

Don't stop. Never stop.

She came in a violent wave that drew the water from the air and wet her skin. She kept coming as Lucien roared his final release and collapsed against her. The rock beneath them trembled, shuddered, then stilled.

He remained in her, the frenzy at rest. Hunger assuaged for the moment. Lucien kissed her over and over till their lips were swollen and aching. Makeda held him trapped with her legs. Bound by her arms. She didn't want to separate from him even for a minute. His blood lived in her as hers lived in him.

They were one.

They were eternal.

Chapter Twenty-One

Crotone, Italy

The sea was around them, held back by the ancient stone of the fortress that had been Andreas's prison and Lorenzo di Andros's grave. Fires burned in the meeting room, food and wine had been laid out, but the scent of old blood could not be erased. Kato sat at the table, Saba at his side as Filomena Salvatore and Emil Conti, the vampire lords of Naples and Rome, sat across from them.

Lucien was aware of his mate when he entered the old castle. Aware of her when he sat down at the table. Aware of her movements when she waited in another part of the castle with Ziri and Arosh. His awareness threatened to overwhelm him.

In another time and another place, he would have stolen her away for weeks. He'd have hidden them in a cave by the sea and let their blood settle as they learned each other and learned who and what they were together. He was no longer alone. She lived in his blood as he lived in hers.

But they didn't have that time or that space. Their love had been birthed in violence and politics and strife.

You are my peace.

She'd whispered that in Lucien's ear the night before when she'd taken his blood before she slept at dawn. Lucien had held her as she closed her eyes and he listened to her breath still. Her body fell silent. The only thing he could feel was his blood living in her body, her amnis woven inextricably with his own.

He prayed he would always be her peace, because she had become life to him.

"This council you speak of," Filomena was saying. "How does it differ from the Athenian council already in place? You ask for tribute and treasure, but what is it you offer to us?"

Lucien would have thought the vampire impertinent if she'd spoken with the attitude he'd expected. But the question, though unforeseen, was spoken with sincerity. Filomena was a new ruler, slowly breaking the insular Neapolitan court of its paranoid tendencies, and Lucien sensed she truly wanted to know what Kato and Saba were offering in exchange for her fealty.

"We offer stability for a region that has too long been rife with infighting and petty jealousies," Saba said, looking toward Emil Conti. "And opportunity to trade without the onerous hand of the Greek. We are more reasonable, and we have no quarrel with either of you."

Lucien knew both Filomena Salvatore and Emil Conti had been hit hard by Laskaris's tariffs through the Bosphorus because both were heavily invested in shipping.

Conti said, "Trade concerns are of utmost importance to my people. But they are not the only consideration."

The Roman regent had taken over from Livia when her treachery with Elixir had been exposed and was widely regarded as one of the most stabilizing and influential European vampire powers. But even with his reputation, he had not been able to completely wipe out the Elixir virus, and the whole of the Iberian Peninsula had been affected.

"I also offer you a cure," Saba said. "A cure *only* I can offer."

Conti looked directly at Lucien. "Does it work?"

"Yes." The fact that they were still waiting to hear could not color his response. At all.

"There," Saba said. "You have heard my son. And while this might mean a loss of the afflicted from your aegis, once you have an alliance with Alitea, there is no true loss. Your sons and daughters will be safe. Your businesses will flourish."

Conti looked between Saba and Kato. "You seek to copy the Eastern model of rule. That is not how the Western world has ever operated."

"The elders of Penglai govern their region with an iron hand," Kato said. "This has leant stability but also a lack of independence."

"Independence cannot be taken for granted," Conti said. "Athens is no longer the power it once was. Laskaris and I have quarreled regarding tariffs, but I have no dispute with the rest of the council you want to usurp. Why should we offer our loyalty and resources to a court that has faded from influence? You would have us trade sovereignty for assumed stability in a region you have not ruled for over a thousand years."

He saw Saba curl her lip in irritation. This was not going as Lucien had planned. He'd thought the meeting in Crotone was no more than a formality. Filomena and Emil would make their demands, negotiations would commence, and the Iberian Peninsula would be a powerful gem in Kato and Saba's growing crown.

Filomena looked between Saba and Emil. Lucien noted the calculating glint before she turned to Kato and said, "Kato, most ancient of kings, you have my fealty and the backing of my court."

Kato held out his hand, and Filomena kissed it. Lucien could hear waves battering the rocks outside.

What was she playing at? And what would Emil say? Lucien had expected their unity in the matter, but Filomena was a new leader and still testing the boundaries of her power. What did she know about Emil that Lucien didn't?

"I challenge you," Emil said to Kato.

Lucien tried not to react, but it was difficult. Formal duels happened so rarely that the practice was nearly extinct. But then Emil was a Roman, and an old one. This wouldn't be the first challenge he'd offered, nor were his words spoken rashly.

It was, however, a hopeless challenge.

Nevertheless, Kato treated it seriously. "I accept your challenge. Meet me on the ramparts in ten minutes, and I will teach you humility, child."

Emil stood and left the room without another word. Filomena followed him, a smile ghosting her face.

"Did you expect this?" Saba asked Lucien.

"No."

"Neither did I," Kato said. "But it is not unwelcome. I have not faced an opponent of my own kind for many years. It is better I face Emil Conti before I face Laskaris."

Lucien realized Kato had not been in battle since his recovery from the Elixir virus. "*Theio*, will you—"

"I'll be fine." Kato smiled. "Bring your pretty mate up and have her watch. This will be an education for her."

Lucien positioned himself next to Makeda as they watched Emil and Kato stand across from each other on the rampart on the far side of the courtyard. Lucien, Makeda, Filomena, and both their entourages stood to witness the duel. The water vampires had stripped to nothing but breeches, and water coated their chests. Emil, smaller and leaner than Kato, was still a fierce and able fighter. His body was scarred from his human life, unexpected for the nobleman Lucien knew he had been.

They stood on either end of the high wall separating the fortress from the sea. Waves churned beneath them with the occasional waterspout shooting high above their heads. The air was quiet as Ziri hovered over the gathered immortals.

"He can't win," Makeda said under her breath. "Even I know that."

"No."

"Will Kato kill him? I thought Emil Conti was one of the good guys."

"Good and bad aren't terms I'd use for either of them," Lucien said. "But Emil has challenged Kato. He must know death is a possibility."

"Isn't Emil a friend of Giovanni Vecchio's? And isn't he a friend of Saba's?"

"Yes."

She shook her head. "I don't understand vampire politics at all."

"Watch," Lucien said. "This is strategy, not aggression."

No words were spoken, but Emil held his hands out and reached for his element, throwing a spear of water toward Kato that would knock him off the rampart and into the courtyard below.

The water never hit the ancient. He held up a palm, and the water shot back to Emil, who threw it with his other hand while grabbing for another wave from the rocks below. Lucien recognized Emil's strategy at once. He could never match the older vampire in power, but he might stand a chance with speed. If he could hit Kato with a flurry, he might last long enough to accomplish whatever purpose he had. The Roman was surprisingly quick. As he moved, even Lucien had trouble tracking him.

The spear of water circled up and over their heads, tossed back and forth by Emil and Kato while the ancient heaved his shoulders, pulling the waves higher and higher against the old fortress walls.

Lucien saw Arosh and Saba watching from the opposite wall. Saba looked curious but unconcerned. Arosh simply looked bored.

Kato lifted his arms, and the whole of the ocean seemed to follow him, rising above their heads before it crashed down over Emil. The younger vampire held up both arms, holding back the water longer than Lucien would have predicted.

"Oh my God," Makeda breathed out. "How...?"

"Age and practice."

The water crashed over Emil, but it did not carry him out to sea. He flipped and rose on a crested wave, riding the water toward the old sea god. Kato held up a hand and the water halted, but Emil didn't. He leapt toward Kato, twisting in the air above him and falling past the edge of the rampart and into the water.

For long seconds there was only the crash of waves below.

Then another jet appeared, shooting Emil up and back onto the rampart before Kato shoved him back into the sea with a grasping wave. Emil came up again, but Lucien could see he was tiring.

"Yield," Kato shouted.

"No!" Emil rose again, flipping over Kato's head and aiming a spear of water at the old vampire's back. Then another. Then another. The triple shots were too fast for Kato to dodge and they knocked him over. The old vampire landed in a cushion of water and sprang back to his feet, turning as Emil brought another spear, this one aimed at Kato's face.

"Yield," Kato commanded again, batting the shot to the side, "and I will spare your children."

Emil dove into the sea again, only to rise on another wave, this one even larger.

"He's far stronger than I thought," Lucien said.

"And determined," Makeda added.

Emil's wave broke over Kato, but it did not knock him down. He stood with the water lifting him from the rampart, the waves crashing over the edge of stone and splashing into the courtyard below.

The ancient water vampire was laughing. "Yield, young one! Give me your fealty. For I would have you as a friend, Emil Conti."

Emil hung from one of the old towers, water dripping from his black hair and coating his skin. Hanging from the tower put him face-to-face with the ancient as the water lifted him.

"Make me second only to you," Emil said, "and I will give you my glad fealty, ancient king."

Kato's eyes narrowed as he examined the vampire who was still hanging on, unyielding before the awesome power of the ancients.

"You will be challenged," Kato said.

"I will face those challenges as I have faced you."

Kato spread his hands, and the water lowered him to the old stone rampart. "Yield to me, Emil Conti, and you will be second to me in power over the ancient sea."

Emil jumped down, walked over, and bent to kiss Kato's outstretched hand. "My lord."

"You are a worthy opponent. Rise and greet your king."

Emil stood, and Kato bent to kiss both his cheeks.

"What just happened?" Makeda said. "Kato's not going to kill him?"

"Emil is very smart," Lucien said. "And possibly more rash than

I'd anticipated. But it worked out for him in the end."

"How?"

"All the others bowed without challenge," Lucien said. "By challenging Kato—even if he didn't win—he has risen above the others in Kato's estimation and reputation in our world. The court in Rome will be second only to Alitea when Kato and the others take control."

Lucien put his arm around Makeda and steered her back toward the fortress. The air was damp and misty, churned up by the battle they'd witnessed. A fire would be very welcome.

"Kato could have killed Emil," Makeda said. "He wasn't even struggling."

Lucien kissed Makeda's temple. "But he didn't. And Kato respects him more for taking the chance. Plus, it gave Kato an opportunity to stretch his muscles."

"A practice run before Laskaris?" Makeda shook her head. "Nothing in this world is simple, is it?"

"Simple?" Lucien glanced over his shoulder to see Emil and Kato deep in conversation, their earlier fight forgotten. "What would be the fun in simple?"

Two hours before dawn, rough agreements with both Naples and Rome were settled, and warriors from both courts were traveling to Crotone to join Kato and Saba. Emil had left after promising a large yacht to take their party across the Ionian Sea, and Filomena had departed after him. Lucien was feeling remarkably sanguine about their upcoming assault on the fortified compound of Alitea, but Makeda was pacing the ramparts.

"We should have heard by now," she said. "We should have heard something."

"We've been traveling all over the place," Lucien pointed out. "If a messenger was sent, he might not be able to find us."

"But the pilots all have mobile phones. Dr. McTierney has their numbers."

The fact that they'd heard nothing about the success of the Elixir trial was beginning to worry Lucien as well. Saba had staked her authority partly on the ability to cure the afflicted. If it came to nothing, her position would be weakened, and her word would no longer be seen as reliable.

"I could try to call Carwyn," Lucien said.

"There's no phone here! When you said it was medieval, I had no idea how literal you were being."

He shrugged. "Send a message to the pilots to call them."

"I did! He hasn't sent a message back." Makeda kicked the stone wall, and Lucien gently moved it back into place with a touch. "What is McTierney thinking?" she griped.

"Makeda?"

"What?"

"I'm not going to do this."

"*What?*"

"Placate you when you're determined to be irritable." He walked toward the open door of the tower that led back to their chamber. "I can think of far better ways to make you relax if you're interested. If not, then I'll leave you to rant."

Her eyes flashed, but she didn't take the hand he held out.

"Fine." He turned his back to her and walked to the head of the stairs.

"Lucien."

He turned.

"I hate that I'm not running this trial. Everything about it is out of my control. I can't monitor the patients. I have no idea whether a slight change in a single drug could affect how the treatment goes."

"I know."

"I hate feeling helpless!"

He walked to her and put a hand on her cheek. "My love, I know."

"How can I be so powerful now and so much weaker at the same time?"

He brought his arms around her and forced her stiff body into a hug. "Something has to keep you humble, Dr. Abel. You'd probably become insufferable otherwise."

"You mean like you?"

He couldn't stop the smile. "We'll know when we know, Makeda." Lucien drew her mouth to his in a kiss, hoping to sooth her troubled spirit.

"Very philosophical, Doctor," said a voice from the courtyard.

Lucien looked down, and even in the gloom and shadows, he could spot the flash of bright hibiscus and hula girls.

"Are you still wearing those hideous shirts?" he called. "Hasn't your wife confiscated them by now?"

Quick bursts of fire flew from a small woman at Carwyn's side to the torches set in the walls of the fortress. "I burn one up and he finds another," Brigid said. "I've given up at this point."

Lucien let out a breath. He'd been a little wary that Giovanni Vecchio might join them despite the scholar's normal aversion to violence and politics. If Carwyn was around, Vecchio often was as well.

But so was Arosh. And two male fire vampires in one war party was never a good idea.

Luckily, instead of his friend, the Welshman had brought his wife. Brigid and Arosh would rub each other the wrong way—most fire vampires did—but they weren't likely to kill each other. Especially with Carwyn to keep Brigid occupied and Saba to distract Arosh.

Lucien turned his head toward the slow, familiar step he heard on the stairs. Baojia walked through a shadowed doorway, his eyes locked on Makeda. She turned immediately and flew to his arms.

"Heya, Mak," he said quietly, wrapping his arms around Lucien's mate.

Makeda laughed and cried at the same time, holding on to her sire with both arms. "I didn't know you were coming. I'm so glad you're here."

Lucien couldn't resent the obvious joy and affection between them. Baojia might not have been Makeda's master, but his blood still flowed in her veins. When Lucien walked toward his old friend, he felt nothing but profound gratitude. For Makeda's life. For Baojia's friendship.

Baojia released Makeda and held his hand out to Lucien, but Lucien enveloped him in a hug.

"Thank you," he said quietly. "I can't even tell you how much."

"So you finally figured it out, huh?"

Lucien pulled away. "You knew."

"Of course I did," Baojia said. "I'm not an old codger like you, but I've got eyes in my head." He smiled at Makeda. "I'm happy for you both."

"We didn't know you were coming," Makeda said.

"I made a promise a long time ago," Baojia said. "Someone called it in." He squeezed Makeda's hand. "Plus I had to make sure you hadn't killed Lucien yet."

Makeda laughed and wiped her eyes as Carwyn and Brigid joined them on the rampart.

"So what now?" Makeda asked. "Are we the JV team or something?"

Lucien frowned. "The what?"

Makeda shook her head. "Never mind. We don't have a wind vampire anyway."

"Says who?"

Lucien looked up and saw the ancient, birdlike woman perched on the top of a tower. He hadn't heard her or felt her when she arrived. But then concealment was one of Tenzin's skills.

"I told you someone called in a favor," Baojia said. "Apparently she didn't trust me to follow through."

"Don't be offended," Tenzin said. "Besides, my presence here serves several purposes. None of which you want to be without."

Lucien said, "Are you and Ziri going to argue?"

Tenzin curled her lip. "Is *he* here?"

"He's part of the new council," Makeda said. "Who are you?"

Tenzin flew down and danced in the air before Makeda.

"Officially? I'm a representative of the elders of Penglai Island, who will establish a relationship with the new council of Alitea as soon as Laskaris finally kicks it, thereby solidifying the council's position as the equal and balancing power to the elders in the East."

"Not that they need your stamp of approval," muttered Lucien.

"And unofficially?" Makeda asked.

"Here I am now"—Tenzin bared her odd, raptor-claw fangs —"entertain me."

Lucien tried not to shudder. Sometimes the old wind vampire was amusing. Other times... she was just creepy.

"Well, until we can provide Tenzin with entertainment," Carwyn said, "perhaps you'd like to hear the news from Brenden."

Lucien and Makeda's eyes both locked on Carwyn.

"What?" Makeda asked. "What is it? Is everything all right? I've been waiting to hear if the transplants—"

"Good news and bad, my girl." Carwyn gave Lucien a rueful smile. "Isn't that always the way? But I think in this case, the good outweighs the bad."

Chapter Twenty-Two

"The good news." Carwyn started talking once they'd taken shelter inside and gathered around a fire Brigid lit in one of the fireplaces in Lucien and Makeda's quarters. "It's working on the immortals. Both the peripheral..."

"Peripheral stem cell transplantation?" Makeda prompted.

"Yes, that one. Both that and the marrow transplants are working."

Lucien asked, "Equally well?"

Carwyn drew a folder from the messenger bag Brigid carried. "Well, you can see his full report here, but—"

Makeda snatched the folder from him and opened it.

Carwyn's eyes widened. "The short answer is yes. It appears they're both working equally well."

She scanned the report from McTierney. "Replication proceeded even faster than I'd predicted."

Lucien looked over her shoulder. "The marrow actually replicated more slowly than the PBSCT. That's surprising."

"Not significantly so," she said. "We're only dealing with six test subjects. It's possible it will vary with the patients."

"But since peripheral cells are so much easier to collect—"

"Treatment on a larger scale could go much faster than we'd anticipated." Makeda looked up. Her natural skepticism couldn't temper the smile on her face. "Lucien, it's working."

Brigid said, "And it's working quickly. The treated vampires are having more than a little trouble with the transition—all but two of them were water vampires—but they're recovering."

"They're like newborns," Carwyn said. "Murphy is working with my daughter Deirdre to mentor them until they can come to Saba."

"Bloodlust?"

"That's the one thing that doesn't seem to be affected," Brigid said. "All of them have newborn hunger, but none of them have uncontrollable bloodlust."

"It's behavioral more than biological," Makeda said. "Because they've already developed the coping strategies to be around humans, they've conquered the bloodlust. The hunger is something they can control because they're already used to the scent of humans."

"Speaking of coping strategies." Brigid nodded at Makeda. "I'd never expect a newborn to be as rational or focused as you. I'm practically a baby myself, so I remember that stage. Whatever you're doing, keep doing it."

Lucien put an arm around her shoulders. "Makeda is an imminently rational scientist, Brigid. She won't allow herself to lose control."

"Imminently rational?" Carwyn poked Brigid's side. "Well, there's your problem, love."

"Says the man who pretends professional wrestling is real," Brigid said.

Makeda didn't feel worthy of the praise. "When you're forced to adapt to something quickly, you don't have a choice," she said. "None of this has gone according to plan. I'm just coping." She flipped to the next page of the report and felt her heart sink. "And there's the bad news."

Lucien leaned closer. "What is it?"

"The human patients."

"Damn."

Makeda skimmed Dr. McTierney's notes. The team in Ireland had followed roughly the same protocols with the human and immortal patients. The chemotherapy. The stem cell treatments. "None of the treatments are killing the virus."

Lucien took a deep breath and squeezed the arm around her shoulders. "We knew it might not work. They were always more at risk than the immortals. At least we know one thing that will work for them."

"It's not fair."

"I know, *yene konjo.*"

Brigid sat up straight. "What will work? Why haven't you tried it yet if you think it will work? Why hasn't Brenden been trying—"

"Saba's blood," Carwyn said, lacing Brigid's hand with his. "It's Saba's blood, isn't it? That's the only thing that will cure the virus."

Lucien and Makeda both nodded.

"Damn," Baojia said, rubbing a hand over his eyes. "So in order for a human to be cured of Elixir..."

"They have to take Saba's blood."

Tenzin said, "But humans can't take vampire blood."

"Not unless they're turned," Lucien said. "Humans with Elixir poisoning *can* be saved. But only if they turn. And only if Saba sires them."

"So they die or they're made a vampire?" Brigid said. "That's not fair."

"Nothing about this is fair," Baojia said. "At least it's an option they didn't have before. We give them the option. They take it or they don't. It's more than what we had before."

"How do we know it'll work?" Carwyn asked. "No offense to the brilliant minds here, but other vampires have tried. They've drained the infected blood and given their humans their own. It didn't work. They died of blood loss because their bodies couldn't make the transition."

"They didn't use Saba's blood," Makeda said. "She's the only one with antibodies that work."

"Is she?" Tenzin's eyes glinted. "I wonder."

"She's the only one we've tested," Lucien said. "So she's the only one that matters." Lucien rose. "Okay, it's getting near dawn. Does everyone have a secure room? Baojia, if you don't, you're welcome to rest in our quarters, but the rest of you need to leave."

Tenzin smirked. "Protective much, Thrax?"

"Yes," he said. "Not that you would understand."

"Now that's just mean."

Makeda watched the tension between the two vampires. Lucien

had told her Tenzin was thousands of years older than he was, but somehow she seemed more childlike. Or perhaps she was simply more playful than Makeda's serious mate.

"We've all been taken care of," Brigid said. "Saba's people are frighteningly efficient."

"I believe one of Inaya's daughters has taken over hosting logistics," Makeda said. "Every place we go, we gather more people."

Carwyn asked, "What is the plan for Athens?"

"Boat," Lucien said. "But we'll talk logistics tomorrow night. For now, all of you get out."

Makeda woke to Lucien stroking up and down her spine with long fingers. He was awake but silent. She let herself sink into the comfort of his body. The warmth. The possession. The long, smooth line of his legs and his skin pressed against hers. His blood stirred in her, and she felt her heart beat twice.

"What are you thinking of?" she asked quietly.

"Infected humans."

Knowing what must have been weighing on his mind, Makeda asked, "Will she agree to it?"

"I don't know."

They'd never directly asked Saba about siring humans affected by Elixir, but Makeda had a feeling the ancient immortal knew it was a possibility. Saba was too intelligent to not see the connection. If her blood was the only thing that could heal immortals, why would it be different for humans? They'd hoped, but the backup plan had always been Saba.

"She can be... mercurial. At best," Lucien said. "It will likely depend on why the human was infected. Our patients in California who were infected against their will? She would have sired them if they wanted it. Young people who took Elixir looking for a new thrill? I doubt it."

"That's not how medicine works," she said. "We don't get to pick our patients."

"But this isn't medicine. It's Saba. And siring a human in the traditional manner—even if that human is weakened from Elixir poisoning—has a myriad of consequences."

"Can we do the stem cell treatment instead?" Makeda asked. "Is there any reason the procedure we use on the vampires wouldn't work on humans?"

"Maybe." He frowned. "If it's not blood, it might... It's worth looking into."

"And we will." Makeda took a deep breath and said, "When this is over, you and I will look at all the options. At least we have one solution, Lucien. We didn't have that before."

"I know." Lucien's hand tightened on her shoulder. "I want to crush Laskaris. Wipe him from the planet. From history. I want his name to be forgotten."

"You will."

"No, I imagine Kato will. Or Saba." He huffed. "I doubt they'll give me the chance. But this evil he spread over the world..."

"Saba will end it."

"I hope so." He hugged her closer. "I hope it's not too late."

Makeda thought of the ship Emil Conti was sending from his port in Civitavecchia to Crotone. The immortal army Kato had gathered would travel by boat from the Ionian Sea to the Aegean. There was little doubt the council of Athens knew they were coming, but no one seemed to know what that would mean for the physical assault on the island.

"I'm glad Baojia is here," Lucien said.

"Because it'll mean there's someone else watching out for me?"

"Yes."

She shook her head. "One-track mind."

He sat up, taking her with him. "We should feed and join the others. No doubt there will be more excitement tonight, especially now that Carwyn and Tenzin are here."

"Lucien?"

"Hmm?"

"When this is over, what will we do?"

"Go back to work. Between the two of us, I know we'll find the answers to put all this to rest." He paused, then he kissed her hard. "And then we'll do whatever we want."

❖

Makeda watched Lucien from the corner of the room. When it came to planning battle, she had little role to play. She felt Baojia settle next to her and cross his arms, watching the older vampires argue over a map.

"You're not in on this?" she asked.

"Me?" He shook his head. "I'm a grunt. Nobody's going to listen to me."

"I thought you did a good job protecting the compound in California."

"Except the little mistake about missing the Greek agent who was living right next door to you?"

"Well..." She shrugged. "Nobody's perfect."

"I'm surprised Katya didn't have my head for that one," he muttered. "It was a mistake to not do a deeper background check."

"What's done is done."

He paused. "Are you really okay? I know you didn't want this. Natalie would tell you I've been in a mood for months now worrying about you."

Makeda took a long breath. "I never would have chosen this," she said. "And if I hadn't..." She watched Lucien. "I would have missed him. Missed all of it. So... maybe I need to be thanking my dear friend Philip after all."

"That would be easier if he wasn't crab food."

She sniffed. "I can't find it in my heart to be sorry about that."

He nudged her with an elbow. "You're going to make an excellent vampire."

"Once I get the hang of it?"

"You're already most of the way there."

She turned back to watch the arguing immortals. "How is Katya?"

"Treating your family with kid gloves at the moment. I'd expect that to continue. Nobody wants to piss off Lucien and his mom right now."

"Has she heard about the Elixir treatments?"

Baojia tried to hide his smile but he couldn't. "Everyone in the world heard about the Elixir treatment even before it started to work. So yes, she's heard about it. And no, she's not happy."

"There's no money in stem cell therapy."

"No. But the fact that you didn't cure it is soothing the pain."

She frowned. "What?"

"Testing kits, Mak. People are still ordering testing kits. Until this virus is completely dead, they'll be ordering a lot of them, and Katya's the only one that has them. So while curing the virus might have been the goal... maybe just detecting it will pay the bills better."

Makeda shook her head. "Leave it to Katya to find a way to make money off of failure."

"Not failure," Baojia said. "Not even close."

Lucien met with "the B-Team," as Baojia had jokingly started to refer to them, after the meeting. Carwyn, Brigid, and Tenzin joined them in Lucien and Makeda's room again.

"We're splitting into two teams," Lucien said. "The main group—with the four ancients, Makeda, and me—will be taking out Alitea with Kato's new army."

Tenzin said. "And us?"

"The plants," Brigid said. "All the factories. They want us to take out the plants making Elixir, don't they?"

"It's possible Laskaris has already begun to move his production, but I don't think so. He's too arrogant, and Ziri said his informants report Livia's original plants are still going."

Carwyn said, "Fleeing would make him appear weak. He can't do that and retain any of his allies. Not to mention the other members of the council."

Baojia raised a hand. "Problem."

"Yes?"

"Do we know if Elixir can be weaponized?"

No one had an answer.

Lucien said, "I don't *think* so, but..."

Makeda immediately saw the issue. "If it can, we need to make sure anyone going in is safe. Baojia, Lucien, and I have living sires. Carwyn, Brigid, and Tenzin?"

"I do," Brigid said. "Carwyn, you're out."

"I can—"

"Forget it," Lucien said. "Brigid's right. If we need an earth vampire, I'll go in and you can take my place with Kato and Saba."

Carwyn sulked. "Fine."

"Tenzin," Lucien asked, "what are you thinking?"

"I'll risk it." She did a somersault in the air. "I'm a little curious if I can catch it, to be honest."

"Let's not make a game of it, shall we?" Lucien looked at Makeda. "I want you to stay with Carwyn and the ancients."

She was shocked. And a little offended. "What? Why? If you're going to the plants—"

"Then there will be at least one of us there to make sure we've taken everything out," he said. "But I want you with Kato and Carwyn. Not only can they protect you, but there will likely be far more humans at the plants than on Alitea."

"That's true," Tenzin said. "Hunting is always done off the island. There are very few humans there."

"You'll be more focused if you stay with the others," Lucien said. "And I trust Carwyn to watch out for you."

"But—"

"Makeda, this is the best option." He turned and handed a printout to Brigid. "These are the blueprints I have. Do you think we can find anything better?"

Carwyn held out his arm to Makeda, who was still standing

behind Lucien, gaping at him.

"Hello," he said. "My name is Carwyn ap Bryn, and I'll be your earth vampire for the battle."

Makeda forced a smile, but she was angry that Lucien hadn't even consulted her before he'd made his decision. She might not be as experienced a soldier as he was, but she had a good idea what she could handle. As Lucien broke away to strategize with Brigid, Tenzin, and Baojia, Makeda stayed behind, sitting next to Carwyn.

"Be kind," Carwyn whispered. "Taking out the plants is more dangerous than going into battle with four of the most ancient immortals in the world."

"I know." *That's why I want to go with him.*

She was sitting on the rocks below the fortress, watching the fishing boats as they made their way into the open ocean. Dawn was two hours away, and their navigation lights dotted the harbor as the boats headed south into the black water.

She felt Lucien walk down to her. He sat on the damp rocks and leaned his elbows on his knees.

"We'll leave tomorrow evening."

Makeda was silent.

"Are you angry with me?"

"I don't like being ignored."

"I'm not ignoring you."

"Disregarded then."

He reached over and took one of her hands, playing her fingers between his own. "Do you understand why?"

"I understand you're being very high-handed and I'm the junior partner here, so everyone is ignoring me."

He sighed. "I'm sorry. You're right. You have every right to be angry."

"But not sorry enough to take me with you."

"No."

She fell silent and watched the boats.

Lucien's fingers suddenly gripped tight. He folded both his hands around her own and brought them to his mouth, pressing his lips against her fingertips.

"Lucien?"

"It's an odd sensation," he said quietly, "to give your heart completely to another. I feel as if my soul is tied up with yours. If something happened to you, I genuinely don't think I would have any motivation to continue living."

"Stop," she whispered. "That's not fair."

"But it's true." He relaxed his hands. "I can live with your anger, Makeda. As long as I don't have to live without you. I don't have a human family. I don't have offspring who depend on me. I have only Saba, and soon she will have many other children. But if something happened to you, I would have nothing."

Makeda was reminded of the angry, arrogant man she'd first met, the focused vampire who lived only for his patients. The intense man with a shadow of despair behind his eyes. "Have you ever tried to end your life?"

"Yes."

Fear stilled her heart. "Why?"

"I was sick. It wasn't just that I was losing my mind, though that was bad enough. I was... tired. I'm *so* old." His face, though unlined, had never looked more ancient. "I've seen nearly everything you can imagine. I've had thousands of lovers and friends, and most of them are gone. I was so very *tired*, Makeda."

"You can't be tired." She felt the tears at the corners of her eyes. "Don't you know? I'm depending on you to keep me company."

"My mother saved me. Finding a cure for the Elixir gave me a focus. Baojia and Natalie made me curious again. But it was you, Makeda..." He smiled a slow smile and pulled one of her curls. "You brought me back to life, *yene konjo*."

"You lived to irritate me?"

He shrugged. "Everyone has to have a purpose. Do you understand why I don't want to imagine the world without you?"

She turned and kissed him slowly and thoroughly. "I will be your purpose. And you will be mine. We will live together. Explore together. You can show me your world."

"There are wonders," he said. "Things you would hardly believe."

"I want to see them all."

He nodded. "I can live with that."

"You'd better."

They fell silent again, but this time they were in each other's arms.

"You're still angry with me, aren't you?" he asked.

"Take me to bed and give me a reason not to be."

She felt him smile against her temple. His fangs were already down. "You drive a hard bargain, Dr. Abel."

"Then you'd better deliver, Dr. Thrax."

Chapter Twenty-Three

They took the plane to Bulgaria after a heated farewell between Lucien and Makeda. He left his new mate in his mother's care and flew away with an unstable Irish fire vampire and a water vampire as reluctant to leave Italy as he was.

The crazy wind vampire refused to board the plane and insisted on meeting them in Plovdiv.

"I don't like it any more than you do, but it was the right call," Baojia said, leaning up against the insulated bulkhead of Giovanni Vecchio's plane. "Carwyn will keep her safe."

"She's angry with me."

Baojia smiled. "Would you like me to list the number and ways in which I've pissed my mate off in the short four years we've been together? Makeda will get over it. According to Brigid's intel, the human presence is high, even in the middle of the night. You made the right decision."

Lucien tapped his foot. "Laskaris will be expecting something."

"He won't be expecting Tenzin and Brigid."

Lucien shook his head. "But he'll be expecting *something*. Our move is overdue. Saba suggested we take out the plants after we left Turkey."

"You didn't, which could play to our advantage."

"Or it could mean he's had more time to prepare."

Baojia shrugged. "I'm not in charge of this operation, so I'm just following orders at this point."

"We should have brought more people."

"I don't think so." Baojia closed his eyes and crossed his arms over his chest. "Rest, Lucien. Going in circles will accomplish nothing."

❖

Makeda watched the plane take off with Saba standing behind her. The faint scent of the pilots and ground crew lingered in the air, but Makeda was learning to ignore it.

"He'll be fine," Saba said. "Do you think I'd send my favorite son off into a battle he couldn't win?"

"My sire and my mate are both on that plane. Do you expect me not to worry?"

"I expect you to focus on the task at hand," she said. "And part of that means leaving your worry here and focusing on what you must do to ensure our victory."

Makeda faced Saba. "And what is that? Because so far, no one has given me any combat training. As far as I know, all I'm supposed to do is stay out of the way. I'm not sure why anyone even wants me there."

"Because it will be easier to protect you if you're with us, of course. And it will be your job to address the court. Tell them I hold the key to their healing should any of them become infected."

Makeda blinked. "You act as if they're just going to let us walk up to the gates and reason with them."

"They will." Saba shrugged. "They have to."

"Says who?"

"Protocol. Tradition."

Makeda said, "Saba, why do you think that means anything to the council of Athens at this point? They've poisoned humans and undermined vampire governments all over Europe. They've killed important people and made enemies everywhere, all in a quest to regain some kind of importance to the larger vampire world."

"They'll open the gates to us because we're old like them." She smiled, both fangs down. "Plus they know we can rip the gates off should we want to."

Lucien could feel her hovering. "Just ask what you want to ask and leave, Tenzin."

"I can't leave. I promised Giovanni I'd help with this." She landed beside him, pouting. "I do have better things I could be doing, you know."

"I'm so sorry we're interrupting your busy social schedule."

She leaned toward him and stared at his face. "You're so much like him, you know."

"Who?"

"Giovanni. You're very... What's the word my life coach would use? Uptight. You're uptight."

Lucien closed his eyes. "You have a life coach?"

"Kind of. So your human—"

"I don't have a human."

She waved a hand. "Your new mate. She was human recently, yes?"

"Yes."

"And you changed her against her will?"

He snarled a little. "It's a complicated story."

"They always are." She lifted off the ground a little. "But tell me, how long did it take for her to forgive you? Not long, I'm assuming, but you are mates, so that could have something to do with it. Were you having sex with her when she was human?"

"I am not going to share any of this with you."

"Fine, ignore the sex question. But really, how long did it take?" she asked. "I'm asking for a friend."

Lucien lifted one eyebrow. "Right."

"What? I am."

He rose and went to find Brigid. She was studying a schematic that had been delivered to them when they'd landed. They were currently holed up in a warehouse that smelled like ash. Lucien suspected it belonged to the Russian fire vampire, Oleg, but he didn't know, and frankly, he didn't really want to. His mother's connections were vast. It didn't mean he had to keep track of them.

"What do we know?" he asked Brigid.

"According to our little spies—who have no reason to lie—the lightest shift happens right before dawn."

"Makes sense."

"So we'll go in right after shift change when everyone is getting oriented." She pointed to the roof. "Easiest access is there."

"What about the ground?"

Brigid shook her head. "Concrete slab six feet deep. Livia built the factory and she built it with vampires in mind."

"Six feet is nothing," Lucien said. "I can break through that."

"But can you do it quietly?" Brigid asked. "Because I'm married to one of you earth boys, and nothing he does is quiet."

Lucien shrugged. "Stealth and breaking rocks rarely go together."

"The roof." She pointed to it again. "There's a helicopter pad and roof access that was left over from the previous owner. Livia didn't use it—neither did Laskaris—but it's there. Tenzin will take you and me up while Baojia secures the water system."

"The water system?"

"According to our source, Laskaris rigged the plant to blow up and dump any remaining Elixir into the local water system. Kind of a last 'fuck you' to humanity, I guess. Baojia will take care of that while you identify what I need to burn up and Tenzin kills anyone who gets in our way."

"Sounds like a fun night."

She shrugged. "It's not political wrangling followed by death and destruction, but it should keep us busy for a couple of hours."

"Does Tenzin know that some of these humans are likely to be hired guns and maintenance staff? We shouldn't kill them just because they're ignorant of who they're working for."

Brigid smiled. "She's not as ruthless as she pretends to be."

"I heard that!" came a voice from across the warehouse. "And yes, I am."

Lucien couldn't see her in the shadows, but clearly she was listening. "Don't kill the humans just for fun, Tenzin."

"I'm not a sociopath." She paused. "Or would that be a

psychopath? I'm honestly not sure what the difference is."

"Don't kill anyone unless they try to kill you," he said. "How's that?"

"What about the scientists who are making this poison?"

"I'll take care of them," he said. "Right now let's focus on shutting this down." He turned back to Brigid. "How many plants?"

"Two more. Oleg has taken care of them. This is the largest and the one farthest from his territory. It's also the one where the final Elixir is produced. The others are satellite plants that make some of the serums that are blended here with the vampire blood to activate the formula."

Lucien looked over all Brigid's plans, but he couldn't find fault with any of them. "This looks good. Clean. In and out with minimum engagement."

"High praise coming from you, General."

"Who told you about that?"

"Carwyn." She grinned. "And I thought you were just an egghead."

Lucien knew that Brigid Connor was a girl that Ioan had loved like a daughter. The fact she was immortal and appeared to be happy would have pleased Lucien's old friend. "Ioan would have been very proud of you," he said. "He loved you so much."

The swift grief rose up in her eyes, but just as quickly, it was wiped away by fierce pride. "Thanks. I know."

They boarded the boats in Crotone, vampires of various elements and wide allegiances, all joined in a single purpose: depose the Greeks and set up a new world order... which was actually more like an old world order.

"This is mad," Makeda said. "Have you ever heard of an army going off to war with this little stealth?"

Carwyn said, "You have to remember, all of them conquered in a time before stealth technology and radio silence. When they needed to communicate, they used horns and drums."

"But the Athenian council—"

"Is expecting them," Carwyn said. "Yes. And they know that. Look at them, Makeda. Do any of the ancients look concerned?"

Arosh lounged on the deck with two nubile young vampires— Elia's daughter, Kiraz, and a vampire from Inaya's harem—hanging on his arms. He looked alternately bored and amused.

Ziri hovered overhead, a silent shadow perched on the bridge. Makeda hadn't even tried to read him.

Kato sat on what could only be called a throne, conversing with several of the soldiers who'd been sent by various vampire lords. There were around twenty waiting to speak to him, no doubt all wanting their share of the glorious new regime.

And Saba was swimming naked in the pool while curious young vampires watched from the edges.

"It looks like a party boat," Makeda said.

Carwyn chuckled. "And welcome to ancient conquest, my dear. As much pageantry as battle. If all goes according to plan, our ship will be welcomed into the hidden harbor of Alitea, and Laskaris will know his time has come to an end. He'll bargain for exile or something that will leave him alive, and Kato and Saba will take over the way they intend."

"But will Kato and Saba grant him exile?" Makeda tried not to sound horrified. She was far from bloodthirsty, but Laskaris and his people had killed her, murdered countless humans all over the globe, and driven hundreds of vampires mad.

"Oh no," Carwyn said. "I'm sure they're going to kill him."

"Doesn't he know that?"

Carwyn cocked his head to the side. "Probably."

"Then why on earth does *anybody* think this is going to go according to some plan?"

The next night, Tenzin dropped Brigid and Lucien on the roof of the factory on the outskirts of Plovdiv. From the outside, it looked like any number of cosmetics factories in the region, but Lucien could smell it immediately.

The sickly-sweet smell of pomegranate permeated the air.

He saw Brigid curl her lip and knew she'd smelled it too.

"Just the scent of it...," she muttered, and he felt her heat up.

"Calm," Lucien said. "I know it's hard to resist."

"I forget that you were infected too."

"I survived. Others will too."

"I hope so." Brigid stepped lightly as they crossed the roof.

Lucien could feel a human on the other side of the door, no doubt taking his turn to check the roof as their surveillance had indicated. Brigid waited for him to open the door, then she grabbed the gun pointing from behind the door, yanked it forward, and before the man could call for help, she had her hand on his neck. He could see the heated imprint of her hand on the human's skin.

"Brigid..."

"Quiet," she whispered, curling her hands around the guard's neck. "Sleep."

The human went limp, and she placed him on the ground behind the door.

With quick hand movements, she entered the dark stairwell and motioned for Lucien to follow. Since she was doing an excellent job so far, he decided he'd let her take the lead. Baojia was below, already working to isolate the plant from the city water system. Tenzin was... somewhere, doing things Lucien decided he probably didn't want to know about.

When they reached the floor, he saw some of them.

Five humans were stacked like cordwood against one wall.

"They're not dead," came a whispered voice from above. "But they'll be out until dawn at least."

Tenzin swooped down and grabbed another human. As she rose in the air, the man's kicking legs fell still. "They all keep coming to look, then I can grab more of them." She grinned. "It's very entertaining."

Brigid hissed. "But what about—"

"Vampire." Lucien grabbed Brigid's shoulders and angled her toward the swiftly approaching immortal in black. Brigid's fire shot out and engulfed the running vampire. He screamed and the fire alarm blared, all at the same time.

"Oh sure," Tenzin yelled. "And she was worried *I* wouldn't be stealthy enough."

"Shut up, Tenzin!" Brigid looked up as the pipes above her hissed. The sprinkler system kicked on, a dense mist that enveloped Brigid and the surrounding area but did not flood the warehouse. "Oh, for fuck's—"

"Here!" Tenzin blew the mist away, and Brigid emerged looking like she'd just walked through a wind tunnel. "You're welcome."

"Let's not delay," Lucien said, running toward an office he saw in the distance. "You two take care of the guards, and I'll find the finished product. We'll need to destroy all the records too. Tenzin, start moving the humans to a safe location. Once Baojia makes the water safe, Saba wants this plant razed to the ground."

❖

"We'll be there by tomorrow evening," Carwyn said. "There's nothing else to do tonight."

"When will we hear from Bulgaria?"

"I don't know."

She was staring into the distance at a horizon that was speeding ever closer as they neared a battle she couldn't even begin to comprehend. They would be anchored off the island of Alitea by nightfall the next night. Makeda knew she should go below and secure herself in her quarters, but the bed felt too empty without Lucien.

"So," she said, "any tips about being mated to a really old guy?"

Carwyn chuckled. "Be patient with us. We don't generally know what we're doing any more than the young ones do."

"That's almost inexcusable considering how many years you have on us."

"Ah, but my dear girl, a woman is the greatest of adventures. No relationship can prepare you for meeting the love of your eternal life."

Makeda smiled at Carwyn. "Smooth."

"I try. She won't let me get away with anything." He winked. "I love her madly."

"You're both very lucky."

"It took us a while to come to grips with it," he said. "We fell in love at a distance, my Brigid and me. Actually living together was a thing neither of us were prepared for. Hence my advice for patience."

She thought. "Lucien and I have spent a lot of time with each other. We worked together for months before I turned."

"Well, you're ahead of where Brigid and I were then."

"But we fought most of the time."

Carwyn said, "That just makes things interesting, doesn't it?"

"Do you *ever* see the dark side of a situation?"

Carwyn burst out laughing. "What would be the point in that? My Brigid is the pessimist. No use having two of them."

Makeda wondered who was the pessimist between her and Lucien. Probably her. Maybe him. Maybe they could just take turns.

"I can't imagine being with the same person for eternity," Makeda said. "Just the forty-some years my parents have together seems crazy."

"But it's life, isn't it? I don't think any of us can grasp living with and loving a person for that long. But then you turn around, like one of my daughters, and you've been with the same person one hundred years. And they're the other part of you. You wake up one morning and it's been four hundred. Then five." He smiled slowly. "What glorious fun! To have a partner like that. To know without a doubt that there is one person in the world who always has your back. I can't imagine a greater adventure, Makeda, than the one you and Lucien have just begun."

"If we can survive this battle."

He threw an arm over her shoulder. "Stick with me, my girl. You have nothing to worry about."

❖

Lucien stood surrounded by empty crates, Baojia standing next to him, his hands on his hips. "It's not here."

"Nope."

"Is the factory disconnected from the local water lines?"

Baojia nodded. "Even if we blow the place sky-high, nothing will leak."

"Then let's do it," he said.

"What?"

"Blow the place sky-high." Lucien had already destroyed the servers where the formula was kept, taken any documentation on how to produce it to Brigid, who delighted in lighting it all in a great bonfire in the center of the factory. She didn't even make a face when the fire sprinklers went off anymore. She and Tenzin were having too much fun.

"If Laskaris's stores of Elixir aren't here," Baojia said, "then we both know where he moved them."

"Alitea." Lucien stepped away from the empty crates and headed toward the doors. "Make sure all the humans are out," he said. "Then tell Brigid to destroy it all."

Chapter Twenty-Four

The grey island rose from the sea, a massive fortress of natural rock hewn by time and immortal hands. From the outside, it looked like nothing more than a solid wall of rock. Kato stepped from the yacht, his arm around Saba, and walked across the water to the massive stone wall. The sea calmed beneath him. The ocean swells fell flat. They walked toward the fortress of Alitea in silence.

Saba raised a hand, flicked her wrist, and a massive groaning crash sounded across the water. The gate of the fortress moved aside slowly, revealing a dark passage concealed by the wall.

Long rowboats left the yacht as one, propelled toward the dark passage by water vampires in each one. Kato walked into the darkness ahead of them, Saba at his side as Arosh and Ziri flew behind them.

"With me." Carwyn put a hand on the small of her back. "Stay with me, Makeda."

Carwyn had also taken the gentle Kiraz under his wing. She was a little thing, and her eyes were huge. She gaped at the yawning chasm they entered, clearly frightened of the battle to come.

Makeda didn't feel frightened. She didn't feel anything. She'd locked down her emotions like she did in all emergencies, calming her heartbeat that wanted to rage and focusing on one very important thing.

Staying alive.

Like Kiraz, Makeda was no warrior, but she did have Kato's training. If she needed to, she could dive to the bottom of the ocean and sit there for days, she'd decided. Lucien would find her eventually.

The glow of the night sky greeted them as the tunnel opened up to a large harbor surrounded by high stone walls.

Alitea was a fortress out of some ancient fantasy.

She had no idea how they hid it from above, but inside the stone walls lay a massive harbor fronting a city straight out of Greek mythology. Rows of marble pillars—garishly painted with gold and deep jewel tones—lined the dock where their boats came to rest.

Along the seawalls surrounding the harbor rose a city built into the cliffs, shielded from the sun by a massive rocky overhang that must have been held by immortal energy because Makeda could see no other reason it didn't come crashing down. Trees and vines grew on sumptuous terraces hanging over the harbor. Flowers tumbled from balconies. Hundreds of immortals stood on the walls of the city, watching Kato as he stepped ashore.

Every one of them was silent.

Makeda did everything in her power to remain impassive, but the overwhelming grandeur of Alitea stole her breath away. The docks embraced them, two giant arms of dressed white stone curling into the harbor where their boats floated. Along the docks, armed guards in helmets and breastplates stood holding torches. More torches lined a pathway bordered by more pillars, fountains, and statues, stunning works of art unlike anything Makeda had ever seen.

Far from the blank stares of white marble she was accustomed to, these statues were painted to vivid life, with eyes that seemed to follow their party as they mounted the stairs and walked toward the massive stone temple nestled against a steaming mountain.

"Is that... a volcano?" she asked Carwyn.

"Yes."

"And they live here?"

"Many live here. The volcano belongs to Eris," Carwyn said.

On the slopes, Makeda saw dense greenery spreading. Fragrant flowers joined the smell of citrus and sweet wine. She saw figures darting among the buildings and narrow streets that angled off the main thoroughfare, but she heard no buzz of conversation or bustling carts. All she could hear was the faint and growing strains of harp and lute.

"Sofia holds the island together," Carwyn continued, "and conceals it from prying eyes. Jason is... Jason. He's barely conscious most of the time. But it's Laskaris we need to worry about."

"Four members of the council. Four elements?"

"I believe Lucien thinks the blood needed to make Elixir is coming directly from the four members of the council."

They walked up the broad stairs and into a massive temple with five thrones raised on a dais at the end. On the thrones were four brightly colored statues where vampires bowed in worship and prayer. Makeda saw them, coming and going from the sides of the hall, bearing baskets of fruit and fish. Wineskins and goblets were placed at their feet.

Makeda's eyes widened when she caught the scent. "Is that blood? Why would they be giving statues—"

"Not statues." Carwyn nudged her shoulder. "Watch."

If she hadn't been watching, she would have missed it. The frozen woman on the throne to the right of center appeared to blur for a moment, then came back into focus. The goblet of blood at her feet had tipped to the side, and a slight flush stained the woman's lips.

"They're alive," Makeda said. "*That* is the council?"

"Yes."

So ancient they appeared as statues. So fast she'd almost dismissed the movement as her own imagination. Makeda examined the four immortals.

"Why are they frozen?"

"They're not frozen," Carwyn said. "They're still. If you or I wanted to—if we were content to simply exist—I suppose we could look the same. But that seems..."

"Somewhat insane?"

Carwyn shrugged. "Ask Tenzin. I've heard rumors that she once remained motionless for a thousand years."

"I don't think I'd classify Tenzin as sane," Makeda said. "At least not from what I've seen so far."

"Smart girl."

She stepped closer, her eyes locked on the statue-like vampires. "Who are they?"

"Jason commands the sky," Carwyn said. A pale, nearly white-skinned man with a fall of gold curls stared into the heavens.

"Eris, the fire-starter." A dark-eyed, olive-skinned woman glared at a point somewhere in the distance.

"Sofia." Carwyn's voice was sad. Softer, but still frozen, was the woman in the center who had drunk the goblet of blood. Her skin was a deep olive, like the glaring woman, but her eyes and features looked more Egyptian than Greek.

Next to her was another pale man, his skin nearly blue in the moonlight, his dark brown beard falling down his chest. His skin glowed with a sheen of water, and his eyes—like his fellow elders—were fixed to a point high over the heads of those who worshipped him.

"And that is Laskaris."

❖

Lucien didn't wait for Brigid. He had no idea how the fire vampire was getting to Alitea, nor did he care. He held on to Tenzin's hand as they flew across the Aegean Sea, knowing Baojia swam beneath them.

"We're not going to beat them there," Tenzin yelled.

"I know."

"What do you think he's planning to do with it?"

"I don't know."

And Lucien truly didn't.

According to all accounts, vampires couldn't be infected by Elixir by any means except human blood. The human had to become infected, then pass the virus to an immortal. Lucien was racking his brain, trying to figure out how Laskaris could plan to use the Elixir against the ancients, but he just couldn't see it.

Burn it? Vaporize it? Would breathing it trigger the virus? It was possible. They'd never tried it, and Lucien feared the result.

Unless Laskaris had infected a massive number of humans and let them loose on the island to infect his enemies, nothing else made sense. And letting loose that many drugged humans on your own population made no sense at all... unless you had a death wish.

Did Laskaris have a death wish?

Lucien didn't know much about the ancient Greek. If he saw his end in sight, he might just want to take all his people with him along with any vampires who'd joined Kato and Saba's side.

"Fly faster," he yelled.

❖

Kato stepped forward. "Laskaris, rouse yourself."

No answer from the throne.

"We come in conquest," Kato continued. "Rise and parley with us, or face your end with honor."

No response. The guards waited on the edge of the temple, as still as statues themselves. The worshipers had halted, seemingly frozen in their movements.

Kato said, "Surrender your throne, and I may let your children live."

Saba walked to a young woman, leaned in, and drew a deep breath. Her shoulders tensed, but the woman did not step away.

A rasping sound came from the thrones. Makeda realized it must have been one of the frozen vampires drawing a breath.

Laskaris didn't move anything but his mouth. "Why do you come to me," he wheezed, "king of my father's fathers?"

"Surrender your seats," Kato said. "And we may let you live."

Laskaris's chest rose with aching languor. By the time he spoke again, every eye had turned toward them. "Why... would I surrender... my throne?" His eyes were fixed on the ceiling of the temple. "Do gods... surrender... to kings?"

Makeda looked up to see an elaborately decorated fresco of the four Athenian immortals drawn in their glory. Laskaris rode a brilliant curling wave from a wind Jason blew from the corner of the scene. Behind them rose a mountain wreathed in fire with Eris's face taking the place of the sun and Sofia's body the verdant green island in the background. A menagerie of animals bowed along the edges. Cheetahs. Elephants. Lions and zebras. Human figures knelt at the vampires' feet, dropping flower petals and palm fronds in worship.

And Makeda realized the four immortals had been staring at their own images painted in glory for hundreds—perhaps thousands —of years. As vampires around them bowed and worshipped and offered sacrifices to them, they'd been gazing at their own images, lost in the contemplation of their renown.

"Talk about believing your own press," Makeda muttered.

Saba walked in front of Sofia and stared at the woman.

"What is she doing?" Makeda asked.

"Sofia is her daughter's daughter," Carwyn said. "She is Laskaris's mate, but she's of Saba's direct line."

A sweet fragrance drifted on the air, curling around Makeda and distracting her. She blinked and looked over her shoulder.

A blank-eyed woman stood behind her, holding a goblet of blood. "Drink," she whispered, lifting the goblet to Makeda's mouth.

Carwyn gripped Makeda's arm and pulled her away, snapping her out of the odd trance the scent had produced. She looked around and throughout the temple, immortals in various states of undress were holding goblets out to their party, most of whom recoiled in disgust.

"Carwyn, what's going on?"

Then Laskaris began to laugh, a grating, awful sound that sent chills down Makeda's spine.

Arosh snarled, "You madman."

Ziri landed beside him, and Makeda saw him draw in a deep breath. "What have you done? It is everywhere. Did you infect them all?"

The volcano shot out a plume of smoke, drawing Makeda's eyes away from the four seated figures and up to the top of the mountain. She looked at the glaring woman. Though she didn't move, waves of heat spread through the room.

Arosh stepped forward, raised his hand, and Eris's head shot back at a painful angle as she dodged the spear of flame that came from his palm.

The heat died down as Kato raised his hands and a cool mist settled over the growing crowd.

Carwyn moved in front of Makeda.

"They wanted... to die..." Laskaris wheezed. "...with their gods."

Saba turned, her expression a frightening combination of agony and disgust.

"They're all infected," Carwyn said, drawing Makeda and Kiraz behind him and backing away from the goblet-bearing vampires who surrounded them. "He's infected them all with Elixir."

Kiraz said, "These poor creatures!"

Makeda wasn't only seeing the dozens of immortals who stood around her, she was seeing the humans who must have been infected to feed them. Sacrificial lambs on the altar of a madman.

"This cannot be forgiven." Kato's hand rose, his palm out, and Laskaris jerked forward in his seat. At his movement, the other council members stood. They moved so quickly it was as if statues had come to life.

Saba stepped forward to stand at Kato's side.

"Enough," she said, glaring at the council. "And to think others urged mercy in the face of your madness."

Laskaris continued to laugh and laugh. Dread curled in Makeda's belly.

"Wait!" Makeda yelled, turning to shout at the vampires surrounding them. "Abandon your council! Surrender to Saba! She can heal you. We found a cure! We can heal—"

"Enough!" Saba's hands rose and the floor buckled beneath her, the earth rose up, and water shot through the stone. Laskaris gave a frightening roar before the pillars rocked and everyone in the hall started screaming.

❖

Lucien saw the smoke and fire before he heard the screams. Tenzin flew over the harbor and dropped him in the water. As he fell, he surveyed the scene before him. Wind vampires from the cliffs took to the sky behind him. Water vampires jumped into the sea and fled. Those belonging to earth ran haphazardly toward the temple or toward the few boats docked in the harbor. Lucien swam toward the shore and came out of the water running.

He had to find her. Had to get her away from the destruction that would soon rain down. The ancients were at war, and the people of Alitea were fleeing. He could feel his mother's amnis in the ground beneath his feet.

Saba was holding Alitea in her grasp.

"Makeda!"

The volcano that had formed the fortress island so many millennia ago pulsed with a low rumble. Then a sound like a cannon echoed against the seawalls as an eruption shot ash and pumice into the air. He could see fire streaking up the side of the volcano and knew Eris and Arosh had come face-to-face.

Baojia ran to him, water dripping from his hair, his eyes wide in horror. "My God, it's Atlantis falling into the sea."

"Where do you think they got the idea in the first place?" Lucien yelled over the crash of tumbling marble. "You think this is the first time this has happened?"

Baojia's eyes went wide, but Lucien knew where the chaos centered. He ran toward the council's temple, fighting through the crowds of vampires who were fleeing the battle. The sickly-sweet smell was everywhere. He could sense Makeda's panic. He felt the gusty wind overhead and knew Ziri and Jason were battling in the skies. Whether Tenzin had stuck around to join the fight was anyone's guess.

Baojia ran after him. "Where are we going?"

"Follow me!" Lucien yelled over an explosion that nearly knocked him down. The dark sea was churning and splashing in the harbor, waves crashing up the marble pathways and upending statuary as the water crawled toward the two ancient water vampires. Lucien trudged through a foot of water, heading toward the main hall, Baojia following him, immortals streaking out of the temple just as the burning timbers of the roof cracked.

"No!" He ran and placed his hands at the steps, forcing his energy into the stones as the massive blocks holding up the ceiling started to shake. Baojia steadied him, holding back the waves threatening to crash over his legs and swamp him. He could feel another immortal's amnis joining his to hold back the falling rocks. "Makeda!"

❖

She couldn't believe what she was seeing. Makeda wanted to run, but Carwyn had told her to stay with him at all times, and he was holding up the building. Saba's amnis split the earth in two, rocking the foundation of the temple and bringing small pillars tumbling down around them. She saw vampires crushed under the falling marble. Others fell into giant crevices that opened beneath their feet.

This was no battle. This was destruction on a scale Makeda had never seen.

"Hold back the water!" Carwyn yelled.

Makeda turned and saw a wave of water heading toward them along with three helmeted guards with swords drawn. It wasn't graceful, but she fell to her knees and *shoved* the water back, jolting the soldiers off their feet and hopefully helping to keep Carwyn stable. Other guards she could see in the shadows and flickering fire, their swords drawn against the screaming population of Alitean vampires. The vampires who had worshipped the elders were cut down if they tried to run. Their blood washed into the churning currents flooding the streets, turning the white marble pink with the blood of immortals.

Carwyn had both hands spread, holding two of the pillars at the entrance to the temple, his massive frame straining even as his feet began to slip. She saw more seawater coming from the harbor and didn't know who was calling it.

"Help me!" she yelled at Kiraz, but the girl was already running toward the door, abandoning Carwyn's protection and taking her chance with the Alitean guards.

"Hold back the fecking water!" Carwyn roared. The current was above his knees.

Makeda tried her best, but there was too much of it. Was it Laskaris or Kato?

The two water giants were locked in battle. Far from the spears of water Emil Conti had commanded, Laskaris and Kato emptied the harbor. Maybe they were pulling from the sea itself. The two immortals threw walls of water at each other, knocking pillars from their foundations and tossing lesser vampires into the air.

Makeda planted her feet in the water, shoving it back in any way she could, trying to keep Carwyn free to hold up the ceiling as vampires fled screaming.

"Can't... hold— *Aaaaaargh*!" Something overhead gave a giant *crack,* and Carwyn heaved and stretched, his hands gripping the pillars as two pieces of the temple pediment flew into the air, launched toward the distant walls of the fortress. As the weight of the massive overhead block left, the pillars beside Carwyn stabilized, but the roof was beyond hope. Plaster and wood fell in burning chunks that turned to soaked cinders when they hit the water-drenched floor.

Carwyn's eyes swept the battle. "Someone is here."

"Makeda!"

"Lucien!"

Lucien walked through the piles of marble, his arms sweeping the rubble to the side as he strode toward her. He grabbed her and kissed her hard, shoving her face in his neck and squeezing her so tightly she could barely breathe.

"Are you all right?"

"Laskaris infected them all!" she yelled. "The whole city. They wouldn't listen. They think they're gods. What are we going to do?"

"Where is my mother?" he shouted over the crashing temple.

Makeda pointed toward the center of the chaos.

Lucien's eyes went wild, then he shoved Makeda toward Carwyn and yelled, "Get her out of here!"

"What? No!"

Carwyn grabbed Makeda around the waist and lifted her off her feet, running past toppled guards and headless vampires. Running away from the rumble of the smoking volcano and toward the harbor. Makeda struggled in his arms, watching Lucien walk toward the heart of the battle, his shirt torn in shreds and his eyes locked on the burgeoning hill rising where the temple had once stood.

"Lucien!" She lost him in the smoke and falling water. She struck Carwyn's shoulders. "Put me down!"

"Sorry, dear girl, I can't do that when the world might be ending."

Pure rage was all she felt. *"Lucien!"*

"Carwyn!"

She heard her sire's voice and turned. Baojia was helping people into the boats they'd brought from the yacht, shoving them toward the gaping portal to the open sea.

"Give Makeda to me!" he yelled.

"No!" she yelled. "Don't you dare! Put me—"

Carwyn tossed Makeda toward her sire, who caught her in his arms and immediately ducked, shielding her from a piece of flying rock. It clipped his head and blood spurted from his temple.

Carwyn shouted, "Both of you, take shelter. Head to the boat."

"Lucien!"

Lucien ignored his mate's cry, knowing his mother was on the edge of destroying everything. It was Axum again. He could hear the cries and smell the blood.

If Saba chose to abandon reason, the whole of the island could be swallowed in a massive explosion. It could sink into the sea as others had before, leaving nothing but rubble at the bottom of the ocean.

Lucien could feel Sofia's amnis batting at the edge of Saba's wrath. Sofia, Laskaris's mate, who was once seen as the wisest and most moderate of the Alitean council, was screaming in rage, blood dripping down her face from the cuts and slices of the marble rocks flying around her. A stone hand reached up from the ground and gripped her in its fingers. Cracks formed in the gray marble only to seal up almost immediately. Water and mud swirled around her in a massive cyclone from Laskaris and Kato's struggle. Lava and sparks flew across the night sky where Arosh and Eris battled.

Saba stood, staring at the blood-soaked rock at her feet. The earth rose and rippled around her like a giant flexing his shoulders beneath the earth. Tears streaked her muddy face. Blood poured from cuts on her skin. She was a bleeding angel resting in a hurricane of destruction.

Lucien walked through the chaos and knelt at his mother's feet. "*Emaye.*"

She looked at him, her forehead creasing. "*Yene Luka*, what are you doing here, my beautiful son?"

He looked up. "You must stop, Saba."

Pain and disgust curled her lip. "He has infected them *all*. His own people. His own mate. Everyone."

Lucien had smelled it as soon as he reached Alitea, the scent of pomegranate only growing stronger as immortal blood spilled in the water. He knew what Laskaris had done with the remaining Elixir. He'd infected the whole of his island and his people, a suicide pact of his own choosing, condemning all of the island to die if he was going to lose his seat of power. It was madness of the most evil kind.

"But you can cure them, remember? Makeda and I found the cure."

Saba shook her head. "They must be *cleansed*."

"Saba—"

"Tell me *why!*" she said. "Tell me why I would show mercy to this vile and corrupt world."

What reason could he give her? The course of history never changed. Empires rose and fell. Humans and vampires both seemed determined to kill each other in the most horrendous ways. Greed was rampant. Children cried. The rain fell on the just and the unjust alike.

Saba knew all those things. The pain of countless millennia lived in her eyes.

"But Saba, children still laugh." He swallowed the lump in his throat. "Humans explore the stars. Mothers nurse their babies and fight for them. Boys sing and dance." He let out a breath. "And even warriors can fall in love."

Saba's face softened.

"The earth has not given up on humanity, despite every abuse we hurl at it," Lucien said. "Maybe someday it will be time to wipe all of us from existence," Lucien said. "We may reach that night. But not tonight, *Emaye*. Not when so many innocents will be lost."

"There are no innocents."

"Then have mercy, Mother, on those who are still learning." He took her hands between his own. "Have mercy on me."

"I have given them"—Saba choked—"so *many* chances. And they refuse to see the beauty before them. The gift of life and death."

Lucien pressed her hand to his cheek, anchoring her with his blood. He knew that, should she want it, Saba might be able to break the earth from the inside out. Plates would shift. Rifts would form and tear the continents in two. "Mother, do you hold the earth?"

"Always."

"Then hold it gently," Lucien asked. "For me."

She turned her eyes from the destruction around her to his face, and he felt her touch soften.

"Hold it gently, *Emaye*. For my mate. For our children."

"So much you ask of me, my son."

"I would have a little more time to love her," he whispered. "If you would give me that."

Roaring silence swirled around them, the elements at war with themselves. The sea roiled. The wind churned. Fire lit the sky above them, and the earth buckled beneath his knees.

Kato came to stand beside him, Laskaris held by the neck in the giant immortal's grasp. "What would you have me do with him, my queen?"

Saba's eyes flared. "Kill him."

Kato squeezed, and Lucien tried not to wince when the spray of blood splashed across his face. The sea calmed around them, and the water crept back.

Ziri landed in similar fashion before Saba, kneeling before her with Jason held across his legs. He took a curved blade from his robe. "My queen?"

"Kill him."

A quick slice and Jason was no more. The wind died down and ash fell in fat flakes.

A scream sounded in the distance, then a massive fireball rose from the mouth of the volcano. Arosh appeared seconds later, soot staining his face and his hair singed at the ends. "I killed her." He put his hands on his hips. "I didn't need your permission."

Saba walked to Sofia, and the earth around the other vampire tightened. Cracks formed and receded like waves in a sea made of stone.

"We are their mothers," Saba whispered to Sofia. "What have you done to your children, Sofia?"

Sofia's eyes drifted closed, and her smile glowed in the darkness. "Laskaris," she whispered. "We shall be gods."

Saba reached up and stroked her hand across Sofia's cheek before the stone hand circling the vampire constricted, and Sofia's head fell to the ground.

The earth beneath Saba came to rest.

Makeda was soaked to the skin, Carwyn and Brigid next to her on the yacht, Tenzin flying back and forth between the boat and the rumbling island of Alitea, giving them progress reports of the battle.

She held on to the thread of Lucien's energy, knowing as long as that thread was there, he was alive. She couldn't face his death even if she was furious with him.

And she was very furious with him.

The battle continued in the water and the air around her. Many of the Alitean guard had been crushed by the collapse of the temple; Makeda was surprised there were enough left to fight. But Kato's forces were kept busy by the water and air vampires loyal to Laskaris who continued to attack the few boats of survivors from the island who held up their hands and begged for mercy. Baojia had joined Kato's forces, helping vampires into the hold below and sequestering them until Kato could decide what steps he wanted to take.

"He infected them all," Makeda said. "They were supposed to die with him."

"He was evil," Brigid said. "He killed so many people. Human and vampire. His ambition had no mercy. I'm glad he's going to die."

The volcano gave one last rumble and fell quiet. The sea calmed. The sky went still.

The conquest of Alitea was over.

Chapter Twenty-Five

"How many?" Lucien dragged himself onto the boat minutes before dawn. Saba, Kato, Arosh, and Ziri had remained on the ruined island, taking shelter in the mountain and in each other's arms. "Inaya's daughter said there were survivors."

"Thirty-two," Baojia said quietly.

Lucien stopped in his tracks. "Thirty-two?" By his estimate, there were over two hundred immortals who'd been living on Alitea.

"The ones who got out... Laskaris and Jason had guards waiting for them. The guards killed whoever they could find, most before we could reach them. Some of the survivors swam toward the Alitean guard with their throats bared."

"They wanted to die." Lucien closed his eyes. "This evil—"

"Has come to an end." Baojia put a hand on his shoulder. "You have ended it, Lucien. You and your mother. Our world can make a fresh start. We'll find whatever stockpiles of Elixir are left and destroy them. No one will dare defy Saba when word of this spreads. You've found a cure for the survivors. We can begin again."

But he hadn't found the cure. Not on his own. "Where's Makeda?"

"In your quarters."

"Has she barred the door?"

Baojia raised his hands. "This is where I back away slowly and find someone who can call my mate."

"There should be a satellite phone on the bridge," he said. "Try that."

"Thanks. And good luck."

Lucien knew she'd be furious with him, but all he wanted was to crawl beside her, lose himself in her touch, and wipe the horror of this night from his mind. If he was very, very persuasive, he might put off the dressing-down he probably deserved until the following night.

If he was lucky.

He knocked on the door when he found it locked. A few moments passed, and he heard slow movement inside.

"Lucien?"

"It's me, Makeda."

Beeping followed by clicked release. She was swaying when she opened the doors, and he realized how close to dawn it must have been. She was barely conscious.

"Sorry." He scooped her up and brought her to the bed, laying her down before he went to secure their quarters.

"Mad... at you."

"I know." He stripped off his clothes and got in bed beside her. "I deserve it."

"Mad..."

"Sleep," he said, kissing her temple. "Be mad at me tomorrow. For now, rest."

And know that you are my world.

He held her tightly through the day, his body resisting the daily torpor of the sun. His mind flashed to the battle the night before. The hail of rain and ash, the surging of earth and sea. In that moment, Lucien had truly understood how delicately balanced it all was. It could crash around him. Seas could rise and the earth sink. His very existence, the air he breathed, was an incalculable and precarious gift.

The complex dance of life had never seemed so fragile. He was spun and woven into it, a tiny thread in an endless tapestry. He could break. They all could.

And they could begin again.

Sometime when the sun reached its apex, he fell asleep only to wake when he felt Makeda stir in his arms. Her amnis rose and reached for his. He was selfishly grateful they were mated. Though she could seethe and rage at him, they were already tied in a way that would make true detachment nearly impossible.

"Makeda?" he whispered.

"You are lucky I love you so damn much, Lucien Thrax."

He let out a long breath. "I know. For the record, I'm sorry."

"No, you're not."

"I'm sorry, and I'm not."

She punched his shoulder. "When you walked into that mess last night—"

"I knew I might be the only one who could make my mother see reason." He kissed her forehead. "And she might not have. She might have pulled the island into the sea, and if that had happened—"

"I am a water vampire. I would have been fine. You were being irrational."

He let out a long breath. "Only ever with you, Dr. Abel."

"Do you think"—she turned in his arms and looked straight into his eyes—"that I want to live in this crazy world without you? That if you had... *died* that I would just move on, find another—"

He kissed her hard. "You have a family. Friends. You have important, *vital* work to finish. And I only have you. You cannot ask me not to risk my life for yours. Not when I've just found you, Makeda."

"We risk together," she said. "We fight together. We search for answers *together*. That is the only way I can do this, Lucien."

"You're not a warrior," he said.

"Then teach me."

Kato's words of warning came to him. *If you try to change who she is, you will learn to hate the thing she becomes.*

"Don't you think I can learn?" she asked.

Kato was right. And he was also wrong.

"You, Dr. Abel?" He gripped her hip. "You told me once that you never forget a lesson. Of course you can learn."

"That's right. Don't forget it."

Kato was right because Makeda's humanity defined her as a healer. But he was wrong because Makeda was also a protector.

She was no longer human. She had eternal life in front of her, and change would now be her constant. Change *brought* life. Perhaps he'd forgotten that for too long.

"If you want to fight with me," he said, "I will teach you. But right now..." His hand moved down her back to cup the rounded bottom he loved so much. "Make love to me, Makeda. Let me make love to you."

She pushed Lucien to his back and moved over him, straddling his hips with her long legs. She kissed his chest over his heart. His neck. His jaw. His lips. Lucien put his hands on her hips and watched her love him, marveling at the play of light over her skin. The wild curls on her head. The soft, blood-flushed lips kissing every inch of his body. She took him in her mouth, making him close his eyes at the heady pleasure of it. He was mindless to anything but her tongue and her hands and the bite she sank into his thigh. He lay before her, a willing offering.

And when he was mindless, she rose over him, sinking onto his erection, her heat a tight, languid caress. She gripped his hands, brought them to her breasts, and rode him.

For hours.

"Makeda, please."

He begged for her bite, but she teased him, punishing him for his arrogance the night before.

Please.

He was dying. He needed her. He was losing his mind.

Then Makeda bent down and offered her neck to him.

Lucien bit viciously and flipped her over, taking control as he thrust a hand in her hair and rode her. Kissed her. Tasted her amnis as it flooded his blood and skin.

She cried out and came hard around him.

Lucien didn't stop.

By the time he came, her neck and breasts were swollen from his lips and fangs. His teeth had marked her, high on her breast, on the curve of her shoulder, the soft skin behind her ear. She was panting and shivering.

Lucien was shivering too. The combination of their blood was a heady thing, as close to intoxication as he'd ever felt since he'd become immortal. She'd wrecked him with slow pleasure. Then he'd wrecked her in the most gratifying way possible.

"Lucien." She curled her body into his, goose bumps covering her skin, her hands and arms trembling.

"Queen," he whispered, wrapping his arms around her and holding her tight. "*Yene Makeda*, you are my queen."

They passed the rest of the night in mindless pleasure, and no one knocked on their door.

❖

Sadly, that didn't last the second night.

Lucien felt Carwyn before he heard him. "The father is here."

Makeda blinked her eyes. "Who?"

"Carwyn. Didn't I tell you he used to be a priest?"

"With those shirts?" Makeda frowned. "You know, somehow I can see it. It's weird, but I can see it."

He walked to the door, cracked it open, and came face-to-face with the pale, redheaded man whose fist was raised to knock.

"Hello!" Carwyn's voice was loud enough to cause a wince. "Get that out of your system yet?"

"Is sex something that's supposed to get out of your system?"

Carwyn grinned. "Not if you're doing it right. You've been summoned though, both of you."

"To the island?"

"Yes."

He took a deep breath and tasted the air, but he couldn't smell his mother or any of the ancients. "Fine. Give us thirty minutes and have a boat ready."

"Your mate doesn't need a boat."

Makeda shouted, "His mate is in the process of taming her

disastrous hair, so a boat is definitely needed."

Lucien raised one eyebrow. "You heard her." Then he shut the door.

Makeda was already in the small bathroom in their quarters, showering the sweat and blood off her body.

"Your hair could never be disastrous," he said. "Just so you know."

"Spoken like a man."

He didn't try to argue with her. Thousands of years had given him that much wisdom at least.

The shower was too small to join her, so he waited until she was out to take his turn. When she left the bathroom wrapped in a towel, he was smiling.

"What is it?" she asked.

"I like this."

She frowned. "What?"

"Living with you."

She shared a shy smile with him before he took her place in the shower. When he emerged, she was already dressed and her hair was "tamed." Lucien found it difficult not to muss her again, but as he valued his life, he decided not to chance it. He took Makeda's hand and led her down the steps to the lower deck where a boat was waiting to take them to the island.

Life seemed to have sorted itself out the previous night. Or Inaya's people really were that good at hosting.

Vampires lounged near the pool with trays of fruit laid out. Silver carafes—containing blood if he had to guess—and bottles of blood-wine were also scattered about the deck. Lucien saw their allies conversing quietly or laughing in corners. Kiraz lay on a pool float, flirting with one of Emil's men. Inaya's daughter held court in the corner, quietly advising several newcomers Lucien didn't recognize.

"Battle one day, party the next?" Makeda asked.

"Most of these vampires have been in enough battles to know when it's time to relax."

"Is anyone going with us?"

"Tenzin and Carwyn will come."

"Where's Baojia?"

"Trying to get home, according to Carwyn." Lucien helped her down the last set of steps. "Apparently Brigid is being stingy with the plane. I think she's still mad we left her in Athens."

The boat to the island was a sleek wooden vessel that came with Emil's yacht. It buzzed toward the great mass of rock that only two nights before had been a smoking pile about to explode. The sea gate stood open, its rock-hewn edges concealing the harbor within.

Tenzin flew overhead. Her task that night was to formally greet the new council of elders at Alitea and report back to those at Penglai. No doubt she was mostly curious what disaster Saba had wrought.

But as they passed through the stone gate and entered the harbor, the last vestiges of worry fell from Lucien's shoulders and his heart finally felt peace. The earth was a resilient and powerful thing.

The ancient streets of Alitea were no more. The cracked marble and ruined statues had been swept into the harbor. Lucien saw their shadowed forms standing silently beneath the sea, testament to a god's folly. He looked up at the cliffs, and instead of white balconies rising from the walls of the sea fortress, vines crawled and flowers fell from balconies taken over by lush greenery where birds were already flying.

The manicured order of Alitea had been swept away, and the earth had sprung up new in its place. The land sloped down from the mountain into the harbor, a symphony of green plants, grey rock, and brown soil dotted with stones. There were no animals. No people. The boat came to rest in the shallows, and Lucien, Makeda, and Carwyn climbed out, splashing over a pebbled beach until they reached the smooth pathway bordered by cypress.

"When she talks about remaking the world, she doesn't joke around," Carwyn said quietly.

"No," Lucien said. "She does not."

Makeda looked around. "What happened to... everything? There was a city here. Roads. Buildings."

"She's never liked those things," Lucien said. "If this is her new kingdom, it will be a very different one from the old."

He linked Makeda's hand in his and walked up the path toward the smell and sounds that were home to him. Distant chatter in a variety of tongues. A campfire. Roasting coffee.

Saba, Kato, Arosh, and Ziri sat on blankets under a spreading olive tree. Kato leaned against a stone, and Arosh lay with his head in Saba's lap as she stirred a pan over some coals. The queen of the vampire race was roasting coffee on an island she'd remade in one night.

"Are you well, *Emaye*?"

"I am well, *yene Luka.*"

Arosh sat up and smiled at Lucien. "It is better, is it not?"

Lucien could feel the volcano's energy. It wasn't dormant, but it was calm. The earth was verdant and the air full of life. The waves rolled gently against the shore; he could hear the sea lap against what was left of the carved marble blocks piled along the harbor. The breeze carried the hint of citrus blossoms and salt air.

Lucien looked around the island and nodded. "It is good."

Ziri was perched on a tall rock that might have been a pediment once. The smooth white marble was already covered in moss. "We will build a city again. Eventually. For now, the vampires we have gathered may stay in the cliff rooms."

"The ones the birds are trying to take over?"

Saba shrugged. "My children would do well to share with the other living things of this world."

Lucien sat next to her. As soon as he did, Carwyn and Makeda sat next to him. Tenzin, who'd been following silently, perched in the olive tree.

"Did you have any questions, daughter of Zhang?" Saba said.

"No."

"And what will you report to your father?"

Tenzin floated down from the tree and sat across from Saba as the smoke rose between them.

"I will tell my father that the ancient sea is at rest once more,"

Tenzin said. "And our mother still gives us life."

"For now." Saba's eyes narrowed. "For *now*, daughter."

"I understand."

"Not yet." Saba leaned against her rock. "But you will."

Without another word, Tenzin took to the sky and disappeared into the night.

Lucien leaned back against the rock that grew behind him and pulled Makeda between his legs. He wrapped his arms around her waist and leaned his cheek on the hair she'd tried to tame. The sea air had already teased it loose from the knot she'd attempted. Lucien fell silent and listened to the conversations of his mother and his friends. Of priests and queens. Spies and kings. Healers and assassins.

The earth was a living thing beneath him. He closed his eyes and felt the new roots his mother had planted steal down into the soil. He listened to the slow circulation of blood in his woman's veins and the air that filled her lungs.

Lucien held his mate for hours on the earth his mother had made new. He held her, and he knew peace.

Epilogue

Northern California

"This is ridiculous."

Makeda turned to see Natalie standing in the doorway. Makeda flew back and plastered herself against the back wall of the lab.

"What are you doing?"

Natalie shrugged and pulled Baojia into the room. "See? I told you."

"It wasn't me. I told you, Mak was the one who—"

"She is not supposed to be in here!" Makeda pointed accusingly at Natalie. The very human, still-somewhat-appetizing Natalie. "What are you thinking, Baojia?"

"I'm thinking that you're going to be fine," Baojia said. "You're ten months old and you haven't had a single incident of losing control. If you weren't a vampire, I'd say you're inhuman." He frowned. "But you are a vampire, so that's an obvious statement."

Natalie squinted. "What are you talking about?"

"It made more sense in my head." He turned on his heel and left. "I'll go get the kids."

Makeda's heart took off at a gallop. "No!"

"Calm down," Natalie said, stepping farther into the room. "He's not going to bring them here. We wouldn't freak you out that much."

She banged her fist on the lab table and made a note to smooth the stainless steel out after Natalie had left. "You are not supposed to be here. I told you twelve months."

"You are paranoid. You've been locked in this lab for six months. Ruben and Baojia say you haven't had a single slipup." Natalie

304

stepped closer. "Besides, it's you. I trust you."

"You shouldn't. Because right now you smell like dinner."

Natalie scrunched up her face. "Be honest. Is it the 'give me that burger now or I'll cut you' kind of hungry, or a 'hmm, is someone barbecuing?' kind of hungry?"

Makeda took a deep breath and realized that—though it was two months before the time line she'd set for herself and though yes, Natalie smelled highly appetizing—she did not detect any feral reactions to the unexpected stimuli. Her heartbeat after the initial shock of seeing her friend had slowed to three beats per minute, which was her typical baseline during waking hours. Her fangs were not extended. Her eyes remained undilated, and no evidence of visual exclusion was present.

"Barbecue, not burger," she finally said.

"I could have told you that solely from the time it took you to answer me. Trust me, I've been around uncontrollable vampires before."

Makeda held up a hand. "Stop. I really don't want to know about your sex life."

Natalie's eyes widened before she burst out laughing. Makeda smiled herself.

She hadn't seen Lucien in nearly three months. While her mate had remained in Europe, Makeda had returned to the US, longing for the calm isolation of her lab after the turbulence of the previous four months that had turned her world upside down. So while Lucien flew between Ireland and Greece, coordinating treatment for the Elixir patients and helping Saba with the political transition, Makeda had returned to the lab.

She worked every night with Ruben and the two other immortal assistants that Katya had hired. She continued perfecting the protein test for Katya, improving the detection factor for Elixir with the updated information on the virus and overseeing its production.

She worked. She slept. She video-chatted with her family on the new Nocht-compatible laptop she'd acquired.

And she missed Lucien.

"I missed you!" Natalie said, wiping her eyes. Walking over, she held out her arms, and Makeda carefully stepped closer.

"I just wanted to be sure," Makeda said, hugging her friend. "You know hurting you or the children would kill me."

"We'll wait on the kids so you don't stress out, but I'm so glad I can see you again."

"You saw me before."

Natalie pulled back, glaring a little. "With a glass wall between us. I felt like I was visiting you in prison."

"Purely a precaution for your own safety."

"Fine." Natalie pulled up a stool and perched at the edge of Makeda's worktable. "Can we just get back to being normal again, please? You're safe around humans. George is more wild and crazy than you, Mak."

"Again"—she sat on the stool across from Natalie—"I don't want to hear about your sex life."

"Too bad, because I want to hear about yours. Spill."

Makeda smiled. "It's pretty slow at the moment."

Natalie's expression was immediately sympathetic. "How much longer?"

"He doesn't know." She shook her head. "It's turning out to be a lot more complicated than he thought."

"Isn't it always?"

She took a deep breath and battled back the curl of hunger at Natalie's scent. "I miss him, Natalie. So much."

"You sleeping okay?"

"Oh yeah. I mean, newborn-vampire sleep is kind of the best. I wake up at night feeling completely rested. It's great. I still haven't figured out if I'm having normal sleep patterns or not, but there must be *some* kind of pattern because without REM—"

"Focus, Mak. Lucien?"

She blinked. "Right. The short answer is, there are dozens of vampires petitioning Saba for healing, and he has to evaluate all of them before he sends them off to Dr. McTierney—Patrick Murphy agreed to continue treating the Elixir patients in his facility—and that takes time because he's Lucien and he's thorough."

"Thorough is good."

"It is. It's also time-consuming. And in addition to all the medical stuff, he's also trying to set up some kind of administrative infrastructure for the new council to deal with current business holdings. Not to mention all the responsibilities associated with overseeing what is basically a federal kind of government over the local vampire leaders in the Mediterranean. Though it sounds like Emil Conti's been really helpful with that."

"That's all good, but—"

"And he has some leads on the business side too. I guess there's someone in Cyprus—"

"Makeda."

"Yeah?" She blinked and stopped tapping her fingers. It was a habit that had become entirely more destructive as a vampire. The edge of her desk was in splinters.

Natalie was staring at her with concern. "Baojia said you finalized the stuff the doctor in Ireland needed. Is that right?"

"I did. Lucien and I decided that since he was the one who'd run the vampire trials with Saba's stem cells, he should run the human trials too."

"That's great." Natalie smiled. "I'm so glad you're back here and that you had time to... level out, you know? It was kind of crazy how you turned."

"It was." She nodded. "I needed to establish a regular schedule again. Change is always difficult for me, and when it all came so rapidly—"

"Stop." Natalie raised a hand. "Listen. Love you. Glad you're back, but... Honey, you need to go to your mate."

Makeda's heart started to beat more rapidly. "Do you think so?"

"Don't you want to?"

"Yes!" She took a breath. "I want very much to go to him. In my opinion, he's not operating at full capacity because he's worried about me and he doesn't have enough help."

Natalie's eyes narrowed. "Then why are you still here?"

"I was finishing the work to send to Dr. McTierney."

"But you're done now."

"And... I thought my presence could be distracting. I didn't know if I was safe around humans. Lucien needs to travel and interact with humans for his work and I was worried..." Makeda took a deep breath and realized she hadn't thought about Natalie's scent for over five minutes.

Natalie's smile grew. "I don't think you need to worry about that, Mak. I'm pretty sure you're going to be okay."

"I should go to Lucien?"

"You should go to Lucien."

Alitea

Lucien lifted his hands from the wind vampire's neck. "Thank you. I have a good idea of your level of infection. I can run the blood test for you, but it will likely confirm what we already know."

"And?"

"It's as you thought. Infection occurred two years ago?"

"Before the tests. I didn't realize..." The vampire shook her head. "It doesn't matter now."

Though the immortal's amnis was erratic, it had not yet reached the critical state where she was losing time or wandering in a fugue, which meant she could wait on the island until some of the more critical Elixir cases were seen to. Lucien had sent four immortals to McTierney the week before. He'd need to wait at least a month before he sent more.

Which, for this vampire, might be a good thing.

"You have time to decide."

"But this is the only option, isn't it?" the Algerian woman said. Her skin was light brown, and intricate tattoos marked her flawless skin. Long wavy hair fell around her face, and her eyes were a stunning blue that reminded Lucien of the sky. In fact, everything about the woman, from her wind-blown hair to her soft, airy voice, reminded Lucien of the sky.

She owed her fealty to Inaya, but her blood beat with the desert wind.

"We have time," Lucien said. "Ziri is your grandsire. You could petition him, and we could try treatment with his blood, but there are no guarantees that it would work. And if it doesn't..."

"I might not have enough strength to accept Saba's cure."

Saba's cure was what immortals around the world had come to call the procedure that Brenden McTierney had perfected in Ireland that killed off the living bone marrow of the infected immortal and replaced it with stem cells harvested from Saba's blood. Saba's cure worked on anyone. There had not been a single failure, even in the most advanced cases.

But it also changed them.

"Tied to the earth...," the wind vampire whispered. Her hand reached down, and her fingertips dragged in the dust. "Never to walk the sky again." There was a wild panic in her blue eyes.

"You have time."

She rose. "Thank you, healer. You have given me much to think about. I will consider all this if you will allow me the time."

"Of course. You've introduced yourself to Ziri?"

"I have."

"If you stay on the island, we will guarantee your safety while you are here."

She bowed to Lucien and left his office.

Built from recovered marble he'd broken and shaped into bricks, his office backed into the hills of Alitea. He'd dug a comfortable series of tunnels, one of which led to the harbor, thinking of the time when Makeda might be able to join him.

He ached with missing her.

When he was working alone, he talked to himself, half-expecting her to answer. She didn't. She was at home in the US, working on the human stem cell trial protocols and acclimating to human interaction with her sire watching over her. It was good that she was with Baojia.

He steadied her and was a fierce protector. Lucien knew Makeda was safe, learning valuable lessons she would carry into eternity. It was good that she could visit with her family. Soon she'd be able to see them in person, and he knew from introducing himself to Makeda's parents that it would be an eagerly anticipated reunion on both sides. They adored her.

And he missed her horribly.

He heard someone coming down his path. He reached out and felt a familiar energy. Saba entered and sat on the narrow bed where he examined his immortal patients.

"I saw Inaya's woman flying back to the shelter," she said.

"Infected."

"And?"

He took a deep breath. "I don't know. She is very much a creature of her element."

Wind vampires had, so far, been the most reluctant to accept Saba's cure.

"A bird who has tasted the sky will fight to keep her wings," Saba said. "This does not surprise me."

"I know. I just wish..."

"Did you and your brilliant mate find anything else that could cure these children?"

"No."

"Then allow yourself to rest. There is a cost to everything. I offer healing to creatures who have already lived unnaturally long lives. They will take it or they will not. Their decision is not your responsibility."

"I know."

"I would have you smile again," Saba said.

He lifted an eyebrow. "Then summon my mate to me, *Emaye*."

Saba's eyes sparkled in the candlelight. "Is that all?" She clapped her hands. "And it is done."

He frowned at her playful smile. "Saba..." He fell silent when he felt Makeda's step on the island. Smelled her scent on the breeze. Sensed her amnis waking within him.

Mate!

Saba's laughter chased Lucien out the door and down the path. He raced toward the ocean and the scent of her. Cinnamon and citrus. Earth and salt. He raced past stone buildings and lush gardens, the beginnings of new civilization on the island. He leapt over rocky hills and ran down the slopes leading to the harbor.

Makeda stood on the pebbled beach, shaking the water from her hair. Her smile was brilliant in the moonlight.

She raised her face and laughed as Lucien tackled her into the sea.

❖

Chencha, Ethiopia

"Tell me about the princess again," Lucien said, tickling her neck with the rough whiskers he allowed to grow when he was in the mountains.

Makeda couldn't stop the smile. "She lived in the mountains in a cave. And all her guards had teeth." She snapped her teeth at his chin.

"Are you calling me a hyena?" he asked.

"Are you calling me a princess?"

"Definitely." They slept in the round tukul high in the mountains where the clouds made islands of the peaks. The tukul was windowless and warm, trapping the heat from the wood stove on one wall. Thick cotton and wool blankets covered them, and the rhythmic syllables of her mother tongue dropped like raindrops on dusty ground.

After a year of work in Alitea, Lucien had taken her back to her childhood home. They'd escaped the traffic and crowds of Addis to climb mountains and swim in rivers and lakes, diving with the crocodiles and laughing at angry hippos. She'd rediscovered the birds that had sung her childhood lullabies and the air that smelled of eucalyptus and cedar. She tasted wild honey and mango again.

Lucien and Makeda went to Sidamo to visit her grandmother, who was so old she didn't question why her American granddaughter only visited at night. Makeda tasted fresh injera and her grandmother's *shiro wat*. She sat and chopped onions at her grandmother's feet, listening to stories she hadn't heard since she was a child while Lucien roasted meat outside with her uncles. She stored away the memories, knowing that someday, like Lucien, her human memories would fade and all she would have left were the pictures she took with her mind and the old camera Lucien found for her.

One night they walked down the mountain to the twin lakes of Chamo and Abaya and climbed the mountain that rested between them. Lucien settled on the hillside facing east to watch for the sun.

"They call this the Bridge of God," Lucien said.

"Why?"

He frowned. "I don't know."

Makeda smiled. "Really? You've never asked?"

He shrugged. "Does it matter?"

"Yes."

"Hmm." He settled his arms around her. "Okay, I will tell you the story."

"I'm all ears." She leaned back against his chest and felt their amnis join and dance in the grey dawn air.

"When the earth was newly born, God took many years to create the world and every creature, fashioning each to fit its unique place. But he knew there was something missing. So he wandered over Africa for days and nights, because this land, he decided, was the most beautiful of all his creations, and he loved it very much. The lakes we see today are his footsteps, didn't you know?"

"Are they?" Makeda watched the sky go from grey to blue while Lucien kept talking.

"They are. God walked up the great valley, his feet pressing into the damp ground, and water filled the holes where his feet had stepped. He walked and he walked until his feet had gathered so much clay he had to shake them off. The mud he shook off his feet made those mountains behind us."

"You're a good storyteller."

"I know. Be quiet and listen."

Makeda laughed and watched the sky go from blue to purple.

"After walking and thinking for so long, God decided to make humans, mortal and immortal, and put them here, because in the great valley there is everything. There is earth and water. High mountains that touch the air and the fire of the sunrise every morning. That is why every one of us came from here. No matter where we have wandered, mortal or immortal, this place is our true home."

The purple turned to pink on the edges of the horizon.

"So after God put his people in the great valley, he decided to rest here on this bridge between the two lakes and watch the sun rise, because he knew in all the world"—Lucien's voice fell to a whisper and his arms tightened around her waist—"there was no more beautiful place than this."

Orange and yellow clouds lit the sky, nearly blinding Makeda's sensitive eyes. She shivered in excitement. Being on the hillside facing east as dawn brightened the sky felt like walking on the edge of a cliff. Frightening, exhilarating, alive.

So alive.

Lucien's arms tightened again. "Sitting here and watching the sun rise, *yene konjo*, is like watching the world being born."

She gripped his hands, felt his lips touch her neck.

"I'm ready," she said.

"If you're sure."

"Yes."

"Yes."

The burning edge of the sun peeked over the horizon just as Lucien grabbed Makeda and fell back into the earth, closing world over them as Makeda's eyes went blind from the flare of sunlight. She saw nothing. She was blind to everything but Lucien's touch as he carefully formed the soil in a comfortable cave around them. She laughed with wild abandon, her heart raced, and Lucien covered her face in kisses.

"Not a scratch," he said. "I promise. Not even a singed hair."

She couldn't stop laughing.

"Makeda?" Lucien was laughing too. "Are you okay?"

"That was"—she gasped—"amazing!"

"Want to do it again tomorrow?"

"Yes!"

His laughter shook the earth. "I think I've created a monster."

Her voice began to slur with exhaustion. "This is like... the vampire version of extreme sports."

"You have no idea."

She turned her face to his and lifted her mouth for a kiss. He very quickly obliged.

"I want to see... everything," she said, her voice growing softer. "I want to climb all the mountains. I want to swim to the bottom of the sea. I want to find... caves and scramble... up trees. I want to see it all, and... I want you to show me."

His forehead pressed to hers. "Done."

"Thank you for my life, Lucien."

"No, Makeda," he whispered. "Thank you for mine."

The End

A note from the author

Dear Elemental World readers,

Once again, we come to the close of another chapter in the Elemental universe. While the Elixir storyline is finished, I hope you can tell from hints given in this book that my work in this world is far from over. My very next project is working on the Elemental Legacy series featuring Ben Vecchio and everyone's favorite wind vampire, Tenzin.

There are currently two prequel novellas that tell what has happened to Ben after the Elemental Mystery series. A lot of time has passed for the young boy adopted by vampires. Ben is all grown up and ready for his own adventures. Who better to keep him company than a vampire who loves starting trouble?

The first of five books featuring Ben and Tenzin will be out in the fall of 2017. Until then, I hope you'll look for their stories, *Shadows & Gold* and *Imitation & Alchemy,* available now at major retailers in e-book and paperback. A third, *Omens & Artifacts,* will be published in early 2017.

And after that, who knows? As long as there are stories to tell in this world, I will keep writing in it. I hope you'll come along for the journey.

Be well, and thank you for reading.

Elizabeth Hunter
November 22, 2016

Acknowledgements

At the end of every series arc, there always seems to be so many more acknowledgments than usual, and this particular book has benefited from the wisdom and eyes of so many individuals, I'm almost positive I'm going to miss some.

But here is my attempt to try to remember most.

To my editing team, Lora, Anne, and Linda. Every book you challenge me to be better, and this one was no exception. Thank you for your professionalism, dedication, and critical eyes. I could not write my books without you. Any mistakes left in this book are probably mine from trying to mess with your beautiful work.

To my cover designer, Damonza.com. I thank you for the truly gorgeous cover for *A Stone-Kissed Sea*. You captured the color and beauty of this book and these characters. Thank you.

So many people contributed to the extensive research for this book, but I especially wanted to thank everyone from National Geographic Expeditions, who introduced me to the inspiring country of Ethiopia. Thanks to Anne Butcher, Henok Tsegaye, and David Scott Silverberg for their expertise and generosity. Their guidance through the complicated history, anthropology, and geography of Ethiopia and the East African Rift was extraordinary.

Effusive thanks to two wonderful writers whose work informed and inspired me, Rebecca Haile and Lemn Sissay. And fangirl adulation to the many musicians whose work was my soundtrack for this book, Baaba Maal, Gigi, Salif Keita, Mumford & Sons, The Very Best, Nina Simone, FKA twigs, and The Gospel Whiskey Runners.

I want to thank my beta readers for this book, particularly Cat Bowen and Pamela Bonsu, who not only checked my voice for this story and offered encouragement and insight, but also reassured me that the MAGIC!science made at least a little sense and that scientific research professionals were as awkward and as wonderful as I imagined. I cannot thank them enough. Additional thanks to all my many readers in STEM fields that helped me with details in this book.

To my beautiful David, thank you for showing me your Ethiopia. Thank you for being you.

To my family, I want to thank you for putting up with all the travel I did during the research for this book. (My patient son, especially.) I cannot wait to bring you along on the next adventure... as long as you're not in school.

To my readers, thank you for following me on this journey. Thank you for your support and encouragement. Thank you for having extraordinary imagination and insatiable curiosity.

You are my people.

ELIZABETH HUNTER is a contemporary fantasy, paranormal romance, and paranormal mystery writer. She is a graduate of the University of Houston Honors College and a former English teacher. She once substitute taught a kindergarten class but decided that middle school was far less frightening. Thankfully, people now pay her to write books and eighth graders everywhere rejoice.

She currently lives in Central California with her son, two dogs, many plants, and a sadly empty fish tank. She is the author of the Elemental Mysteries and Elemental World series, the Cambio Springs series, the Irin Chronicles, and other works of fiction.

ElizabethHunterWrites.com

Also by Elizabeth Hunter

Made in the USA
Las Vegas, NV
20 March 2024

87510214R00189